MURDER IN MIND

Sophie Bradford is pretty, blonde and an accomplished flirt. When her body is found dumped in a ditch on a lonely West Country road, Jamie Mullin is the prime suspect. He was her latest boyfriend and they'd had a very public row just before she disappeared.

Jamie protests his innocence but soon spirals into a breakdown fuelled by frustration, self-pity and drink, and it is left to his friend, Matt Shepherd, to fight his corner. Can he find the truth behind what appears to be a motiveless murder?

As Matt begins to uncover some dark secrets— secrets that someone will kill to protect—he soon learns that loyalty at all costs carries a lethal price.

MURDER IN MIND

Lyndon Stacey

WINDSOR
PARAGON

First published 2007
by Hutchinson
This Large Print edition published 2008
by BBC Audiobooks Ltd
by arrangement with
The Random House Group

Hardcover ISBN: 978 1 405 68736 2
Softcover   ISBN: 978 1 405 68737 9

British Library Cataloguing in Publication Data available

Printed and bound in Great Britain by
CPI Antony Rowe, Chippenham, Wiltshire

In memory of the real Taffy; of Herbs, Mo Mo, Sula, Starsky, Gerty, Shadow and the many other *special* dogs who have enriched the lives of their human companions beyond belief, and who continue to be sorely missed.

ACKNOWLEDGEMENTS

As usual there are many people to thank for their willing and enthusiastic help. This time, top of the list must come Robert 'Choc' Thornton for giving me an insight into the life and work of a National Hunt jockey at the top of his game. Also, thanks are due to Roger Hart, physiotherapist Jacqueline Flexney-Briscoe, Melanie Scott at Weatherbys, Joan Gardiner, Mark Randall, Earle Garner and Julie Cooke.

1

The turf was racing by in a blur of green and brown in the instant before Matt Shepherd hit it, shoulder first, and slammed over onto his back.

Years of practice had him instinctively curling into a ball and rolling to cover his face and stomach, but emerging unscathed from a steeplechasing fall is always a matter of luck, and, on this occasion, luck wasn't entirely with him.

He'd been near the front of the field, riding the favourite, when he'd approached the last fence in the back straight, with only three fences left to jump and every expectation of lifting the prestigious Camberley Gold Cup for the second year running. But, three strides out, he knew it was not to be. Kandahar Prince was wrong at it—totally wrong—and it was too late to do anything but sit quietly and hope the horse could sort it out for himself.

To be fair to Prince, he might have done, had the horse immediately behind not been so close. A Herculean effort saw him clear the tightly packed birch, but he landed too steeply and, as he stumbled, the following horse cannoned into his hindquarters, sending him pitching forward onto his nose and then down, catapulting Matt some ten or twelve feet further on.

For a moment, as he pressed close to the track, his whole world diminished to a chaos of thunderous noise, flashes of colour, and the thudding blows of galloping hooves.

It was a big field—twenty-five runners, to be

exact—and it seemed to Matt that they all managed to clip him in passing, the last one giving him such a clout that he was rolled over twice more before he stopped moving.

An eternity passed in seconds and, as the drumming hoofbeats receded into the distance, Matt lay still for a moment, grass tickling his nose and the earthy aroma of bruised turf filling his nostrils. Somewhere behind him he heard Prince get to his feet and set off after the other horses.

'You all right, old boy?' a voice enquired, and, lifting his head cautiously, Matt saw a blur of scarlet and yellow close by, which presently resolved itself into the shape of another jockey, sitting up and watching him with a level of concern that belied the jokey tone he'd used.

Matt blinked, and the jockey became, more specifically, Jamie Mullin, Irishman and his own good friend.

Matt opened his mouth to speak, paused, spat a quantity of grass and gritty soil, then said, 'Fancy meeting you here! Do you come here often?'

Jamie's face widened into a characteristic grin.

'Not if I can help it. You?'

'Unfortunately, yes.' Matt uncurled, gingerly testing each limb for function.

'Got all your fingers and toes?' Jamie stood up and came over, undoing the strap on his crash cap and taking it off to reveal a quantity of thin, spiky blond hair and the dark smudge of a goatee beard.

'Yep. Think so.' Matt waggled them experimentally and felt pain spread through his left ankle and foot. 'Damn! Some bugger's stepped on my ankle.' Holding his hand up, he balanced on one foot as Jamie pulled him to his feet, and then

2

stood holding on to his friend while he tried putting a little weight on the injured foot.

The result wasn't encouraging.

'Bugger! I've got Secundo in the next.'

Jamie pursed his lips. 'Or . . . not.'

'Shh-hit!' Matt said.

The racecourse medics, who had been hovering on the other side of the rails, now ducked under and approached, bags in hand.

'Everything OK?' they wanted to know.

*   *   *

After a precautionary visit to A&E for X-rays, which showed his ankle to be badly bruised but not broken, Matt found Jamie waiting in the hospital reception area when he was wheeled out in a wheelchair, a walking stick held in his lap.

'Thought you'd have gone home ages ago,' he said, surprised. There had been a lot of waiting around and it was gone six o'clock.

'We came in *your* car this morning, if you remember. Your valet gave me the key. Anyway, it's the least I could do for the bloke who stepped aside to give me my third winner of the day,' the Irishman declared jauntily. 'Or should I say—hopped aside?'

Matt favoured him with a parody of a smile. Secundo had been his own best prospect of the day—a horse he'd nursed through the uncertainty of the first outings as a novice, and who he'd been looking forward to partnering in the first big trial of its career. But such disappointments were part and parcel of jump racing and, if someone had to benefit from his misfortune, he would rather it was

Jamie than anyone else. At twenty-two, the Irishman was still hovering on the fringes of success.

'Oh well. At least it gives you a taste of what it's like to be a *proper* jockey,' he retorted.

'Nice try, but you can't put me down today; I'm on a roll! Three winners this afternoon, two decent rides on Monday—one courtesy of Matt Shepherd Esq.—and a date with the gorgeous Sophie tonight. Things are definitely looking up!'

Jamie drove fast, patently enjoying the powerful engine and sweet handling of Matt's MR2, and, in less than forty-five minutes, they had reached the tiny village of Norton Peverill and were turning in through the gateway of the Somerset cottage that Matt shared with his fiancée, Kendra Brewer. Jamie also had a room there, which he used whenever he was riding in the south of the country for a few days; this was one such time.

Built of the local golden stone with a brown-tiled roof, the cottage sat end-on to the lane and was approached from the left-hand side via a wooden gate in the stone wall. Once in the yard, there was garaging for three cars on the left, built into an old timber-framed barn. Ahead was a five-bar gate, which led to a concreted yard with three stables and a second barn, and, beyond that, another gate into a lane and the first of three paddocks where he hoped, one day, three or four thoroughbred brood mares might graze. At the moment they were playing host to a couple of yearlings, bought on impulse at a recent sale.

To the right, as they drove in, the cottage sat illuminated by the soft sunlight of early evening. Now, in mid-September, the narrow flowerbeds either side of the front porch were bursting with late-summer colour: blowsy pink dahlias, elbowing their way through the drifts of goldenrod; asters and lavender, all bobbing and bowing in a lively breeze.

Matt regarded the beds with satisfaction. He'd lived at Spinney Cottage for just over three years, but the garden had been left more or less to its own devices until a few months ago, when Kendra had moved in.

Jamie stopped the car in front of the wooden doors of the garage to allow Matt to get out.

'What'll you do about the party tonight?' he asked.

'Oh, I expect I'll go,' Matt said, climbing stiffly out with the aid of the stick. 'Doogie would be very disappointed if I missed it. But I might not stay till the end. I'll see how I feel.'

Leaving Jamie to put the car away, he limped across the brick-paved yard towards the cottage. When he was still several feet from the door, it opened and a slim blonde girl stepped out to meet him. Just as the sight of the cottage gave Matt a lift each time he came home to it, so it was with Kendra. Just turned twenty-one, with fine-boned features, hazel eyes, and elbow-length hair of the palest gold, he continually blessed whatever quirk of her personality had made her fall for him.

'Hiyah. Are you OK? What did the hospital say?' Her concern showed in the tiny crease between her eyes. She rarely came to the racecourse and never watched his races on TV—saying that it made her nervous—but he'd rung to warn her that he'd very likely be late home.

'Just bruised, but I'll be signed off for a day or

two. Secundo won,' he added, ruefully.

'Oh, what a shame!' She put her arms round his neck and kissed him. 'Well—not that he won, obviously—but you know what I mean. You've worked so hard on him.'

'Yeah. Still, there'll be other races. And Jamie's not complaining.'

He followed her into the cottage, limping through the lounge with its oak beams, ochre walls, and stone fireplace, and was almost knocked over by the welcome from the dogs as she opened the kitchen door. There were four of them, though sometimes, when they were whirling excitedly, as now, it seemed as if there were twice as many.

He spoke to them all, reserving his fondest welcome for his own special dog, a German shepherd bitch called Sky. Rocko and Patches, the collie crosses he'd adopted from the local rescue centre, were always first in the queue for attention, but Kendra's dainty sheltie waited back until the fuss died down before coming forward demurely to receive her greeting.

'Hallo, Taffy.' He bent gingerly to ruffle her fur, the action reminding him of the buffeting he'd received.

'It's not just your foot, is it?' Kendra observed astutely. 'C'mon, my lad. Let's get you upstairs and into a hot bath.'

*   *   *

Kendra was going out for the evening too, to the hen night of an old school friend, and was picked up by a minibus just after eight, leaving Matt and Jamie to drive to the party in her car. It was an

6

automatic, which meant that if—as was probable—Jamie went on to spend the night with his girlfriend, Matt would be able to get himself home with only one good foot to operate the pedals.

'Wouldn't you do better to get a taxi?' Kendra had asked, on her way out.

'I'll be OK. I've no intention of getting sloshed anyway, unlike our young friend here!'

An evening spent socialising was not number one on Matt's wish list after the day he'd had, but the party was to celebrate the seventieth birthday of Doogie McKenzie, the trainer who had been his mentor and who'd given him his first break as a jockey. They'd had many successes since those days. Indeed, there was a photograph on the wall at Spinney Cottage that showed the two of them standing beside Blackavar in the winners' enclosure after the Champion Hurdle. In the picture, Doogie had his arm round Matt's shoulders, and Matt, still wearing his cap on his short brown hair, chinstrap undone, had the widest of wide smiles on his lean countenance.

Although Matt had moved on from Doogie's yard to a much bigger one, they remained firm friends, and it would have taken a far more serious injury than the one he'd received today to make him miss this particular bash.

The party was being held in the function rooms of a livestock auction house two or three miles from Charlborough. The venue stood back from the road, surrounded on three sides by parking and having what looked like a couple of acres of covered livestock holding pens on the other. It was approached along an unlit stretch of B-road with fields on one side and an area of private woodland

7

on the other.

Doogie had been in racing all his life and was an extremely well-liked man, as was evident by the number of cars in the car park. When Matt and Jamie entered the building, they found upward of two hundred people jostling for space on the dance floor, seated at tables around the perimeter, or queuing at the bar. The music pounded uncompromisingly loud, keeping time with the throbbing pulse of Matt's headache.

Jamie's eyes were alight with anticipation of an evening's enjoyment, but Matt, whose taste ran more to classical music than the relentless rhythm of club anthems, regarded the next hour or two as something to be endured, and was surprised that Doogie should have wanted a celebration along such lines.

The main function room was lit only by table lights and the flashing coloured bulbs of the DJ's rig, but, even so, Matt recognised several faces. Kendra's younger brother, Deacon, was there and, in the centre of a group by the bar, he could see the ever-popular figure of ex-jockey Harry Leonard in his wheelchair. A good friend of Matt's, Harry was also the son of and assistant to the trainer he usually rode for, and he'd rung whilst Matt was awaiting attention in hospital, to check that he was all right.

As Matt paused just inside the doors, Jamie tapped him on the shoulder, pointed across the dance floor, and moved away. Almost immediately, a stick-thin, gaunt-faced man took his place, leaning close to speak in Matt's ear.

Bob 'Bully' Jennings had yet to reach thirty, but could have been taken for a man twice his age, his features ravaged by a dozen years of struggling to make the weight required of a top-ranked jockey. His teeth were misshapen and discoloured, and, in the daylight, his skin looked sallow, but he invariably wore a smile. Matt liked him a lot, and wished, without much hope, that he would hang up his boots and give his body a chance to recover. Matt was no stranger to the weight battle himself, but, at six foot, Bully had the disadvantage of being at least three inches taller, and his nickname was rumoured to result from a past struggle with bulimia.

'Good to see you up and about,' Bully told him. 'I heard you'd been carted off to hospital. What's the verdict?'

'Just bruised. I'll be back in time to ride Tortellini next week, so don't start getting your hopes up.'

'I never even gave it a thought!' the other jockey protested, unconvincingly. 'By the way, Doogie's in the other bar, if you're looking for him. I'm stopping here to see if I can get lucky.' He winked, waved a hand, and turned away.

Matt looked round for Jamie and saw him weaving his way through the throng towards the place where a platinum blonde in a slinky red dress was dancing with her hands above her head, flaunting her ample curves for the delectation of whoever might care to watch. From what Matt could see in the fluctuating light, a number of people cared, almost all of them men. Shaking his head slightly, he turned away. He had no doubt that Sophie Bradford would give Jamie the runaround—it was her stock-in-trade—but he supposed it would do him no harm in the long term, and he had to learn.

Hobbling into the smaller bar and lounge with the aid of his stick, Matt saw Doogie McKenzie seated at a circular table, attended by a group of mainly older men and women. When he caught sight of Matt, he stood up and waved, his weather-beaten face splitting into a huge smile.

'Matt! You made it! Come over here, lad,' he called, in his broad Scottish tones, and Matt saw, with amusement, that he had come to the party in a kilt with a tartan tam o' shanter atop his shock of unruly white hair.

As he approached the table, the other guests shifted up to clear a space for him on the red leatherette corner seat.

Doogie accepted Matt's bottle-shaped gift bag with thanks and waved a hand to a hovering member of staff.

'Can we have some more drinks over here? What'll it be, Matt? Don't tell me Diet Coke—this is a celebration! Have some champagne!'

Matt smiled, easing himself gratefully into the waiting space. His ankle was beginning to protest strongly, in spite of the painkillers he'd dosed himself with.

'Thanks. Just one, though. I'm driving.'

'So what's the damage?' Doogie asked, gesturing at Matt's foot, then, before he had time to answer, turning to the other guests and saying, 'Matt used to ride for me, you know. You could say I discovered him. Best bloody rider I ever saw—even at sixteen! Ran away from school and turned up on my doorstep, he did. Knew what he wanted and went for it—a man after my own heart!'

Matt smiled faintly at the polite murmurs of

interest from those closest, most of whom would have heard the story many times before, and let the trainer get on with it. It *was* his birthday, after all.

*   *   *

After a couple of hours in the company of Doogie and his friends, trying not to look at the well-laden buffet table from which most of the guests were helping themselves at regular intervals, Matt felt he'd done his duty and was only waiting for the right moment to make his apologies and leave. His head was still aching and he had, for at least half of that time, been politely but firmly repelling the advances of a not so young redhead who became more amorously inclined with each glass of wine. The cottage and his bed had never seemed more desirable.

'Think I'll make a move now,' he told Doogie, as soon as the chance arose.

'Feeling a bit sore?' the elderly trainer asked, bushy white brows drawing down over eyes that were chips of brilliant blue. 'I'm not surprised. Looked a bit nasty, that fall. Thanks for coming— I'm sure you didn't feel like it.'

Matt shrugged. 'Oh, I'm OK. And I certainly wasn't going to miss your birthday bash. But I must admit I'll be thankful to get this shoe off and put my feet up.' He stood up, hopping a little as he took the bulk of his weight on his right foot.

'Oh, you're not going already?' The redhead rose with him, making a moue with lips from which scarlet was beginning to bleed into the surrounding lines. 'The party's only just started.

11

Stay with me and I'll make you forget all your troubles . . .'

'Ah, sorry. Another time, perhaps.' With his free hand, Matt lifted her arm off his shoulders and draped it, instead, over Doogie's.

'Thanks, pal,' the older man muttered, and Matt was chuckling as he turned away.

In the main function room the music was still as thumpingly loud, and the track, from Matt's point of view, was indistinguishable from whichever one had been playing when he first arrived. He glanced round for Jamie, even though they had already arranged that Matt should take the car when he was ready to go; Jamie would probably get a taxi home from Sophie's flat sometime the next day.

Suddenly, to Matt's right, there was a ripple of movement in the crowd by the bar, and, at its centre, he saw Sophie's blonde head forging through towards the dance floor with Jamie hot on her heels. Seconds later, Jamie caught up with her, grabbed her arm, and pulled her round to face him.

Whatever passed between them was lost in the unremitting pounding of the music, but the result was plain for all to see. With an ugly expression twisting her carefully made-up features, Sophie swung her arm and slapped Jamie hard across the face, rocking him back on his heels. Wrenching her arm free, she turned away, but Matt could see that Jamie wasn't going to let the matter rest and, sure enough, he recovered his balance and headed after her.

Matt groaned inwardly. Jamie had a quick temper at the best of times, something that had undoubtedly hindered his career once or twice in

12

the past, and alcohol and high emotion were a combustible combination. He watched helplessly, too far away—even without the handicap of his injured ankle—to intercept his friend before he reached the girl again.

The altercation hadn't gone unnoticed by the club's security, however, and, to Matt's relief, a burly figure stepped into Jamie's path, halting his forward progress in the nick of time by dint of placing a meaty hand on each of the young man's shoulders.

Jamie didn't take kindly to the intervention and made that abundantly clear, but, as combatants, they were woefully ill-matched. In the absence of a sling and pebbles, the smaller man took the only course available to him and swung a punch at the face some eight inches above his own.

The bouncer swayed back in a way that suggested time spent in the boxing ring, fielded the flying fist, and twisted it up behind Jamie's back. Shaking his head with grim amusement, the bouncer then steered him, with no further ado, towards the exit.

Matt let out breath he hadn't been aware of holding. He turned to follow and almost walked into a corpulent figure with sparse grey hair arranged over a shiny brown pate and weak eyes behind bottle-glass spectacles.

'Ah, Matt! Just the chap I was looking for!' the man exclaimed triumphantly. 'Didn't think I'd see you after that nasty-looking fall, but Doogie said you were here. No wonder they call you India Rubber Man!'

Matt paused, producing a smile. Roy Emmett, Tortellini's owner, was a kindly and generous man,

13

but one infamous for never making do with half a dozen words where twenty or thirty would do. He was also—although Matt personally had no problem with it—what Kendra's father disgustedly termed a 'Raving Poofter'. With a glance at the door through which Jamie and the bouncer had just disappeared, Matt resigned himself to at least twenty minutes' delay.

'Hi, Roy. How are you? And how's that horse of yours?'

Emmett beamed. 'He's well, Matt—very well. That's what I wanted to talk about . . .'

Twenty minutes turned out to be a conservative estimate; it was, in fact, nearly forty before Matt managed to get away, and then only by taking advantage of the distraction offered by the appearance of Emmett's partner.

Pleading weariness, he made his excuses and left the party behind, making as much haste as was politely and physically possible. He emerged into the car park and looked round without much hope for Jamie. A light high on the side of the building illuminated the immediate vicinity, revealing one or two snogging couples, and a dozen or more smokers, braving a blustery wind to get their fix. Jamie was not amongst them.

Matt approached the nearest group, one of whom was a young jockey he vaguely recognised.

'Hi. I'm looking for a friend . . .'

'Well, try Internet dating,' one of them suggested, and the whole group fell about laughing.

Matt smiled. 'Very good. No, this guy came out maybe half an hour ago. He was, er . . . shown out by the bouncer.'

14

'Oh, Jamie Mullin?' a girl in an eight-inch skirt and hooped earrings said, sobering up. 'Yeah, I saw him. He, like, hung around for a while and tried to get back in, but the bouncer was, like, waiting for him? Then he wanders off.'

'Did you see which way he went?'

'Nah, sorry.' She chewed gum and looked Matt up and down appraisingly. 'I could help you look, if you like.'

'Thanks, I'll manage,' Matt said.

'Suit yourself. I think he went that way.' She waved a hand in the general direction of the car park and road out before losing interest. As Matt turned away, he saw her remove a cigarette from the lips of the boy next to her and slip it between her own, drawing in a deep lungful of pollution with evident enjoyment.

Matt made his way to the corner of the building and stood, taking most of his weight on his good foot, scanning the rows of cars and the exit road. As far as he could see, there was no one in sight. If Jamie had gone that way, he was long gone.

Taking his mobile from his pocket, Matt keyed in Jamie's number, but the network's answering service cut in immediately. He left a message for Jamie to call back and returned the phone to his pocket. The only sensible course of action seemed to be for him to collect the car and head for home, keeping an eye open for Jamie as he went.

Sighing, Matt did just that, checking the vicinity of the parked car before he left. Unsure of how much his friend had had to drink, he felt it was just possible that he could have sat down to wait for him and fallen asleep, but he wasn't there.

Driving slowly, Matt scanned each side of the

road all the way down to the junction with the highway. Here he paused for a moment, the engine idling. The road he was joining had originally been the main one into Charlborough from the south until a road-straightening project had cut this section out and left it almost redundant, serving only a garden centre, the cattle market, and a newly built business park some half a mile further on. Consequently, at this time of night, it was deserted, the businesses shut and the businessmen gone home.

It seemed most likely that Jamie had either decided to walk to Charlborough or called a taxi to take him there and, irritated that he hadn't thought to let him know, Matt pushed the gear lever into *Drive* and turned left towards the town. As he pulled onto the open road, he became aware of just how much the wind had strengthened since the afternoon, the trees on the edge of the wood bowing and waving, and a few early fallen leaves scurrying along the kerb line towards him. Fifty yards or so from the junction there was a lonely bus stop followed by a stone bridge over a stream, and then the pavement came to an end, leaving any walkers to take to the road or stumble along the grass verge.

Even with his lights on main beam, Matt might easily have missed the flash of white in the trees at the side of the road, had he not been keeping an eye open for just such a thing. He pulled in with two wheels on the grass about a car's length beyond the bridge and, retrieving the stick from the passenger-seat footwell and a torch from the glove compartment, got out and made his way back.

The white turned out to be not Jamie's shirt with Jamie inside it—as he'd half hoped—but a piece of white satiny material with a fringe: a lady's evening wrap caught on a branch in the shrubby undergrowth at the side of the road. The fringed edge of the shawl was decorated with something that sparkled in the light; someone would undoubtedly be upset at having lost it.

Shrugging, Matt disentangled it from the bush it had caught on and turned back to his car. As he crossed the bridge, he could hear the rush of a fair amount of water and, drawn by it, shone the torch over the parapet into the darkness below.

He could see the river maybe fifteen or twenty feet down, foaming as it tumbled over a lip of stone under the bridge. On each bank vegetation crowded darkly and Matt would have turned away had the torch beam not sparkled on something at the edge of the water. He leant over the wall, holding the torch at arm's length, wishing the bulb had more power.

There it was again—a bright glint, as of light reflecting from the multifaceted surface of a jewel. Moving the torch from side to side, Matt scanned the surrounding area.

And froze in shock.

The beam, suddenly less than steady, had found the unmistakable outline of a woman's stiletto-heeled evening sandal and, just visible amongst the tangle of plant growth, the long smooth shape of a leg.

'Christ!'

Matt propped the hospital's walking stick against the parapet of the bridge and, using his free hand, retrieved his mobile from an inner pocket and dialled three nines while he flashed the torch to and fro over the side, seeking a way down.

By the time the emergency operator answered, Matt had decided that the left-hand side, with a scattering of saplings to hold onto, looked the better bet.

Cutting through her attempts to follow procedure, Matt gave the operator his location and requested an ambulance before returning the phone to his pocket and beginning the descent.

Climbing over three strands of wire and negotiating a steep slope, thick with vegetation, wouldn't have been easy in daylight and full fitness, but, with an injured ankle and a torch in one hand, it was going to be touch and go whether he reached the bottom on his feet or his backside.

Tripping and scrambling, covered in nettle stings, and with bramble-torn clothes and skin, he did indeed lose his footing, and slid the last three or four feet to land knee-deep in the edge of the river, swearing vociferously as the action jarred his swollen ankle.

The route Matt had chosen landed him on the opposite bank to where the woman was lying, so it was now a case of wading across the remaining six or eight feet of water and climbing out. This, in itself, presented a challenge. In the centre, where the current was relatively strong, the streambed was stony, but Matt dreaded to think what the consultant at the hospital would have said if he'd been witness to the spectacle of his patient plunging his handiwork into the thick, stinking silt near the banks.

Shining the torch into the reeds and brambles ahead of him, Matt scrambled out onto the marshy margin of the river. From here he could see both of the woman's legs, one outstretched, one bent at the knee, and the hem of a dress or skirt riding high over her hips. Chivalrous instinct bade him pull the material down to hide the skimpy white underwear that left little to the imagination, but he resisted the urge, knowing that, if she were dead, and her death was in any way suspicious, the police wouldn't be happy to find that he had tampered with their crime scene.

Treading carefully, he approached, directing the torchlight over the woman's body toward her head. She was lying on her back, with one arm outflung and the other twisted under her, a long glittering earring trailing over her neck and into her blonde hair. A dark smudge of dirt or blood discoloured the skin of her cheek and, catching the light, her eyes gleamed half-open and still. With a sense of disbelief and a sinking heart, Matt recognised her.

It was Jamie's girlfriend, Sophie.

2

Steeling himself, Matt moved forward until he was close enough to reach down and press two shaky fingers against the cool skin under the girl's jawbone. There was no detectable pulse and, with rising dread, he noticed a thin trickle of blood running blackly from her ear. It brought back painful memories of the death of a fellow jockey, kicked in the head in a horrific fall. No breath issued from her slightly parted lips to warm the back of his hand and, feeling nauseous and a little

19

panicky, he straightened up and reached into his pocket for his mobile phone. He wanted a paramedic—someone, anyone—who could tell him what to do.

The phone lit up in his trembling hand as he slid it open but could find no signal in the gully by the river. Matt cursed under his breath and forced himself to think rationally.

By his reckoning, it was getting on for ten minutes since he'd stopped the car by the bridge, so Sophie must have been lying at the bottom of the bank for at least a quarter of an hour. There had been no discernable warmth in her skin, but he didn't know how significant that was. It was a cold, windy night, and he had a fair idea that his own skin would have felt cool to the touch if he'd lain in this damp hollow for that long. Even so, there was no doubt in his mind that the girl was dead.

He shone the fading torch on her face once more. It was criss-crossed with bramble scratches, as were her arms and bare legs. How had she come to be there? Although it was just conceivable that someone looking over the bridge parapet might have overbalanced, surely then they would have fallen into the river? From the position of her body, the possibility that Sophie's death had been accidental began to look exceedingly remote.

Matt turned and regarded the bank up to the road, noticing for the first time a narrow path of smooth earth winding steeply upward through the tangle of briars and nettles. As he began the ascent, gritting his teeth against the pain in his ankle, he could hear the first sounds of a siren in the far distance.

*   *   *

To Matt, who hadn't started it in very good shape, the night seemed to stretch on interminably.

The first of the emergency services arrived, in the shape of a paramedic in a fast-response car, just as he scrambled up the last few feet of the slope and squeezed through the wire fence. Its occupant asked a few brief questions and made a call on his mobile phone before disappearing into the darkness at the side of the bridge, shining a powerful torch ahead of him.

Feeling cold and shaky, Matt went to wait in Kendra's car, and he was there when, some minutes later, a bevy of sirens and flashing blue lights heralded the advent of two police cars closely followed by an ambulance.

Suddenly the lonely spot was buzzing with activity, as the police officers donned their fluorescent-banded Day-Glo jackets and swung into action.

Matt was approached by a young WPC who, after establishing the essentials, took him to sit in one of the police cars whilst she and her partner held a conversation over the parapet with the paramedic down below. A third officer secured the scene, reeling out a quantity of orange-striped tape around the bridge area and placing cones in the road. The ambulance crew, after consultation with the police, climbed back into their vehicle and drove away, their departure confirming Sophie's demise.

In due course, someone produced wire-cutters and made an opening in the fence beside the bridge, whilst another began rigging up lighting to illuminate the scene.

A passing car slowed to view the spectacle, the driver winding down his window to call a query, only to be moved on by an officer who then took up traffic duty.

Cocooned in the police car, with the multiple flashing lights having an almost hypnotic effect, Matt had a strange sensation of detachment, as if he were watching it all on TV.

The female officer returned, sliding into the driver's seat with an accompanying rush of cold air and an apology for keeping him waiting. She introduced herself as WPC Deane and, producing a clipboard with a form attached, told him that she needed to ask him a few questions. She was about his own age—in her mid to late twenties, Matt judged by the soft glow of the car's inside light— her face boyish and her dark hair cut in short layers beneath the peaked cap. She ran through the basics of who he was, where he lived, and how he had come to be there, and then, under her sympathetic but thorough probing, he was obliged to relate the story of Jamie's row with Sophie. He felt like a traitor, but knew they would have the story soon enough, whatever he did or didn't say, and he had no wish to bring down any suspicion on his own head.

The paramedic reappeared fairly quickly, and Deane excused herself to go and speak to him, but, on her return—to Matt's frustration—she refused to divulge any information as to the probable manner or cause of Sophie's death.

Outside the vehicle, much urgent communication was carried out over radios and, as

WPC Deane made notes on the form, Matt saw two more cars arrive, pause while their occupants spoke to officers already at the scene, and then race on in the direction of the club. He supposed they had been despatched to begin questioning the partygoers, and imagined the consternation that would break out as news of Sophie's death filtered through. The racing world would be humming with it for days to come.

Moments later an unmarked BMW saloon arrived bearing a large man in civilian clothes, and it was immediately evident to Matt that the newcomer was significant. All heads turned his way and one or two of the officers hurried to meet him. The man looked up at the sky, reached into his car, and took out a mackintosh, which he put on whilst walking towards the taped-off area around the bridge. An instant later, Matt heard the first patter of rain on the roof of the car.

After a few minutes, presumably briefed on the situation, the big man turned and came towards the vehicle that Matt occupied.

WPC Deane stepped out of the car to meet him and, after they had exchanged a few words, during which Matt heard Jamie's name mentioned, the plain-clothed man bent down and his heavy-featured face appeared in the open doorway.

'Mr Shepherd, I'm Detective Inspector Bartholomew of Charlborough CID. Can you tell me where Jamie Mullin is now?'

Matt shook his head.

'No, I'm sorry. I haven't seen him since he left the club. I was looking for him when I found Sophie.'

'And he hasn't been in contact by mobile phone?'

'No.'

'Have you tried to contact him?'

'Yes, but there's no answer.'

'May I have a look at your mobile phone, please?'

Silently, Matt reached into a pocket and handed it over.

'Thank you.' The DI dropped it into an evidence bag held open by another officer. 'Do you have any idea where he might have gone?'

Matt shook his head again.

'Sorry.'

'I understand that Mr Mullin lodges with you. Is there anyone at home now?'

'The dogs. And my fiancée might be back by now. Why?'

'We'll need to take a look round.'

'What for?' Matt bridled at the thought of people—albeit police officers—rummaging through the contents of his home. 'Sophie's never been there.'

'Nevertheless, I'm afraid it has to be done. If Jamie hasn't been back there since the party, it shouldn't take too long.'

'Well, can I at least warn her?' Matt was pretty sure he already knew the answer to that one.

'I'm afraid not, but don't worry, there'll be a female officer with them. Meanwhile, I'm going to have to ask you to accompany us back to the station for further questioning, Mr Shepherd. We'll go in my car.'

'You're asking? Does that mean I have a choice?'

'Well, I wasn't going to arrest you, but I can if you'd prefer . . .'

Resignedly, Matt transferred to the DI's BMW,

where he sat in the back next to the WPC on seats that smelt of cigarette smoke. Bartholomew turned the car round and drove up to the junction with the main road where a roadblock had been set up. There he spoke briefly with the officer in charge before continuing towards Charlborough.

*   *   *

At Charlborough Police Station, Matt was given a change of clothes, his own—the trouser legs stiff with dried river silt—having been taken and bagged up for forensic examination. He was then shown to a small room furnished with a table, three chairs with bright orange upholstery and wooden arms, and a large wood-effect cupboard with sliding doors. Here, Deane asked him to wait and promised that someone would be along shortly with a cup of tea. Glad of the chance to take the weight off his ankle once more, Matt sank into one of the chairs and looked around him.

The room was in the heart of the building and had no window to the outside world. The floor wore a speckled blue carpet, the walls were covered with crime prevention and neighbourhood watch posters, and two fluorescent tubes radiated a harsh blue-white light from the yellowing Artexed ceiling.

Apart from the portly, middle-aged sergeant who brought him a mug of builders' strength tea, Matt saw no one for a good twenty minutes. The shakes had subsided now, leaving him both mentally and physically exhausted. An electric heater under the desk was billowing out heat and, with that and the soporific murmur of voices from beyond the closed door, he was more than half asleep by the time Bartholomew reappeared.

He came in carrying a mug and a clipboard and, for the first time, Matt got a good look at him in the light. He was built on impressive proportions—his burly frame well over six foot tall and dressed in a rather creased brown suit. The top button of his black shirt was open above a slightly crooked, loosely knotted tie. His hair was thick, untidy, and a nondescript shade somewhere between dark blond and brown, and his face showed signs of dissipation, even though Matt estimated he was not much more than forty.

The DI settled in one of the orange chairs, placing his mug on the carpet by his feet, and a second officer came in, stood a tape-recorder on the table, pressed a button to set it running, and retreated to stand by the door.

After a moment or two, Bartholomew gave the time and date before saying thoughtfully, '*Matt Shepherd*—jockey. I've heard of you, haven't I? Didn't you win the Derby or something?'

'No. I'm a jump jockey.'

'Would've thought you were a bit tall for a jockey . . .'

'Not for a jump jockey,' Matt informed him patiently. It was a common misconception. 'The flat-race jockeys are the little guys.'

'Oh, I see. Was it the Grand National then?'

'No. It was the Champion Hurdle.'

'Ah yes, of course.' The Inspector nodded sagely, but Matt wasn't fooled. He sat quietly, waiting for the policeman to get down to business.

'So why do they call you Mojo?'

Matt's surprise must have shown, for

26

Bartholomew added, 'My officers have been talking to your colleagues at the social club.'

'Well, we all have nicknames—mine's short for Eskimo Joe.'

'Ah. A cool customer.'

'Or maybe just a good actor,' Matt said, and the DI pursed his lips and nodded slowly.

The interview with Bartholomew more or less followed the same format as the earlier one with WPC Deane, although this time the DI informed him of his rights first.

'Am I under arrest?' Matt's heart rate had stepped up a notch, the phrases familiar from countless movies and TV shows.

'No, no,' Bartholomew soothed. 'There's a procedure to follow, that's all. Now, I know you've already been through it with my constable, but, for the tape, could you just run through the events of this evening, starting at the time you arrived at the party at . . .' he consulted his notes '. . . at The Cattle Market Social Club near Charlborough. Take your time and tell me everything you can remember—even if it doesn't seem important.'

Matt did so, and Bartholomew listened, interrupting occasionally to get him to clarify something. The detective's demeanour through-out was matter of fact and calm to the point where he sounded faintly bored.

'Was it your impression that Mr Mullin had been drinking heavily?' he asked, when Matt told him how the young jockey had been thrown out of the club.

'He'd obviously had a bit to drink, but it was a party; I'd have been more surprised if he hadn't. He didn't have to drive. I expected him to go home

27

with Sophie.'

'Is he normally a heavy drinker?'

'About average, when he's not riding, but we have to be very careful.'

'Why, particularly?'

'Because we can be tested at the track—randomly; it's just not worth the risk. Look—what happened to Sophie? How did she actually die?'

The DI regarded him thoughtfully.

'I'm not at liberty to discuss details with you—indeed, I don't *know* the details until a proper examination has taken place—but it appears that she suffered severe head injuries, and that's all I'm prepared to say.'

Behind Bartholomew the door opened and someone leaned round it to have a few quiet words with the officer standing inside. He nodded and, as the door closed, came forward to relay the message to the DI.

'Have you found Jamie?' Matt asked, catching a word or two. 'Is he all right?'

'Yes, we've found him,' Bartholomew confirmed. 'He's being brought in now. Tell me, in general, how does drink affect Jamie? Does he get argumentative? Violent?'

'No. A bit loud, perhaps, but that's all. He wouldn't hurt anyone.'

'Yes, well, unfortunately, Mr Shepherd, most of us aren't really aware of what we ourselves are capable of, let alone other people, however well we might think we know them. Alcohol and jealousy are a potent combination.'

Matt shook his head.

'I'm sure he didn't kill her.'

Bartholomew inclined his head. 'Well then, he's

28

got absolutely nothing to worry about, has he? But if he did . . .' He left the possibility hanging in the air between them and pushed himself to his feet, making ample use of the chair arms, which creaked in protest. 'Well, thank you for your time, Matt. That'll be all for now. We'll just get those fingerprints and a DNA sample and I'll see if I can find someone to run you home.'

Matt stood up.

'And what about Jamie?'

'Mr Mullin will be spending the night with us. We need to speak with him and we can't do that until he's had time to sober up. He'll be left to sleep it off for now and we'll see how he is in the morning.'

He opened the door and stood back to allow Matt to pass.

'Is he under arrest?'

'We'll speak to him in the morning,' the DI repeated. 'Goodnight, Mr Shepherd.'

*   *   *

A further hour had passed by the time arrangements had been made to get Matt home. When he enquired about Kendra's car, he was told that, like his clothing, it was classed as evidence and would have to undergo forensic tests. He realised with a shock that they wanted to check that the Honda hadn't been used to transport Sophie, or her body, to the bridge.

'Did the doctor say you were fit to drive?' Bartholomew asked, casting a doubtful look at Matt's ankle as he got up stiffly from his seat in reception.

29

'I didn't ask him.'

'Hmm. Perhaps you should have.'

'It's an automatic,' Matt pointed out. 'That's why I borrowed it.'

Bartholomew merely raised his eyebrows, so he gave up and hobbled out to the squad car with WPC Deane. Settling himself and his stick into the passenger seat, he sat back with his eyes closed, looking forward to home, a decent cup of tea, and a long overdue dose of painkillers.

It was half past three in the morning when the police car turned into the yard at the cottage. During the journey, Deane had made sporadic attempts to engage him in conversation, which lent some weight to Matt's suspicion that Bartholomew had hoped he would open up to her when he relaxed. As it was, in spite of his anxiety about Kendra, Matt was so tired that he found himself nodding off more than once and Deane gave up before they were halfway home.

At Spinney Cottage, a light glowed behind the curtains in the sitting room, but there were no other vehicles in the yard. It appeared that the police had finished their search.

'Thank you for your help, Mr Shepherd, we'll be in touch,' the WPC said, as Matt eased himself out of the car.

'Yeah, well—thanks for the lift.' Matt turned away, and, by the time he reached the front door, Deane had gone.

Letting himself in, he found Kendra curled up on the sofa, wrapped in a duvet. She appeared to be asleep, but woke up soon enough when Patches picked up a squeaky toy and started parading round the room with it to celebrate Matt's return.

'Oh, thank God you're back! Are you OK?' she said, standing up and shedding the quilt. 'The police were here for ages. I had to go next door with the dogs. Woke Terry up—but it was either that or the police station. They wouldn't tell me what they were looking for. What's going on, Matt?'

'I'm sorry. I wanted to warn you, but they wouldn't let me.'

Kendra came over and Matt enfolded her in a big hug.

'I was terrified when they turned up. I thought something had happened to you,' she said, tucking her face into the side of his neck.

'I'm sorry,' he said again. His ankle was throbbing and he was beginning to feel a bit light-headed.

'God, where on earth did you get this jumper? It's not yours, is it? It smells musty.'

'Police lost property, I shouldn't wonder,' Matt said. 'They promised me it was clean, but they took my clothes for forensic tests.'

'So what's going on? They were asking about Jamie—if I'd heard from him. Said they were working on an enquiry. Is he OK?'

Matt sighed.

'Yeah—physically, at any rate. He's at Charlborough Police Station. Sophie Bradford's dead.'

It came out more bluntly than he intended and Kendra pulled away to look at him, her eyes wide. 'Sophie? How? I mean—what happened?'

'It looks like she left the party on her own and someone attacked her.'

Kendra's eyes opened even wider.

'What? She was murdered? Oh my God! That's awful!'

'What's worse is that, at the moment, they think Jamie did it.'

'But that's ridiculous! Why would they?' Kendra exclaimed. 'Jamie wouldn't hurt anyone.'

'Well, unfortunately he and Sophie had a bit of a set-to at the party last night, in full view of everyone,' Matt told her. 'So, I suppose it's not surprising he's their number one suspect.'

He hobbled to the nearest chair and collapsed into it.

'Sophie . . .' Kendra said wonderingly. 'It's hard to believe. Poor girl! I mean—I won't pretend I ever really liked her—but you wouldn't wish something like this on anyone, would you?'

'Just at the moment, all I wish for is to get this shoe off before my ankle explodes. Everything else will just have to wait,' Matt said wearily.

*　　　*　　　*

One of the few drawbacks of being stable jockey in John Leonard's yard was that it placed Matt under the controlling influence of Kendra's father, Charlie Brewer. Brewer's string of thirty or so thoroughbreds represented nearly half the horses in training at the Rockfield yard and—as the businessman wasn't above reminding Leonard when they experienced a difference of opinions— the trainer owed his success and ongoing career almost entirely to him.

Leonard, ex-RAF and son of a gentleman farmer, had already been training racehorses at the time Kendra's father had first met him, desperately struggling against an ever-increasing tide of debt that had been set in motion by crippling inheritance taxes. Brewer, for his part, had just made the decision to spend a little of his considerable wealth on a racehorse or two, and was looking around for a trainer. His eye had alighted on Leonard's struggling yard at Rockfield Farm, less than a dozen miles from Brewer's home, and, within a very short space of time, he had bought the farm and stables, taken the trainer onto his payroll, and added half a dozen well-bred youngsters to the eleven animals already there.

Six years on, Rockfield ranked amongst the most successful yards in the country, and Brewer's string of horses were the envy of many a more established owner. And if, in due course, Leonard had any reservations about this wholesale takeover of his home, life, and career, he had never shared them with Matt in the three years he'd known him, and no doubt felt it to be a small price to pay in return for the many advantages of the arrangement. In his early sixties, he could now face the prospect of retirement with equanimity and the comfort of knowing that his disabled son was assured of a job.

Matt was aware that it was a source of irritation to Brewer that he couldn't control Matt in the same way, more especially since he had become engaged to Brewer's daughter. Matt knew he wasn't the man the social-climbing businessman had hoped for Kendra to settle down with and had resisted the attraction himself for some time, wary of the implications of marrying the boss's daughter, but, in the end, the chemistry had been too strong.

True to his character, when Brewer had realised that he couldn't stop the relationship developing, he sought instead to manage it. Here, too, he had been thwarted. Matt had remained politely but stubbornly independent, rejecting his future father-in-law's handsome offer to build them a home in the shadow of his own, Birchwood Hall, in favour of staying on in Spinney Cottage, some twenty miles away.

For a while after this disagreement, Brewer had been a little cool towards him, but Matt had affected not to notice it and lately the businessman had shown a measure of acceptance.

One dictate that he and Kendra did bow down to was that they should join the rest of the family for the Sunday evening meal at Birchwood Hall. This doubled as a social occasion and a chance for Brewer to discuss with his jockey the timetable and prospects for the week ahead.

The day following Doogie's party was no exception, and seven o'clock found Kendra parking Matt's car on the broad sweep of gravel in front of the Brewer family home.

Birchwood Hall was a Regency-period country house of some stature and importance with an imposing three-storey façade and a colonnaded front door sufficient to satisfy the most ostentatious of occupants. With upward of thirty main rooms, numerous outbuildings, a stable block, and an orangery that had been converted into a swimming pool, it stood in formal gardens, surrounded by about seventy acres of park and farmland.

Much as Charlie Brewer would have loved to claim it as a family seat, handed down through the generations, the truth was that he'd bought it less than twenty years before; his own antecedents having eked out a far less privileged existence as farm labourers in Suffolk. Her grandfather, according to Kendra, had been a second-hand car dealer.

She and Matt were met at the door by the Brewers' butler-cum-occasional-chauffeur, Greening, who informed them that the family were assembled in the drawing room. They always were at this time on a Sunday evening, but the politenesses had to be observed.

It was typical that the first person Matt saw as he followed Kendra into the elegant reception room was her father. At forty-six, tanned and bald-headed, he was a muscular six foot or so, with shrewd blue eyes in a strong face that sported a designer moustache and close-cut goatee beard. There was no denying that he was a striking figure, and it was easy to see, in the middle-aged man, the good-looking young lad-about-town who had swept a seventeen-year-old debutante off her feet at a summer ball some twenty-five years before. The intervening period had added to that charm an indefinable presence born of success, so that he seemed to inexorably draw the eye, dominating any gathering at which he was present.

Reclining in a gold brocade wing chair, with a glass of red wine in his hand, Charlie Brewer looked up as his daughter and her fiancé entered, but it was his wife, Joy, who stood and came to meet them across the immaculate cream carpet.

'Ah, here they are. Hello darling! Oh dear! How's that ankle of yours, Matt?' she asked in quick sympathy, her brows drawing down over a

35

pair of fine brown eyes. Slim, with long blonde hair, she was often mistaken for an elder sister rather than the mother of her four grown-up children. Matt was extremely fond of her.

'It'll be fine in a day or two,' he assured her, as they exchanged kisses.

'Wouldn't have happened if you hadn't ridden Smythe's horse,' Brewer commented from across the room. 'Missed out on Secundo, didn't you?'

'Yes. That'll teach me, won't it?' Matt observed, with a quizzical smile. 'Still, Jamie did a good job on him.'

Brewer grunted. 'That horse would have won whoever was on his back, but that's not the point. You're the stable jockey.'

'Yes, well let's not start the evening with an argument, darling,' Joy put in. 'Matt didn't hurt his foot on purpose, I imagine.'

Matt was grateful to her. As stable jockey, he was technically employed by Leonard and answerable to him alone, but, because of the trainer's dependence on Brewer, the issue was a little confused. Brewer was strongly of the opinion that Matt should ride for Rockfield and no other yard, even to the point of offering to subsidise him for any loss of income, but Matt wasn't prepared to sign up for that. He liked to be busy; he liked variety; and he was also very wary of placing all his eggs in one basket. Besides which, as his reputation continued to grow, he was getting some really good rides from other yards. The Champion Hurdle win had been on a horse from Doogie McKenzie's yard and the Scottish trainer had a number of youngsters that he was looking forward to riding.

Kendra left his side to go and give her father a kiss and, glancing round the room, Matt waved a hand and voiced an all-encompassing greeting. He did a swift head count. There would be eight sitting down to dinner on this occasion, as the whole family was present. He knew Kendra's two elder sisters, Grace and Frances, and her younger brother, Deacon, who was seated in one of the wing chairs with one of his two Persian cats on his lap. The only person he didn't recognise was a young man who was sitting on the settee next to Kendra's eldest sister, Grace.

'Come and meet Rupert,' Joy said, taking Matt's arm and steering him towards the pair.

As they approached, the young man rose to his feet and Matt found that he was of a similar height and age to himself, with receding blond hair and rather weak, pale blue eyes. His carefully casual clothes screamed money, from the Calvin Klein polo shirt down to the toes of his Timberland leather trainers.

'Rupert Beaufort,' the young man announced, before Joy had a chance to introduce him. He stretched out a beautifully manicured hand. 'And you must be the jockey.'

'That's right,' Matt agreed, shaking the soft-skinned hand and quelling an impulse to tighten his grip and wipe the slightly patronising smile off Beaufort's face. 'Matt Shepherd.'

'Rupert's father is Jarvis Beaufort,' Grace announced, in the tone of one imparting a golden nugget of information. She stood up and came forward to put her hand on Beaufort's designer-jacketed arm. 'He owns Beaufort's the Jewellers.'

And diamonds are a girl's best friend, Matt

thought dryly, raising his eyebrows and inclining his head in a spurious show of interest.

Three years older than Kendra, Grace was stick-slim and, in Matt's estimation, the smile on her face was about as natural as the blondeness of her hair. She had her father's colouring and rampant ambition, but little of his charm.

'Rupert has promised to take me on a private tour of the London showroom and studios,' she said. 'It'll be wonderful.'

'Oh, how exciting!' Kendra exclaimed, coming over in time to save Matt from having to find something polite to say.

Grace positively glowed with satisfaction, and it occurred to Matt, not for the first time, that she was a little jealous of her younger sister.

When they sat down to dinner at the fifteen-foot-long, mahogany table, under the lights of three cut-glass chandeliers, Matt was pleased to find himself next to Kendra's second sister, Frances. At twenty-three, she was just a year younger than Grace, but couldn't have been more different. Taller, bigger built, and plainer than her siblings, she wore her shoulder-length brown hair unbleached, and a minimal amount of make-up and jewellery, but she had an attraction all her own. Intelligent and practical, with a sharp wit, which she wasn't averse to sharing, she was, to her father's eternal mystification, training to be a child psychologist.

'So, what do you think of Grace's latest conquest?' she murmured to Matt as they began the meal. 'Impeccable qualifications, wouldn't you say?'

He glanced at her in amusement, not pretending

to misunderstand.

'Oh, definitely. Diamonds and an Eton accent—perfect.'

At the head of the table, Brewer cleared his throat.

'Nasty business that, last night,' he commented, breaking a roll to dip into his asparagus soup. 'Deacon had already left, but I think Harry got caught up in it. It was a hell of a business, I gather. Were you there when the police turned up?'

'No, I'd already left too,' Matt said.

Kendra looked at him, raising her eyebrows infinitesimally, but didn't say anything.

'That poor girl!' Joy said.

Grace was less sympathetic. 'It was on the news earlier. They made her sound like such an innocent little thing, but you should have seen the way she was dancing—she was asking for it.'

'Oh no—you can't say that!' her mother responded. 'God knows she wasn't a saint, but no one deserves that!'

'I didn't see you at the party,' Matt remarked to Grace. He'd declined the soup, knowing from experience that it was rich and creamy. With two further courses to come, he had to watch his fat intake.

'Oh, Rupert and I just popped in for a few minutes. We were passing and there was someone he wanted a word with. Sophie was dancing on one of the tables when I saw her, and Jamie was looking as mad as fire. No wonder; she can't have had much on under that dress.'

'I think she looked beautiful,' Deacon put in.

He was sitting diagonally across the table from Matt, and had been very quiet until then. Even

39

now he spoke as if to himself, his dark eyes dreamy under the fringe that flopped over his fine-boned face. At nineteen he was heir to a business empire worth millions, but, as yet, had shown no great desire to become involved in the running of it. With uncharacteristic patience, his father had been heard to say he had no doubt the lad would come to it in time.

'She was a slut!' Grace declared.

'Now, come on,' Joy intervened. 'I think that's enough. Whatever else she was, she was someone's daughter and nothing excuses the taking of a life. Let's talk about something else, shall we?'

There was an uncomfortable silence for a moment, broken only by the chink of cutlery on china, and then Grace spoke again.

'No prizes for guessing who the number one suspect will be, anyway,' she remarked, and Matt could cheerfully have throttled her.

Her father pushed his empty bowl aside.

'Who?'

'Well, Jamie Mullin, of course. She's been leading him round by the nose for weeks and they had an almighty row last night—right in the middle of the dance floor!'

'That doesn't mean he killed her!' Kendra protested. 'Jamie wouldn't do anything like that and you know it!'

'I didn't say he would. I just said he'd be the prime suspect.'

Greening came in with a heated trolley, removed the soup bowls, and replaced them with plates for the next course. When he'd departed, leaving the diners to help themselves to a roast dinner of generous proportions, Brewer stated that nothing

40

would surprise him about Mullin.

'Oh, darling, that's not fair!' his wife said reproachfully, and Matt kept his temper with an effort, knowing that the businessman had disliked Jamie ever since the Irishman had told him, with debatable tact, that one of his most expensive horses would never make the grade. In Matt's opinion, Jamie would almost certainly be proved right in the long run, but, for the sake of a good working relationship, the opinion would really have been better left unaired.

'I like Jamie,' Deacon said thoughtfully. 'Top bloke!'

Kendra looked across curiously. 'Are you hungover, Deke?'

'I hope not!' Brewer frowned heavily, and Matt caught Rupert looking from one to the other in surprise.

Joy had evidently noticed as well.

'Deacon suffers from migraines,' she explained to the newcomer. 'He's supposed to stay off the alcohol, aren't you, darling?'

'Oh, bad luck, old boy,' Rupert commiserated, but Deacon merely shrugged, looking philosophical.

'So, have the police spoken to Jamie yet?' Grace was like a dog worrying at a bone.

'They're speaking to everyone who was there,' Matt hedged, helping himself to a modest helping of roast chicken and veg.

'I heard they'd arrested him.'

'They've taken him in for questioning, that's all,' Matt said, ruthlessly suppressing his natural honesty. 'It's just routine. They've already spoken to me, and I expect they'll be after you and Rupert

41

before long.'

'What for? *We* didn't see anything, we were only there about twenty minutes.'

'Well, I don't suppose Jamie saw anything either.'

Grace subsided, looking annoyed, and then, with a sweetly malicious smile, picked up the dish of crispy roast potatoes and offered them to Matt.

He returned her smile with a sarcastic one of his own and shook his head. Potatoes, especially roasted or chipped, were one of the things he had to ration when he was racing, and to give in to temptation was to set foot on the slippery slope that would mean long, dreary hours spent in the sauna.

'No? Oh—*sorry*, I was forgetting, you have to watch your weight, don't you? How silly of me.'

'Grace, you're a bitch,' Frances said flatly, but her sister just laughed.

'That's enough!' Brewer finally took a hand, apparently dismissing Sophie's demise as of no further interest. 'So what did the doctor say about your ankle, Matt? Will you be fit to ride Cheddah on Wednesday?'

'Can't see why not. It's just badly bruised, that's all.'

'You'd have done far better resting it last night, instead of going out partying,' he groused, balancing three Yorkshire puddings on the edge of his plate, out of the gravy.

Matt didn't rise to the bait. Brewer had always been a little jealous of his enduring loyalty to Doogie McKenzie. He'd have been even less pleased if he'd been privy to Matt's nocturnal scramble to the riverside.

'Yeah, you're probably right,' he agreed, evenly.

Having had the wind effectively let out of his sails, Brewer subsided and applied himself to his meal.

* * *

When Matt and Kendra got back to Spinney Cottage just before midnight, they found Jamie sitting at the kitchen table, head on arms, asleep. A mug of something that had once been hot stood in front of him, untouched. It seemed that he had slept through the commotion of the dogs' greetings, but he raised his head sleepily when Matt said his name.

'Are you OK?' Kendra asked. 'When did you get back?'

Jamie rubbed a hand over his face. He looked pale and there were dark circles under his eyes.

'Absolutely shattered. Got back about ...' he looked at his watch, 'an hour ago.'

Kendra put a hand on his arm.

'I'm so sorry about Sophie, Jamie. What a horrible thing to have happened.'

'They think I did it,' he said bleakly.

'Is that what they said?' Kendra asked indignantly. 'That's ridiculous!'

'If they really thought that, they wouldn't have let you go,' Matt reasoned.

'Well, they haven't got any evidence, have they? Only circumstantial—nothing definite.'

'Well, that's all right then, because they won't find any, will they?' Kendra took the fabric of his shirt between her fingers. 'Did they dress you from lost property, too?'

43

Jamie glanced down at the red and black checks.

'Yeah, they took my clothes for forensic testing. It was either these or one of those white boiler suit decontamination things you see them wearing on telly.' He looked at Matt. 'They took your clothes too then. Have they questioned you?'

'Yeah. Last night. It was me that found her.'

'*You*? Where was she? They wouldn't tell me. I think they thought I knew and were hoping I'd let it slip.'

'Just a couple of hundred yards down the road from the club; there's a bridge over a river—she was at the bottom of the bank.'

'So how come you were there?'

'I was looking for you and I saw Sophie's shawl-thing caught in the bushes as I drove by,' Matt told him, taking the kettle to the sink and filling it. 'Where the hell had you got to, anyway?'

'I went the other way. I wanted a drink and I thought there was a pub up the road, but it was closed—boarded up and everything. I started walking back and then this lorry driver stopped and offered me a lift. I was feeling really pissed off by then, so I thought—why not?'

'So did anyone see you, apart from the lorry driver?'

'No. That's what the police asked me. There's nothing much up that way, except that industrial estate and the pub. Well, not even that now. I didn't see a soul. There weren't even many cars on the road.'

'And what about the lorry? Do you remember anything about that?'

Jamie shook his head.

'You don't see much when it's coming towards

you, just lights. It was foreign. The driver didn't speak much English. I think he might have been Romanian or something. To be honest, I didn't take much notice, I was just grateful not to have to walk. He dropped me in Charlborough and I went to a nightclub. Gino's, I think it was. I just wanted to get blotto.'

'And is that where Bartholomew's lot found you?'

'Yeah. I came out for a smoke and there was a car sitting outside with a couple of coppers in it. I think they were just there keeping an eye on the clubbers, but they must have had my description.'

'I thought you'd given up smoking,' Kendra put in, accusingly.

'Yeah, well I have—mostly. Anyway, these coppers wandered over, kind of casually, and asked me my name. I told them. I mean, I didn't know what was going on—not knowing about Sophie. And then they arrested me. God—what a shock! I couldn't believe it.'

'Tea or coffee?' Matt's hand hovered over the tea caddy.

'Er . . . Tea's fine.'

'Me too,' Kendra said. 'So, what started it all? I mean, what was the argument about?'

Jamie pulled a face.

'Her ex-boyfriend was there—at the party. Darren something-or-other. She was flirting with him when we got there and then she danced with him. God, you should have seen them! His fucking hands were all over her. I told her I wasn't happy about it, that's all.'

'And she said . . . ?'

'She said it was my problem, not hers, and I

45

could fuck off for all she cared.'

Matt could imagine Sophie saying that. He was sure there was nothing she'd have liked better than to have two men fighting over her, especially in public.

'So you grabbed her and she slapped you,' he said. 'You should have let it go, you know. She wasn't worth it.'

Jamie groaned.

'I know, but I'd had a couple of drinks—I wasn't thinking straight. But she's never been like that before. It's not like her.'

In Matt's opinion it was *just* like her, but he didn't say so. Jamie would find out soon enough; there was bound to be talk.

'There you go.' He put two mugs of tea on the table.

Jamie looked at his without enthusiasm.

'Actually, I think I'll just shower and go to bed. Do you mind? I feel kind of dirty.' He stood up and looked at each of them in turn, the strain of the last twenty-four hours plain to see. 'I didn't do it, you know.'

'Well, of course you didn't!' Kendra exclaimed. 'Nobody doubts that.'

'Oh don't they?' Jamie retorted bitterly. 'Nobody except DI Bar-fucking-tholomew and his mob, maybe. I tell you, you're so knackered by the time they've finished with you, you're even beginning to doubt yourself. Whatever happened to "innocent until proven guilty"?'

'They don't know you,' Matt reminded him. 'And you must admit, from their point of view, it doesn't look good.'

'But it was just a stupid quarrel. We'd have

46

kissed and made up in a day or two, most likely.'

'You were drunk. People do stupid things when they're drunk. After all, no one's saying you meant to kill her. It could have been a tragic accident.'

'But I *didn't* kill her. I told you what happened. I never saw her again after I left the club. I kept telling the police that, but they wouldn't believe me.'

'It's just ridiculous!' Kendra protested. 'Why don't they ask around? Anyone would tell them you'd never do something like that.'

'Would they, though?' Matt countered. 'You might think so, but plant a doubt in their minds and I suspect a number of people would think twice about being a character witness. Don't forget, almost everyone at the party saw the row.' He hated to play devil's advocate, but he felt Kendra was being naïve.

Kendra stared challengingly at him, but Jamie nodded.

'You're probably right. I expect I'd be one of the first to point the finger, if it was someone else.' He picked up his mug and headed for his room, pausing in the doorway to add, 'But thanks anyway, Kennie—you're a sweetheart.'

As the door closed behind him, Kendra squared up to Matt hotly.

'What Jamie needs now is support—not you doubting him too!'

'I'm *not* doubting him. I fought his corner as hard as I could with Bartholomew last night, but I think he has to face facts. Things don't look good and I don't think he can count on everyone sticking by him. If only he'd waited and had it out with Sophie in a less public place. Bloody woman!

I did try and warn him about her, but I feel guilty that I didn't try harder. Not that he'd have listened. And, when all's said and done, I expected her to mess him around, but there's no way I could ever have foreseen this.'

3

'JOCKEY'S GIRLFRIEND FOUND DEAD AFTER FIGHT AT PARTY'

The headline screamed at Matt as he pulled the newspaper through the flap of the letterbox the next morning. He groaned, opening it out. The text was bordered on each side by a photograph. On the left, there was one of Sophie Bradford, taken some years earlier, looking virginal in a floaty white dress, and, on the right, a picture of Jamie, scowling over his shoulder, as he entered the weighing room at one of the racecourses. Possibly Chepstow, Matt decided, wondering how long it had taken someone to trawl through the archives for that shot. Quite a while, probably; Jamie was generally sunny-natured and nearly always produced a wide, engaging grin for the cameras.

Taking the paper through to the kitchen, he scanned the article. It wasn't helpful. He read that 'sources at the party' were quoted as saying that Sophie was a 'popular young woman' and that 'Irish steeplechase jockey Jamie Mullin' had appeared 'moody and jealous' during the evening and had 'a violent disagreement with her' shortly before the attack. The only good news was that no mention was made of Matt's part in the night's events. It was believed that a passing motorist discovered the body, the paper reported.

Jamie was still in bed, able to slip in and out of the early-rising habit in a way that Matt envied. His own inner alarm clock woke him religiously at half past five whether he was riding or not, though, on most mornings, he would be riding 'work' for one trainer or another. It was an integral part of being a jockey, helping the trainer assess the race-fitness of his horses, and giving himself the chance to get to know the youngsters before riding them on the track for the first time. Matt would have been riding that morning, if he hadn't felt it sensible to rest his ankle for a couple more days.

Leafing through the newspaper over breakfast, he toyed briefly with the idea of throwing it away before Jamie appeared downstairs, but knew that it would only be postponing the inevitable; he would have to face up to the inflammatory needling of the press sooner or later—better that it happened in the sanctuary of Spinney Cottage than in public view on a racecourse.

Jamie's reaction to the article was one of voluble indignation. He held forth for several minutes on the subject of what measures he would take against the editors of the *Daily Standard*, each idea as doomed to failure as the last. Matt bore the tirade with patience, aware that beneath the bluster there was a rippling undercurrent of panic.

'Don't try and take the papers on,' he advised, when Jamie's first outburst had spent itself. 'All you'll do is give them more to write about. There's nothing they'd like better.'

'So what the hell am I supposed to do? Sit back and let them write lies about me?'

'Yeah—basically. It's all you can do.' Having been in the public eye longer than Jamie, Matt had had more experience in dealing with the press. 'Keep your head down and get on with your work. People who know you won't believe all that stuff anyway. I'm sure the police will come up with something before long, and you'll be off the hook.'

'I don't like that Bartholomew,' Jamie muttered, staring broodingly into his coffee mug.

'You don't have to like him! I'm not asking you to bloody sleep with him—just trust him to do his job and get on with yours!'

*   *   *

The following day—the Tuesday—saw Jamie riding at Aylesbury. Matt saw him off with mixed feelings. His ankle felt a lot better and it was hard to see someone else taking his rides, but, on the other hand, it would take Jamie's mind off Sophie's death and the police enquiry.

'Be careful with Tulip Time,' he told the Irishman over the breakfast table. 'If you have to use your whip, make sure you keep it behind your leg. If you wave it near his head, he'll stop; he's a moody bugger! And you'll need to keep Inkster covered up for the first circuit. The owner will tell you to take him to the front, so just nod and ignore him. If you give him too much daylight early on, he'll pull your arms out and not look where he's going. First time I rode him, he got away from me and went arse over ears at the first fence!'

'But you won on him last time out, didn't you?'

50

'Yeah. Well, I do try not to make the same mistake twice. He's a good enough horse—you just have to time your run right. I shouldn't think there's much in the field to trouble him.'

'Except Rubblestubble.' Jamie had done his homework. In spite of his happy-go-lucky image, he was very serious about his racing and studied the form.

'Rubblestubble isn't proven on the fast ground,' Matt said. 'And, with his action, I don't think it'll suit him.'

He was going by the general rule that horses that galloped with a higher knee action found firmer ground more jarring, which often took the edge off their enthusiasm. It couldn't be regarded as an absolute science, because temperament had to be taken into account; some horses would ignore the discomfort and suffer for it afterwards. To avoid the risk of long-term damage, a sensible trainer wouldn't race such horses on firm ground unless the stakes were very high.

Jamie left the house mid-morning, but he didn't take all the tension with him. In spite of his advice to carry on as though nothing had happened, Matt knew it wasn't going to be easy for his friend, and couldn't help worrying about him. The morning's headlines wouldn't have helped, either. The *Daily Standard* had discovered that Sophie Bradford was related to one of the top brass in the Jockey Club—racing's ruling body—and led with the headline 'ROADSIDE ATTACK VICTIM WAS LORD KENNING'S NIECE'. Listed as riding at Aylesbury, Jamie was going to be a sitting duck for the media, many of whom would no doubt be trying to provoke some kind of reaction—

51

something juicy to put in print. Matt could only hope his friend would be able to keep a rein on his volatile temper.

As the day wore on, it became clear that some helpful soul had divulged the fact that Jamie lodged with Matt and, after the fourth call from snooping reporters, Matt left the receiver off the house phone and turned his mobile on instead.

The afternoon's racing was broadcast on television, and Matt watched Jamie pilot Tulip Time to a respectable third place and then ride a brilliant race on Inkster to win by two lengths. With the last of Jamie's three races being run after TV coverage had finished, Matt switched off, thinking that he'd have to watch his back if the boy was going to ride too many more like that.

When Jamie returned later that afternoon, Matt was sanding down a window frame in the newly built extension at the back of the house. The Irishman sought him out as soon as he got in, and Matt could see straight away that he wasn't happy.

'Hiyah. What's up? Should have thought you'd be over the moon. Two good results.'

'Fliss Truman had two spare rides this afternoon because Rollo had a hard fall in Tulip Time's race, but she put Bully up instead of me.'

'Well, she's allowed to,' Matt pointed out reasonably.

'Yeah, I know, but she always uses me.'

'Well, did you ask her why?'

'Yeah. She said the owner asked for someone else. No prizes for guessing why.'

'You don't know that. Maybe they wanted a more experienced jockey. It happens,' Matt said.

52

'I won on one of those horses in the spring,' Jamie said bitterly. 'I remember, because the owner gave me a twenty-quid note. Now, suddenly, he doesn't want to know me.'

Matt sighed.

'OK, so you're getting a bit of fallout from the weekend, but it'll blow over, give it time.'

'How much time?' Jamie demanded. 'Until the police find the bastard that killed Sophie? What if they never do, huh? What then? People will look at me for years, and wonder if I did it.'

'I'm sorry, I don't have all the answers. I know it isn't easy, but I don't see that you have a lot of choice,' Matt said, adding more brightly, 'Inkster went well for you, didn't he? I watched on telly. You'll be taking that ride off me, if I'm not careful.'

'Oh God, yes—TV! They wanted to interview me after Inkster, but I managed to dodge them. Did they say anything about—you know?'

'It was Ted Barker. He just said you were bound to be a bit upset because you'd just lost a close personal friend. He's a good bloke, Ted.'

Jamie grunted, flopping down on the extension's only piece of furniture, an old dust-sheeted chair, and levering his right shoe off with the toe of his left. As he repeated the operation with the other foot, Kendra's little sheltie, ever sensitive to distress, padded into the room and laid her head on his knee. He stroked her soft fur absent-mindedly.

'It was really weird today. The bloody reporters all wanted to talk to me and everyone else treated me like a leper.'

'The lads in the weighing room were all right

though, weren't they?'

'Yeah, mostly. Razor made a few remarks.'

'Well, I shouldn't let that worry you. Everyone knows what he's like.' All the jump jockeys had nicknames and Geoff Hislop's was a direct result of his acerbic tongue and cruel wit. He was a man with few close friends.

'Yeah, but he's a jammy git, too. Did you see him trying to box me in on Inkster? I was shouting for some light, but the bastard knew I had the better horse and he wasn't going to let me out. That guy has the luck of the devil with the stewards! If that had been you or me, we'd have been hauled up and handed a suspension before we knew where we were!'

Matt shrugged.

'They're just doing their job. Don't take it personally.'

Jamie nodded glumly. He had a bit of a persecution complex where the stewards were concerned. Each race meeting had three stewards, usually local people of some standing, who were responsible for overseeing fair play under the guidance of the Stipendiary Steward, in whose hands the final decision was left. In Matt's own experience, their judgements were generally fair, but the system wasn't perfect and, on some occasions, you just had to accept the punishment and put it behind you. There was the option to appeal, but, unless the stakes were very high, it was rarely taken up.

Matt felt sorry for Jamie.

'Hey, don't let them get you down, kiddo. Give the police a couple of days and they'll probably have taken someone in for questioning and then the heat'll be off you. They'll find who did this, don't worry.'

*   *   *

Matt's words were only intended as a reassurance for the moment, which was just as well, because the following morning's paper put paid to any good they might have done.

The two of them had risen early and driven over to Rockfield in Jamie's ageing MG Roadster to ride work and do some schooling for John Leonard on the all-weather gallops, half a mile from the yard. The session had gone well, with all the horses seeming to be fit and happy in their exercise, and Matt was pleased to find that the strain of riding produced no more than a dull ache in his ankle. Dull aches were nothing—in a sport where you can expect an average of one in ten races to end in a fall, injuries were commonplace and bruises practically the norm. Coping with the wear and tear was all part of the game, and having a body that could take the punishment and repair itself quickly one of the necessary qualifications.

Peeling off his outer layer of clothing in the warmth of the kitchen at Rockfield Farm, Matt breathed in the heavenly aroma of grilled bacon and exhaled with a sigh of contentment. Irene Leonard had years of experience in cooking for jockeys and stable lads, and he knew the bacon would be lean and cooked over a drip tray. The farmhouse kitchen was like a second home to Matt, its old-fashioned cream-painted cupboards and dresser, uneven flagged floor, and green checked curtains as familiar to him as the more

55

modern, fitted one at Spinney Cottage.

'Good mornin' to you, Reney,' Jamie said cheerfully, broadening his accent comically. 'You're looking as pretty as a May morning, so you are! How do you do it?'

Irene looked up from stirring teabags in a huge earthenware pot. She frowned at him and prodded the air with a long-handled spoon. 'You're a disrespectful young varmint!' she scolded, but there was a glow of pleasure about her. 'Wash your hands, sit down, and keep your Irish charm for someone naïve enough to be taken in by it!'

'My, but you've a sharp tongue about you, gal!' Jamie shook his head mournfully.

'Old Brodie reckons Temperance Bob won't like the ground,' John Leonard reported, following Matt and Jamie into the kitchen with the paper open at the racing page. He took his cap off to reveal a sunbronzed pate ringed by a fringe of grey hair. Old Brodie was a well-regarded tipster with a regular slot on the racing page of the *Standard*. 'He should have come up and watched him work the last few days.'

'Certainly didn't *feel* like he had any issues with it,' Matt agreed. The horse had been pulling hard on the gallops that morning.

'Wash up and sit down,' Irene told her husband, putting the teapot and three mugs on the table. In her late fifties, she had collar-length reddish-blonde hair, a stout figure invariably clothed in a navy pinafore dress, and a face as smooth and pink-cheeked as a child in a storybook.

The trainer obediently headed for the sink, dropping the paper beside his place-setting, where it was instantly fielded by Jamie.

56

Matt watched him as he scanned the pages and could see by the change in his expression that he didn't like what he found.

'Listen to this . . .' Jamie exclaimed. ' "Mullin was riding at Fontwell yesterday, for all the world as though nothing had happened." What did they expect me to do? Go around bawling my eyes out? And here, it says I'm "surly and secretive". What the hell is that supposed to mean? Just because I didn't want to spend all day being interviewed by reporters? How can they say that? And listen: "Today, Mullin, who often steps in when Gallagher is injured, was passed over in favour of Bob Jennings, who made a very good job of riding two for Fliss Truman." No mention of my ride on Inkster at all!'

Matt's heart sank. Jamie had been pretty much his normal upbeat self so far that morning, but, in a few short moments, the article had brought his sense of fear and grievance jangling back to the surface.

Leonard turned away from the sink, drying his hands on a tea towel. Tall and trim in corduroys and a checked shirt, he was an intelligent man who was generally liked and respected, both around the yard and by his peers in the racing world.

'It's only one person's opinion, lad,' he said calmly. 'And it's their job to sensationalise—you know that. Take no notice.'

'Trouble is—other people take notice,' Jamie pointed out. 'I already missed out on two rides yesterday. You know I rely on picking up last-minute rides; they're just not going to happen, if this goes on.'

'Well, you've got two decent rides today for Mr

Brewer, so concentrate on those and let the future take care of itself,' the trainer advised, and Jamie nodded glumly.

'Where's Harry this morning? Did he have a bad night?' Matt asked as Irene put a slice of wholemeal toast with bacon and tomato in front of him. After his accident, Harry, the trainer's wheelchair-bound son, had suffered debilitating bouts of sleeplessness, when the pain from his damaged spine had kept him awake, sometimes for nights on end. Nowadays, these episodes were a rarity, but it was unusual for Harry to miss watching the morning gallops, and Matt was concerned.

'No, he's fine.' Leonard speared one of two fried eggs with his fork and dunked his toast in the yolk. 'He's gone on ahead in the car. Said he wanted to call in on someone on the way—can't remember who. Oh, and he's going to pick up some bits and pieces from Greaves, you know—the saddler.'

'That car of his has been a godsend, hasn't it?' Matt said, trying not to look at the forbidden eggs. As a personal friend of Harry's, he knew that the most devastating consequence of his accident had been the loss of his independence, and the funding of a specially adapted MPV by the Injured Jockeys' Fund had been a tremendous boost to his mental recovery. If only his physical recovery could follow suit, Matt thought sadly, but it seemed the doctors were at a bit of a standstill as regards that.

'Saved his life, I shouldn't wonder.' Having seen to everyone else, Irene finally sat at the table with a slice of toast and a mug of tea.

'Was it that bad?' Matt knew Harry had been depressed, but he had had no idea it had been that serious. Harry hid his feelings well, and Matt experienced a twinge of guilt that he hadn't made the time to find out how his friend had *really* been coping.

'I don't think it was quite *that* tragic,' Leonard moderated, with a frown at his wife. 'Harry's a tough lad. He just had a low spell. It's not surprising; it can happen to anyone.'

*   *   *

'Jamie's here, then,' Jim Steady commented, as he laid out the silks for Matt's first race. Steady was Matt's racecourse valet. They were in the weighing room at Worcester racecourse and all around them were jockeys in various stages of undress, preparing for the coming afternoon's racing. The weighing room was actually a misnomer for the changing room; the area where the jockeys actually weighed out being known as 'The Scales'.

'Yeah, he's got two rides,' Matt said, in answer to the valet's remark. He was surprised. Steady surely knew that; he usually valeted for Jamie, too.

Steady grunted. 'I know, I just thought . . .'

'You thought what?'

The valet looked uncomfortable. 'Well, I don't know nothing about it, but there was this rumour going round this morning that he'd been arrested.'

Was there indeed? Matt looked across to where Jamie was taking off his jacket, noticing that, where he would normally have been part of a lively crowd, now he was isolated, or as isolated as it was possible to be in the fairly cramped changing area. The tide of busy, chattering, laughing men and boys was parting around him, as though he were a

59

rock in a stream. The young Irishman was keeping his head down for the most part, although, as Matt watched, Jamie glanced up and caught his eye, shrugging slightly. The look on his face might have fooled the casual observer, but Matt knew him well and could tell he was intensely unhappy.

'So, what else are they saying?' he demanded of the valet. Jamie was generally well liked, and the other jockeys were usually pretty supportive when one of their number was in trouble. Something was going on, and he suspected he hadn't been told because he was known to be Jamie's particular friend.

Jim Steady wouldn't meet Matt's eyes. He muttered something about having others to see to, and would have made his getaway if Matt hadn't caught his arm.

'Jim! Tell me.'

'Oh look—I don't really know; I wouldn't like to say. It's none of my business really.'

'Well, which is it? You don't know, or you don't want to say?'

'Look, I'm not saying I believe it—I've always thought he was a nice lad, but what I heard was that the girl that was murdered the other night was raped before she was killed. And they're saying that Jamie did it. I don't believe it, mind,' he added hastily.

'That's absolute rubbish!' Matt said. '*Who's* saying it? Who told you?'

'I'm not sure I remember. So she wasn't raped?'

'No! I mean—I don't know about that, but it definitely wasn't Jamie, anyway. You must know who told you.'

'I'm keeping out of it. I'm glad it's not true

though.' Steady was edging away and Matt let him go. On reflection, it was unrealistic to expect him to divulge any names; he had to work with a lot of the jockeys and wouldn't want to lose their trust.

With the first race looming, Matt was occupied with changing and weighing out before they were called to the paddock. There, his attention was claimed by the trainer and owners, so he didn't have time to exchange more than a couple of words with Jamie until they met up down at the start.

Here, as they circled, keeping the horses warm and supple whilst waiting for the starter to mount his rostrum and call them forward, Matt sought Jamie out, bringing his bay gelding alongside the Irishman's grey horse.

'Hi, kid. How're you doin'?'

'Bloody awful!' Jamie muttered. 'You must have heard what they're saying. I'm not just a murderer, now I'm a fuckin' rapist, too!' His agitation transferred itself to his horse and it tossed its head, nervously.

'Shhh! It's just talk. I know it's hard, but you're here to do a job, and you have to keep your mind on that.'

From the rostrum, the starter called out, 'Goggles!'

'It's easy for you,' Jamie protested, putting up a hand to pull his protective goggles into place. 'It's not you everybody's whispering about.'

'And, of course, I don't give a damn,' Matt observed.

'I'm sorry, it's just so fuckin' unfair!'

'Well, if it isn't Mutton!' someone exclaimed, using Jamie's nickname. 'Been let out for the day

61

for good behaviour?'

Unseen by either of them, Geoff Hislop had ridden up on Matt's left and was now grinning unpleasantly across at Jamie. He had a thin, sharp-featured face that only served to make his own nickname more apt.

'Fuck off, Razor!' Jamie responded, snatching his own mount up short and turning away.

Before Matt could say anything, the starter called out, 'All right, jockeys, make a line and walk in. Right, keep to line, walk . . . walk.'

Within moments the horses were all turning towards the starting line. The starter called, 'All right, come on!', the elasticised tape pinged aside, and, with a surge, they were away and powering towards the first fence, some two hundred yards distant.

As always with Matt, he left all the business of everyday living at the starting line; his world narrowing to the strip of lush green turf down which he was travelling, the pounding rhythm of the horse beneath him, and the urgent, jostling presence of the other runners around him.

The bay gelding was a fairly experienced campaigner and, tucking him in behind the leaders, Matt was able to settle him quite quickly and approach the first fence at a sensible pace. On his outside, Razor—on the favourite—was swearing at his mount, who was pulling hard with its mouth open and head low, and, glancing over his shoulder, he could see Jamie's grey horse, two or three lengths behind. The only sounds were the thudding of hooves, the short, sharp snorting breaths of the horses, and the odd word from one of the jockeys. The wind whipped past Matt's ears and small chunks of turf hit his chest and face, thrown up by the leading animal, some three lengths ahead.

The first fence loomed, the runners rose like a Mexican wave of horseflesh over the clipped birch, touched down, and were away towards the second. A buzz of exhilaration fizzed through Matt. Even after nearly ten years of racing, the thrill was still there, the painful consequences of his last race forgotten in the excitement of the present.

The bay gelding gave Matt a super ride, taking all the fences in his stride and moving forward smoothly as they rounded the last bend to take up a position just behind Razor on the favourite. Heading for the second last, Matt became aware of someone else moving up on his outside. A grey horse. Jamie's.

Razor looked back, saw him coming, and gave his mount a sharp crack of the whip, just behind his leg. The pace picked up a notch or two, but Jamie's horse, not shaken off, moved up alongside the favourite and they approached the last fence together, rising in perfect synchronicity with Matt close behind.

As they landed, Matt saw Razor's horse, ears back, beginning to falter, so he switched his own gelding to the outside so as not to be hampered by the slowing animal.

They approached the furlong pole almost in a line, with Jamie's grey a fraction in front of Razor's horse, and Matt barely half a length adrift, and he saw Jamie sit down and urge his horse forward. Under pressure, the grey surged ahead, veering towards the rails in front of the struggling favourite, and, yelling abuse, Razor made a big show of pulling his horse back, and quickly dropped out of the reckoning.

Pulling his whip through to keep the bay straight, Matt pushed him on with hands and heels, and had the satisfaction of overhauling Jamie's grey and putting a length between them at the finishing line.

Both horses slowed to a canter and then to a ragged trot, and Matt patted the bay's sweaty neck and looked across at Jamie.

'Gotcha!' he said, with a grin, and Jamie grinned ruefully in reply.

As they turned back to meet the approaching handlers, Razor rode between the two of them and leaned towards the Irishman.

'You fuckin' took me out, you moron!'

Jamie looked astounded.

'I did not!' he protested, but Razor was gone. 'I didn't,' he said again, turning to Matt.

'Just ignore him.'

They slowed to a walk and heard the public address system issue the ominous two-tone chime that presaged a Stewards' Enquiry.

Jamie grimaced. 'Oh God, that's all I need!'

Fred Pinter, Rockfield's travelling head lad, materialised at the bay's head and took his rein to lead him back to the winner's circle, glowing with pleasure at the reception they received. As a close second favourite, there had been a fair amount of money on him, and the punters were loud in their glee.

By the time Matt had dismounted, had his photo taken next to the horse, been hugged by the lady owner, spoken to Leonard, and unsaddled, he had to hurry to weigh in before the fifteen-minute deadline. As he made his way through the drifts of people, collecting the occasional pat on the back, he became aware that the TV presenter, Ted Barker, was interviewing someone over the PA system.

'Well, I've got Geoff Hislop here. Geoff, you were on the beaten favourite, Louisiana Lou. You came in fourth—was that the ground? Does she prefer a bit more cut in it?'

'Yeah, I think she does.' Hislop's Yorkshire accent was unmistakable. 'But she still had a bit of fuel in the tank. What really finished her off was being hampered on the run in by Mullin's horse. I had to snatch her up and come round him, and it completely ruined her rhythm. When you're that close to the line, there's no time to recover.'

'You're saying Jamie Mullin's horse—that was Penselwood, wasn't it?—hung across to the rail and forced you to pull up? Are you saying you think Louisiana Lou still had a chance of winning at that point?'

'She might have, if Mullin had had his mind on the job. We all know he's going through a rough patch right now—and, of course, we wish him well—but he can't let it affect his riding. It's a dangerous enough game as it is without loose cannons in our midst.'

Matt could see the tall figure of Ted Barker now, just yards away, and, in spite of the waiting scales, when he drew close, he slowed up to lean over Razor's shoulder.

'Bad luck, fella,' he said, clapping the other jockey on the back.

'Ah, Matt—Matt Shepherd. Have you got time for a quick word?' Barker asked, as Matt had hoped he would. Wearing his trademark cream suit and trilby, he was a well-known and well-liked figure around the racetracks and on the BBC's racing team.

'Er . . . Just a very quick one,' Matt said, and Hislop moved aside to make way for him.

'You rode the winner, Temperance Bob. Well done! Was that as easy as it looked?'

'Pretty much. He's a very honest horse; always gives his best.'

'Geoff reckons he had an unlucky run—could you see what happened?'

'Yes, I was right behind them.' Matt cheered, inwardly. Never one to miss an opportunity for controversy, the presenter had given him just what he'd wanted. 'It's true, Jamie's horse did hang left, but, in my opinion, Hislop's horse wasn't going anywhere by then. She looked good and tired, to me.'

'It did look as though Hislop had to take a pull on Louisiana Lou,' Barker persisted, pushing the microphone towards Matt again, hazel eyes sharp with interest in his pleasant face.

'Yeah, but sometimes these incidents can look a lot worse than they actually are,' Matt replied lightly. 'Look, it's up to the stewards now. I'd better get weighed in, OK?'

'Of course. Thanks for talking to us, Matt.' Barker smiled and turned away to speak directly to camera and, carrying his saddle and crash cap, Matt hurried towards the scales and the waiting officials.

By the time he'd changed into his colours for the next race, the stewards had announced no change to the finishing order, and the presentation to the connections of the winner could get underway.

Slipping Temperance Bob's colours back on over the top of the ones for his second ride, Matt went out to join Leonard and receive his prize.

* * *

After his success in the first race, Matt's afternoon settled into the usual mix of fortunes, with two runners unplaced, and Charlie Brewer's hope, Cheddah, beaten by a short head. Jamie's second ride trailed home almost last and Matt saw little of him until he was legged-up onto his mount for the final race and spotted the Irishman over the heads of the crowd, walking away from the paddock in company with a bulky figure in a brown suit.

With a sinking heart, Matt recognised the man. DI Bartholomew. Damn! What did *he* want?

It was the best part of an hour before Matt was able to seek Jamie out. The runners were held up at the start because one of them cast a shoe and the farrier had to be called to replace it and, after the race, when he emerged from the weighing room having showered and changed, the owner of his last ride collared him, wanting to discuss the animal's form.

Free at last, Matt finally ran Jamie to ground in the Tattersalls Bar, alone and slouching on a barstool amongst a scattering of people who were lingering after the racing to celebrate bets won or dull the pain of money thrown away.

He got to within six feet before Jamie looked up and saw him and, straight away, Matt could tell that he'd sunk more than a couple of beers. His body language was lacklustre and his eyes heavy lidded. When he saw Matt, he raised his half-empty glass.

'Gonna join me?'

'No, I'm not. One of us has to drive, remember?' Matt was annoyed. His ankle was aching and had swollen again, and they had agreed that morning that Jamie would drive home. No chance of that now. He reached out and removed the glass from Jamie's hand. 'You've had enough, too. Don't forget you've got a ride tomorrow.'

'*Did* have,' Jamie said, reclaiming his beer. '*Did* have a ride. Not anymore.'

'Why? What happened?'

'Emmett says the ground's too firm for the filly.'

'Oh. Well, it *is* pretty hard,' Matt temporised.

'Bollocks!' Jamie said into his glass. 'Didn't want a rapist riding his horse, more like!'

'Don't be ridiculous! And keep your voice down. Anyway, he wouldn't scratch the horse if that was the case—he'd get someone else to ride it.'

Jamie shook his head. 'Emmett's not like that— he's too *nice*,' he said, turning the last word into a sneer.

Matt reluctantly had to acknowledge the truth of that, but he still didn't accept Jamie's interpretation of the matter.

'She's a young filly; I expect he's just looking after her legs. You can't blame him, she cost him a fortune.'

Jamie grunted and drained his glass.

'What did Bartholomew want?' Matt asked, waving away an expectant barman. 'I saw you talking to him earlier.'

'More bloody questions! Kept on and on about where I went when I left the party. I told him where I went. Not my fault no one saw me. If I'd

68

known I was going to need a fuckin' alibi, I'd have taken someone with me!'

'I hope you didn't say that to Bartholomew.'

Jamie shook his head. 'No, I didn't. That bloke's had a sense of humour bypass.'

'I don't suppose he thinks it's a laughing matter,' Matt pointed out. 'Did he have anything else to say? What about the rape story?'

'Oh, that—no, that wasn't true. Shouldn't be surprised if Razor made that up himself.'

'So they haven't found the lorry driver, then?'

'No, they haven't. I think Bartholomew thinks I made that up, too.'

'Well, how else does he think you got to Charlborough? You couldn't have walked it in that short time. Come on, let's get going. I want to get home and put my feet up.' Matt took the empty glass out of Jamie's fingers and stood back, but the younger man didn't move.

'Bartholomew did say one other thing,' he said, his eyes fixed broodingly on the bar top. 'He told me that Sophie was pregnant.'

'Pregnant? Oh God!'

Jamie didn't seem to have heard. He looked up with eyes that were suspiciously bright. 'I could have been a father, Matt.'

Could have been was about right, in Matt's opinion. He reflected that, in Jamie's position, he'd have wanted a paternity test before he shelled out maintenance for any child of Sophie's.

'He asked me if I knew. Do you know—he actually asked me if I'd killed her because of the baby!' Jamie said bitterly. 'Christ! How sick is that?'

'It's probably not unheard of,' Matt said. 'Don't

forget, blokes like Bartholomew are mixing with the bum-end of society all the time—being cynical is the cornerstone of his job. As of a few days ago, he'd never even heard of you; you can't really blame him for thinking that way.'

Shaking his head, Jamie got to his feet and walked past Matt towards the door, but he didn't say anything else until he slid into the passenger seat of the MR2, and then the words burst from him as if they'd been under pressure.

'Why did this have to happen? Why didn't she tell me she was pregnant? I would have stood by her. It's what I've always wanted—a family. Not yet, obviously, but it's one of those things—if it happens, it happens. If she'd just told me, none of this would have happened; everything would have been all right.'

Matt didn't think Jamie really expected an answer, and he didn't attempt one. After all, what could he say that the Irishman would want to hear? That, had she lived, and by some miracle the child was proven to be Jamie's, Matt could have forecast nothing but trouble and heartache? When he'd first come into contact with Sophie, some years before, she had already earned herself the nickname of the Bradford Bang, and, from what he'd heard, the sobriquet had become more apt with each passing year.

He wouldn't have wished her fate upon anyone, but, at the same time, he couldn't be sorry that Jamie had been freed from her clutches, once and for all. It was a very black cloud indeed that didn't have *any* silver lining.

70

4

In spite of Matt's best efforts, Jamie didn't get up in time to ride work for Leonard the following morning. By the time Matt had had a cup of coffee and taken the dogs for their early morning stroll with Kendra, it was six o'clock and time to set out for Rockfield, but Jamie was still in bed and answering only in grunts and groans.

'Oh, I should leave him. I expect John will understand,' Kendra said, twining her arms round Matt's neck to kiss him goodbye. 'It's only fair to cut him some slack after what happened.'

'Are you going to be here?'

'This morning I will, but this afternoon I was planning to go over to help Mum. She's got a delivery coming in and I said I'd lend a hand.'

'Oh, right. How's that all going?' Joy Brewer had started her own millinery business just six months before, with an eye to capitalising on the family's racing contacts. It was based in a converted outbuilding at Birchwood Hall, where potential customers could come, drink coffee with Joy, and try on hats at leisure.

'It's going really well,' Kendra told him. 'She's got more work than she can cope with. She was talking about taking on a part-timer to help.'

Matt thought he detected a wistful note in her voice.

'So, how many hours would you do?' he asked.

Kendra looked up into his face, her eyes hopeful.

'Would you mind?'

'No. Why on earth would I? It's up to you. I

71

expect you get bored hanging around here, anyway.'

'Well, sometimes. It would be nice to help Mum and I love the hats.'

'Then go for it,' Matt advised, kissing her once more and lightly slapping her behind.

'But what about Jamie . . . ? Are you worried about him?'

'A little. He was really down yesterday. Finding out that Sophie was pregnant really shook him up—he seems to have taken it for granted that the baby was his. Personally, I have my doubts, but what I'm trying to get him to see is that he mustn't let all this stuff affect his career. He's been doing so well lately, but he needs rides to get rides. Out of sight is all too quickly out of mind. He mustn't stop trying, just because a couple of people are reacting like idiots.'

'I suppose he's bound to take it hard,' Kendra said. 'He's only a kid and not everyone's as single-minded as you are.'

'He's older than you,' Matt protested.

'I'm not talking numbers. Go on, you'd better get going or you'll be late.'

*   *   *

Matt's day was busy. After riding out with the Rockfield string, and having breakfast with the trainer and his wife, he travelled up-country with Leonard, where he rode five horses, notching up two winners and one second place. It was the day of Tortellini's run in the Midlands Gold Plate, and the horse didn't disappoint, romping home five lengths clear of the field, much to the delight of

Roy Emmett, who pressed two fifty-pound notes into Matt's palm after the prize-giving.

It wasn't until the lull in between the presentation and going out to the paddock for his last ride of the day that Matt had the time to phone home and see how Jamie was. It was a weighing-room rule that mobile phones were switched off during racing and he had to wheedle permission from security. Taken to a separate area, he tried twice, but both times the answering service cut in, and he was left wondering whether Jamie was still under the covers or had got up and gone out somewhere.

By the time he returned to the cottage that evening, it was nearly eight o'clock and a light was glowing a welcome from behind the closed curtains in the sitting room. Parking the MR2, Matt limped wearily across the yard and let himself in, fending off the tidal surge of dogs in the porch and calling a greeting to Kendra.

'Hi!' She came through from the kitchen wearing an apron that announced 'Chief Cook & Bottlewasher' in large blue letters and, holding her hands up out of the way, leaned forward for a kiss. 'Well done on Tortellini. Can't hug you, I've got tomatoey fingers.'

Matt obliged with the kiss. 'Mm, something smells good—hope it's not fattening. Have you seen Jamie at all? I tried to ring him earlier, but there wasn't any answer. I see his car's gone.'

'No, I haven't seen him,' Kendra said, turning back into the kitchen. 'And I've been back about an hour. I didn't know whether to cook for him or not. There was nothing on the fridge,' she added, referring to their customary practice of leaving

73

Post-it notes on the refrigerator door to keep each other informed as to what was going on.

By the time the meal was ready, Matt had begun to feel a little uneasy. It had to be said that Jamie wasn't always the most considerate of people when it came to notifying them of his plans, and normally Matt would have seen nothing alarming in his absence, but the current state of affairs was far from normal.

There had still been no word at eleven o'clock when Matt took the dogs into the paddock for their late night comfort walk. Back in the cottage, he tried Jamie's mobile number one last time before following Kendra up the narrow staircase to bed.

*   *   *

Nothing was heard from Jamie the following day, by which time Matt's anxiety was mixed with a fair measure of annoyance. He'd managed to get Doogie McKenzie to consider putting the Irishman up on one of his runners at the weekend—as his regular jockey had picked up a suspension for careless riding—but Jamie's disappearance had seen that chance go begging and done his ongoing prospects no good at all. He still wasn't answering his phone, and a phone call to his landlord at his other digs produced the information that he hadn't been seen there for a week. Matt went to bed wondering how soon he could officially be listed as a missing person, and reluctantly decided that, if Jamie hadn't made contact by the following evening, Bartholomew should be told.

It was just before three in the morning when Matt was dragged back from the depths of sleep by the insistent trill of the telephone on his bedside table. Putting out a questing hand, he located the receiver and brought it to his ear.

After a certain amount of crackling, hissing, and a couple of beeps, someone asked, 'Matt? Izat you?' The voice, though thickened and slurring, was undoubtedly Jamie's. 'Matt?'

'Yeah, it's me. Where are you? And where the hell have you been all this time?'

'I don't know . . .'

Matt sat up and switched the bedside light on, blinking at the abrupt change.

'What do you mean—you don't know? You must have some idea, surely.'

'Erm . . . Bournemouth. I'm in Bournemouth.'

'What are doing there—apart from getting drunk, that is?'

'I need you to come and get me,' Jamie said, adding as an afterthought, 'Please?'

Matt's heart sank.

'Do you know what time it is? Can't you get a taxi?'

'I haven't got any money. S'all gone—everything.'

'Listen. Call a taxi and tell them I'll pay when you get here, OK?'

'I can't. They've taken everything. I only had 50p in my pocket and I've used that to ring you. I need you to come and get me—please, Matt.'

'Who are you talking about? Who's taken everything?' Seriously worried now, Matt sat up straight, his heart thumping.

'I don't know who they were; I didn't see them. It was too dark. They took my wallet and my phone

75

and my keys—everything.'

'Have you called the police? You should call them.'

'Oh, God no!' Jamie groaned. 'I just want to come home. Please, Matt.'

Matt hesitated, but he could sympathise with Jamie's reluctance to spend another night in a police station answering questions.

'All right,' he said eventually. 'But you'll have to give me some idea whereabouts you are. Bournemouth is a big place.' He was out of bed now and reaching for his clothes.

Kendra turned over and blinked sleepily.

'What's happening?' she asked, but Matt waved a hand to silence her.

'Jamie? Are you there?'

'Yeah . . .'

'Where are you?'

'I'm, er . . . down the bottom, on the seafront . . . There's a big cinema thing . . .'

'The IMAX, you mean? Are you near the IMAX?'

'Yeah, I was on the beach . . .'

'What on earth were you . . . No, forget it. Stay where you are. I'll be there as soon as I can.' He switched the phone off, tossed it on the bed, and began to pull on his trousers.

*   *   *

Bournemouth in the early hours of a Saturday morning was a busy place and, unsure of his way, Matt saw rather more of it than he intended. Groups of the young and not so young hung around outside clubs, wandered in rowdy drunkenness through the streets, and pissed and vomited in doorways and dark corners. Matt found his lip curling in silent distaste at the mindlessness of it all. A fat teenager wearing an England football shirt pulled his tracksuit bottoms down and mooned at the car as it passed, apparently providing riotous entertainment for half a dozen other youngsters, who lounged, drink cans and cigarettes in hand, against the railings beside the road.

'Get a life!' Matt muttered, swinging the MR2 round a roundabout and heading on downhill towards the seafront.

Passing the IMAX cinema, he slowed to a crawl, eyes darting from side to side. Two men walked by, hand in hand, and a couple of kids were kissing on a wooden bench, but there was no sign of Jamie until the car turned away from the beach once more and, for a fleeting second, its headlights illuminated a figure sitting in the shadow of a wall.

Matt slammed the brakes on and backed up.

Caught in the full beam, the man threw up a hand to shield his eyes. Light, spiky hair, goatee beard, blue jeans, faded red sweatshirt, and white Nike trainers.

Jamie. It had to be.

Matt hauled the steering wheel hard left, driving the car up onto the kerb and wincing as he heard the undercarriage scrape on the concrete. He dipped the headlights, switched off, and, within moments, was crouching down beside his friend.

'You OK?'

He didn't look OK. One eye was blackened and his lip was split. He blinked at Matt, squinting against the sudden brightness.

77

'I'm sorry. They took everything. I had to call you—didn't know what else to do.'

'That's OK, don't worry. What did they do to you? Are you hurt?'

Jamie shook his head, waving a hand vaguely towards his face.

'My head aches. I didn't see them coming. They pushed me into the wall. Akshly, I think I'm a bit pissed,' he confided.

'You don't say.' Matt put a hand under Jamie's arm. 'Do you think you could get up, if I helped you?' He cast an anxious look back towards the car and two youths who were approaching, eyeing it speculatively. Thank God he'd removed the ignition key.

'Yeah—I'm OK,' Jamie mumbled. 'Juss give me a moment . . .'

'We don't have a moment. We're going now,' Matt told him firmly, exerting upward pressure. To his relief, the Irishman made an effort and came staggering to his feet, clutching the front of Matt's jacket for support.

After an initial spell of dizziness, Jamie rallied and, with a fair bit of help from Matt, made it to the passenger seat of the MR2.

'Where's your car?'

'I'm not sure. It's here somewhere.' Jamie swung his arm in a gesture that Matt took to encompass the whole of Bournemouth. 'They took the keys . . .'

'Well, unless you told them where the car is, I guess it'll be safe. Whatever, I'm not driving round Bournemouth half the night looking for it.'

Glancing at the younger man's face as they set off for home, Matt wished he'd brought the old

78

Spinney Cottage Land Rover instead. They kept it for transporting dogs, horse feed, and bales of hay and, consequently, the very real prospect of Jamie puking on the way home wouldn't have been quite as grim as it was amidst the gleaming leather upholstery of the sports car.

As it turned out, Jamie was only sick once, and managed to get the door open in good time, before settling back in his seat with his eyes closed and apparently sleeping for the remainder of the journey. Uneasily mindful of the possibility of concussion, Matt woke Jamie once, and was rewarded by a reasonably coherent response, which partially satisfied the niggling voice that was telling him he should really be taking him to A & E.

Back at the cottage, Jamie seemed to have revived a stage or two, and was able to make his way to the front door with only minimal assistance. Sitting him down at the kitchen table, Matt gathered cotton wool, warm water with a dash of antiseptic lotion, and some sticking plaster, and set about cleaning him up.

'What's going on?' Kendra was standing in the kitchen doorway, a towelling bathrobe wrapped about her and sheepskin slippers protecting her feet from the chill of the stone flags. Her long hair was untidy from bed and her eyes sleepy. 'Oh my God! What on earth have you been up to, Jamie?'

Jamie merely shook his head slightly, so Matt answered for him.

'From what I can gather, he was walking along the beach—having drunk himself stupid—and some kind souls shoved him into the wall and nicked his wallet, phone, and car keys.'

'Fucking bastards!' Jamie put in.

'Exactly,' Matt agreed.

'Here, let me do that.' Kendra came forward and took the bowl of water and wad of cotton out of Matt's hands. He moved aside, gratefully.

'So what's happened to the car?'

'We don't know. Jamie can't remember where he left it. I suppose we'll have to go back and look for it in daylight. I've rung the police and told them that Jamie dropped the keys—he couldn't face more questions, and I can't say I blame him. If it was kids, they'll never catch 'em anyway—even if they bother trying.'

'So they took your wallet? Did you have any cards with you?' Kendra asked, bringing a practical viewpoint into the mix. 'Because, if you did, you'll need to get them stopped.'

'They won't find much,' Jamie responded. 'Enough to buy a slap-up meal at Burger King and that's about it!'

*   *   *

By the time Jamie had been cleaned up and his card companies notified, it was getting on for six o'clock. Matt had made tea and Kendra took hers and went sleepily back to bed, recommending that the others follow her example. Matt was very ready to do so, aware that a busy day awaited him, but Jamie, it seemed, wanted to talk.

'Do you think she was a slut?' he asked, as Matt stood hopefully with the door to the stairs open. 'Sophie, I mean. Razor and the others—they said everyone knew she slept around. Did you know?'

'Well . . .' Matt hesitated, unwilling to lie but not

80

feeling the time was exactly ideal for being bluntly honest.

Apparently Jamie wasn't expecting an answer.

'I know she wasn't an angel,' he went on. 'But she was trying to change. If she'd had a child, I think she'd have been different, don't you?'

'Mm. Maybe . . .'

'All right, she *was* a slut!' Jamie said suddenly, explosively. 'She was a lying bitch and everyone could see it except me! They were laughing at me. Were you laughing, too? Huh? Were you?'

'No,' Matt said quietly.

Jamie looked up at him, his face bitter. '*You* knew she was sleeping around—why didn't you tell me? Why did you let me make a fool of myself? That baby wasn't mine. Why did I ever think it could have been?'

'You don't know that,' Matt countered, more to calm him than through any conviction. He closed the door and came back into the room, placing his mug on the table opposite Jamie and sliding wearily into a seat.

'Yes I do. Bartholomew rang earlier. The DNA didn't match. It wasn't my baby. God knows whose it was—take your pick, really.'

'I'm sorry.' Matt wasn't sure if that was the right thing to say. Was it right to commiserate because the baby—which had never had a chance at life—hadn't been Jamie's? At this time in the morning, it was too much for his sleep-deprived brain to sort out.

'*I'm* not,' Jamie stated, taking a sip of his tea, but, as if to prove him a liar, tears welled under his lashes and one escaped to run down his cheek. He brushed it away, impatiently. 'What am I going to

81

do, Matt? People were just starting to ask for me to ride their horses—not because I happened to be available, but because they actually wanted me. But they won't want me now. This has ruined everything. Why won't anyone believe I didn't do it?'

'People *do* believe you. I do, Kendra does, John and Reney do, and loads of other people. I think Bartholomew probably does, too, or he'd have charged you by now.'

Jamie shook his head.

'No, he doesn't. He was trying to get me to confess. Said it would be in my best interests. Now he thinks I killed her because the baby *wasn't* mine. Bastard!'

Matt wasn't sure what to say, and, after a moment, came up with a suggestion that was near to his own heart.

'Look, why don't you get some sleep. You're not thinking straight—which is hardly surprising after the night you've had. Let's leave it till later, huh?'

'Yeah, maybe.' Jamie showed no signs of moving.

'Jamie, come on . . .'

'You go on.'

Matt sighed and tried again.

'You know, drinking yourself into a stupor isn't the way to deal with all this. It won't solve anything.'

'So what do you suggest, Matt? How would *you* deal with losing your girlfriend—who, it turns out, was fucking half the county behind your back— losing your job—as near as dammit—and having all your mates look at you as if you'd just crawled out of a sewer! I feel like shit and drinking is the only thing that makes it go away.'

'But it *doesn't*, does it?' Matt said, exasperated. 'You have to stop sometime, and, when you do, it's still there. If I were in your shoes, I'd stop whingeing and protesting my innocence, and prove it.'

'How?' Jamie looked up. '*How* can I prove it?'

'By finding out who did kill Sophie.'

Jamie frowned, but there was a spark of interest in his eyes.

'How?'

'I don't know—I'm too tired to think at the moment.'

'Will you help me, then?'

Having an uncomfortable suspicion that he might have started something he would come to regret, Matt pushed his chair back and stood up.

'If I can. Now, will you go to bed?'

'All right—but you *will* help?'

'I said yes, didn't I? Go to bed!'

*　　　　*　　　　*

Any hope that a few hours' sleep would have erased all memory of their conversation from Jamie's head was swiftly banished when Matt encountered him later that morning. Surprisingly, considering the hour at which they'd finally gone to bed, this was at the breakfast table, just after nine. Matt had left a text message on Leonard's phone to excuse himself from riding work, before falling into bed at the time he would usually have been getting up. Even though he managed to sleep for a couple of hours, he awoke feeling anything but rested and could have happily done without a return to Jamie's problems over the coffee and

83

toast.

'So, what do we do first?' Jamie looked like a morning-after boxer with an impressive black eye and a cut and swollen lip, but it seemed that Matt's promise of positive action had acted like a tonic.

'What *you* do first is go and look for your car,' Matt told him. 'I can give you a lift down there, but you'll have to find your own way back, because I'm riding this afternoon. Have you remembered where you left it?'

'Yeah, I think so. But what I meant was where do we start with clearing my name?'

'Give me a chance!' Matt exclaimed, last night's premonition growing ever stronger. 'Just when am I supposed to have come up with a plan of action? In my sleep?'

*   *   *

In spite of having formulated no plan, the first chance to make enquiries on Jamie's behalf presented itself that very afternoon and in an entirely unexpected way.

Rockfield had sent runners to two courses—Leonard had taken a promising young horse to run on the flat at the Ascot Festival; whilst Harry and Matt were at Maiden Newton, where Matt was booked to ride two for Kendra's father and one for another owner.

The afternoon started badly when he was hailed by Mick Westerby, a wiry ex-jockey-turned-trainer he'd ridden for on several occasions when he was starting out, who offered him the ride on a novice in the first.

'Nice sort. Been showing a lot of promise at

home,' Westerby told him. 'Randall's been schooling him over hurdles for me. Jockey's called in sick this morning.'

Matt wasn't keen. Although it went against the grain to turn down a riding fee, he hadn't the greatest regard for Westerby's skill in bringing on youngsters, and jump racing was a risky enough business anyway without taking on a ride that had every chance of ending in a fall. Still, Nick Randall was no fool, and if he'd been schooling him . . .

'Chap who owns him has just bought Peacock Penny,' Westerby added casually. 'You know, the mare who wiped the floor with the field in the Devon Stakes. I expect he'll be looking for a jock to ride her soon . . .'

'You're a devious bastard!' Matt declared. 'All right, but if this animal goes flat on its face at the first, I'll feed your bollocks to my dogs!'

'He'll be fine. Just keep a hold of his head. I'll give the colours to your valet.' Westerby began to turn away, then hesitated. 'Er . . . How many dogs have you got?'

Matt leaned close.

'Four,' he said. 'And they always seem to be hungry . . .'

*   *   *

The first race of the day was a two-mile novice hurdle. The ground was good to firm and Westerby's youngster, who went by the name of Khaki Kollin, cantered quite smoothly down to the start, so Matt began to relax a little, until one of the other jockeys called out, 'Have you packed your parachute, Mojo?'

85

He turned to see Irishman Tam Connelly riding towards him on a neat-looking chestnut.

'Do you know this fella, then?' he asked, with a feeling he wasn't going to like the answer.

Connelly laughed.

'You remember old Fletch bust his collarbone a couple of weeks back? Well, guess what he was riding . . .'

Matt groaned.

'That bugger Westerby swore he was a good 'un. Said Nicko had been schooling him.'

'Nicko rode him once,' Connelly said. 'Told 'em to take him to the glue factory. Have a nice day!'

'Oh, cheers, mate!'

The starter called them in; Matt pulled his chinstrap a little tighter and shortened his reins; the tape flew up and they were away.

It seemed Khaki Kollin's smooth progress to the start had been misleading. As soon as the race got underway, all his manners went out the window, and, with them, any chance of a comfortable ride. 'Keep a hold of his head,' the trainer had said. That was a joke! Matt found himself with a choice between letting the animal have its head, in which case it seemed probable Khaki Kollin would burn himself out within a mile—always supposing he didn't come crashing down at the first hurdle—or trying to control the speed, which option was almost certain to result in a pitched battle all the way to the first with much the same outcome.

In the end, he compromised, but his efforts to tuck the horse in behind the steadier runners met with little success. Kollin barged about, seemingly with little regard for his own safety, finally clipping the heels of the horse in front, causing it to

86

stumble and drawing a curse from its jockey. Matt steered his mount wide again, gritting his teeth and holding on tight as the first hurdle loomed.

The jumps used in a hurdle race are made of gorse woven into a wooden frame and driven into the turf so that they flatten if they are hit hard enough, which is exactly what Kollin did. Executing something between a skip and a jump, he barely attained half of the necessary three foot six and lost his back end on landing, throwing his head up and thumping Matt in the face with his neck.

Matt swore and caught sight of Tam Connelly's grinning face looking back at him as the rest of the field passed by. The mistake at the first would have been almost worthwhile if Khaki Kollin had learnt from it, but, once he regained his stride, he set off for the second hurdle with undiminished enthusiasm, leaving Matt with the feeling that it was not so much *if* they came to grief, as how soon.

He wasn't left wondering for long. The second hurdle was negotiated, if not stylishly, then at least without drama, but as they approached the third, which would also be the last jump when they had completed a circuit of the track, Kollin had caught up and was running hard on the heels of the field. Matt made the decision to leave the horse to its own devices and hope that self-preservation took a hand.

It didn't.

Khaki Kollin was either too excited or too stupid to think of anything but getting past the other horses and, for the second time, he completely failed to jump high enough. This time gravity won out. The horse stumbled, tipped onto his nose, and ended up skidding along the turf on his side.

For Matt, propelled over Kollin's shoulder to bounce and roll to a halt some twenty feet away, the thing was a run of the mill affair, barely bruising, and, as he watched the horse scramble to its feet and gallop after the others, he felt no great sense of disappointment. The fall had been a foregone conclusion and, as such, it was just as well that it had happened here, where it was a short walk back to the weighing room, than way over on the other side of the course. He would receive his riding fee and there was no damage done—it could have been a great deal worse, but, even so, he had a bone to pick with a certain trainer.

Climbing to his feet, he loosened the strap on his crash cap and headed for the medical room and the compulsory checks, and then the pleasure of a confrontation with Mick bloody Westerby.

*   *   *

In fact, it wasn't until after Matt's last ride of the day that he finally caught up with Khaki Kollin's trainer, coming face to face with the ex-jockey round a corner.

'Matt!' Westerby exclaimed, in unconvincing tones of happy surprise.

'Mick,' Matt responded, somewhat more heavily. 'Do you remember our little conversation? You told me that horse had been showing a lot of promise . . . Promise of what? I wonder.'

'Randall thought he was going nicely.'

'I have it on good authority that Randall said he should be consigned to the knacker's. And remember Fletch?'

'Ah. Perhaps I was thinking of a different horse.'

'Perhaps you were,' Matt agreed. 'But please don't tell me you were mixed up about getting me the ride on Peacock Penny.'

'No, no,' Westerby assured him hastily. 'I was just talking about you with the owner yesterday.'

'Well, mind you talk to him about it again soon. I think you owe me that,' Matt said.

'Mick? Is there a problem?' A cultured voice spoke from behind Matt, and he swung round to see the tall, grey-suited figure of Lord Kenning, Sophie Bradford's uncle. 'Ah, Matt. Didn't realise it was you. How are you? Nice win on that black horse of Emmett's earlier . . . Er, what's its name?'

'Coneflower,' Matt supplied. 'Thanks, yes—he's a good horse. Er . . . Lord Kenning, could I possibly have a word with you?' He glanced at Westerby, who muttered something about having horses to see to and scuttled away, patently relieved to have been let off the hook.

'Yes, Matt. How can I help you?' Lord Kenning held out one arm, palm forward, to indicate that Matt should walk on with him, and he did so, wondering how on earth to broach the subject uppermost in his mind.

'Well, actually, it's about Jamie Mullin,' he began. Out of the corner of his eye he saw the peer's face harden and hurried on. 'I think he's being given a raw deal.'

'Oh?' Kenning's tone wasn't encouraging.

'The press have picked him out as a suspect, purely because he was Sophie's boyfriend, but he hasn't actually done anything wrong, and I thought if you—as Sophie's uncle—were to demonstrate support . . .'

'Who *says* he hasn't done anything wrong?' Kenning demanded. 'Of course, *he* does—and you do too, I suppose, as he's a friend of yours—but how do *I* know that? As far as I know, he could well be her killer. He picked a fight with her in front of everyone at that party, and he was quite plainly drunk. Everybody knows he has a sparky temper; it seems to me he's the obvious suspect. The only thing I can't understand is why the police haven't got him under lock and key!'

'Because there's no evidence,' Matt countered. 'And that's because Jamie didn't do it. Look, I know Sophie was your niece, but how well did you actually know her? Were you close?'

Kenning's brows drew down over his pale grey eyes and his colour rose alarmingly.

'I think you've said enough, Shepherd! I'll not stand here and listen to you repeating unfounded rumours about my family, and, if I were you, I'd be careful whom I did speak to on the matter. Your career may be on a high at the moment, but it could just as easily go the other way, if you get my meaning. Good day.'

He stalked off, leaving Matt staring after him in complete bewilderment. What on earth had prompted that reaction? It was true he hadn't held out much hope of winning Lord Kenning's support, but he had thought it worth a try. He certainly hadn't expected a rebuff on that scale.

While he stood in momentary confusion, a voice hailed him from behind.

'Matt. Hi!'

Matt turned. Harry Leonard was approaching, smiling up at him from his wheelchair. Around

90

thirty, with wavy brown hair and an engaging grin, he was a good-looking man who'd received plenty of attention from the ladies when he'd been a jockey and Matt thought that, now he'd stopped wasting to make his riding weight, he looked better than he had ever done.

'Hiyah,' he responded, putting Lord Kenning's strange behaviour to the back of his mind for the time being.

'Join me for a drink to celebrate Coneflower's win?' Harry suggested.

'Er, yeah, OK.' He'd wanted to get back at a reasonable hour, just in case Jamie suffered a relapse into his depressed state of the day before and decided to go out on the town again. Still, Kendra was going to be around and had promised to keep an eye on him, and it was a while since he'd had a chance to catch up with Harry, socially.

Ensconced in the owners' and trainers' bar, with a white wine spritzer in his hand, Matt relaxed with a deep sigh. A party of thirty-somethings were noisily celebrating a win on the other side of the room, and at the bar two or three solitary drinkers appeared to be doing the opposite, but there were more staff than customers around at this time of day, collecting glasses and wiping tables now the rush was over.

'Not a bad day, I suppose,' he said, as Harry manoeuvred his chair closer to the table. 'Although Panda Feet was a bit of a disappointment. I just couldn't get him interested at all. Have you spoken to Toby Potter since the race?' Panda Feet was usually a reliable stayer, but today he'd trailed home twelfth of seventeen. His owner, a vet who'd been an enthusiastic amateur jockey in years gone

91

by, normally collared Matt after the race for an in-depth discussion of his horse's performance, but today he'd been nowhere to be seen.

Harry shrugged.

'No, I haven't seen him. Perhaps he was on call and an emergency came up.'

'Where does he work?' Matt asked, helping himself to two or three peanuts from a dish on the table.

'Bristol vet hospital.' With a small smile, Harry moved the nuts beyond his reach.

'Didn't I hear he's started doing some new mumbo-jumbo therapy? Can't remember who told me.'

'Sounds like something Charlie might have said,' Harry said dryly. 'He doesn't believe in anything that hasn't been tested, re-tested, and the figures produced in triplicate for his scrutiny. Toby's a physio; you make him sound like a witch doctor! Anyway, you mad bugger, what on earth made you take the ride on Mick Westerby's no-hoper?'

'Well, obviously I was the only person on the racecourse who didn't know it *was* a no-hoper. I knew about Fletch, of course, but, for some reason, I just didn't connect the two. Peacock Penny was held out as a carrot, and I'm going to make damn sure he honours that promise.'

'I don't think Khaki Wotsit has finished a race yet—but I might be wrong. Still, it could have been worse.'

'Yeah, it was about a grade three,' Matt replied. In the years when they had both been riding, they'd formed a habit of grading their falls from one to ten, according to pain and damage, with grade one being a step-off, four a case of bad bruising, and five upward being broken bones of varying severity and number. It had all been a joke until Harry had suffered his crippling fall. Matt remembered the first words the trainer's son had spoken to him in hospital, whilst still hooked up to a myriad of tubes and monitors. 'Guess that was a ten,' he'd said sleepily, the morphine keeping his sense of humour alive. At that point, he hadn't been told the grim report of the surgeon. With an effort, Matt had smiled, but their joke had turned sour.

'So, where's Jamie today? Not riding?' Harry's query brought him back to the present.

Matt shook his head. 'No one wants to touch him at the moment with this Sophie Bradford thing going on.'

'Oh, that's a bit unfair!' Harry exclaimed. 'The police don't *really* think he had anything to do with it, do they? Seriously?'

'I'm not sure. They're certainly keeping the pressure on. And, you have to admit, it didn't look good, he and Sophie having that row less than an hour before she turns up dead. I mean, they couldn't have picked a more public place, could they?'

'No, I guess not, but, actually, I was out getting some fresh air. Typical, isn't it? The highlight of a dull evening and I missed it!'

'There wasn't much to it, really. She'd been winding him up all evening, flirting with an ex-boyfriend. Jamie grabbed her, to try and make her listen, and she slapped him and walked off. He went after her and the bouncer stepped in, so Jamie swung a punch at him.'

Harry chuckled. 'He's game, I'll give him that. I

should imagine the bouncer wiped the floor with him, didn't he?'

'No, just frogmarched him out.' Matt took a sip of his drink. 'I gather you were still there when the police arrived.'

'Only just. I was out by my car. I'd had enough at that point and was on my way home, but I wasn't quite quick enough and ended up back inside. They wanted to question everyone, which took forever and was a complete waste of time, considering I didn't see the famous bust-up and I'm hardly in a position to have followed the poor girl down the road and attacked her. Would you believe the cops asked me if I actually needed the wheelchair? I felt like saying, "No, I just use it for fun!" ' He shook his head at the memory. 'Lucky you left when you did. You were well out of that.'

'Yeah, except I got caught up in it anyway. It was me that found Sophie's body.'

'*You* did? I didn't know. God, how awful!'

'It *was* pretty grim. I was actually looking for Jamie, because I thought he might need a lift home. As you can imagine, I got stuck with the police for hours.'

'Have they got you down as a suspect, too?'

'Lord knows! I expect so. But they seem to be concentrating on Jamie at the moment.'

'So, what did old Kenning want, just now?' Harry was carefully balancing his wine glass on the arm of his wheelchair as he spoke.

'Oh, that.' Matt explained his abortive attempt to get the peer on Jamie's side. 'I must say, I didn't expect quite such a strong reaction,' he finished. 'Nearly snapped my head off!'

'Ah, I take it you didn't hear the rumours then?'

94

'What rumours?'

'Christ, Matt! You should learn to pay more attention to weighing-room gossip. Couple of years ago—just before my accident, it would have been—there was a rumour going round that our friend Kenning was more than just a doting uncle to pretty Miss Sophie Bradford, if you know what I mean. I can't believe you didn't know.'

'I don't remember it. Perhaps I was injured or suspended or something. No wonder he turned nasty when I asked him how close they'd been. Was there any truth in the rumours?'

Harry shrugged. 'God knows. It was a one-minute wonder, anyway. The lads had moved on to something else in a day or two. I think it was Razor who started it—it usually is—but I don't know where he got it from.' Looking at his watch, he drained his glass and stood it on the table. 'Well, I'd better be going—got a date.'

Matt raised his eyebrows. 'Well, well. Anyone I know?'

Laughing, Harry reversed his chair, then tapped his nose with his index finger.

'Ah, that would be telling. See you later.'

Left alone to finish his spritzer, Matt pulled the forbidden bowl of peanuts closer once more, helped himself to a handful, and gazed thoughtfully out of the window. Below, the horses were just being led back to the stables after the last race and the crowds were rapidly dispersing, leaving behind a mess of discarded betting slips, racecards, and food wrappers on the trampled grass.

Matt took some more nuts and wondered at the sheer laziness of the masses. Bins abounded, and

95

yet it seemed that most people couldn't be bothered to walk the few steps necessary to use them. A disparate movement caught his eye—Harry in his wheelchair, moving swiftly along the tarmac path. The guy should try the Paralympics, he thought with a smile, watching his rapid progress.

The chair continued to follow the path, moving nearer to the building and almost out of Matt's range of vision. Idly, he leaned closer to the window to keep it in view and saw it come to a halt in front of the Tote kiosks, where a figure in a flat cap and tweed jacket was standing waiting. With a sense of disappointment, Matt wondered if this was the date Harry had referred to. He'd hoped his friend had found himself a girl. Losing interest in the unheard conversation below, he was about to look away when the man in the flat cap glanced up momentarily at the sky as if considering something.

It was Toby Potter, owner of the disappointing Panda Feet, Matt realised in surprise. That was strange, after the conversation they'd just had. If Harry had known he was going to meet the man in a few minutes' time, why on earth hadn't he said so?

5

It seemed Matt was destined to be late home, for, as he headed across the now sparsely populated car park, a diminutive figure in skintight jeans and a pale blue Puffa jacket stepped out from behind a

96

Land Rover and hailed him by name.

'I'm sorry. Do I know you?' Matt looked down at the tousled red hair and freckled face of the female who'd spoken and was pretty sure that he didn't. She looked to be about sixteen, and he waited for the expected autograph book to appear.

It didn't. The female put out a freckled hand to be shaken, and announced, 'Casey McKeegan,' as if it were a name with which he should be familiar. Her accent was every bit as Irish as Jamie's.

He shook the hand, because it seemed churlish not to.

'And what can I do for you, Ms McKeegan? I have to warn you, I'm in a bit of a hurry.'

'I'll walk with you,' she offered, not in the least put off. 'I'm a journalist, and I wanted to ask you—'

'A what?' Matt broke in, wondering if he'd heard right.

'A journalist.'

'A journalist, huh? OK. Can I see your press card?'

The girl frowned.

'Why?' she asked, tilting her head slightly.

'Because I don't just talk to *anyone* who comes up and asks . . .'

'OK.' The redheaded girl flashed a laminated rectangle in his direction and would have stowed it back in her pocket just as quickly if Matt hadn't clicked his fingers and beckoned for her to produce it again. He scanned it swiftly. The girl in the photo did indeed look like the one before him, but the name of the paper was a bit of a shock. The *Daily Standard*.

'You don't look old enough. How did you wangle that? Does Daddy own the paper?' Matt enquired.

97

'I'm nineteen. Not that it's any business of yours,' she said hotly.

'You don't look it.'

'Are you always this rude, Mr Shepherd?'

Matt stopped and turned to face her.

'The *Standard* isn't exactly on my list of favourite papers at the moment—strangely enough. But then you knew that, didn't you? That's why you tried to whisk the card away before I had time to read it properly.'

'I thought you might not talk to me,' Casey admitted, looking up at him from under her untidy red fringe.

'And you were right, so don't bother trying the lost puppy dog act on me. It won't work.'

'I'm not!' she stated indignantly. 'Look, can we talk about your friend Jamie Mullin?'

'So you can drag him across the coals again? No, I think not.' Matt started to walk away. 'As I said, I'm in a hurry.'

Casey hurried to catch up. 'That wasn't me. That was Dave—Dave Rossiter—he's only interested in stirring up trouble, *I* want to get to the truth.'

'Well, you're probably in the wrong job then,' Matt told her, without stopping.

'*No*,' she cried in frustration. 'I *like* Jamie. I met him once in a pub. He bought me a drink. And, anyway, if he's your friend, don't you want to put his side of the story across?'

Matt slowed a fraction.

'Yes, if I thought for one moment it would be done straight. Give me one good reason why I should trust you . . .'

The girl's freckled brow furrowed.

'Well, what am I supposed to say? That I'm

98

honest? You wouldn't believe me. What if I said I know something about you that you'd sooner I didn't tell? Would you talk to me then?'

'That would be blackmail,' he observed.

'But would you?'

'Depends what it was.'

'All right. I know it was you who found Sophie Bradford's body.'

Matt stopped and looked down at her through narrowed eyes. She looked as fresh-faced and wholesome as a kid in a Walt Disney film, but there was clearly a sharp brain behind those candid green eyes.

'Were you eavesdropping on my conversation in the bar?' He searched his memory but couldn't recall having seen her.

'I might have overheard,' she replied, meeting his gaze unashamedly.

'And that's supposed to make me trust you?'

'No. It's supposed to make you see that I mean business and I'm good at what I do. You want to clear Jamie's name and I might be able to help you.'

Smiling slightly, Matt shook his head.

'I was wrong. You're in just the right job,' he said. 'OK, I'm listening. What exactly do you want to know and how do you think you can help me?'

*   *   *

The following day was fine and dry, and Matt managed to persuade Jamie to accompany him to Rockfield to ride work for Leonard. His search for the MG had proved abortive and a couple of hours spent schooling novices over a line of low, stiff brush fences did more to restore Jamie's spirits than any pep talk Matt could have come up with. Unfortunately, chatting about the ongoing plans for the horses afterwards, over coffee in the Leonards' kitchen, only served to remind Jamie that those plans might well not include him, and he quickly sank back into gloom until Irene Leonard dropped a copy of the *Daily Standard* onto the table in front of Matt.

'Well, you're a dark horse, aren't you? What's this? Matt Shepherd—Private Eye?'

'Let's have a look.'

Before Matt could react, Jamie had pinched the paper from under his nose.

'Wow!' He glanced sideways at Matt. 'Your pint-sized journo certainly came through with the goods. You've got a slot on the front page: "Sophie Bradford's Murderer—Top Jockey on the Trail!" When you say you're going to do something, you don't hang about, do you?'

'You're kidding! It doesn't actually say that, does it?' Matt had told Jamie about his meeting with Casey McKeegan on the way over.

'Yep.' Jamie began to read. ' "When I caught up with top National Hunt jockey Matt Shepherd this afternoon, I naturally expected him to defend his fellow rider, Jamie Mullin, who rumour has linked with the murder—after all, they are friends, and Jamie sometimes lodges at Matt's Somerset home—but I didn't expect the twenty-six-year-old to be quite as fired up as he was. Although, perhaps 'fired up' is the wrong phrase to use. Matt, known in the weighing room as 'Eskimo Joe', was indeed ice-cool as he told me of his determination to find the culprit behind the senseless attack and

100

bring him—or her—to justice. To be honest, jockey-turned-sleuth sounds like something out of a thriller, but take a good look into those steady brown eyes, and I, for one, wouldn't bet against him getting the job done." ' He stopped and looked at Matt in awe. 'Wow! She really knows how to lay it on, doesn't she?'

Matt groaned. 'The words *with a trowel* spring to mind. I never dreamed she'd write all that rubbish. I just wanted a couple of lines to take the heat off you.'

Irene looked concerned.

'Was that such a good idea? What if the real murderer reads that and thinks you're coming after him?'

'I don't suppose for one moment that he will, but if he does, he'll probably laugh himself silly at the idea that I think I can do better than the police, as will a number of other people, I have no doubt,' Matt added, grimacing in anticipation of his next visit to the weighing-room.

' "Take a good look into those steady brown eyes," ' Jamie quoted with relish, slanting a look at Matt. 'If you ask me, she's got the hots for you, my friend.'

Matt pulled a face. 'She's not much more than a kid. Actually, you've met her. She said she'd met you in a pub.'

Jamie pursed his lips and shook his head. 'Don't remember it . . .'

'Don't know what Mr Brewer will think about this,' John Leonard said doubtfully. 'I don't imagine he'll be too pleased.'

Matt thought he was probably right, but the deed was done now, and only time would tell whether it had been a good idea or a bad one.

*　　*　　*

Back at Spinney Cottage, an hour or so later, the first layer of fallout from the article landed on the front doorstep in the person of DI Bartholomew. Jamie was out, having been persuaded to walk across the fields to the village to buy a pint of milk.

The dogs gave the alarm, performing a mass exodus from the kitchen and tearing through to the sitting room, where they began to bark furiously at the front door.

'I'll get it.' Glancing through the window on his way to the door, Matt saw Bartholomew's black BMW pulling up in front of the cottage. 'Damn!' he muttered, then called over his shoulder to Kendra, 'Can you call the dogs in there? It's bloody Bartholomew.'

By the time the DI jangled the bell a couple of minutes later, the dogs were safely in the kitchen, a fact that he ascertained before inviting himself in.

He ducked under the lintel and came into the low-ceilinged room, making it seem even lower than it was. His suit—the same brown one Matt had seen before—looked as though it had been slept in and his eyes were heavily hooded. He was on his own.

'Are you here to see Jamie?' Matt asked, shutting the door behind the officer. 'Because he's not here at the moment.'

'No, Mr Shepherd. As a matter of fact, this time it's you I wanted to talk to,' Bartholomew said, turning to face Matt. He produced a folded sheet

102

of newsprint from his pocket. 'I see you've set yourself up as some kind of private investigator. Would you mind telling me what that's all about?'

'Ah,' Matt said, stalling for time. He should have guessed that the article would bring Bartholomew running. 'It's not really how it sounds—it's just a reporter getting a bit carried away. You know what they're like.'

'So you're not intending doing any nosing around?' Bartholomew's tone suggested that he would strongly advise against it.

'Well, that depends . . .'

'On what, exactly?'

'On whether you can convince me that Jamie is just one of many lines of enquiry you are actively following. Because it seems to me you've more or less decided that he's guilty and you think, if you put enough pressure on him, he'll confess.'

'I can assure you, that's not how we work,' the DI said, coldly. 'Mr Shepherd, have you ever heard of Holmes?'

Matt frowned.

'As in Sherlock?'

'Yes, but more specifically, as in the computer programme that every police force in this country uses to run murder investigations?'

'No, I haven't,' Matt admitted. 'Er . . . do you want to sit down?' Bartholomew was standing hunched slightly forward to avoid the stripped oak beams.

With no word of thanks, the DI moved across and lowered his burly frame into one of the armchairs. Matt settled opposite him and waited.

'HOLMES—or more correctly, HOLMES 2— stands for Home Office Large Major Enquiry

System,' the detective told him.

Matt nodded, inwardly cringing at the clumsy acronym.

'This system ensures that every possible line of enquiry is followed up. Every single detail of the investigation is entered into the computer: every statement, every fact and scrap of information. HOLMES then generates hundreds of lines of enquiry, which are followed up and the results entered in their turn. For instance, this party last weekend—we entered the details of every single person on the guest list; anyone else who turned up uninvited; all members of staff at the social club, from the manager, bar staff and bouncers, right down to the caretaker and cleaners. It prioritises lines of investigation, links with other forces around the country, and even produces documentation for use in court.'

Matt inclined his head.

'Very impressive.'

'It *is* impressive, but my reason for telling you, Mr Shepherd, wasn't to impress you but to illustrate that, however much we may personally favour one particular line of enquiry, in this day and age, it simply isn't possible for us to ignore any of the others.'

'Computers are all very well, but they can't take character into account, can they, Detective? As far as your HOLMES programme can see, the facts about Jamie would be the same whether he was the popular, easy-going person that he is, or an unpleasant thug, as long as he hasn't anything on record. Isn't that right?'

'But that's precisely what makes it so valuable,' Bartholomew pointed out. 'It isn't swayed by personal prejudice. And, you must remember, it's only an aid to investigation—it doesn't replace the human element, merely complements it.'

'Well, it's the human element that's making Jamie's life a misery at the moment,' Matt countered.

'The fact remains that Mr Mullin is the one person who was seen to fall out with the deceased—er, Miss Bradford—on the evening she was killed. Naturally, he becomes a prime suspect, and, if your view wasn't coloured by a natural sense of loyalty, you would see it the same way.'

'But what's to stop it being a purely random attack?' Matt asked. 'An attractive woman, dressed, er—to impress, shall we say?—walking along an unlit road late at night? Surely that's a scenario made for trouble?'

'And obviously that's a possibility we're following up, but there was no evidence of any sexual assault, and, in the vast majority of these cases, the killer is someone known to his—or her—victim. I'd be failing in my job if I didn't investigate Jamie Mullin's involvement as thoroughly as I could. If he's innocent, he's got nothing whatever to worry about.'

'Except that, in the meantime—until you find whoever did kill Sophie—his whole life is going down the pan! Between you, you and the bloody papers have seen to it that no one in the racing world wants to be associated with him. There are plenty of able young jockeys around just gagging for a chance to show their worth. In our business you need rides to get rides, and the reputation he's been working his butt off for, over the past four years, will slip away in as many weeks if he's not riding. And you hounding his every move isn't helping.' Matt stopped, seeing nothing remotely resembling sympathy in the DI's face. 'Ah, what's the use?' he asked disgustedly.

'I do know what you're saying,' Bartholomew said, after a moment. 'But let's get back to the reason for my visit, shall we? My business is finding out who attacked and killed this young woman, and having an amateur bumbling around isn't going to help. I seriously advise you to get on with your own job and let me get on with mine. We have hundreds of people working on this; across the country—thousands. I don't know what the hell you think you can do that we haven't already done.'

'It's not actually against the law for me to try and clear Jamie's name?'

'No, of course not.'

'Then, I don't see a problem,' Matt said pleasantly. He stood up and went towards the door. 'Is there anything else?'

Bartholomew's eyes narrowed.

'Do you *know* something? Because, if you do and you withhold it, you'll be obstructing a police enquiry, and that—I'm sure I don't need to tell you—*is* against the law. Do I make myself clear?' He got to his feet and moved across to where Matt waited, dwarfing him in both height and bulk, but Matt stood his ground, looking him steadily in the eye.

'I'm not stupid,' he said quietly, opening the front door and stepping aside.

With a final cold glare, Bartholomew left the cottage.

Matt wasn't riding that day. It was Sunday, but the season had yet to get into full swing and the only National Hunt meeting was taking place at the other end of the country. As he'd only been offered one less than thrilling prospect to ride, Matt had made the decision, some days ago, to stay at home and catch up on a little DIY, but any plans he might have nurtured for a peaceful day after the DI's departure were swiftly routed. His attempt to plaster the walls of what was shortly to become the new kitchen were doomed to failure as one phone call after another left the plaster hardening on his mixing board.

The first couple of interruptions came from other newspapers, agog to know if the article in the *Daily Standard* was to be believed. The third, surprisingly, was from Matt's elder brother, Luke.

'Hello stranger, where are you?' Matt said delightedly, noticing that the display showed a London number.

'London. Got in last night. I'm renting a place in Putney until I get sorted out.' Luke's voice held a noticeable New Zealand accent, even though he'd been schooled in England. Matt pictured him— tall, blond-haired, and with a shy smile that masked a confident business brain.

'And Mum and Dad?' It was over a year since Matt had seen any of his family.

'No, just me.'

'So, are you coming to visit, then? It's ages since we caught up, and I want you to meet Kendra.'

'Yes, I will do, but I'm afraid it won't be for a day or two. I'm here to oversee the opening of the

London office and I'm going to be tied up for a few days. Actually, I have a proposition for you, have you got a mo?'

Matt said he had, but, in the event, it was nearer half an hour before he put the phone down, and his unused plaster was useless. As he scraped it into the bin and made up some more, he was turning Luke's proposal over in his mind and wondering how Charlie Brewer would react to the idea.

Moments later, the phone began to ring again.

'Can you get that, Kennie?' he called. 'If it's another bloody newspaper, I'm not at home.'

The ringing stopped and, moments later, Kendra appeared, holding the handset out towards him.

'It's Dad,' she said, with an apologetic grimace. 'I think he's seen the papers.'

Matt rolled his eyes heavenward, wiped his hand on the seat of his jeans, and took the phone.

'Charlie. Hi. What can I do for you?'

'You can start by explaining just where the hell this bloody paper got that story!' Brewer said explosively. 'They've made it sound as though the reporter actually interviewed you—this Casey something-or-other. Please tell me she didn't.'

'Well, as a matter of fact, she did,' Matt admitted.

'Then she obviously misquoted you . . . ?'

'Well, they weren't my exact words, but the gist of it is right.'

'But . . .' The businessman was momentarily and uncharacteristically at a loss. 'What on earth do you think you're playing at? Isn't it bad enough that Mullin has got himself in the shit without you doing your best to join him? Because that's what will happen, Matt. Sophie was a popular girl.'

Matt quelled his first, instinctive, response to this somewhat surprising comment and said merely, 'Jamie hasn't done anything wrong.'

'Yes, yes—so you say, but mud sticks, you know. Best stay out of it, at least in public, don't you think? Lord Kenning says it's only a matter of time before the police take Mullin in; it won't look good if you're seen to be defending him and then that happens.'

'And it'll look better if I desert a mate when he's in trouble? Anyway, what has Lord Kenning to do with this?'

'I was speaking to him this morning, actually.' Kendra's father couldn't help a note of pride creeping into his voice as he reported this.

Bugger Kenning! Matt thought. The man was clever and had gauged Brewer exactly right. Money he had, and aplenty, but it couldn't buy what he wanted most in the world, acceptance by the titled and landed gentry. Kenning had rightly guessed that a personal phone call would soon have Charlie laying the pressure on Matt.

'You'd think he would be pleased that someone wanted to help find Sophie's killer,' Matt said, mildly. 'She was his niece, after all.'

'I expect he thinks, as I do, that it's a matter best left to the police. Good God, Matt! I'm telling you this for your own sake. I don't want to see you mess up your career and neither does he. Quite apart from your marrying my daughter, you're a bloody good jockey and I need you to ride my horses; that's the bottom line.'

'Okay, I hear what you're saying,' Matt said wearily. 'Though I really don't know why everyone

109

is getting so hot under the collar. I was only ever going to ask a few questions, that's all. I'm not planning a new career!'

'I knew I could rely on your good sense,' Brewer stated.

That's why you felt the need to ring, I suppose, Matt thought dryly, but, for the sake of family harmony, he kept it to himself.

'We'll see you this evening, then. Oh—yes, the girls have decided to have a barbeque, so, if you want to come over a bit earlier . . . ?'

Matt said they would, and Kendra's father put the phone down, no doubt satisfied that the matter was closed.

Matt turned to find that Jamie had come into the room.

'So, you've let him talk you out of it, have you?' he asked bitterly.

'No, I haven't said one way or another,' Matt responded. 'He just *thinks* I have.'

'So you'll still carry on?'

Matt sighed.

'Jamie, listen. I'll do what I can to help, but, in spite of what I said to Casey, I really don't know how much that's going to be. Please don't get your hopes up too far.'

*   *   *

In the late afternoon, at Kendra's suggestion, Jamie accompanied them to the barbeque at Birchwood Hall. It couldn't be said that he was a willing participant, but Matt wasn't keen on leaving him alone at Spinney Cottage in his current frame of mind. There had still been no

110

word on the whereabouts of the MG, but he wouldn't have put it past Jamie to call a taxi if he were really determined to go out and drown his sorrows.

Things were just getting underway when they arrived at the Hall, and they rounded the side of the house to find the large, brick-built barbeque alight and being attended to by most of the male contingent; two long trestle tables groaning under the weight of enough food and drink to feed an African family for a year; and the ladies engaged in a light-hearted game of croquet on the lawn. With the backdrop of the Regency building and its immaculately kept formal gardens, the scene had enough upper-class Englishness to satisfy even the most ardent social mountaineer.

All the family were present, with the addition of Grace's new boyfriend, Rupert; John, Reney and Harry Leonard; and a muscular individual with a shadow of shaved hair and one earring, who had once been introduced to Matt as Niall Delafield, and who apparently took care of security for Kendra's father. He had, to Matt's mind, the look of an ex-soldier, and was dressed on this occasion in faded denim jeans, a whiter-than-white tee shirt, and a navy jacket. He appeared at ease mixing with the family and shook hands with a grasp that left Matt in no doubt of his strength and a smile that rivalled his tee shirt for brilliance.

In spite of his reluctance to attend, Jamie was a natural party animal and, once he was mixing with the Brewer family and their friends, he seemed to shed a little of his black mood and allowed Kendra to draw him into a riotous croquet game with her mother and all the younger members of the

111

gathering.

Now that the barbeque was performing as it ought, Charlie drifted away to talk to John Leonard, and Reney, who could never resist the lure of a cooking range—in whatever form—was left with the tongs. Carrying a beer, Delafield retreated to the comfort of a swing seat, apparently content to watch the antics of the croquet players. All in all, Matt decided that the time would probably never be better to broach the subject of his brother's offer with Charlie.

His reaction was more or less what Matt had expected.

'Sponsorship? What do you want a bloody sponsor for? Why didn't you ask me if you wanted to parade some company's name on your breeches? You can have CRB Developments plastered on every part of your anatomy if you want to—but I didn't think you would, you're so bloody independent! Who are these cowboys, anyway?'

'Q&S Holdings.'

'I see.'

Matt hid a smile as Charlie almost visibly regrouped. Q&S Holdings were one of the top ten companies in New Zealand, and had branches on every major continent.

'Did they call you or did you contact them?'

'Actually, my brother is in charge of the new London office.'

Charlie grunted. 'Still can't see why you need a sponsor,' he said peevishly. 'Got everything you need at Rockfield, haven't you?'

'You said it a minute ago,' Matt told him evenly. 'Independence. But I don't see what the problem

112

is—it won't affect my riding for you.'

'Yes—well, we'll see. We'll need to talk it over, but not now.'

'Actually, I've already accepted. Haven't signed anything, of course, but I've said I'd like to go ahead.' Matt smiled, affecting not to notice the heavy frown his announcement provoked. 'Can I get you another drink?'

As he turned away, he caught John Leonard's eye and winked; the trainer's expression was so aghast that Matt was silently laughing to himself as he went towards the drinks table.

*   *   *

As the sun sank slowly behind the oaks in the park and the patio torches were lit, the croquet players came laughing to the drinks table, Deacon and Harry arguing over whether or not a deflection off the wheel of the wheelchair should count as a foul.

'Well, I think *some* allowance should be made for the fact that I'm a disabled competitor,' Harry complained.

'That's rich!' Frances put in, handing him a glass of white wine. 'Considering you were thrashing the lot of us before it ever happened!'

'Luck, that's all,' Harry protested, looking up at her, and Matt was struck by the softness of the glance that passed between them.

Well, well, he thought. Was that the way the wind was blowing? If so, he was pleased for his friend, but with a slight reservation. Brewer had already had to come to terms with the prospect of one of his daughters marrying a mere jockey; Matt had an idea he wouldn't readily take to the idea of

113

Frances going out with a disabled ex-jockey who was, furthermore, the son of one of his employees.

Just at the moment, however, Kendra's father was fully occupied with the barbeque, from whence came the mouth-watering aromas of a variety of sizzling meats, sausages, mushrooms, and fruit and veg kebabs. Reney's influence had ensured that many of the offerings were suitable for jockeys with an eye on the scales, and Jamie and Matt were happily able to join the feast.

By mid evening, everyone was lounging in the cushioned cane furniture that Greening had brought out from the huge conservatory at the back of the house; drinking wine, talking, and enjoying the warmth of the calm September night. Moths fluttered round the patio lights, instinct drawing them heedlessly into danger, and overhead a pipistrelle bat whirled and dived, causing Grace to look up nervously.

Frances was quick to notice.

'Don't worry,' she said, with a sweet smile. 'It won't get caught in *your* hair. Even bats have to draw the line somewhere!'

'You cow!' her sister exclaimed, lobbing a rolled-up serviette in Frances's direction.

It fell woefully wide, but the one sent in reply hit its mark beautifully and a free-for-all threatened.

From the chair opposite, Joy spoke up.

'I think that's enough, girls! Fran, why don't you make us some coffee?'

'Where's Greening, then?' her daughter asked.

'Putting his feet up, I hope. I told him we'd manage this evening. Don't be so lazy!'

Grumbling, Frances slowly uncurled herself from her chair and stood up. 'OK, coffee, tea, hot chocolate, Horlicks, Ovaltine, milk—who wants what?'

There ensued a few chaotic minutes as she collected everyone's orders, in the midst of which it was discovered that both Harry and Deacon had disappeared.

'I'll find Deke,' Delafield volunteered, getting to his feet. 'I was just going in to fetch a jacket.'

'Harry's gone to the loo,' Frances said. 'I sent him to the workshop one, because it's easier access on wheels. Actually, that was a few minutes ago, I hope he found it OK.'

'Oh dear, I wish you'd told me,' Joy said. 'I had a delivery of hatboxes this afternoon and they're all stacked in the back room; he won't be able to get through with the chair. I don't want to offend, but do you think someone ought to go and see if he's OK?'

'We'll go,' Kendra said, getting to her feet and reaching a hand down to Matt, whose chair she'd been sharing. 'I wanted to show Matt the Hattery anyway. He hasn't seen the showroom since you've had it fitted out.'

'I wish you wouldn't call it a hattery. You've got me doing it now, and I nearly said it in front of one of the customers.'

'Give in and call it "The Hattery",' Frances suggested. 'You were looking for a good name for the business.'

Joy made a face.

'I was thinking of something classy,' she said.

Laughing, Kendra and Matt made their way round the back of the house through a brick archway to the old stableyard, most of which was now converted into garages and storage. Joy's workshop and showroom were located in what had originally been the coach house, a building with arched windows and a high ceiling, which provided ample light for working and space for her creations to be displayed to advantage. A light showed behind the blinds.

'Looks like he's still there,' Kendra remarked.

As they approached, Matt paused by another of the doors.

'Delafield's looking for you,' he said conversationally.

'Oh shit!' came a voice from the shadows. There was a faint glow, incompletely shielded, and then the gritty sound of a shoe on concrete.

Matt moved on to catch up with Kendra and, moments later, Deacon moved out of the doorway, lifting a hand in their direction.

'How did you know he was there? I didn't see him,' she said softly.

'Smelt the cigarette smoke.'

'He is naughty. He knows he's not allowed.'

'I expect that makes it all the more pleasurable,' Matt observed. 'I'm not surprised he rebels a little. If I were your parents, I would thank my lucky stars he's not on something harder than tobacco.'

'Actually ...' Kendra began, then apparently thought better of it.

'Actually—what? You don't think he is, do you?'

'Oh no, not now! But, when he was at uni, I overheard Mum and Dad having this enormous row about him, and something they said made me wonder ... They never talked about it to the rest of us. I might have got it all wrong.'

'Well, I wouldn't be surprised if he had tried drugs,' Matt told her. 'The wrong crowd, peer

116

pressure—it happens all the time, and to lads far more streetwise than Deke.'

Finding the showroom door unlocked, they went in. The high-ceilinged room was lit with dozens of spotlights, each angled onto a different stand of hats: narrow-brimmed, wide-brimmed and rimless; veiled, feathered or ribboned—to Matt's wondering eye, every conceivable colour and style seemed to be represented.

Matt uttered a soft 'Wow!' that clearly pleased Kendra.

'Not bad, is it?'

'It's amazing!'

He wandered through the archway to the adjacent workshop, where he could see some of the tools of the milliner's trade laid out on a bench, with a rack displaying dozens of reels of ribbon and thread, and a large ceramic vase that held a collection of ornamental hatpins, like so many metal-stemmed flowers. Matt picked one out, testing the point of the steel pin with his finger.

'Ouch! That's sharp!'

'It has to be, to push through the hat . . .' Kendra observed, as if explaining it to a five-year-old.

'I should think you'd have to be careful you didn't push it through your head!' Matt said, putting the pin back in the vase.

'You forget, these are *ladies'* hats,' she retorted, with a sweet smile. 'We can cope with these sorts of things without killing ourselves.'

'You don't hear of many cases of death by hatpin.' Deacon had followed them into the workshop and was standing leaning against the doorpost. 'But I'm surprised they've not been

117

banned by the EU on health and safety grounds. You can imagine it—directive from Brussels—hatpins shall be no more than two inches in length and must be tipped with rubber.'

'*Made* of rubber, more like,' Matt said, and, while they were laughing, the door to the back room opened and Harry came through, handling the heavy self-closing mechanism with the skill born of practice.

'*Thought* I heard voices,' he said.

'I brought Matt to see the showroom,' Kendra said quickly. 'He hasn't seen it since Mum had it redecorated.'

'Looks really good,' Harry agreed, and it occurred to Matt that he seemed rather flushed and out of breath.

'Are you OK?' he asked. The glimpse he'd had of the back room had shown it to be piled high with boxes, as Joy had said.

'Yeah, of course I am.' The reply was a little abrupt. 'Why shouldn't I be?'

'Just that Joy wasn't sure you could get past the boxes. Sorry I asked.'

In a moment, Harry's likeable smile was back.

'No, *I'm* sorry. I shouldn't be touchy. Actually it *was* a bit tight but—hey ho—I managed in the end. It's just so bloody frustrating sometimes!'

'Yeah, it must be.'

There was an awkward silence, into which Harry said brightly, 'Well, Kennie, m'dear. Are you going to model some of these confections for us?'

When they returned to the patio ten minutes later, the hot drinks had arrived and Grace told the three of them that they'd been within a minute or two of sending out a second search party.

118

Harry glanced sharply at her, and Matt swore silently under his breath. So much for sparing the ex-jockey's feelings.

*   *   *

Returning to Spinney Cottage, just after midnight, the mellow mood of the evening was shattered by the discovery of a police car parked in front of the house.

'Bloody hell! Now what?' Jamie said, echoing Matt's own thoughts, and, as they pulled up beside it, WPC Deane and a colleague got out.

'Have you found my car? Is that what this is about?' Jamie asked hopefully, dispensing with the social graces.

'In a manner of speaking. I'm afraid I have to ask you to accompany us to the station, sir,' Deane said.

'Again? What for? What's happened?'

WPC Deane stepped closer.

'James Mullin, I'm arresting you on suspicion of the murder of Sophie Bradford. You do not have to say anything–'

'Hang on!' Jamie protested. 'You've already questioned me.'

'We have some new evidence,' she told him, then continued with the caution before opening the back door of the squad car and indicating that he get inside. 'If you would, sir . . . ?'

With one last desperate look at Matt and Kendra, Jamie stepped forward and complied.

6

Jamie was taken to Charlborough Police Station and, although Matt and Kendra would have followed, Deane told them there was little point in doing so, as they wouldn't be able to see him.

They let themselves into the cottage feeling tired and dispirited.

'You don't think it really *could* have been Jamie, do you?' Kendra asked. They were facing one another over the kitchen table—he doodling in the margins of the *Racing Post* and she apparently engrossed in centring her half-finished mug of coffee on its coaster.

'No, I don't.' Matt looked up. It was the first time she'd asked and he hoped it didn't mean she was beginning to have doubts.

'No, me neither. Oh, I feel so sorry for him—it's so unfair.'

'I know. It's just so frustrating not knowing what they've got on him.' It had been the recurring theme of the last fifteen minutes. 'If Jamie's told us everything, then I can't see what evidence they *can* have.'

'Well, at least they've found his car,' Kendra said.

'Yeah, but God only knows what condition it's in. Still, with any luck, his insurance will cough up.'

'Even though he told them he dropped the keys?'

'We don't know for sure that whoever took it had the keys,' Matt pointed out. 'They may have hot-wired it. I expect it's quite easy with an old car like that.'

They sat in silence for a moment and then

Kendra spoke.

'So what happens now?'

'Now? Bed, I should think.' Matt got up and tipped the remains of his own coffee down the sink before coming to stand behind her chair and leaning to kiss her silky blonde hair.

'No, I mean with Jamie. Do you think they'll charge him?'

Matt shrugged.

'It depends what they've found, I suppose.'

'Not much more *you* can do, anyway. I guess it's up to the police now.' Matt thought Kendra sounded relieved about the fact.

'Yeah, but I promised him I'd try. After that pep talk I gave him the other day about getting off his backside and helping himself, it's the very least I can do, don't you think? You saw the way he looked at me when they took him away.'

'Bartholomew won't be pleased,' Kendra said, twisting to look up at Matt.

'Bartholomew is supposed to be one of the good guys,' Matt responded. 'Let's not start worrying about *him*.'

'So, where are you going to start?'

'I'm not sure. I suppose, try and speak to Sophie's friends and relations, but the problem is, I don't even know where she lived. I wish I'd thought to ask Jamie.'

'Oh, that's easy. She rents an apartment in Bath—at least she used to. I know her flatmate— Tara Goodwin—we were at school together and I ran into her last year.'

'Brilliant! You wouldn't happen to have her address, I suppose?'

Kendra looked apologetic.

'Sorry. I can give you her phone number, though. You could ring and ask. Or I will, if you don't want to.'

'Hmm. If it's at all possible, I think I'd rather just turn up. It would give her less time to think up an excuse for not seeing me.' Matt kissed her again. 'Right, I'm off to bed. I've got to be at the yard in less than six hours.'

*   *   *

True to her word, Kendra found and wrote down Tara Goodwin's number for Matt before he set off for Rockfield at six o'clock the following morning, although he still hadn't decided quite how to go about approaching her.

There was no racing that day and he spent a busy couple of hours schooling young horses for Leonard. It was a part of the job that he enjoyed very much. Trying the novices over fences for the first time was often the moment when a bright spark of talent began to glow in one of the horses; a spark that, with time and care, could flare into that one in a million horse that would make tracks like Aintree and Cheltenham its own, and bring fame and fortune to all its connections. It took more than talent to make a champion, though, Matt reflected as he rode back to the yard on his last mount of the day. It was a critical blend of ability, courage, luck, and that extra indomitable will to win that only a very few possessed.

The chestnut he was sitting on was ordinary; he might make a fairly decent chaser. It was the third time he'd schooled the horse and he'd taken to fences calmly and sensibly, but Matt hadn't felt that rush of exhilaration that the special ones generated. He patted the warm satiny neck. Most of his rides were like this fella. They were the bread and butter of his job and deserved no less respect than the brilliant ones. It was only the stupid and the wilfully awkward that he had a problem with, but thankfully they were very much the minority.

It had been a chilly morning with wisps of mist lurking in the hollows, reminding him that the days were shortening and the National Hunt season proper was on its way. Coffee and toast in the farm kitchen beckoned enticingly as Matt unsaddled the chestnut and rubbed him down but, as he followed the trainer towards the house, his mobile began to vibrate, silently, in his jacket pocket. He located it with the hand that wasn't carrying his helmet.

'Yeah?'

'Is that Matt?'

'Yeah. Who is this?'

'It's Casey McKeegan.'

'Oh, hi Casey.'

'I just heard about Jamie. That's awful!'

'You just *heard*? How did you hear? It only happened a few hours ago.'

'I have my sources,' came the smug reply. 'So what's the latest?'

'Well, supposing you tell me.'

'All *I* know is they've found Sophie Bradford's credit cards in Jamie's car and they've arrested him. What do you know?'

Her credit cards—so *that* was it. But how the hell did they come to be there? And how the hell—for that matter—had Casey found out?

'So, what? Have you got a bug on Bartholomew's

phone or something?' Matt asked, and Casey laughed.

'I can't reveal my sources,' she said loftily. 'By the way, did you like my piece in the *Standard*?'

'Very good,' he said dryly. 'Especially the bit about my—what was it?—"steady brown eyes". Wasn't that just the teensiest bit over the top?'

'It humanises you. I just wish they'd been blue. "Icy blue eyes" sounds so much more impressive, don't you think?'

'I think you've been reading too many crime novels—that's what *I* think! Look, can your sources do something for me?'

'They might . . .'

'I have a phone number, but I need the address that goes with it. I'd rather you didn't say who's asking, though. Can you do that?'

'Yeah. No problem. What's the number?'

Matt fished the piece of paper out of his pocket and read it to her. 'Have you got that?'

'Yeah. That's a Bath number, isn't it?'

'Yes. How soon can you get it?'

'Right away,' she declared. 'But, if that's Sophie Bradford's flat, I don't need to ask my sources. I know where it is. I can take you there.'

Matt wasn't keen on that idea.

'I'm sure I can find it, if you just give me the address.'

'But that's not how a partnership works,' Casey complained. 'There has to be something in it for me, too.'

'Look,' Matt explained patiently. 'My girlfriend went to school with Sophie's flatmate. With *her* there, she might just be relaxed enough to talk to me; with a journalist in tow, I might just as well not bother going!'

'I could pretend to be your sister.'

'Oh, and you take after our Irish mother, I suppose, whilst I take after our father ... No, Casey, just stay out of it, please.'

'So why should I tell you the address?'

'To prove to me that you're more mature than you look?' Matt suggested.

There was a moment's silence, then Casey said, 'Has anyone ever told you that you're a devious bastard?'

'Not for a day or two. The address?'

Matt's conversation with Casey gave him much food for thought. The business with Sophie's credit cards was perplexing. He still didn't believe that Jamie was guilty, but the odds were stacking against him. Surely, though, Bartholomew wouldn't think Jamie would be so stupid as to keep them in his car if he *had* stolen them? To what end? He'd have to have been unbelievably moronic to think he'd get away with using them with all the hue and cry going on. If he had stolen them—perhaps with the idea of making the murder look like a mugging—the obvious thing to do would be to destroy them as soon as possible. He hadn't had them upon his person when he was first arrested, so where did they think he'd hidden them? Did they—and this made Matt go cold for a moment—think Jamie had had a partner in crime? Because, if they did, it took little intellect to work out who would be top of their list of candidates.

*   *   *

Kendra's reception of the idea that she should pay

125

an unannounced social call on her old school friend was lukewarm at best.

'But I haven't seen her for absolutely ages! In fact, only once since we left school, and *that* was by accident. I can't just go swanning up to her flat and expect to be invited in, especially after what's happened.'

'But she gave you her number,' Matt reasoned. 'She must have meant you to use it, surely.'

'Well, yes . . . but not necessarily . . . I mean—it's a bit like people you meet on holiday. It's a spur of the moment sort of thing, and you don't really expect them to follow it up; in fact, it's a bloody pain if they do! I'm sure I'm the last person Tara wants to see right now.'

'This is for Jamie, remember? It's not a social call.'

'Yes, I know, but . . . Oh, you're a bastard, you know that?'

'Mm, so I'm told,' Matt said smiling. 'Regularly.'

*   *   *

Brock Street in Bath was a road of golden stone houses near the centre of the town. Two thirds of the way along, Matt and Kendra stopped outside a glossy green front door and, glancing up at the number, Matt said, 'This is it. Ready?'

'Not really. But, if we're going to do it, let's get it over with.'

'Atta girl.'

Matt pressed the button beside a brass plate etched with the imaginative words, *The Flat*.

After a short pause, the intercom crackled and a rather indistinct voice enquired, 'Yes? Who is it?'

Matt nodded to Kendra, who leaned forward, saying brightly, 'Tara? Is that you? It's Kendra. Kendra Brewer.'

There followed an even longer pause.

'Kendra Brewer? From Roedale?'

'That's right. I said I'd come and visit, d'you remember?'

'Well, of course! How utterly sweet of you ...' There was the sound of another, deeper voice and a stifled giggle, before Tara said, 'Come on up and have a coffee. Just give me a minute.'

The intercom crackled abruptly to silence and, after the promised minute lengthened to two, the door beside them gave an audible click.

'We're on.' Matt gave Kendra the thumbs up and pushed the door inward, standing aside for her to enter.

'I feel awful,' she murmured, as she stepped past him. 'She's obviously got someone with her. She must be cursing me!'

The hall and stairs were wide and airy, with cream walls, stained glass over the door, and a hard-wearing hessian carpet. As they hesitated, there came the sound of a door opening and shutting somewhere above them, followed by footsteps running lightly down the stairs. Moments later, round the bend from the second flight, a young Asian man appeared. He wore light cotton trousers with a blue shirt undone to four inches above the waist, and a gold chain rippled on the smooth skin of his chest.

He flashed them a gleaming smile as he passed, pulled the door open, and was gone.

Matt looked at Kendra. 'Right, come on, lass. Up we go.'

Tara Goodwin was slim, with fine dark hair down to her shoulders and a face that would have been beautiful if her rather prominent nose had played along. With barely a blink at finding two people in her hallway, where she'd clearly expected one, she invited them both in with a warmth that—Kendra said later—made her feel guiltier than ever.

The flat that, until lately, Tara had shared with Sophie Bradford had a distinctive retro look, harking back to the brash modernism of the late sixties and early seventies. Boxy black leather sofas sat on lush white carpets, the shelves and coffee table were of tubular chrome and smoked glass, while half a dozen fluffy scarlet cushions, and two red-painted, unframed canvasses on the wall, provided bright splashes of colour to lift the mood.

The lounge and kitchen were open plan and, waving a hand towards the chairs and instructing her uninvited visitors to sit down, Tara went to put the kettle on.

'So what brings you to Bath?' she asked brightly, lining up white mugs and a cafetière on the black granite worktop.

'Shopping, mainly,' Kendra said, and then, apparently realising the incongruity of having no bags, added, 'We've dumped the stuff in the car.'

'Oh, what have you bought? Anything nice?' Tara said, then laughed over her shoulder. 'Now, that's a bloody stupid thing to say, isn't it? As if you'd buy something you didn't like.'

'Just stuff for the house. We're doing it up.'

Tara wanted to know where they lived, and, while Kendra described the cottage in some detail, Matt was considering the delicate task of bringing the conversation round to Sophie Bradford. In the

128

event, Tara did it for him. Coming through from the kitchen area with the coffee and three mugs on a tray, she said, 'I suppose you've heard what happened to my flatmate, Sophie? You must have seen it on the news.'

'She was your flatmate?' Matt exclaimed, before Kendra could reply. 'How awful for you.'

'Yeah, well, to be honest, I can't say we were all that close, because she wasn't here half the time and she could be a bit of a pain. But I've known her quite a while, so it *was* a bit of a shock, and, of course, I've been inundated by the police and reporters all week.' She put the tray down on the table and sank back onto the sofa opposite them. 'The things they want to know—I mean, who her friends were; did she get on with her family; what were her hobbies—men, men, men, basically for that one. They even wanted to know where she shopped. I mean, what's that got to do with anything?

'It *is* awful, though,' she went on, before they had a chance to comment. 'I mean, you hear about these things happening—on the news and everything—but you never expect it to happen to anyone you know. It makes you realise it could've been you. You just don't feel safe any-more.'

She took a sip of her coffee, and Matt took advantage of the pause.

'Her boyfriend was a friend of mine.'

'Which boyfriend? Darren?'

'No. Jamie.'

'Oh, little Jamie—that's what she called him— she said he was sweet, but I don't think she was very serious about him. I don't think she was very serious about any of them, come to that. It was all

129

a big game to her. She used to come back here and laugh about them sometimes; about how she could wrap them round her little finger.'

'The police think Jamie might have killedher . . .' Matt let the statement hang in the air.

'Oh my God! But *you* don't—obviously—if he's your friend.'

'No, I'm certain he didn't. Did you know Sophie was pregnant?' Matt asked. As she hadn't recognised him, it seemed they'd struck lucky and Tara hadn't read Saturday's *Daily Standard*.

'How did you know that? The police asked me that, the other day. No, she didn't tell me, but it doesn't surprise me. I mean, she was always forgetting to take her pill. I'm surprised it hasn't happened before now, to tell the truth. She . . . well, let's just say she lived life to the full and leave it at that.'

'So she didn't seem worried or upset about anything?'

'Not particularly. She had her ups and downs, just like anyone else.' She paused, and looked from Matt to Kendra, frowning. 'Look, what's going on? You weren't just passing, were you? What are you doing here?'

Kendra reddened a little under her scrutiny, and Matt made the decision to come clean.

'I'm sorry. No, you're right, we weren't just passing. The thing is, Jamie's a good friend of ours and he's in a lot of trouble. We're just trying to help him, that's all.'

Tara hesitated, catching her lip between her teeth.

'Well, I don't know what I can tell you, anyway,' she said eventually. 'I told the detective—I forget his name . . .'

'Bartholomew?'

'Yes, that's right. Bartholomew, and the woman—Deane, isn't it? I told them, over and over, that Sophie and I were friends, but not close friends. We didn't share secrets or anything. She had days when she was moody, like we all do, but I've no idea if she was worried or just hormonal. More coffee?'

Matt accepted, even though he didn't really want it. He had a feeling Tara might know more than she thought she did, and, now she'd begun to expand, it seemed a shame to stop her.

'Where did Sophie work?'

'Work?' Tara stifled a laugh. 'That's a good one! She did a bit of modelling from time to time— quite often on the racecourses. You know, hired by the sponsors to walk back beside the winners and stand and look pretty while the prizes are given out? I always feel sorry for them, half the time they look bloody freezing! But I don't think she'd done any modelling for ages.'

'Perhaps she got money from her family . . .' Matt suggested.

Tara nodded.

'It's possible. She didn't seem to get on with them very well, but I know they weren't short of a penny or two. There was someone she called Mosie. I think he was quite a bit older than her. I got the impression he was a sort of sugar daddy. There were flowers sometimes, and, once or twice, expensive jewellery. I would tease her, but she'd just laugh and accuse me of being jealous. She was infuriating at times, but you couldn't help liking her.' Tara looked away, picking up her coffee cup

131

and taking a sip; to steady herself, Matt suspected.

'I'm sorry. Would you like us to go?' With characteristic sympathy, Kendra put out a hand to touch the other girl's arm.

Tara summoned a smile.

'No. Please stay. It's silly, but I miss her. I never thought I would, but I do. We shared this place for over three years, and it worked really well, on the whole. Half the time she wasn't here, but knowing she's never coming back makes it seem dreadfully empty, somehow. I still can't believe that she's actually dead; that someone *murdered* her. It just doesn't seem real.'

'Did you ever see this Mosie?' Matt asked, thinking about Lord Kenning and the rumour Harry had told him about.

'No, he didn't come here, except once, to pick her up—but then I only saw his car. It was a Jag. A big, silvery grey one. I remember thinking, *You lucky cow!* And then, when she came back the next day, she told me she'd been with him. "Mosie took me to this sumptuous hotel in the country, but you mustn't tell anyone, Tara," she said, though I don't know who she thought I was going to tell. So I reckon he was married, don't you?'

'Most likely,' Matt agreed.

'Oh, and there was something else—she told me once that Mosie liked to play games.'

'Games . . . ?'

'That's what she said. I didn't ask what—it's not really my scene—I imagine she meant dressing up or something.'

Matt turned the idea over in his mind. If it *was* Kenning and he wanted to keep the relationship quiet, how much worse would it be for him if it was

132

known that there was a kinky element to his liaison with his niece?

'Do you know if she had any other girlfriends; anyone she might have shared secrets with, perhaps?'

Tara pursed her lips and shook her head.

'Not that I ever met. As far as I could see, she seemed to socialise almost exclusively with men. We very rarely went out anywhere together—you know, for girls' nights out or anything. It just wasn't her scene.'

'And there's nothing else you can think of—odd phone calls, anything she said or did that struck you as strange, especially recently?'

Again, Tara shook her head.

'No. That's what the police kept asking, but there was nothing. Everything was normal—or as normal as it ever was with Sophie around. I've been racking my brains all week and I haven't come up with a thing. I'm sorry, I've not been much help to you, or your friend.'

*   *   *

Having taken their leave of Tara Goodwin, a few minutes later Matt and Kendra stepped out through the glossy portal and paused for a moment on the pavement outside.

'She's nicer than I remembered,' Kendra said. 'At school, she used to get on my nerves—she was a bit loud.'

'Whilst you were perfection, of course,' Matt quizzed gently, and was rewarded by an indignant jab in the ribs. 'Ouch! Now what have I said?'

Linking arms, they started to walk back to where

133

they'd left the car.

'So, Sherlock, did you learn anything useful?' Kendra asked.

'Not a lot.' Matt sighed. 'I guess it was daft to think I would, but I had to try. That stuff about Mosie was the most interesting.' He told Kendra what he'd learned from Harry about Lord Kenning.

'Do you think he was Sophie's sugar daddy, then? Why Mosie? What's Lord Kenning's name?'

'Um ...' Matt scoured his memory. 'Edward, I think, but she'd hardly use his real name, given the circumstances. I'd be interested to see what sort of car he drives ...' He broke off, adding explosively, 'Now what the hell is *she* doing here?'

Ahead, where the MR2 was parked in a line of cars at the side of the road, he could see a familiar redheaded figure, seated on the bonnet, apparently studying her fingernails.

'Who is it?'

'Casey McKeegan. That reporter I told you about. I don't know what she's doing here.'

'Waiting for you, I'd say.'

'Oh, ha ha.'

They were less than twenty feet away before Casey looked up and saw them. Instantly, she straightened and greeted Matt with a wide grin, just as if Matt hadn't warned her, earlier that day, to stay away.

'How did it go with Tara?' she asked, before he could say anything.

'Kendra, this is Casey McKeegan. Casey, Kendra Brewer, my fiancée.'

'Hi,' Kendra said.

'Hi.' Casey gave her an unsmiling glance and

134

turned back to Matt. 'So how did it go? What did Tara tell you?'

Matt shrugged.

'Not much, I'm afraid. She couldn't think of anything that would help.'

'So you talked about the weather for an hour and fifteen minutes did you? *Come on.*'

'Have you been watching the flat?'

'Well, I had to do something. And don't try and tell me you were going to ring me and give me an update; I wasn't born yesterday!'

'I might have done, if there had been anything to tell,' Matt hedged. 'Look, I'm afraid we've all had a wasted journey. Sophie didn't take Tara into her confidence. She really doesn't know anything more than what she's told the police.'

Casey's eyes narrowed.

'You,' she said, pointing an accusing finger, 'are not playing fair. I gave you Tara's address; the least you can do is tell me what she said.'

'She's got a point,' Kendra remarked.

Matt cast her a darkling glance, then sighed.

'All right. Let's go and get a coffee or something. But I warn you, you'll be disappointed.'

*   *   *

'She's quite a character, isn't she? Your Casey.'

Matt and Kendra were in the car, heading for home.

'She's not *my* Casey,' Matt said.

'Oh, I think she is—in *her* mind, anyway. I think she's got a huge crush on you.' Kendra slanted a look at him. 'Actually, underneath that tomboyish exterior, I think there's quite a pretty girl trying to

135

get out.'

'Well, it's not trying very hard.'

Kendra laughed.

'That's mean! Still, you can't deny she's bright. And, with her contacts, she could be very useful. If she can find out who this mysterious Mosie is, that'll be a start, won't it?'

'Well, I'm pretty sure it must be Lord Kenning, but, if she can prove it . . .' Matt shook his head. 'I can't work out how she got a job working for a paper like the *Standard*, at her age. It's not as if she even looks her age. She looks about sixteen.'

'Maybe that's an advantage? I imagine she might get under people's guard. Maybe an editor recognised a latent talent; who knows? So what's the next move?'

'I'm not sure. I think maybe I should have a little chat with Razor at Sedgefield tomorrow.'

'Talking of which . . .' Kendra looked at her watch. 'What time are you supposed to be meeting Rollo and Mikey?'

'Three o'clock. Oh shit, I'd forgotten that. What's the time?'

'Ten to two. You'd better get a wriggle on.'

*   *   *

Driving like a man possessed, Matt made it back to Norton Peverill, packed an overnight bag with Kendra's help, grabbed his saddles, boots, and kitbag, and drove on to his rendezvous with the other jockeys, arriving only a few minutes late.

Sedgefield Racecourse in County Durham was a round trip of five hundred miles or more, and not a place to which Matt would consider travelling

136

without sufficient incentive in the form of quantity or quality of rides. On this occasion he had rides in all but one race on the card, but he might still have baulked at the distance, had Rollo Gallagher and young Mikey Copperfield not been travelling north, too.

Because their job involved so much travelling, it was normal for jockeys who lived relatively close together to share the driving to the more distant courses. On a long haul, it was also normal for them to put up for the night in the house or lodgings of one of their colleagues who lived in the area. It was a reciprocal arrangement that, over the course of the year, saved all of them a good deal of money. Long hours spent on the road were tedious and contributed to sky-high insurance premiums but, in most instances, the likely financial rewards on offer for a day's jump racing made the idea of flying to the course a non-starter.

After an overnight stay crammed into the spare room of a seasoned jockey known as Limpet—for his famed ability to stay on even the clumsiest of animals to the bitter end—the four of them made their way together to Sedgefield.

Razor arrived late at the course and then rode the winner in the first, which meant that Matt had no early opportunity to speak with him in private.

Things began to pan out in his favour, however, when one of the other jockeys fell off going down to the start of the second race, and the rest of runners and riders were kept circling quietly whilst the loose horse was rounded up and caught.

Threading through the large field, Matt managed to bring his horse alongside the grey ridden by Razor and engage the jockey in

137

conversation.

On the drive up from the south, Matt had wrestled on and off with the delicate question of how to bring up the subject of Lord Kenning and Sophie Bradford with Razor. If it had been almost any of the other jockeys that he knew, he would have just come straight out and asked, but 'Razor' Hislop was a different matter, and Matt couldn't rely on him to keep the knowledge of his interest to himself.

As it turned out, Matt's own recent publicity had come to Razor's ears, and he wasn't the man to let the chance to mock pass him by.

'Well, well, if it isn't Inspector fucking Clouseau!' he said, as soon as he saw Matt beside him. He continued in a fair imitation of Sellers' character: ' 'Ow is your hinvestigation coming along?'

Matt rolled his eyes. He'd already had to put up with some of the same in the weighing room.

'OK, OK, get it over with.'

'You don't seem to be 'aving much success in clearing Mutton's name, do you?' Razor enquired, still in character. 'Last I 'eard 'e'd been taken down ze nick, but maybe that was part of your cunning plan, *non*?'

'Tell me what you know about Lord Kenning and Sophie Bradford,' Matt said, abandoning subtlety. 'I'm told it was you who started the rumour that they were having an affair.'

'What? That was ages ago.' Razor dropped the silly accent. 'There was nothing to it. It was a mistake.'

'So where did you get it from? Who told you?'

'No one did. I got it wrong, that's all. Kenning explained, I apologised; end of story.'

Matt eyed him thoughtfully. It sounded out of character. The Razor they all knew and distrusted would never normally let something go as easily as that.

'Why d'you want to know, anyway?' Razor said then. 'What's old Kenning got to do with anything? You must be losing the fucking plot if you think he murdered her. Why don't you just accept that your little pal probably did it, and move on?'

'Because he didn't do it.'

Razor lifted an eyebrow and shrugged.

'Well, whatever. But I'll tell you something for nothing. Get on the wrong side of a man like his lordship and you might as well kiss your career goodbye. It's professional suicide, mate, and don't say I didn't warn you!'

Thoughtfully, Matt watched Razor ride away. The warning was to some extent unnecessary. You didn't have to be Brain of Britain to work out that it would be extremely foolish to make an enemy of a man who had considerable influence in your chosen field, and he was surprised that the surly jockey had bothered to deliver such advice. Matt felt it would have been more in character for him to sit back and enjoy the sight of his rival playing with fire.

Before he had time to ponder it further, the starter mounted his rostrum and delivered the thirty-second warning to put their goggles on. Instantly, Matt's brain shifted into racing mode, and everything else was relegated to the area marked pending.

*   *   *

139

The Sedgefield meeting was very successful for Matt, and the three southern jockeys spent another night in the north, using the following day—when there were no jump meetings—to travel home. On the journey, Matt entered into the conversations with Mikey and Rollo in a slightly abstracted way, his mind occupied with Jamie's plight.

He found himself at a bit of a standstill with regards to what to do next. Razor's information had thrown a shadow of doubt upon his own growing conviction that Lord Kenning had been Sophie's Mosie. He'd seemed so definite that it had been a mistake. It was true that Kenning's own reaction, when Matt had mentioned his relationship with Sophie, had been one of intense annoyance, but then the simple fact of Razor's past rumour-mongering could account for that. Razor's easy dismissal of the story still bothered Matt. Had pressure been brought to bear? Would that explain the warning he'd passed on?

After a day's travelling, Matt reached Spinney Cottage feeling tired and looking forward to a quiet evening spent with Kendra, a glass or two of wine, and a DVD on the television.

However, following a rapturous welcome from the dogs, Kendra greeted him with a hug and the information that Jamie had called from Charlborough Police Station, not five minutes before, and wanted to be collected.

'They're letting him go?'

'I imagine so. Unless he's overpowered the guard and escaped,' she suggested with a twinkle. 'I was just on my way to get him.'

Belatedly, Matt noticed that she had a coat over

140

her arm and her car keys in her hand.

'If I'd known, I could have picked him up on my way past,' he complained. He was too weary for repartee. 'I wonder what's going on. Have they charged him, do you know?'

'I don't know. I'm sorry, Matt. I tried to get you on your mobile, but couldn't get through.'

'Yeah, the battery's flat. I forgot to take my charger. Look, can't he get a taxi?'

'He says he hasn't any money . . .'

'Well, he can pay when he gets here, surely?'

'Sorry, I didn't think of that. I'll try and ring him back, shall I?'

'Yeah, do that.' Matt dumped his overnight bag on the sofa, then changed his mind. 'No, forget it. I'll fetch him. It'll only take forty minutes.'

'Oh yes? And the rest . . .' Kendra said dryly. 'Please, Matt . . . Slow down a little—for me? I don't want to lose you.'

Matt glanced at her in surprise. Apart from not liking to watch him race, she wasn't especially given to anxiety. Under his scrutiny she dropped her gaze as though feeling suddenly self-conscious. He thought she looked a little pale.

'Are you all right, sweetheart?'

She smiled brightly at him.

'Yes, fine. It's just . . . you *do* drive too fast sometimes—even with me—and I dread to think how fast you go when I'm *not* in the car. I know you're a good driver, it's all the other idiots I worry about, and when you're driving that fast, you haven't got a hope of avoiding them.' She waved a hand. 'OK, I've said my piece. I'll go and find something for supper.'

Jamie spoke little on the way back from Charlborough, seeming withdrawn and depressed. He recounted that the MG had been found upside down in a field, but, thankfully, not burned out, although even that fact didn't appear sufficient to leaven his mood. As far as Matt could understand it, Jamie owed his continuing freedom to the absence of any of his fingerprints on Sophie's stolen cards, but, beyond saying that the police hadn't had enough evidence to hold him any longer, Jamie volunteered no further information about his three-day ordeal, and, when Matt questioned him, said he didn't want to talk about it. Matt attempted to fill the silence by recounting the events of the past three days, but soon realised that—understandably—neither his non-productive investigations nor his racing successes would awaken much joy in Jamie's heart.

At the cottage, Jamie joined them for the meal Kendra had prepared, but ate little before saying he was tired and retiring to his room.

Matt watched him go, thoughtfully.

'Are you going to be here tomorrow? I'm at Hereford. I'm sorry, but I'm a bit worried about leaving him on his own,' he said, as he and Kendra settled down on the sofa with their coffee. The dogs padded in after them, Sky and The Boys flopping down on the rugs, and Taffy squeezing herself onto the chair with them and laying her chin on Kendra's knee with a satisfied sigh.

Matt caught himself shifting up to give the sheltie more room.

'Why is it I sometimes get the feeling this dog

142

plays the fiddle round here, and we all dance to her tune?'

'That's because she does,' Kendra said, matter-of-factly. 'I *was* going to help Mum tomorrow, but I could stay if you're really worried. I'm sure she'd understand. You don't think he'd try anything stupid, do you?'

'I don't really know. I'd be happier if he was ranting and banging doors. I've never known him quiet like this.'

'I'll give Mum a ring in the morning,' she promised, then leaned towards him and kissed him gently behind the ear. 'Now how about some *us* time?'

'Sounds good to me,' Matt responded, then, with a glance at Taffy, added, 'But do we have to OK it with Madam first?'

7

Matt liked Hereford racecourse; it was a friendly, country course where there was racing all year round. The squareish track was flat and suited horses with a turn of foot, which exactly described the two runners that Brewer was sending there on the day following Matt's return from Sedgefield. Both Brewer and Leonard were attending the meeting, and Matt travelled to the course with the trainer, who informed him that his boss was not in the best frame of mind following Matt's announcement about the sponsorship deal.

'And he's not happy that you're riding Kandahar Prince again, either,' Leonard finished.

143

'Oh God! Not that again! I've been riding him for years and Plumpton was the first time he's ever fallen with me. It's not as if it was even his fault, poor sod! If Brewer had his way, I'd be wrapped up in cotton wool and only taken out when he had a runner, which would defeat the object anyway, because I wouldn't be race fit.'

'Of course you wouldn't,' Leonard agreed. 'That's what I've told him, God knows how many times! He can't expect you to pass up the ride on a favourite, either, just to suit him—it's ridiculous!'

'He knows that, really,' Matt said, as the trainer's Volvo accelerated out of the motorway slip road. 'He's just too bloody controlling to let it go.'

By the time they turned into the owners' and trainers' car park at the racecourse, large drops of rain had begun to splash onto the windscreen, and Leonard rooted amongst the clutter on the back seat to locate a large golf umbrella, under which they made their way to the racecourse buildings.

Matt's first ride of the day was on a horse of Doogie McKenzie's—Tranter, a big angular chestnut with a long, honest head and ears that had a tendency to flop sideways. Doogie wasn't in the habit of telling Matt how to ride his horses, unless there were very specific instructions, and, as he had two runners in the race, he greeted Matt when the jockeys entered the paddock and then left him, in favour of looking after the less experienced lad who was riding his other horse.

Matt wasn't bothered. He stood in the driving rain watching the runners circle, some with heads and tails low, some dancing sideways to try and turn their rumps to the wind, and thought that, even on a pig of a day like today, he would rather

144

be doing his job than any other he could think of.

'Ah, Matt. Lousy weather, isn't it?' a voice commented in his ear, and he turned to find Lord Kenning at his shoulder.

'At least it's not cold, sir,' he replied, wondering what had prompted the man to approach him and trying to quell the distasteful images that Tara's revelations now conjured up.

'Just had a word with Doogie. He says the horse has been working well, so we should have quite a good chance here.'

Matt's brain changed gear. He hadn't realised that the horse was Kenning's. The ride had been arranged by his agent, and, with his mind on other things, for the first time in his career, Matt hadn't done his usual pre-race research in the formbook. Not that he would have turned Tranter down—a ride was a ride, as long as the horse wasn't a serial non-finisher—and he trusted Harper not to book him anything too dangerous.

'He looks a useful sort, sir.' It was the best that could honestly be said of the chestnut at first glance.

'Yes, I think he is. He's got a nice turn of foot, but he'll stop if he sees the light too soon. Keep him handy, tuck him in until a furlong or two out, and then send him on. Got that?'

'Yes, sir.' Matt eyed the horse doubtfully. Somehow he didn't have the look of a sprinter but, in reality, it was difficult to tell, and Kenning was an experienced owner who wasn't accustomed to having his judgement questioned. 'Don't think I've seen him around—have you had him long?'

'Bought him in the summer. Came from Grant's yard, up in Perth.'

145

That would explain it.

The bell sounded, signalling time for the jockeys to mount, and Matt excused himself from Kenning's presence and walked across to Tranter. The horse was being walked round by Doogie's travelling head lad, a man Matt knew well from his days riding for the yard. With practised ease, he flipped the waterproof sheet back onto the chestnut's rump and swiftly legged Matt up into the dry saddle.

'All right, Matt?'

'Yeah, fine thanks, Pete.' Matt's feet found the stirrups. 'So what about this boy? Kenning reckons he needs to be covered up.'

Pete twisted to look up at him, his face registering the equivalent of a shrug.

'I wouldn't know. He's been working OK, but he hasn't shown anything special. This is his first run for us.'

After a couple of circuits of the paddock, the horses were led out onto the track and, with a slap on the neck, Pete let Tranter go. The horse accelerated willingly enough into a long-striding canter, head down into the wind and rain, and they made their way to the two-mile start.

Out on the course, the rain became even heavier and, driven by an ever-strengthening wind, was soon lashing horizontally across the course. After what seemed like an interminable time circling in front of one of the hurdles, getting wetter and wetter, the runners were called through to the steeplechase course and the race got underway.

Bearing Lord Kenning's advice in mind, Matt slotted Tranter into third or fourth place on the rails and prepared to bide his time. The horse

146

didn't give him the feel of an animal that was raring to get to the head of the field, rather, he felt content to hack round with the masses, jumping efficiently and with care. He'd make a super hunter when he'd finished his track career, Matt thought, squinting behind his goggles as mud from the leaders' hooves hit him in the face and chest.

Passing the stands and the winning post for the first time, the field swung round the second bend and away towards the open ditch and the water. Tranter cleared both with no fuss and soldiered on, though Matt winced in sympathy as he saw Mikey Copperfield's horse go down heavily in a tangle of legs. Five fences and three bends later, they were approaching the last with less than two furlongs to go and the chestnut was still holding his position steadily, although Matt had moved him off the rails, aware that several runners were ranging up on the outside.

Tranter flew the last with his best jump of the race, and, as the field spread out in the final charge to the line, Matt pulled a fresh pair of goggles into place, switched his whip, eased the horse out to the left, and waited for the promised surge as the chestnut saw daylight.

It didn't come.

With the leader a length and a half ahead and three or four other contenders picking up speed around him, Matt sat down and rode hard for the finishing post, but to no avail; Tranter plugged on gamely, but could do no better than sixth place.

Matt patted the steaming chestnut neck and let him slow down gradually. The animal didn't feel especially tired; in fact, he felt as though he could have gone round again with no problem. In sixth place, he had finished with more than half the field behind him, but Matt was frustrated, feeling that, if he'd followed his instincts and taken the running on from maybe half a circuit out, he might very well have managed, if not to win, then at least to have improved his position by three or four places.

Pete came out onto the track to meet him as he trotted the horse back towards the stands.

'Looks like the trip was a bit short for him,' he said, as he reached for the chestnut's rein.

'Yeah, I'd say he was an out-and-out stayer,' Matt agreed. 'Well done, Bully!' he called, as the winner rode by.

In the unsaddling area, Doogie came to meet him as he undid Tranter's girths and slid the saddle off.

'Left it a bit late there, Matt,' he said, slanting a look at him from under his bushy white brows. 'Not like you to get it wrong. Kenning's not happy.'

'Well, that's rich! It was him who told me the horse needed to be covered up.'

'Are you sure? He told *me* he was happy to leave it in your hands.'

Matt stared at the trainer, thinking back. Was it possible that he could have misunderstood Kenning's instructions? Surely not, he'd been quite specific—cover him up for a late run.

'Perhaps we got our wires crossed,' he suggested. It went against the grain not to fight his corner, but over the years he had learned that, at certain times, and with certain people, it was better to give in gracefully, even if justice hadn't been served.

'Didn't you look at his form?' Doogie asked, sponging the chestnut's heaving flanks. 'He's a stayer. Normally a front runner.'

Matt shook his head guiltily.

'Sorry, Doogie. I've been kind of caught up in this business with Jamie.'

'Hm.' The trainer turned to him, water dripping from the sponge. 'Look Matt, I'm sorry for the lad—as sorry as anyone—but make sure he doesn't drag your career down with his. I read that bit in the paper the other day and, I can tell you, it makes me uneasy. Owners want to be sure their jockey is concentrating 100 per cent on the matter in hand.'

'And you know I do,' Matt stated.

'Ah yes, *I* know. But you're laying yourself open to criticism. When owners are paying nearly twenty grand a year just to keep their horses in training, it's so much easier to question the jockey's concentration or commitment than accept that the horse had an off day or just plain isn't good enough, and you're giving them just the fuel they need.'

The first person Matt bumped into as he headed back to the weighing room was Josh Harper, his agent.

'Ah, Matt. I was looking for you.' Harper, an ex-jockey himself, was short, growing stout, and hailed from Glasgow. 'I've got you a ride in the last. The doc has stood Copperfield down after that fall, so I had a word with Fliss Truman and she's happy to put you up on Mr Blue Shoes. He's got a good each-way chance.'

'Thanks. Listen, Josh, did you go chasing that ride on Tranter, or did Doogie come to you?'

'Neither. Kenning rang me yesterday and asked for you, specifically. Said it was the animal's first run for Doogie and he trusted you to get a feel for

149

the horse. Why do you ask?'

'Just wondered. I don't suppose he'll ask for me again. Apparently he's just bent Doogie's ear about me not concentrating on the job.'

'Awkward sod! I've dealt with him before. He treats me like I've just crawled out from under a stone. I shouldn't worry. We can do without him, although, having said that, I think you're riding a couple more for him at the weekend.'

'Or not,' Matt observed.

'Yeah, maybe, but I expect he's just letting off a bit of steam to cover up the fact that he's bought a very ordinary horse.' He paused, looking over Matt's shoulder. 'Ah, looks like someone else wants you . . .'

The someone else turned out to be Casey McKeegan, and Matt cursed inwardly. All he wanted at that moment was to get showered and changed, check on Mikey in the medical room, and concentrate on riding Charlie Brewer's horse in the next race.

Something of Matt's irritation must have shown in his face, for, as he turned to meet Casey, her expression became all at once defensive.

'I know you're busy, you don't have to say it. I just thought you'd want to know. I've done a little info gathering on our friend Lord Kenning.'

'Oh—right.' Casting a hasty look around, Matt steered Casey to a quieter spot. 'What've you found?'

'OK: age, sixty-three; born in Esher, Surrey; father Brigadier Kenning; mother the society "It Girl" of the day. Our Kenning did the usual stuff for a toff—public school, Cambridge etc, and then, not surprisingly I guess, on to officer training at

150

Sandhurst. Seems he wasn't cut out for army life, though—he must have been a big disappointment to the Brigadier—because he only made lieutenant. Married late, no children, on the boards of a couple of companies and one or two charities, including one his father set up to help ex-servicemen reintegrate into civilian life. All very worthy and rumours of possible honours in the offing, so he'd be wanting to keep his nose clean, wouldn't he? Anyway, I had a dig around in the archives and found a couple of photos of him where he was pictured with a car, and both times they were Jags; not silver ones—but both of them the current year's registration, so I'd say he changes his motor fairly regularly, wouldn't you? Also—and this is the good bit—guess what his middle name is . . .'

'Um . . . Moses?'

'Maurice!' she said triumphantly. 'Close enough, wouldn't you say? Maurice—Mosie. *And* I asked our senior editor if he ever remembered any talk about Kenning and Sophie Bradford, and he basically told me that, if I wanted a long and glittering career in journalism, I should leave that particular rumour well alone. Which I think points to his lordship doing some pretty heavy leaning, don't you?'

Matt agreed that it did, and he also had to admit, if only to himself, that Ms McKeegan was turning out to be a far more useful contact than he'd expected.

*   *   *

In the event, Brewer's horse proved as big a

151

disappointment as Kenning's had done, trailing home near the back of the field. Matt was at a loss to understand it, unless it was just a combination of the weather and a fast pace. The horse was young and had pulled early on, but hitting a hurdle or two seemed to knock the stuffing out of him.

'He'll maybe improve with a run or two under his belt,' he told the businessman, who had come round to the unsaddling area intent on a post-mortem. Brewer grunted, regarding the horse as if he'd delivered a personal insult, and Matt as if he'd engineered the defeat on purpose.

The rain didn't bother Kandahar Prince in the next, where he made up for his recent fall by winning by three lengths, a fact which didn't improve Brewer's mood at all.

Making his way back to the weighing room after the presentation, Matt found Kendra's brother, Deacon, walking alongside him. He seemed more animated than usual.

'Is that all you get?' he asked, gesturing to the cut-glass ashtray Matt had received as winning jockey.

'Yeah, useful if you don't smoke, isn't it?'

'That's pathetic! I thought it'd be a cup or something. It's almost an insult.'

'Depends on the race,' Matt said. 'It goes from the sublime to the ridiculous. I've got a couple of huge silver cups and a bowl at home, but sometimes it's just a book token. Actually, I preferred the book token, at least it was useful and didn't have to be dusted.'

'Can't you get Kendra to do that?' Deacon said, with the blithe disregard of a sibling.

'We share,' Matt told him. 'I didn't know you

were coming today. Did you come up with your dad?' It was rare for Deacon to attend a race meeting.

'Yeah, and my shadow's here somewhere, too.'

'Your shadow?'

'Niall bleeding Delafield. I've shaken him off at the moment, because I went down to the stables with John. Niall won't go near the horses—he's allergic—but no doubt he'll soon catch up.'

'Does he follow you everywhere?'

'Pretty much—when I leave the house,' Deacon said moodily.

Matt glanced at him, thoughtfully. He was unclear as to exactly what role Delafield fulfilled. Did Brewer imagine Deacon was in particular danger of being kidnapped? If that was the case— why him and not his sisters? Was it because Deacon was the son and heir? But any potential kidnapper who'd taken the time to study the businessman would know that he was just as passionately devoted to his daughters. Matt had spoken to Kendra about it once, but she seemed almost as much in the dark as he was.

'I think Daddy's had some threats, or something,' she'd said vaguely. 'He took Deke out of uni suddenly, halfway through his course, and then went abroad with him. It was just after that that Delafield turned up.'

'Well, I'm surprised your brother puts up with it. A lad of his age wants a bit of freedom, not to feel that his every move is being watched and reported back to his father.'

'Mm, I suppose so. But Deke's very sweet-natured, you know. He does flare up occasionally, but, on the whole, I think he's too lazy to rebel.'

Now, coming to a halt outside the weighing room, Matt turned to Deacon.

'So why d'you put up with it?'

'Oh, I don't know ...' He looked a little uncomfortable. 'I don't have much choice, really.'

'Of course you do! You're what—nineteen? Nearly twenty? Old enough to take charge of your own life, surely?'

'Yeah—I guess Dad's just worried about me. Anyway, Niall's OK most of the time; he's a pretty cool bloke, really. He used to be in the army—special forces. And it's a bit like being a rock star—having a bodyguard.'

Matt shrugged.

'Well, it's your life. Look, I must go, and I'm afraid you can't come in here. It's jockeys and officials only.'

He started to turn away, but Deacon put out a hand to stop him.

'You think I'm scared to move out—I'm not, you know. It's just different in a family like ours. Dad's made a lot of money, but he's probably trodden on a few toes along the way—people that might want to get back at him.'

'But *he* doesn't have a bodyguard following him around all day,' Matt pointed out.

Apparently at a loss, Deacon just stared at him, and Matt felt a little guilty for rocking the boat. After all, it wasn't his boat to rock, when all was said and done.

'I'm sorry. It's none of my business,' he said then. 'Must go. See you later.'

He turned away and came face to face with the muscular bulk and gold earring of Niall Delafield himself. This time the white teeth weren't in

154

evidence.

'Matt.'

It was said with a slight nod, and it was all that was said, but Matt got the strong impression that Delafield had overheard some of the foregoing conversation and he wasn't happy.

'Niall,' he said, similarly cool. 'Must go, I've got a horse to ride.'

'Yes, we've all got our jobs to do,' Delafield said, turning his body just enough to let Matt pass.

In the weighing room, Matt changed into Brewer's purple, gold, and orange colours once again, hoping—for everyone's sakes, not least his own—that he could coax a good run out of Tulip Time in the next race.

Presently, weighed out, and sitting by his peg waiting for the call to the paddock, Matt found himself wondering how Kendra was faring with Jamie. Normally, the moratorium on using mobile phones until racing was over didn't bother him over much. In fact, some days the peace was welcome, but today it was decidedly frustrating. He wondered if he could get Harry to call for him.

'It's still cats and friggin' dogs out there,' someone said disgustedly. 'You wouldn't happen to have a spare pair of goggles you're not using, by any chance?'

Matt looked up. Rollo Gallagher was standing in front of him, tucking his silks into his breeches.

'Yeah, of course.' Matt rooted in his kitbag and found an extra pair. 'Have you seen Mikey lately?'

'Yeah. He's OK. The doc's let him go, but he won't be riding anymore this arvo. Razor's picked up his ride in this one. Reckons he'll make the running. Looks like it'll start favourite, too, the

155

jammy git.'

'Jockeys, please!' The call came from an official by the door, and, with a certain amount of grumbling about the weather, eighteen jockeys headed, in shuffling single file, out of the weighing room, through The Scales, and into the rain.

Brewer was in the paddock watching with John Leonard as Tulip Time stalked round with ears back and head held low. Matt's heart sank. Tulip Time—a head-shy horse—was never the easiest of customers, as he'd warned Jamie the previous week, but today he looked to be in a really foul mood, occasionally aiming a nip at his handler's leg as they walked.

'I hope you haven't put your shirt on him,' he joked, as he joined the two men. 'He doesn't look a happy bunny.'

'I expect he'll be all right when he gets going,' Brewer said. 'Apart from the favourite, there's not much here that should trouble him.'

Matt wished he shared the businessman's confidence.

'He's got the ability, it's the mindset that lets him down. He can be a real bugger when he's in a mood.'

'Well, it's up to you to sweet-talk him then, isn't it?' Brewer suggested, and Matt could tell that he still hadn't forgiven him for winning on Kandahar Prince.

By the time the starter dropped his flag, the weather had improved a little, but, unfortunately, Tulip Time's mood hadn't. He jumped off willingly enough, though, and Matt was able to settle him on the heels of the favourite, where he kept him for the first mile, content to bide his time and hoping that the horse would run himself out of the sulks.

As the field swept round the second to last bend, with four furlongs and three fences to go, Razor's horse slowed a little and the rest of the runners began to bunch up, until there were two horses running outside Tulip Time and one on his inside.

With hands and heels, Matt pushed his horse to move ahead of this first group of runners, knowing that, if he was to drop back, even as far as the flanks of the other horses, Tulip Time might be put off by the waving whips of their jockeys.

The horse responded, pulling ahead of the others to take the next fence half a length clear and maintaining that lead all the way to the second last. As they turned into the final bend with just one fence left to jump, Tulip Time flicked his left ear back and, sneaking a look over his shoulder, Matt saw the favourite gaining ground on his outside, ridden hard by Razor. His own efforts to coax more speed from Tulip Time were rewarded by a flattening of his ears and much tail swishing. Clearly Brewer's horse was running at his limit.

The two horses, now battling side by side, were bearing down on the last fence and, as they drew steadily nearer to the dark mass of birch, Razor's horse drew slightly ahead and the tip of his whip flicked upward just inches from Tulip Time's face.

Instantly, the horse's rhythm faltered as he threw his head up, and the jolt of his shortened stride shook Matt, loosening his grip and making his teeth rattle.

'Watch your whip!' he shouted, but Razor apparently didn't hear, because his horse drifted closer.

Matt swore. With the last fence just yards distant, Tulip Time was running the rail and—unless he could pull him off it—would be squeezed into the white wing of the jump.

'Give me some sodding room!' he yelled furiously, and this time the other jockey responded, correcting his position and allowing Matt to do the same.

Thundering towards the fence, Tulip Time's muzzle was once more level with the toe of the other jockey's boot and, unbelievably, when they were just three strides out, Razor's whip flicked out again, stinging the animal across the nose.

Instantly, Tulip Time threw his head up, hitting Matt in the face, and veered sharply to the right, meeting four feet six of stiff brush on completely the wrong stride.

Dazed, Matt clung to a handful of mane, peering through watering eyes as the horse made a valiant attempt to clear the fence, landing with his hind legs in the top of the birch and kicking himself free. The effort left the horse almost at a standstill on the landing side—which, while it allowed Matt to regain his seat, also placed them firmly in the path of the rest of the field, following just a split second behind.

There was no time to do anything more than gather up his reins before the others came, rising over the fence in a sweating, straining wave of horseflesh, the nearest landing so impossibly close that impact seemed a certainty.

Someone swore, Tulip Time flinched, and then they were past, their pounding hooves showering Matt with wet mud and turf.

As the other horses headed away towards the

finishing line, herd instinct kicked in and Tulip Time pulled himself together and set off in pursuit.

Matt, functioning mainly on autopilot, shifted his weight forward over the horse's withers, grabbing a fresh handful of mane while he fought the whirling dizziness behind his eyes.

*   *   *

'You all right, Mojo?'

A hand rocked his shoulder gently and Matt turned his head, frowning as he focussed with some difficulty on Rollo's familiar features.

'Yeah, fine,' he answered automatically.

Tulip Time had slowed to a jog, and Matt realised that there were horses all around him, breathing hard after their exertions. At some point they must have passed the finishing post, but barely had Matt's muzzy brain registered this fact when Tulip Time, following the general tide of movement, swung round on his haunches and headed back at a canter.

Matt swayed drunkenly in the saddle, only his grip on the mane preventing him from being dumped unceremoniously on the turf. As he caught up with the other runners once more, Tulip Time slowed and a hand reached for his rein.

'Are you okay, Matt?' John Leonard was looking up at him with some concern. 'Looks like he caught you in the face.'

'Bloody Razor!' Matt muttered. 'Waving his fucking whip around!'

Leonard led the horse off the track towards the unsaddling area.

159

'Razor did that? Are you sure?'

Matt put a hand up to his face and it came away thinly streaked with blood.

'No. The horse did it. But he threw his head up because Razor hit him in the face.'

'It happens,' the trainer said philosophically.

'He did it on purpose.'

Leonard glanced sharply at him, eyes narrowed.

'That's a hell of an allegation, Matt. Are you sure?'

'Yep. Twice.'

'So what do you want to do about it?'

Matt didn't know. He shook his head and then wished he hadn't as his vision whirled like the inside of a snow dome.

They entered the unsaddling area, where the horse came to a halt and Matt kicked his feet free of the stirrups and slid off, taking a quick step backward as his knees threatened to buckle.

Leonard put out a hand to steady him.

'Are you sure you're all right?'

Brewer wasn't anywhere to be seen, but Matt didn't know if that was a good sign or not.

'Yeah, give me a minute,' he said, but his reply was interrupted by the announcement of a Stewards' Enquiry.

'There you go—looks like you'll be able to have your say,' the trainer observed. 'But I'd take it easy, if I were you . . .'

He didn't enlarge on the comment, but Matt understood. The weighing-room community was, by and large, a close-knit one, and any jockey considering making an accusation of foul play should be pretty sure of his facts.

He slid the saddle off Tulip Time's sweaty back

160

and laid the girth over the seat to carry it in.

'You all right with that?' Leonard asked.

Matt nodded. His head was clearing now and his legs regaining their strength, but, even so, he was glad to reach the weighing room and collapse onto the bench by his peg. A glance in the mirror on his way through had shown him a pale face with a darkening bruise on the bridge of his nose, but there was little blood in evidence, and, with no ride in the next, he felt confident that he'd be fit for his last two outings of the day.

'Matthew Shepherd and Geoffrey Hislop?' a voice called from the doorway. 'Upstairs, please. The stewards would like to see you.'

Matt looked up and raised a hand, recognising Chris Fairbrother, the Stipendiary Steward or 'Stipe', as the jockeys termed these particular officials. As Stipes went, Chris Fairbrother was generally liked, regarded by the jockeys as being reasonable and even-handed.

Following Fairbrother, Matt and Razor ascended the stairs to the stewards' room, where they were both left waiting outside like naughty schoolchildren outside the headmaster's office. Razor didn't volunteer any conversation, much less an apology, so Matt kept his thoughts to himself too, and, in due course, Fairbrother reappeared and invited them to step inside.

Inside the room, the three stewards were sat in a row behind a table. Opposite them was a large television screen upon which a replay of the relevant portion of the race was presently shown.

After everyone had been introduced, it was announced that they were there to look into possible interference between Razor's horse and

Matt's on the last bend and the approach to the last fence. Over the next few minutes, they all watched the action on the screen from various angles and then Matt was asked to give his account of the incident, which he did, carefully keeping his anger hidden.

Next, Razor was asked for his view and obliged with wide-eyed innocence, saying he had carried his whip in his right hand because his horse had been showing a tendency to hang right and that he had had no idea that Tulip Time would react so violently to his actions.

'Bull!' Matt said explosively, in spite of his resolve to stay calm. 'With respect, sir, I've warned the lads, more than once, that Tulip Time is head shy and ultra-sensitive to whips.'

'Mr Shepherd! I must ask you to wait your turn,' Fairbrother cut in. 'You have already spoken; please let Mr Hislop have his say.'

'I honestly didn't know, sir,' Razor declared, with a convincing expression of earnest apology. 'I thought I was doing the right thing, trying to keep my horse straight.'

'And what do you say to Mr Shepherd's assertion that you actually hit his horse shortly before the last fence? We all saw how it swerved . . .'

'I'd be very surprised if I did, sir,' Razor said, still with that guileless expression.

Matt longed to wipe it off his face. He risked another interruption.

'Sir, I shouted to him—twice—to watch his whip, but he didn't take any notice.'

'I didn't hear you,' Razor said. 'What are you saying? That I did it on purpose?'

That's exactly what I'm saying, Matt wanted to

162

say, but he gritted his teeth against the temptation.

A few moments later they were asked to leave the room whilst the stewards came to their decision.

As the door closed behind them, Razor shook his head, pityingly.

'You haven't got a chance, you know.'

Matt ignored him.

When they were called back, a few minutes later, it was to be told that the decision of the stewards was that, if interference had indeed taken place, it had been of an accidental nature. The Stipendiary Steward added that, as it was impossible to prove that Matt's horse would have beaten the favourite, the placings would remain unaltered and no further action would be taken.

Silently fuming, Matt joined Razor in thanking the stewards, and they filed out.

'Told you.' Razor was full of smug satisfaction. 'No hard feelings, eh?'

'Absolutely not,' Matt agreed, then leaned close as he passed. 'But, if you ever do anything like that again, I'll take you apart piece by miserable piece, and be damned to the stewards!'

He had the brief gratification of seeing Razor's self-satisfied expression falter, but, in truth, as soon as the words had left his lips, he regretted them. Falling out with the other jockey wasn't going to achieve anything useful, no matter how much support he could count on from the other lads in the weighing room. He couldn't imagine Razor ever being a friend, but he had an idea he'd make an uncomfortable enemy.

8

Sitting in the weighing room chewing on an oat bar during the next race, Matt began to ponder the stewards' verdict. Why, he wondered, hadn't they asked for a third or fourth point of view? It was possible one or two of the following jockeys might have seen something, and surely they would have testified to the fact that he'd warned them all about Tulip Time's whip phobia?

Not for the first time, Matt found himself wishing that the whole business of racecourse stewarding could be overhauled. While he felt that, on the whole, they did a very good job, he knew he wasn't alone in the opinion that sometimes the interests of racing might better be served by a panel of professional adjudicators from within the industry.

The rules stated that the placings should remain the same unless there was very little room for doubt that the horse suffering the interference would have won. It was also the case that the further from the winning post the incident took place, the less likely it was that the result would be overturned, but sometimes Matt felt that the letter of the law was adhered to in the face of justice and good sense. However, there was nothing that could be done to change the decision, so he resolved to put it behind him and get on with the business of the day.

His final two rides that afternoon turned in workmanlike but uninspiring performances, both finishing just outside the places, and Matt returned wearily to the weighing room to change into his everyday clothes.

Emerging presently, the first person he saw was Harry Leonard, who waved him over.

'Hiyah. Ouch! That looks sore.'

Gingerly, Matt touched his bruised nose.

'It is, a bit, but I don't think it's broken.'

'Dad told me how it happened. Any luck with the stewards?'

'No. Razor came the innocent. Where *is* your dad?'

'Still at the stables, I think. Look, I was hoping I'd catch you. See that guy over there by the steps—the one with the black leather jacket? That's Darren Wallis. He's the son of Ron Wallis, the bookie, but he's also one of Sophie Bradford's exes; they were inseparable for a time a while ago. I think he was the one she was flirting with at the party. Don't know if it's any help, but I thought you might want to know, if you're still doing your sleuthing bit.'

Matt sighed.

'Thanks. Yeah, I am—in the teeth of opposition. Not that I'm making much headway, though.'

He looked in the direction Harry was indicating, and saw a fairly heavily built man of around thirty, talking to a willowy blonde girl who was leaning close and laughing. It didn't look to be the most propitious moment to approach him on the subject of an ex-girlfriend, but it seemed too good a chance to miss, so Matt took a deep breath and strolled over.

'Darren Wallis?'

The beefy man broke off his conversation and frowned at Matt.

165

'Yeah, who wants to know?' he asked, obviously not recognising Matt in his everyday clothes.

'Matt Shepherd. Sorry to interrupt . . .'

Wallis's expression cleared a little.

'The jockey? Oh, right—hi. What can I do for you?'

'Matt Shepherd?' the blonde broke in, doing something coquettish with her eyes. 'My friend thinks you're hot! I couldn't have your autograph, could I?' She fumbled in an impractically small handbag and produced a pen and an address book.

'Yeah, sure.' Matt reached for the book.'To . . . ?'

'Lucy. With love . . .'

'So what can I do for you?' Wallis repeated.

'Er . . . In private, perhaps?' Matt suggested, handing the address book back.

Wallis's brows drew down.

'I suppose so. Listen, Lucy—run along for a moment, would you?'

The blonde made a moue but did as she was told, stalking away on four-inch stilettos, one hand repositioning the strip of fabric that did duty as a skirt.

Watching her, Wallis sighed.

'Nice totty, but not the brightest button in the box. Now, what's this all about?'

'Sophie Bradford. I understand you used to go out with her . . .'

'Yeah, we were together for a while, but I don't know about going out—we spent more time in, than anything—if you get my drift.'

Matt thought he did.

'When was this?'

' 'Bout eighteen months ago. Can't remember exactly—one blonde seems to blend into another,

166

somehow. So why d'you want to know? Is this something to do with that bit about you in the paper? Said you were trying to solve the murder or something.'

'Yeah. Just trying to help a mate out, that's all. Can you tell me what happened? With Sophie, I mean. Why did you split up?'

'Found out she was two-timing me,' Wallis said disgustedly. 'Caught her with her knickers down, you might say. Not that she wore any, half the time.'

'That's a bit of a bummer.'

'Yeah, but what the heck! 'S not as if I was going to marry the woman,' he said philosophically. 'Hey, don't go thinking I've been bearing a grudge all this time; it wasn't me that topped her—I can tell you that for nothing.'

'I wasn't thinking it,' Matt soothed. 'I gather you were dancing with her at Doogie's party that night, though.'

'Yeah, so what? Your mate Mullin was late, and she hit on me. She wasn't the sort to stand around when she could be having fun.'

'So there wasn't anything going on between you?'

Wallis shook his head.

'Nah, she was just using me to try and make him jealous. Pay him back for keeping her waiting—you know. When I realised what she was up to, I left them to it. I don't want that kind of trouble, and, besides, I had another party to go to.'

'The police have obviously been onto you . . .'

'Yeah, a couple of times, but my alibi checked out, so they lost interest.'

'OK. Well, thanks anyway.' Matt waved a hand

and turned away feeling that the encounter had done no more than reinforce what he already knew of the dead girl's character, or lack of it.

Leaving Wallis, Matt made his way to the racecourse stables in search of Leonard, but was told that he'd left a message for Matt to meet him at the car. Wearily, he threaded through the rapidly thinning crowds towards the exit and, as he passed the door to the stands, it opened and the Stipendiary Steward came out, almost bumping into him.

Matt nodded.

'Mr Fairbrother.'

Seeing Matt, Chris Fairbrother hesitated, colour flooding over his face and into the roots of his sandy hair.

'Matt. Hi. Er . . . I'm in a bit of a hurry . . .'

Matt wasn't surprised the Stipe was embarrassed after his recent highly questionable rulings.

'Yes, I expect you are,' he said regarding the man with a degree of bitterness.

Fairbrother's colour deepened.

'Look—about that, I'm sorry. I didn't really have a choice . . .' He faltered. 'Look, we shouldn't even be discussing it. I really have to go.'

On those words, he ducked his head and turned away, leaving Matt mystified as he headed for the car park. What the hell had he meant—he didn't have a choice? Of course he bloody did! He was the Stipendiary Steward—the final decision rested with him.

*   *   *

With no rides booked for the following day,

Kendra departed to Birchwood Hall for a day's millining—as she put it—and, after a bit of badgering, Jamie rolled up his sleeves and prepared to help Matt with the ongoing work on the kitchen.

The results of Tulip Time's headbutt had flowered into a pink and purple bruise on the bridge of Matt's nose, but, he was thankful to discover, showed no signs of blackening his eyes. Kendra's reaction had been one of sympathy, but also, Matt fancied, a slight deepening of the faint aura of tension that had surrounded her for the past few days. His attempt to quiz her about it produced only a quick denial and he was left to wonder.

Jamie, Matt discovered, had come through his silent mood, although that proved to be a well-disguised blessing, as he proceeded to hold forth at length on the injustices dealt out to him by the police, the press, and those he termed his 'so-called friends'. Matt was more interested in the circumstances that had led to his arrest and release than his sense of grievance, and wanted to know exactly what he had gleaned from Bartholomew, though it seemed that the DI had been cagey with his information.

'He wouldn't say when I'd get the MG back,' Jamie complained. 'He did say he thought it might be salvageable, though. Apparently they found it upside down in a field, so it sounds like kids, don't you think? Bartholomew said I was bloody lucky it wasn't burnt out.'

'Had it been hotwired?' Matt asked, prising the lid off a tin of undercoat and gazing unenthusiastically at the contents.

'I don't know. Why?'

'Well—I just thought, if they had the keys, it would look like that going-over you got in Bournemouth wasn't so random, after all. Did you tell Bartholomew about that?'

'Yeah, eventually. But I'm not sure he believed me. He wanted to know why I didn't report it at the time. Are you saying they mugged me just to get my car keys?'

'Sophie's cards had to get in there somehow,' Matt observed. 'You didn't put them there, so who did? The fact that they didn't set fire to the car seems significant, don't you think? Kids often do, I would imagine. I'd be surprised if Bartholomew didn't take that into account. This might actually work in your favour, in the long run. I mean—why would *you* pinch her credit cards?'

Jamie looked a little uncomfortable.

'I wouldn't, but the thing is, Bartholomew's been nosing in my bank account.'

Matt paused in stirring the paint.

'And . . . ?'

'And . . . he knows I'm not too flush at the moment,' Jamie said, reddening a little. 'Haven't been for a while.'

'OK. Spell it out. You're not in debt, are you?'

'Well, in a manner of speaking—yeah, a bit. But it doesn't make any difference; I still didn't pinch her cards,' he rushed on. 'Bartholomew was trying to make me say that we'd had another row because she found out that I'd nicked her cards. I mean, it's crazy! He said maybe I didn't mean to kill her. Maybe we were arguing and I'd just pushed her, or she'd tripped and bashed her head on the wall. He kept on and on, but it's not true, Matt. I didn't kill her. I wasn't even there—I told the truth in the beginning. The last time I saw her was in the club. *You* still believe me, don't you?'

'Of course I do. But I'm bloody annoyed that you didn't tell me you were in debt. Why the hell didn't you?'

Jamie wouldn't meet his eyes. He picked up a paintbrush and started to run the bristles through his fingers.

'Jamie!' Matt felt more like a father than a friend at that moment, even though only four years separated them.

'Because I knew you'd feel you had to help, and you already do enough for me. Whatever you say, I know I don't pay enough rent and I don't want to sponge off you for cash as well.'

'You haven't borrowed money, have you?' Matt asked suspiciously. 'Please don't tell me you've gone to a credit company . . .'

Jamie shook his head.

'No, I haven't—but I *was* thinking about it.'

'Well, stop thinking about it—it's madness!'

'It's all right for you!' Jamie protested. 'It's easy to take the moral high ground when you've never had to worry about money. Things were just starting to pick up before this happened—I was picking up regular rides and there was a light at the end of the tunnel, but now I've got bugger all coming in and no prospect of it, and I've still got to live. Just what would you do in my position?'

Matt began stirring the paint again, rhythmically following a figure of eight pattern while he sorted out his thoughts. Jamie was right, up to a point. Even though he'd never relied upon his family's money, the very fact of its being there was a kind

171

of mental safety net. How would he feel if, like Jamie, he was the son of a single parent; one of a big family from a Belfast council house? He didn't have an answer. In spite of what he'd said to Jamie, he knew his own pride would get in the way, too.

'I'm not offering to give you money,' he said finally. 'I'll lend it to you. You can pay me back when you're back on your feet.'

'Don't you mean *if*?'

'No. I don't. Now stop vandalising that paintbrush and give me a hand. If you do a good job, I'll pay you ten quid an hour.'

Jamie slanted a calculating look at him.

'Fifteen?'

'You bloody Irish!' Matt exclaimed.

*   *   *

Saturday's racing at Maiden Newton didn't get off to a particularly auspicious start for Matt. He'd barely hung his jacket on his peg in the weighing room when a suited and bespectacled official from the Horse Racing Authority called in to inform him that he was wanted for a drug test.

'Again, sir? I had one a couple of weeks ago.'

The official shrugged, uninterested.

'I don't know anything about that—I'm just passing on the request.'

Matt had no choice but to accept the summons. Drugs tests were an inescapable part of a jockey's life, as in any modern sport. At least one jockey was tested at the start of each day's racing, and, on occasion, all the jockeys at a meeting would be checked. The tests were, however, supposed to be

172

random—unless doubts were harboured about a particular rider—and Matt felt a little hard done by to have drawn the short straw twice in such a short period of time.

With a sigh, Matt made his way to the specially adapted camper van where another official was waiting to conduct a breath test for alcohol and a urine test for narcotics.

When he emerged a few minutes later, having given the requisite samples, he came face to face with the tall, wiry figure of Lord Kenning, so close to the camper van that it almost looked as though he'd been waiting for Matt to appear. His first words gave weight to this suspicion.

'Called in again, Matt? You'd better be careful; people will begin to talk.'

Matt stopped in front of him.

'How would they even know, unless *someone* saw fit to tell them, sir?'

'Oh, I know what the weighing room's like. There's always gossip. It only takes a couple of jocks to tell their girlfriends or trainers and, before you know where you are, it's common knowledge.' He leaned closer to Matt. 'Let's just hope the press doesn't get wind of it and start to speculate. That could be very prejudicial to your career . . .'

Matt held Kenning's gaze for a moment, so angry that he didn't trust himself to answer.

'Excuse me, sir. I have a horse to ride.'

Kenning straightened up.

'Of course you do.' He stepped to one side, adding in an undertone, 'And let's hope those results come back clean, shall we?'

Matt's eyes narrowed, but now Kenning was smiling and moving on to speak to one of his cronies, so that he could almost believe he'd imagined the last remark.

As he changed into his breeches and colours, he couldn't stop his mind replaying the interchange. What had the peer meant by that last comment? Surely even someone with as much clout as *he* had couldn't influence the outcome of a drugs test. Kenning was a big noise in the Jockey Club, not the HRA, and Matt knew it was the HRA who organised the drug testing, although he was pretty sure it was an outside body that actually carried it out. No—Kenning had just been trying to scare him, and what's more he had succeeded, for a heartbeat or two. It would be about a month before a copy of the results would fall onto the doormat at Spinney Cottage, and no doubt it had amused the man to think that Matt would worry about his remark until the day he was shown to be clear.

'Bastard!'

'Whoa! I shall make sure I don't get on the wrong side of you today,' Rollo declared. 'Which particular bastard were you thinking of?'

Matt looked round. He hadn't realised he'd spoken out loud.

'Kenning.'

'Ah, the *smarmy* bastard.'

Matt laughed.

'You like him too, then?'

'Don't know anyone that does, really,' Rollo said. 'At least, not among us lower forms of life in the weighing room. What has he done to upset you?'

'Oh, nothing I could sue him for.'

'OK. Well, I was coming to ask if there was anything you could tell me about Mr Manchester.

174

You rode him last time out, didn't you?'

Matt shook off his anger. It was highly unprofessional to carry a bad mood into the workplace, to say nothing of the detrimental effect it could have on the partnership between horse and rider.

'Mr Manchester? Chestnut gelding—trained by Belinda Kepple?'

'That's the one.'

'So, what does she say?'

'It was Belinda who said to ask you,' Rollo replied. 'She says he shows nothing at home, but you got a sweet tune out of him.'

Matt cast his mind back.

'I don't think there's any mystery to it. He's a front runner. He'll pull like hell from the off, but he'll settle when he's at the front.'

*   *   *

By the time Matt and Rollo strolled out to the paddock, Matt had managed to put Lord Kenning to the back of his mind, and the sight of the ten novice chasers stalking round the paddock with the autumn sunlight gleaming on their burnished hides lifted his mood in the way nothing else could.

He was riding a new horse for Doogie McKenzie—Woodcutter, a youngster he knew the Scot thought a lot of. Looking at him now, a smallish, dark bay gelding with an intelligent head, a sloping shoulder and good clean limbs, he had to admit that he was a nice type, but it wasn't until the horse was led into the centre of the paddock to have his girth tightened and stirrups let down that Matt felt a stirring of excitement. Standing stock-still, Woodcutter lifted his head to gaze out over the heads of the crowd to where the first of the runners was already heading down the cinder path to the track, and Matt saw something in his eye that sent a shiver up his spine.

The look of eagles, it was sometimes somewhat fancifully called, but it nevertheless described perfectly that extraspecial something that some horses have about them. It wouldn't necessarily translate into speed, but it almost always denoted character. Such horses could be exceptional—and they seemed aware of it.

The girths tightened, Doogie came across to where Matt was fastening the strap on his helmet.

'Owner not here?' Matt asked.

'Had to work,' the trainer replied. 'He's a surgeon—last-minute call. So what d'you think?'

'Yeah, he's a nice sort,' Matt replied. 'I can see why you like him. Sorry I didn't make it over to school him. How's he been going?'

'He's an absolute star!' Doogie said. 'Been working like a dream. I don't think you'll have any bother with him, unless he's just a tad overkeen.'

Matt walked forward with the Scot, preparatory to being legged into the saddle. Close up, the horse looked lean and hard-muscled.

'So where's he been? Why haven't I seen him on the track?'

'His owner's been point-to-pointing him,' Doogie muttered disgustedly. 'Until I managed to make him see what a waste that was. Trouble is, now he's saying, if he can't ride him, he might as well sell him, so it looks like I'm buggered either way.'

Matt picked up the reins, rested his hands lightly on the bay's withers, and bent his leg at the knee.

Seconds later, he landed lightly in the saddle and the toes of his soft leather boots found the stirrup irons. Woodcutter walked forward calmly, his short black mane flopping up and down with the rhythm of his stride, and an ear flicking back enquiringly towards his new partner.

'Good lad,' Matt told him.

'It's up to you how you ride him. You'll have to play it by ear,' Doogie said, as he patted the horse's shoulder and moved away.

That was one of the things Matt liked about the Scotsman. Unless there was a good reason to, he never interfered. There was a trust between them that each would do their job to the best of their ability, and the confidence that that best would be enough.

Woodcutter walked calmly beside his lad out of the paddock and down to the track, where he arched his neck and jogged a little as he felt the turf beneath his hooves.

On Matt's OK, the lad slipped the lead rein and they were away. The bay settled into an eager canter as he spied the rumps of the other runners ahead of him. Balanced easily over the horse's withers, his hands resting quietly on his neck, Matt looked forward through the pricked, black-tipped ears, his knees flexing with the rhythm of Woodcutter's stride, and was aware of a tremendous feeling of contentment. The sun was warm, the track a broad strip of emerald between shining white rails, the trees beyond the racecourse were russet and gold, and beneath him was a young horse about to embark on his new life as a steeplechaser. Life, in spite of the recent troubles, was good.

Woodcutter didn't put a foot wrong. Matt made sure he was ready when the tape flew back and settled him in mid-field, seeing Rollo on Mr Manchester leading the way, two or three horses ahead. Maiden Newton was an ideal course for youngsters—the fences were well made and of medium height, the bends fairly open, and the rails opened out in the home straight, allowing the field room to spread across the track, which made it less likely that anyone would get trapped behind a tiring horse in the race to the line.

Woodcutter rounded the last bend still travelling strongly with one fence left to jump. The four runners ahead of him separated as the pace picked up a notch or two, and, as soon as Matt gave him the office, the little bay surged forward. He flew the last birch, gaining half a length in the air, and thundered into the final two furlongs neck and neck with Rollo's horse.

There was no contest.

For a moment, as they drew level, Mr Manchester rallied, finding extra reserves of energy, but Woodcutter was having none of it. Flattening his ears back, he lengthened his stride and, within moments, had left the chestnut floundering in his wake.

As soon as he was clear, his ears flicked forward once more and he would have run on, but Matt steadied him; he didn't want him winning by too large a margin, or he'd be penalised by the handicapper. They passed the finishing post easing down but still three lengths ahead of Rollo's horse, and Matt patted Woodcutter's neck, telling him he was indeed a star.

The lad came out, smiling, to lead the horse in,

and, within a few strides, Doogie was there, too.

'No need to ask how that felt,' he commented, looking up at Matt. 'You're grinning like a Cheshire cat!'

'Did you see the way he went past them?' Matt demanded. 'And he was hardly trying! I tell you, if you put any other jockey up on this boy, I swear I'll never speak to you again!'

Doogie shook his head.

'It might not be up to me, Matt,' he warned, and Matt remembered that the horse might well be sold.

By the time he dismounted in the winner's circle, Matt had made a decision.

'Where's this fella running next?'

'He's entered in the October Cup at Henfield,' Doogie told him, mentioning one of the newest prestige races for novice chasers. 'Why?'

Matt undid the girth and slid the tiny saddle off into his arms.

'If you can get hold of the owner, tell him you might have a buyer for him. I'll speak to you later.'

He walked away, knowing that Doogie was positively bristling with curiosity, but needing time to think before he took the next step.

Time was one luxury that he didn't have an abundance of that day. With a runner in every race, he was locked into a seemingly endless round of changing, weighing out, weighing in, speaking to owners and trainers, and riding.

The big race of the day was third on the card and Matt was riding Charlie's Temperance Bob, who, by virtue of their recent win at Worcester, was the clear favourite. The horse looked well, and, as Matt cantered him down to the start, he felt

179

quietly confident. There was nothing in the field that should worry him, as long as he jumped cleanly, which he normally did.

Matt planned to follow the format that had been proved to suit Bob before, tucking him in just behind the leaders and coming with a late run in the final couple of furlongs, but they had covered barely half of the scheduled two miles when he began to feel that something wasn't right. Uncharacteristically, the horse felt lacklustre and clumsy; if he hadn't known better, Matt would have said he was tired. He had to push him from a long way out, just to keep his position, and, when they rounded the final bend and the field fanned out, he showed no sign of wanting to take advantage of the gap that had opened up in front of him.

After the last fence, the leading horses began the sprint to the line, led by Rollo on a rangy grey, and a gap of four or five lengths opened up in front of Matt's horse. Glancing over his shoulder, Matt saw that there was a similar gap between Bob and the rest of the field, so he eased the pressure and they passed the post in a respectable but disappointing fourth place.

John Leonard was waiting with the lead rein as Matt slowed up.

'What happened there?'

Matt shook his head.

'I don't know—he just had no spark. His jumping wasn't too special, either. I didn't see any point in pushing him.'

'No, you did right.' Leonard slapped Bob's bay neck and glanced back at his flanks. 'He doesn't look particularly distressed—got a bit hot, but then it's a warm day. I wonder what's wrong with the old fella.'

Matt shrugged, calling out congratulations as Rollo rode by.

Back in the weighing room, he was stripping off Charlie Brewer's colours, deep in thought about Woodcutter, when the jockey next to him leaned across and said, 'Hey, Mojo! The Stipe wants you.'

'Oh—sorry.' Matt looked up and saw Chris Fairbrother waiting in the doorway, eyebrows raised.

*　　　*　　　*

Matt's session with the stewards was uncomfortable, to say the least. Not entirely surprised that they should want an explanation after such a poor show from a strong favourite, he expected that he and John Leonard would be asked a few questions about Temperance Bob's fitness and health, but he wasn't prepared for the accusatory slant the interrogation took, and he certainly wasn't prepared to be handed a two-day suspension for failing to ride out the finish.

As the door of the stewards' room closed behind him, Matt looked across at the trainer in bewilderment.

'What was that all about? How the hell can they justify giving me a suspension—I came fourth, for Christ's sake!'

'Sshh!' The trainer took his arm and steered him towards the stairs.

'Well, what were they looking at? Any fool could see that horse wasn't comfortable, even if they didn't want to take *my* word for it.' Matt was incensed, the effort of remaining calm and subordinate, in the face of what he felt to be gross injustice, now finding its outlet. 'I used to think Fairbrother was one of the better Stipes, but he seems to have it in for me lately. That's the second time in two days!'

'Careful! You're beginning to sound a bit like Jamie,' Leonard warned. 'Seriously, Matt, just let it go. You get runs of bad luck in racing—you should know that.'

Matt took a deep breath and sighed, consciously trying to relax.

'Sorry, John. It's just—well, I thought the stewards saw it my way. They seemed to, from what they were saying, especially that tall guy.'

'I must say, I thought so too, but there you are. I've got no problems with the way you rode him and I'm sure the boss won't have, either.'

They'd reached the bottom of the stairs now and the trainer paused.

'Right, I'd better go and see how Ron's getting on with Parsley Pete. See you in the paddock.'

Matt lifted a hand and went on through The Scales to the weighing room, where a sudden hush fell over the group nearest the door.

He paused, looking at each in turn, amongst them Razor, Mikey, Rollo and Bully.

'OK. Who's going to tell me what I've walked in on?'

'It's nothing—'

'It's my fault—'

Rollo and Mikey spoke together and stopped together, then Rollo started again.

'Razor was just giving us the benefit of his explanation for your horse's poor show,' he told

182

Matt.

'Oh yes?' Matt asked, softly. 'And would he care to share it with me?'

'I was just telling the lads that I had a phone call the other evening . . .'

'What sort of phone call?' Matt asked, although he was pretty sure what was coming.

'Someone who knew I was riding the favourite in the last on Thursday,' Razor put in. He didn't elaborate. He didn't really have to; they were all familiar with the concept of being offered money to lose, even if it hadn't happened to them.

'And?' Matt prompted.

'Oh, I don't think you need me to spell it out, do you?'

Suddenly Matt found that no one cared to meet his eye, and the anger the stewards had induced rose again. Perhaps reading the signs, Rollo put a restraining hand on his arm, but Matt shook it off.

'You bastard!' he exclaimed. 'I rode that horse to win, but it wasn't his day. End of story.'

Razor lifted his brows.

'Whew! Not so cool, Eskimo Joe,' he muttered, but Matt affected not to hear him.

Back at his own peg and trying to get his fury under control, he was approached sheepishly by Mikey. He dug deep and produced a smile for the youngster.

'Hiyah, kid.'

'I'm sorry, Matt. It was my fault before.'

Matt rummaged in his kitbag for a clean pair of gloves.

'How so?'

'Well, me and Rollo were wondering what the stewards wanted you for and I said, if you'd eased

183

down on Temperance Bob, there must have been a good reason, and Razor comes by and says, maybe someone offered you a good reason. But I knew you hadn't—I mean, you wouldn't . . .'

Matt smiled and shook his head.

'No, I wouldn't. Don't worry about it, Mikey.'

*   *   *

The day that had started so promisingly continued on its relentless downhill slide.

Matt's fourth and fifth rides of the day turned in uninspiring performances, both finishing out of the money, and his sixth and final ride folded up on landing after the final flight of hurdles, dumping him in the path of a field of fourteen, who were all, at that point, behind him.

Sitting up when he was sure that the coast was clear, Matt undid the strap on his crash hat and used his whip to vent his frustration on the hoof-torn turf beside him.

'You all right?' a voice called, and he looked across to where an ambulance car waited, engine idling, a medic poised to come to his aid if necessary.

He nodded and waved a hand.

'D'you want a lift?'

'Thanks.' Matt got to his feet wearily, the action pinpointing one or two areas that would be sore later. It was only a few hundred yards back to the stands, but it had been a long day, and he wasn't about to turn down anything that would make life easier.

The weighing room, after the last race, was comparatively empty. A handful of jockeys were

184

just leaving as Matt went in, most of them acknowledging him with a nod or a word as they passed. He crossed to his peg and sat down heavily on the bench beneath it, wishing he was already showered and changed, and that someone else was driving him home.

'Matt?' It was Jim Steady, his valet.

'Hi, Jim.'

'You all right?'

'Yeah, thanks. Just feeling a bit sorry for myself, that's all.'

'A kid outside asked me to give you this,' the valet said, holding out a piece of folded, lined notepaper, such as might have been torn from a spiral-bound pad. It had his name pencilled on the outside and was stuck down with Sellotape.

Matt took the paper and unfolded it. It was written in capital letters with a pencil, and suggested that, if he met the sender in the Paddock Bar in half an hour's time, he might find out something about a certain set of credit cards. It was unsigned.

'Who gave you this?' he asked. 'A kid, you say?'

'Yes. Young lad, about twelve or thirteen. He said someone told him to make sure you got it. He was gone before I could ask him who.'

'He probably didn't know. Thanks, anyway.'

The valet hesitated.

'Not bad news, I hope . . .'

'No. Nothing like that.' Matt wasn't about to satisfy his curiosity. A wonderfully efficient valet he might be, but he provided the service for dozens of jockeys during a normal week, and Matt placed no great reliance upon his discretion.

185

The Paddock Bar was all but deserted when Matt walked in. At the end of the bar, a red-faced man in a suit but no tie was deep in contemplation of his spirit glass, and in one corner a middle-aged couple sat holding hands. Two of the young staff, dressed in black with short white aprons, were collecting glasses and wiping tables, while another was doing something with the till and a wayward roll of paper.

Matt walked across to the bar and, finding himself suddenly thirsty, ordered a black coffee. He sat on one of the stools and angled himself slightly towards the red-faced man, who glanced at him uninterestedly and then returned his attention to the half-inch or so of brownish liquid he was hoarding. Matt was relieved, he'd been hoping the man wasn't his contact.

The coffee arrived and, as Matt felt in his pockets for some change, a familiar voice spoke in his ear.

'That'll be disgusting; it's the end of the day, so they won't have made fresh. I'd send it back.'

Casey.

Matt took a sip. She was right, it was horribly strong. He made a face and pushed the cup back towards the young man, who'd apparently caught the gist of Casey's comment and was scowling at her.

Unabashed, she climbed onto the stool next to Matt.

'Maybe I'll have tea instead,' he suggested, then turned to Casey, who seemed to have done something different with her hair. It suited her.

186

She looked older and a little more sophisticated. 'Was it you who sent me that note?'

A calculating look came into her eyes.

'It might have been . . .' she said slowly.

'But it wasn't,' Matt decided. 'Not quite quick enough, Ms McKeegan. And no, I'm not going to discuss it with you now. If you're a good girl and make yourself scarce, I might just tell you about it afterwards.'

'Don't you dare patronise me!' she returned hotly.

He grinned.

'I knew you'd rise to that.'

'Oh, but—'

'No buts. I'm here to meet someone, and, if they see I'm not alone, they'll more than likely shy away.'

'I'll sit in the corner.'

'Out,' Matt said firmly.

'But I wanted to see you . . .'

'OK, but later. Please, Casey. This could be important.'

Looking slightly sulky, Casey slid off the stool and headed for the door.

Whatever the author of the note had been going to tell him, he or she had obviously had second thoughts. Matt waited half an hour before giving up, and left the bar staff trying to convince the red-faced man that he should also go home.

'But there's no one there,' Matt heard the man say in mournful tones as the door closed behind him. 'My wife left me. She says I drink too much . . .'

Outside, the sun was sinking fast behind the autumnal trees that Matt had so admired when

187

he'd cantered Woodcutter to the start.

Woodcutter! Damn! He'd meant to catch up with Doogie before he left. Too late now. Glancing around, he was surprised and not a little relieved to note that Casey was nowhere to be seen. Presumably she'd given up waiting and gone to wherever she called home, which was precisely what he intended to do.

Where *did* Casey live? he found himself wondering, as he left the racecourse behind and headed across the owners' and trainers' car park in the gathering dusk. He imagined a town-centre flat close to the pubs and clubs, though, at her age, she could just as possibly still live with her family, he thought, realising he knew absolutely nothing about her.

He looked ahead and, just for a moment, couldn't see the MR2 amongst the twenty or thirty cars that remained but, as he walked on, it came into view on the far side of a dirty white transit van that hadn't been there when he'd parked.

Taking the keys from his pocket, Matt operated the remote button, walked between the two vehicles and bent to open the door.

He fumbled and stopped short; it was as if the handle had just disappeared.

Closer inspection revealed that it had. Some kind soul had filled the recess with what looked like Polyfilla.

Matt turned his eyes heavenward and groaned, 'Oh, for fuck's sake!'

In that first instant, annoyance and disbelief filled his mind to such a degree that he didn't pause to wonder why someone should have chosen *his* car to vandalise and, even when the sliding

188

door of the van behind him opened, he didn't immediately apprehend danger. He was in the act of turning when someone caught hold of the collar of his jacket and slammed him, face down, onto the low roof of his car.

9

The attack was so unexpected that Matt didn't have a chance to get his arms up to protect his face, with the result that his left cheekbone and temple connected painfully with the cold metal. Half stunned, he was easy prey to his attacker, and, before he could gather his scattered wits, his right arm was grasped and twisted up behind his back until his hand was somewhere in the region of the nape of his neck.

Pressure was applied, and he gritted his teeth, glad that he'd always been loose-jointed—something that had saved him from broken bones on many occasions.

Leaning hard, so that Matt's body was sandwiched between him and the unyielding side of the car, the man behind growled, 'I'm gonna to keep this short, 'cos we're just here to deliver a message, and it goes like this: Lay off the snooping and stick to riding the pretty horses, while you still can. Understand?'

Matt wasn't in a position to nod and his lung capacity was severely limited by the weight of his interrogator, but he managed a breathy affirmative.

Keeping up the pressure on Matt's arm, the man

bounced his bodyweight against him once more, rocking the car on its suspension.

'Sorry. Didn't catch that. Come again . . .'

'Yes!'

'Yes, what?'

'Yes, I understand,' Matt said, through his teeth.

'Good.'

The man stepped back, pulling him upright, and air found its way back into Matt's lungs. It seemed that he took Matt's prompt acquiescence for submission, for, releasing the arm lock, he swung him round and sent him crashing into the side of the transit van.

Following him, the man leaned forward, as if to deliver a postscript to the message, and Matt found himself facing a stocky character in combat fatigues and a woolly hat, with a neck like a rhinoceros and an attitude to match. Matt was hazily aware that another figure stood to one side looking on, but his full attention was taken by the man in front of him.

Whether it was just that the attack came at the end of a long, frustrating day, he couldn't afterwards be sure, but, finding his arms free, he discovered within himself a fierce aversion to being manhandled and, without further thought, launched a powerful if unskilled uppercut into the face that jutted so aggressively towards his.

The stocky man grunted, staggering back, and Matt—a little off-balance himself—followed his opening gambit with an unscientific shove, which nevertheless sent his opponent sprawling backward across the low bonnet of the MR2.

It was the last fleeting moment of satisfaction that Matt was allowed, for now the silent partner got involved and what he lacked in loquacity he certainly made up for in action. In the blink of an eye and without quite understanding how he got there, Matt found himself lying on his back on the uneven turf of the car park, gasping for breath like a landed fish.

His instinct for survival was strong, however, honed by many years of dicing with serious injury amongst the hooves of racing thoroughbreds, and, even as he fought to breathe, he was aware of how horribly vulnerable he was in that position. Pulling his arms and legs in, foetus-like, and tucking his head between his elbows, he turned onto his side just a split second before the silent man's boot thudded into his ribcage.

At this point, Matt acknowledged, with a kind of fatalistic calm, his options weren't good. To move from his defensive curl would be to lay his belly and face open to potentially life-threatening injuries but, on the other hand, it would only take one hefty kick to the kidneys or spine and the outcome could easily be the same.

Somewhere around the third or fourth blow, he came to the decision that, if he didn't move soon, he might never do so again. He knew the first man could only have been temporarily incapacitated by his inexperienced punch and, once he was operational again, Matt's chances, already minuscule, would be non-existent.

'What the *fuck* are you doing?' The stocky man sounded furious, and the onslaught faltered.

Matt opened his eyes and peered through the gap between his upper arms. There was nothing within his field of vision other than grass and one of the front wheels of the van.

'Deliver the message and put the frighteners on him—that was the brief—not kick the shit out of him. We don't want a murder on our hands!'

'He asked for it,' the other one replied, punctuating his sentence with another kick, albeit with slightly less vigour, and Matt heard himself grunt.

'Cut it out, I said!'

Matt decided not to wait on the outcome of this dispute. The sight of the van wheel so close had given him an idea and, straightening out suddenly to full length, he rolled once, twice, and fetched up beneath the dark, oily-smelling underbelly of the transit.

Wriggling sideways until he estimated that he was halfway between the wheels, he stopped, face down and chest heaving—partly from exertion and partly from fear. Incidental injuries in the course of his job were one thing, but never before had he been on the receiving end of a concerted effort by one of his own kind to do him harm, and the sensation was immeasurably shocking.

What would they do next?

It seemed likely that, with the temptation one step removed, the stocky man would be able to cap his colleague's more murderous tendencies, but Matt wasn't about to bet on it. What might they have in their van that could make life under it untenable? The way he felt now, nothing short of a shotgun would induce him to leave the comparative safety of his bolthole.

He watched as one pair of boots hurried round to the other side of the van and then their owner knelt down and peered under.

'He's still there—in the middle. Shall I drive

forward?'

Matt's heart leapt painfully. How stupid had he been to think he'd found refuge? One man to drive forward and one to pounce; he'd gained nothing.

Just as he was wondering if he could roll out again in the moments before the van moved—or even if he had the nerve to try—Matt heard the other man say urgently, 'Sshh! What was that?'

There was silence for a moment, even Matt holding his breath in anticipation, and then, from some distance away, someone called, 'Matt? Is that you?'

Casey!

Shit! He'd have to warn her, but would she hear if he shouted from under the van?

He started to edge forward, swearing as he bashed his head on some protruding piece of metalwork.

'Come on, we've done enough—let's go,' the man on the left suggested. The side door slid shut with a crash and, shortly after, the nearside cab door opened and the suspension dipped as he got in. Another dip, the two doors banged shut and the engine was gunned.

Matt stayed where he was, pressing the right side of his face to the grass, and folding his arms over his head, resisting—with extreme difficulty—the urge to draw himself up into a protective ball. Hoping against hope that the only way out for the van was directly forward, he shut his eyes and tensed his whole body, as if by doing so he could prevent injury from the rolling wheels and the ton or so of vehicle they conveyed.

For a moment nothing existed except noise, fear, and darkness, as the engine roared and the van pulled away over the rough ground. One of the wheels grazed Matt's elbow, dragging at the sleeve of his jacket, and then it was gone, the chaos replaced by silence and a degree of light.

Deliverance had been so sudden that relief was mingled with disbelief and he lay still, struggling to trust in his altered circumstances.

'Matt?' Casey's voice sounded breathless and much nearer, and he felt, more than heard, her running footsteps approaching. They stopped. 'Matt? Oh my God, are you OK?'

Matt wasn't sure. Compared with half a minute ago, he was terrific, but it had been a close call and, now that the terror was ebbing from his system, his brain was allowing the messages of physical trauma to get through. He wasn't looking forward to moving. In fact, given solitude and a less public place, he would have postponed the decision until he felt more in control, but Casey was waiting, her concern very evident as she repeated his name.

Matt gingerly raised his head three inches.

'Just give me a moment,' he told her, surprised at the normality of his voice.

'What happened? Who were those men? Shall I call the police?'

Realising he wasn't going to be allowed the luxury of breathing space, Matt pushed himself up onto his elbows, wincing a little as all the major muscles of his torso protested in unison.

'I should call the police,' Casey said, but she didn't sound convinced.

'Not yet. I need to think.'

With an effort, Matt turned partly onto his side, brought his legs up, and got as far as one knee, where he paused, waiting to catch his breath.

Casey stepped forward, offering her hand, and, leaning on her a little, he got to his feet and managed the five or six feet across to his car. Once there, he remembered the state of the door handle and swore.

'What's up?' Casey looked at him. 'Haven't you got the keys?'

'Yeah ...' As he said it, Matt remembered that he had been holding them when he was attacked. He glanced down at the grass in the failing light. 'Actually, I dropped them, but anyway, the bastards glued up the handle.' Feeling unequal to initiating a search, Matt turned round, leant against the car, and slid down it till he was sitting on the ground with his back resting on the bodywork. He felt shaky and unutterably weary.

'You can't sit there!' Casey exclaimed.

'Just for a moment.'

She looked down at him, her hair falling forward a little around her face, and Matt squinted through the twilight, thinking—for the second time that day—that something was different about her. Apparently working on the *If you can't beat them, join them* philosophy, Casey watched him for a second or two more, then moved over to the car, turned round, and sat down beside him.

'So, who were they? What did they want?'

Matt shook his head slightly.

'I've never seen them before, and, if I never see them again, it'll be too soon.'

'Well, didn't they say anything?' Casey was beginning to sound impatient, but Matt's scattered wits were reassembling and he recalled her vocation.

195

'Listen, I don't want a whisper of this in tomorrow's paper.'

'Oh, that's not fair! You can't ask me to pass up something like this.'

'Not a whisper. Promise?' Matt looked hard at her through the gloom.

At first she returned his gaze, but then she rolled her eyes heavenward and sighed.

'Oh, all right. So what did they want? Were they sent to warn you off?'

'Apparently.'

'But that's great! It means we've got someone worried. So now we just have to figure out who sent them.'

Matt wished he could view the affair as matter-of-factly as she seemed to.

'And do you have any bright ideas as to how we go about that?' he asked, leaning his head back and closing his eyes.

'Well, the van registration might give us something,' she said, studiously casual.

Matt's eyes snapped open again.

'You didn't . . . ? You got the number?'

'Part of it,' she said. 'Echo Tango November, and I think there was a two or a five—it was a bit dark. But it might be enough.'

'You little . . .' He couldn't think of a suitable epithet, and finished, 'Well done! That's brilliant!'

Casey glowed.

'So what about the police? Aren't you going to tell them?' she asked.

Matt groaned. The thought of a session with Bartholomew, when all he really wanted was a hot bath and a stiff whisky, wasn't inviting. After all, what could he realistically report?

'No, not tonight. I will sometime.'

'Bartholomew won't be pleased . . .'

'So what are you, my conscience?' he demanded. 'What can I tell him anyway? That I was set upon by two men—one of whom I didn't get a good look at, and one who looked like any other tough Joe—but that I don't know who sent them, or why. He's bound to think I'm not telling him the whole story. It'll take all night. Let's wait and see if the registration throws up something, then I'll tell him.'

'OK.' Casey didn't seem unduly perturbed by the prospect of bypassing the authorities. 'Well, hadn't we better see if we can find your keys?'

'Actually . . .' Matt shifted his weight a little. 'I think I may be sitting on them.'

To Matt's great relief, they found the handle on the passenger door was clear and, edging across from that side, Casey was able to open the driver's door from within, but she then stubbornly refused to budge, insisting that Matt was in no fit state to drive home.

Aware that she was probably right, Matt nevertheless didn't relish the idea of the youngster at the controls of his precious car, even though the racecourse was his closest, being a bare thirty-five or forty miles from Spinney Cottage. However, Casey assured him that she had her licence and was perfectly capable, and so it proved; in fact, she drove the sports car so carefully that Matt was moved to ask her, as she headed along the A37 at a steady forty-five, what kind of car she herself owned.

'I haven't got a car, as such. Not yet, anyway,' she admitted, not taking her eyes off the road.

197

'So when exactly did you pass your test?' Matt asked, with a growing conviction that he didn't want to hear the answer.

'Um—in August.'

'*This* August? Last month? Why the hell didn't you tell me?'

'Because you wouldn't have let me drive, if I had,' she pointed out with inescapable logic.

'Too right!'

In spite of her inexperience, the short journey was accomplished without mishap and Casey pulled up in front of the cottage with an unmistakable air of triumph.

Kendra met them at the door and was visibly shocked at Matt's condition. He knew from the car's sun visor mirror that a rapidly purpling bruise on his cheekbone now matched the one on the bridge of his nose and, however much he tried, he couldn't disguise the stiffness that had set into his damaged muscles on the journey home.

'What's happened? Jamie said you'd had a fall—he saw it on TV—but he said it didn't look too bad. Oh—hello Casey,' she added, raising her eyebrows in mute enquiry as Matt stepped past her into the room.

'Casey drove me home. We need to call her a taxi,' he said, knowing that the explanation was woefully insufficient.

'That was kind of her.' Kendra led the way through to the kitchen. 'My God, Matt! What on earth have you been up to?'

Matt looked down at his clothes, becoming aware—for the first time—of the grass and mud stains on his beige trousers and the elbows of his jacket. He sighed.

'I—er . . . had a spot of trouble,' he said.

*   *   *

A quarter of an hour later, when the taxi arrived, Kendra was in possession of the full story and, due to Casey's interjections, far more of the details than Matt had intended she should have. Her reaction had been less pronounced than he'd expected, but it clearly wasn't an accurate gauge of her emotions for, as soon as they had seen Casey off, she got straight down to business. They were back in the kitchen, where he was finishing a cup of coffee to which Kendra had added a good slosh of whisky. It was making him feel drowsy, and he was looking forward to a hot bath.

'I want you to stop this, Matt,' Kendra said suddenly.

'Stop . . . ?'

'You know damn well what I mean. Stop this messing about—playing at being a private eye! I know *why* you're doing it, and I love you for it, but it's getting scary now. You could have been killed today, and for what? You say you don't even know why they attacked you. It's crazy! If Jamie's innocent, he'll be OK. The police will find out who did do it; it's their job. Those men were right— *your* job is riding horses, as if that wasn't dangerous enough . . .'

'Hang on,' Matt cut in. 'What do you mean *if* Jamie's innocent? Don't you believe it anymore?'

'Well, of course I *want* to believe he is—but how can we be 100 per cent sure?'

'*I'm* sure,' Matt stated quietly. 'And you were, last time I heard. You've certainly changed your

199

tune.'

'I haven't. Oh, don't change the subject! We were talking about you getting beaten up—for nothing.'

'But, don't you see? This means I'm getting somewhere. Somebody's scared of what I might find out; that's what this was all about. Why else would they go to all that trouble?'

Kendra, who had been pacing round the room, stopped and made an exasperated noise.

'But how does it help, if you don't know what prompted it and you don't know who sent them?'

'We'll wait and see what the registration number throws up,' Matt said.

'No. Give it to the police. If this was just a warning, what'll these people do next time?'

'I'll be more careful now,' he promised. 'And I *will* tell Bartholomew, if Casey comes up with something.'

Kendra pulled out a chair and sat on it, abruptly, heavily, as if all the strength had gone from her legs. She pushed back her long blonde fringe and Matt was shocked to see tears in her eyes. She rarely cried.

'What's this all about?' he asked gently. 'It's not just what happened today, is it? You've been on edge for a while. Can't you tell me about it, Kennie? Maybe I can help.'

'No, it's not just what happened today,' she admitted. 'It's everything—Sophie, Jamie, you doing this stuff, Deacon's cat, everything. I just feel scared all the time and I should be so happy—especially now . . .'

Matt's attention sharpened.

'Especially now?' he asked, the penny teetering on the edge.

'Because I'm pregnant,' Kendra announced, and burst into tears.

'But that's brilliant!' Matt exclaimed. 'Are you sure?'

'Of course I'm sure!' she sobbed. 'Oh—and I wasn't going to tell you like this—I wanted it to be special . . .'

'It *is* special.' Matt leaned over the table, reaching out to take and hold her hands, oblivious—in the joy of the moment—to the discomfort of his bruises. 'It's absolutely amazing! When's it due?'

'About May-time, I think.'

'Oh, wow! This is incredible! *You're* incredible!'

'Well, you had a little something to do with it,' Kendra told him, with a flash of a watery smile.

'That's a relief to hear,' he joked. 'But, you know, that's why you've been so anxious lately. You're hormonal.'

'Oh—that's it! Now you're happy,' she exclaimed. 'The male answer to every female emotion—hormones.' She pulled her hands free and wiped her eyes.

Matt prudently changed the subject.

'One thing still puzzles me. Where does your brother's cat fit into all this?'

'Oh, that was so sad. The poor little thing got run over.'

'Not by Deacon?'

'No. It was Niall, I think—Niall Delafield. Deacon was devastated. I didn't see him, but Mum says it brought on one of his awful migraines. He stayed in his room all day.'

'Oh, I'm sorry. Poor Deke!' Matt wasn't a cat man, but he knew how he'd feel if it happened to one of the dogs. 'By the way, when are we going to

201

tell your family the news?'

'Not just yet, I think,' she said. 'Let's keep it to ourselves for a little bit longer, shall we?'

With the conversation back to Kendra's exciting revelation, they spent some little time marvelling and making plans before Matt finally rose stiffly to his feet and headed upstairs for the longed-for bath.

In spite of his aches and pains, he felt wonderfully content. They hadn't planned to start a family so soon, but, now that it had happened, he wouldn't have had it any different. The only cloud on his horizon was their unresolved disagreement over his efforts to clear Jamie's name, but he decided, with a complacency born of exhaustion, that he'd deal with that another day.

*   *   *

Unfortunately, 'another day' turned out to be the very next day and, furthermore, first thing in the morning, over the breakfast table.

Unusually for him, Matt had slept late, and Kendra had let him, informing him—when he awoke in a panic—that she had already rung Rockfield and excused him from riding out.

'You didn't say anything about what happened last night?' Matt asked in alarm.

'No, I just said you'd had a problem with the car and didn't get in until late. I also said you'd picked up a few bruises from your fall yesterday. Well, John's bound to notice, with you moving around like an eighty-year-old!' she added, as he started to protest. 'And that's another reason why you should

202

leave this Sophie business to the police. If you won't do it for me and the baby, you should do it for yourself. If you get yourself all beaten up, you won't be able to ride. I know you're in demand right now, but only as long as you deliver the goods. Look what happened to Jamie. If word gets about that you're not as fit as you might be, they'll drop you like a shot.'

'That sounds like your father talking,' Matt said, the knowledge that she was right giving his voice a bitter edge. 'Anyway, they just caught me by surprise yesterday. I'll be more careful in future.'

'Oh, and that'll be all right then, will it? From what Casey said, they were big powerful men. Just how do you propose to deal with them if they come looking for you again?'

'She's right, Matt.' Unseen by either of them, Jamie had come to stand in the kitchen doorway. 'God knows I'm grateful for what you've been trying to do, but I don't want you to muck up your career on my account. Bad enough that one of us is on the breadline. And I don't want you guys falling out over me, either. I've been thinking it might be better if I head off back to Cambridge.'

'Oh? And what are you going to use for rent money up there?' Matt enquired. 'You're skint, remember?'

'I dunno—get myself a paper round or something. Anyway, I think you two deserve a bit of space. Or should I say, you *three*—sorry, I kind of overheard you last night. Congratulations, by the way!'

Matt wasn't keen on the idea of Jamie being so remote while he was still see-sawing on the edge of depression. Who would watch out for him if he drank himself into a stupor again?

'Thanks,' he said. 'But I think you going up to Cambridge is a bad idea. Besides, you haven't worked off what you owe *us* for rent yet.'

He didn't pitch it any stronger, unsure of how Kendra would view the situation, but she rose to the occasion as he'd hoped she would.

'And I call it bloody ungrateful to waltz off just when I need a bloke around the house to do the heavy lifting for me when Matt's not here.'

She didn't say just what heavy lifting she had in mind and nor did either of the others question it.

'Well, if you put it like that,' Jamie said, glancing at each of them in turn. 'Of course I'll stay.'

*   *   *

It being a Sunday, early evening found Matt and Kendra heading for Birchwood Hall and the family dinner. There was still some tension between them, but Kendra hadn't returned to the contentious matter of Matt's extracurricular activities, and *he* certainly wasn't about to.

At the Brewer home, the atmosphere wasn't much better. Deacon was still indisposed and missing from the pre-dinner gathering, as was Charlie, who—Joy told them, as she greeted Matt with a kiss—was in his office dealing with a matter of business.

'Oh dear. You look as though you've been in the wars,' she remarked, stepping back to arm's length and taking a good look at him.

'Been fighting with the horses again?' Grace enquired from the sofa, where she was sitting within the circle of Rupert's arm. 'Or has my sister

204

been beating you up?'

'Oh Grace, you're so not funny,' Frances told her.

'How long do you think Charlie will be?'Matt asked. 'I was hoping to have a word with him.'

'Well, he said ten minutes or so, but that was half an hour ago,' Joy told him, consulting her watch. 'So you could go and see. Only don't keep him too long or dinner will spoil.'

'And I'm hungry,' Grace added in a plaintive tone.

'Oh well—that'll certainly make me hurry,' Matt said, sending a private wink Frances's way as he headed for the door.

Charlie Brewer's study was on the first floor, at the end of an impressive corridor flanked on both sides by items of antique furniture bearing numerous objets d'art. On the deep-red walls hung an extensive collection of portraits—amongst them, one each of the Brewer family in sumptuous evening wear and painted in the old style. The door stood slightly ajar and, as Matt approached, the noise of his footfalls lost in the dense pile of the carpet, he could hear voices emanating from within the room. He hesitated—Charlie wasn't alone, and, by the sound of it, there was some pretty significant business being conducted.

Matt was debating whether to postpone his own business with Kendra's father or whether to cough loudly, knock on the door, and go in, when the sound of Charlie's angrily raised voice temporarily distracted him from either course.

'I don't care how politically incorrect it is; in *my* house, *I* make the rules, and I say get rid of him.'

'You're overreacting. He's never been here—and

205

never would have.' The second voice was calmer and sounded familiar to Matt, although he couldn't immediately put a name to it.

'It's not up for discussion. If you want to keep your job, you know what to do.'

Matt started to turn away. This quite plainly wasn't any of his business and it just as plainly wasn't an auspicious moment to raise his own point of contention with Kendra's father.

The other voice came again.

'That's an empty threat, you know you're not going to fire me.'

'And *you* know you can't talk,' came the response. 'Not now.'

There was a long silence, during which Matt leaned closer, etiquette forgotten in the face of this fascinating exchange. He'd recognised the second voice now. It was Niall Delafield, Charlie's security man.

'Well, just make sure you keep your end of the bargain, or we'll all be fucked!' It was Delafield who eventually spoke, and so much nearer to the door that Matt was shocked into swift retreat.

The corridor was way too long to traverse in the second or two he might have, so, to be spared the ignominy of being caught eavesdropping—albeit accidentally—he waited until he saw the door open, and then began to walk forward.

'Oh, hello!' he exclaimed, on coming face to face with Delafield.

Delafield glowered, nodded briefly, and stood back to let him pass.

Charlie was sitting staring at his desk when Matt knocked on the open door. He looked up.

'Oh, hello, Matt. I didn't realise it was that late.'

He glanced at the ornate Regency carriage clock on the mantelpiece and got to his feet. 'I'd better come down. Er . . . did you want something?'

'No. Just to say the meal's ready,' Matt told him, and Brewer, his mind clearly distracted, seemed to find nothing odd in this.

*   *   *

The mood at the dinner table that evening was edgy and uncomfortable, a state of affairs which Grace did nothing to improve. It was clear to Matt that he and Kendra were not the only ones wrestling with problems; even had he not overheard the exchange in the office, he would have guessed that something was bothering Kendra's father, because he spoke little and his usually prodigious appetite had apparently deserted him. Joy, too, seemed tense and unhappy, displaying dark circles under her eyes, as if she hadn't slept well.

With conversation floundering, it was left to Grace to hold the floor, which she did by regaling the company with the details of her visit to Rupert's father's jewellery showrooms. Since, for her, the most memorable aspect of the tour seemed to have been the extravagant prices of the various sumptuous pieces on show, Matt very quickly grew bored, but Joy and Kendra exhibited the requisite wonderment—whether real or feigned—so Grace was encouraged to continue. When she had exhausted that topic, though, she reverted to her usual pastime of stirring up trouble and, as was often the case, Matt was her target.

It was as the dessert was being served that she

casually dropped the most unwelcome nugget of information into the silence.

'So, Matt, Kendra tells us you've been tangling with thugs.'

Surprised and disappointed, Matt looked across at Kendra, who coloured up, saying, 'I didn't! I was talking to Mum. You shouldn't have been listening, Grace. You bitch!'

'Should have kept your voice down then, shouldn't you, little sister?' Grace replied, and Matt saw Rupert looking a little uncomfortable, as though for the first time he were seeing another side to her. For his own part, he couldn't imagine what had taken the man so long.

'Girls, *please!*' Joy pleaded.

'That's enough!' Charlie thundered from the head of the table. It was the first time he'd involved himself in the conversation, and it produced instant silence. 'I don't much care who said what and who shouldn't have been listening, but I do want to know why I wasn't told about this. Matt? What's this all about?'

Matt hesitated, wondering how little he could get away with, and Grace answered for him.

'A couple of men attacked him in the car park after the races. That's where he got those bruises.'

'Is that true?' Charlie frowned heavily at Matt, who had no option but to give an affirmative.

'Well, what did they want? Did you report it? Why wasn't I told?'

'It was a private matter,' Matt stated. 'No real damage done. Everyone's making a mountain out of a molehill.'

Across the table Kendra looked intensely unhappy and he gave her a quick reassuring smile.

Her father paused, regarding Matt thoughtfully through narrowed eyes, and, for a moment, he thought he might just have got away with it, but Grace hadn't finished yet.

'It wasn't anything to do with *Matt Shepherd— Private Eye*, then?' she asked, her face the picture of innocence.

'Was it?' Charlie demanded.

'Like I said a minute ago, it's private.'

'Not when it affects your riding, it isn't!'

'It hasn't affected my riding. It happened last night, after the meeting. Look, can we just drop this?'

'This whole damn thing is affecting your riding,' Charlie argued. 'Look at the way you rode Kenning's horse the other day, and what about Temperance Bob yesterday?'

'I don't know what was the matter with Bob—but it certainly wasn't down to me,' Matt protested.

'Not what the stewards thought, was it? And what about the others, huh? Not exactly the performance we've come to expect from you, was it?'

Matt stared, a little hurt. Surely this wasn't still fallout from the upset about the sponsorship deal. Charlie was brusque by nature, but he knew what an up-and-down business racing was, and he was normally very supportive.

'Well, what about Woodcutter? Nothing wrong with my riding there, was there?' he asked, forced to defend himself and, as he said it, remembering that he still hadn't contacted Doogie about the horse. Events had put it right out of his head.

There was a sudden scraping noise as Kendra pushed her chair back and got to her feet. She

209

mumbled something with her hand half covering her mouth and hurried from the room.

'Excuse me.' Matt rose to follow her, glad of the chance to escape, and, as he rounded the end of the table, Joy looked up and put out a sympathetic hand to touch his arm.

'We'll talk about this another time,' Charlie promised grimly.

From the corner of his eye, Matt could see Grace smirking quietly and, for the first time in his life, he contemplated doing violence to a woman. He'd liked to have rammed her face firmly into her bowl of apple pie and custard.

10

Matt arrived at Rockfield bright and early the following morning to ride out, determined not to give anyone fuel to criticise either his fitness or commitment. In truth, although his muscles were still extremely sore, it was the kind of tenderness that you grit your teeth and work through, rather than a sharp pain that causes weakness and disability. He was confident that his performance wouldn't be in any way affected.

When he'd run Kendra to ground the previous evening, he found she'd taken refuge in the kitchen with the family cook and a cup of hot chocolate. Although Matt didn't take her to task over spreading the tale of his beating, she was clearly feeling wretched for having brought the wrath of her father down on him, and wouldn't rest until she was sure she was forgiven. This was so out of character for her that Matt returned to the dining room to make their excuses and then took her home.

This morning she had seemed much more composed when Matt took her a cup of tea in bed and kissed her goodbye, and he had experienced a surge of optimism that perhaps she had come to terms with the situation and everything would be all right.

As he turned into the yard at the stables, his lifting spirits suffered a knock-back. To his surprise, alongside John Leonard's grubby Volvo and Charlie's spotless Land Rover was parked a red hatchback he didn't recognise. The first thing he saw, when he got out of his car, was Brewer himself, standing in the open doorway of Secundo's box, in company with a slight figure in navy jodhpurs and a fleece jacket. They both glanced over their shoulders and, with a shock, Matt recognised Ray Landon, a young jockey who some were predicting to be the next hotshot. Landon raised a hand to Matt, looking a little sheepish, and Matt had a sharp premonition of trouble ahead.

The trainer hurried across to Matt, who nodded towards the visitor.

'What's he doing here?'

'Er . . . Charlie wants him to put Secundo over a few fences,' Leonard said, as if it were the most natural thing in the world for a newcomer to take over the schooling of one of the best young horses in the yard from the stable jockey.

'So when was this decided?'

'I don't know. He's only just told *me*.'

'And did he say why?'

211

'Er . . . Something about it paying to keep our options open,' Leonard said, adding quickly, 'Look, can you do me a favour and go and see where Harry's got to? He hasn't appeared yet and the Guv was asking where he was.'

'But Secundo's *my* ride!' Matt protested. 'Apart from the last time, when Jamie took over, I've always ridden him.'

Leonard nodded unhappily.

'I know. You'll have to take it up with the Guv, but please Matt . . . Harry?'

Even though he was sure it was a diversionary tactic, Matt assented, turning his back on the yard and going down the cinder path to the farm cottage where Harry lived.

He found the door unlocked and opened it, calling, 'Harry? You up?'

'Yeah. Just coming.' The voice came from the bedroom at the back of the house.

'You OK? Anything I can do for you? Brewer has graced us with his presence and your pa requests your immediate appearance. In other words, *shift your butt!*'

He heard Harry laugh, just as, on the kitchen table, his mobile started to play the James Bond theme.

Matt chuckled.

'Your phone, Mr Bond!'

'Oh, shit! Can you get it for me?'

'Righty ho.' Matt picked it up. 'Hello?'

'Harry, it's Toby,' a voice said immediately. 'Look, I'm sorry but I can't make our session today. We've got a mare coming in with a possible twisted gut, any minute now, and I'm in surgery this arvo. I'm afraid I'll have to postpone . . .'

212

'Actually, it's not Harry,' Matt said, when he got the chance. 'But I can pass the message on for you or pass you over, if you like.'

'Shit! Look, the mare's here—can you pass on the message? Must go.'

The phone clicked and went dead, and Matt wasn't sure if Toby's exclamation of annoyance was due to finding that he'd been talking to the wrong man or because his patient had arrived before he was ready for her.

'Who was it?' Harry came wheeling into the kitchen just as Matt put the phone back on the table.

'Toby Potter. Said he can't make it today, he's got an emergency.'

'Oh.' Harry looked momentarily disconcerted. 'Er . . . thanks.'

'Trouble with one of the horses?' Matt enquired. 'He's not your usual vet, is he?'

'Er—no, he's not, but he's a bloody good physio and he was going to have a look at Bob's back for us.'

'Temperance Bob?' Matt asked, his interest sharpening. 'You think that's the problem? Charlie was trying to tell me it was my fault, but I knew damn well it wasn't.'

'Yeah, well—it's a possibility. He didn't look 100 per cent comfortable yesterday when he walked out of his box.' He retrieved his phone from the table and a coat from a low hook by the door. 'I like your jacket. Is that the new sponsor?'

'Yeah. Quite striking, isn't it?'

The navy blue, fleece-lined canvas jacket had arrived the day before and was decorated with the distinctive red and white rings that formed the

213

logo of Q&S Holdings.

'Very snazzy! So, what happened to your face? That wasn't all from Tulip Time the other day, was it?'

'No . . .' Matt hesitated, but Harry was bound to hear the story sooner or later. 'I had a spot of bother on the way home Saturday night.'

'Oh? What sort of bother? You didn't crash the car?'

'No. I was late leaving the course and a couple of charmers were waiting for me in the car park. It seems someone is taking my efforts on Jamie's behalf seriously and they want me to stop.'

'You're kidding! So, what happened?' They had started down the path to the yard, but now Harry stopped the chair and looked up at him.

Matt looked away.

'Oh, just a bit of rough stuff and some threats. No lasting damage, but it's not something I'd care to repeat in a hurry. Look, we should get on—they'll be waiting.'

He took a couple of steps, then glanced back at Harry and found him still watching intently, his eyes screwed up against the sun.

'A bit of rough stuff, eh?' he said. 'No, I think it was a bit more than that. I know you, my friend, and you're really rattled. This has got to you, hasn't it? How bad was it?'

'All right, I admit for a moment or two I thought I'd had it, but I don't think that was the plan,' Matt said, reluctantly. 'I don't think I was expected to fight back.'

'They didn't know who they were picking on.' Harry's chair began to roll again. 'But this has got to be good for Jamie's case, hasn't it? What did the

214

police say? You did report it, I hope.'

Matt grimaced.

'I will do. It's just such a palaver, and the last thing you feel like when you've just had a drubbing like that.'

*   *   *

Matt had no opportunity to speak to Charlie till the horses had all been worked and were being settled back in their stables. Even then, the businessman stood talking to Ray Landon for several minutes before the jockey waved a cheery goodbye and headed for his car. Charlie then showed every sign of doing the same until Matt called out, 'Charlie! Have you got a minute?'

Charlie pushed back his sleeve to look at his watch.

'Well, not really. Can't it wait?'

'No, it can't. I want to know what's going on.'

'Going on?'

'You know what I mean—with Secundo and Ray.'

'Oh, not here, Matt. This isn't the time.'

'*Yes*, here. You owe me an explanation.'

Charlie turned to face Matt and sighed.

'All right—you asked; I'll tell you. You know I've not been happy with the way you've been riding lately . . .'

'Ever since Lord Kenning called you, in fact,' Matt put in.

'I'm well able to make up my own mind about it,' the businessman retorted hotly. 'But—since you mention it—yes, Lord Kenning is concerned, as are several other people.'

215

'Name them,' Matt said promptly, and had the satisfaction of seeing Charlie thrown off his stride briefly.

He was swift to recover.

'Certainly not; they spoke to me in confidence—and, anyway, it's beside the point. The fact remains that, ever since this business with Jamie and that woman, you've not been giving your full attention to the job, and I expect anyone who works for me to be 100 per cent committed.'

'I've never been less than 100 per cent,' Matt said, in a low, furious voice.

'Until lately, I would have agreed, but people are losing confidence in you.'

'Again—these nameless people. So what are you planning to do? Jock me off and give my best rides to Landon? What sort of message does that give out?'

'You were warned, Matt.'

Matt was struggling to believe what he was hearing.

'You can't do this. I'm Rockfield's jockey. It's not just *your* horses.'

'Yes, well the other owners are obviously free to do what they think fit, but, of course, John Leonard works for me. Ray's a good jockey and very keen. I think we'll find he's a popular choice with all the owners.'

'So, you've had this in mind for a while, have you?'

'Actually, I rang him just last night. He said yes on the spot.'

'I don't doubt it. But I'm the stable jockey here. We have an agreement . . .'

'I didn't sign anything,' Charlie pointed out. 'And

216

neither did you.'

'You know that's not how it works! You can't just step out of the arrangement without a bloody good reason.'

'Which I consider I have. Oh, I don't doubt there'll be some tongue-clicking and shaking heads, but they'll get over it. It's amazing how quickly people forget. Look Matt, I don't like having to do this, because you're family, but racing is a business, just like any other, and no business can afford to carry dead wood. Once something or someone ceases to be an asset, they must be cut loose. I'm sorry, but it's the only way to survive.'

'I don't believe I'm hearing this. What are you saying? That you're sacking me? Please tell me this hasn't got anything to do with my sponsorship deal.'

'No, of course not—though I see you're parading their logo already. All I'm saying is that I can't afford to have you ride my horses the way you have been. If you'd just given up this stupid crusade of yours when I told you to, and let the police do their job, then it wouldn't have come to this. You have only yourself to blame.' He looked at his watch once more. 'Now, I really must go, I've got a busy day.'

Matt stood and watched the Land Rover leave the yard, his head whirling with the massive injustice of Charlie Brewer's words. His pointed observation that Leonard worked for him just about covered it all. However much the trainer disagreed with what Kendra's father was doing, Matt doubted that he would risk sticking his neck out to say so. Having no written contract to safeguard his position as the Rockfield stable jockey was not unusual. Matt didn't know of any of his contemporaries who had anything more than a verbal agreement, but it was generally regarded as solid. But maybe Brewer was right; given the negative spin he and Kenning were putting on his career, would anyone seriously blame him for long?

Feeling slightly shell-shocked, Matt turned his steps towards the farmhouse.

The kitchen enfolded him with its usual combination of warmth and mouth-watering cooking aromas, but, as Matt closed the door behind him and stripped off his padded jacket, it became clear that even this haven had been affected by the ripples of unease radiating out from the arrival of Ray Landon. The atmosphere was strained and it was obvious—from the way John Leonard was avoiding Matt's gaze—that he'd been made privy to his boss's intentions whilst he and Charlie had watched the horses work from the vantage point of the Land Rover.

'Well, I suppose you're up to speed on Charlie's plans now,' Matt said.

Leonard looked even more uncomfortable.

'I'm sorry, Matt. I don't know what to say. I don't know what's got into him.'

'I do. Lord bloody Kenning!' Matt said. 'You know Charlie thinks the sun shines out of the arse of anyone with a title, and Kenning has had it in for me ever since I asked for his support for Jamie. Boy, was that a big mistake.'

'But surely he can't blame you for standing up for a friend,' Reney declared, wrapping a dishcloth round her hand and bending to open the oven.

'He can!' Harry interjected. 'I remember

218

Kenning from *my* racing days. He regards jockeys as some form of low life, regrettably necessary, but not entitled to views and opinions of their own. If someone could devise a way of getting the horses to race on their own, no one would be happier than him.'

'So, how is Jamie, anyway?' Reney asked, coming across to the table as Matt settled into his usual seat and reached for the cafetière. 'It's ages since he's been over. Never thought I'd miss having that cheeky monkey around, but I do.'

Matt poured coffee.

'He's still pretty low—but not about to self-destruct at the moment,' he said, as Reney slid a plate in front of him.

Thanking her, his thoughts drifted back to Kenning. Why *had* he taken against Matt so completely? Was it really about his relationship with Sophie? He recalled his conversation about the man with Razor at Sedgefield. 'You must be losin' the fuckin' plot if you think he murdered her!' the other jockey had said, in his endearing way, and, at the time, Matt had agreed that it was unlikely, but now—for the first time—he seriously began to wonder. Why else would Kenning be going out of his way to discredit Matt, unless he had something to hide? Had he and Casey perhaps been on the right track when they had discovered the probability that Kenning was the sugar daddy Sophie's flatmate had spoken of, who liked 'dressing up'? Kenning was a well-respected man who occupied a number of influential positions. Had Sophie perhaps tried to blackmail him— threatening to reveal his secret activities? Reluctantly, Matt decided that maybe it was time

219

he shared the idea with Bartholomew.

For several minutes there was silence at the table apart from the chinking of cutlery on plates as they all busied themselves with the hot food.

'So, Harry says old Temperance Bob is a bit stiff in his back,' Matt said presently. 'I gather Toby Potter is coming out to have a look at him sometime.'

Leonard frowned at his son.

'That's news to me. When was that arranged?'

'Oh, it was just an idea—nothing definite.'

Matt regarded his friend thoughtfully, but made no further comment. On the phone, Toby had certainly sounded like someone breaking a fixed appointment, but Harry didn't seem bothered, and Matt had more pressing matters occupying his mind.

'Am I still on Cantablay tomorrow?' he asked Leonard.

The trainer nodded.

'Yeah. I've already made the declarations for the next couple of days, so you should be safe.'

'Thanks.' It was something, he supposed. 'How many of the owners will stick with me, do you think?'

Leonard shrugged.

'I've not had any complaints, as yet. But, if word gets round that the Guv has lost confidence in you—well, you saw what happened to Jamie.'

'But Matt's been riding for them a hell of a lot longer than Jamie had,' Harry put in. 'Doesn't that count for anything?'

'It should do,' his father said. 'I'll do my best for you, Matt—you know that—but at the end of the day . . .'

'Yeah, I know. It's Brewer who pays your wages,' Matt said. 'Don't worry, I know your hands are tied.'

When he left Rockfield, Matt drove to Charlborough to see DI Bartholomew and, surprisingly, was shown into his office almost straight away. The reason was made clear to Matt immediately.

'You just caught me. I can give you five minutes and then I have an appointment with a golf course,' the detective said, waving his hand to suggest that Matt sit in the black leather-look chair in front of his desk. 'So, have you come to reveal the identity of Sophie Bradford's murderer?'

Matt sat down. The office was smallish with black and chrome furniture, a grey Venetian blind at the window, and a bank of filing cabinets against one wall. A crime-fighting slogan bounced across the computer monitor as a screen saver and paperwork was piled on every flat surface. It had about as much warmth of character as Bartholomew himself.

'I thought your computer was going to do that,' he countered.

'It takes time, and HOLMES is only as good as the information we feed it.'

'Well, have you tried feeding it with Lord Kenning?'

Bartholomew's eyes narrowed.

'Of course, as one of Sophie Bradford relations.'

'Well, how about as her lover? Her sugar daddy, to be more specific.'

'And exactly what makes you think that?'

Matt explained what he'd found out from Tara Goodwin about the mysterious Mosie; from Casey

221

about Kenning's middle name and his ongoing love of Jaguars; and about the rumour that Razor had started about Sophie and Kenning.

'Razor—that is, Geoff Hislop—swears he made a mistake, but I don't believe him. Casey says she was warned off the subject in no uncertain manner by her editor. I think pressure was brought to bear. The man has a lot of clout.'

'Well, I'm not surprised. Nobody wants that kind of publicity. It doesn't prove there's any truth in the rumour. Even if there was such a relationship—and, personally, I think your link is tenuous—Lord Kenning wasn't at the party that night and he has a rock-solid alibi.'

'But you will speak to him?'

'Oh, I'll have a word with him,' Bartholomew said, nodding. 'This very morning, in fact. I'm playing golf with him in half an hour.' He stood up. 'Was there anything else?'

It had been Matt's intention to tell the detective about the attack at Maiden Newton, but, in the face of this revelation, his resolve wavered. His original doubts resurfaced. With no evidence to present in support of his tale, except a partial registration plate, was it worth incurring a lashing from Bartholomew's acid tongue over his failure to report the incident straight away?

He hesitated. He hadn't heard from Casey yet. Perhaps he should wait and see what she turned up.

'Mr Shepherd?'

'No, nothing,' he heard himself say.

*   *   *

222

Matt drove home fast, finding an outlet for his frustration in pushing the limits, but any hopes he had that the mood at Spinney Cottage would be an improvement on the one he had left behind at the yard were doomed to be dashed.

He found Jamie and Kendra in the kitchen with the breakfast dishes still on the table, and the expressions on their faces warned him of a fresh catastrophe in store.

'If it's bad news—I don't want to hear it,' he said, straightening up from greeting the dogs.

Mutely, Kendra held up a copy of the *Daily Standard*. It was open and folded back on the racing pages, which were dominated by a large photo of Matt's fall in the last at Maiden Newton, with a superb action shot of the horse sprawling on his knees and Matt himself headed turfward. Above this masterpiece were the words 'How Low Can Mojo Go?'

Matt shrugged.

'Very funny. Just some hack with a warped sense of humour and way too much time on his hands.'

'No. Read it,' Jamie said.

Reluctantly, Matt held out his hand for the paper.

The article opened with an account of the race leading up to the pictured fall, somehow managing to convey—without saying it outright—that it had been through some fault of Matt's that the animal had fallen. Conveniently passing over his victory in the first, it described his poor results in the other three races of the day, making it sound as though his two-day suspension for failing to ride out the finish on Temperance Bob was the just reward for a series of poor efforts.

'But could there be a more sinister reason why such a capable jockey has suddenly started to lose races?' it went on to ask. 'Is there more to this than meets the eye? It hasn't escaped our notice that Matt Shepherd has been singled out for two drug tests in the last month. What are we not being told? Regular readers will remember that Matt Shepherd is the jockey who famously claimed that he would beat the police to discovering the identity of socialite Sophie Bradford's killer. We are still waiting—but, in the meantime, is Matt's mind really on the day job?

'We wouldn't like to say, but rumour has it that trainer John Leonard is getting jittery, with several of his owners—most notably millionaire businessman Charlie Brewer—asking for another jockey to ride their horses. Is Mojo's promising career going down the same drain that claimed that of his close friend, Jamie Mullin?'

It was no surprise to find that the piece had been written by Dave Rossiter, the journalist Casey had told him was responsible for the damaging articles about Jamie.

'How the bloody hell did they find out about the drug tests?' Matt demanded. 'That bastard Razor, I bet!'

'But how can they say that about Daddy?' Kendra asked, disregarding his remark to concentrate on the issue that concerned her most closely. 'He wouldn't do that to you.'

Matt didn't know quite what to say, so he said nothing, but Jamie was watching him closely and had no such reservations.

'My God! He already has, hasn't he? He's pulled the rug out from under you, like he did me!'

'That's not true!' Kendra's blue eyes beseeched him to deny it. 'Matt?'

'He had Ray Landon try out Secundo this morning,' Matt told her, loath to shatter her faith. 'But they can't have known that.'

'But why?'

'He says he's not happy with my riding anymore.'

'Bollocks!' Jamie said, explosively.

'That doesn't make sense,' Kendra protested. 'He's always said you'd be champion jockey one day . . .'

'Apparently he doesn't believe I'm totally committed to my job,' Matt told her, failing to keep the bitterness out of his voice.

'But Daddy wouldn't do that to you,' she repeated. 'They must have got it wrong. You must have misunderstood. I'll ring him.'

She swung round, then paused as she found the base unit empty.

'It's in the new kitchen, on the windowsill,' Jamie said. 'I remember seeing it yesterday.'

As Kendra disappeared in search of the handset, he turned to Matt.

'This is all because of me. I know what you said yesterday, and I appreciate it, but I really should go. No—' he said, forestalling Matt's protest. 'I won't go to Cambridge. Pete, down at The White Bull, has offered me some bar work and there's a room if I want it. I think I should take him up on it. You two need some space. But you have to leave this Sophie thing now and concentrate on your career.'

'Jamie . . .'

'No, Matt. I'm serious. I appreciate what you've done for me, but there's no sense in both of us

225

fucking up our lives. You've got Kendra and the baby to think of. Maybe, if I go, you can get back on track with Brewer and, after all, I *am* innocent, so, sooner or later, they'll find the bastard who really did kill Sophie and then maybe we can get back to where we were before this nightmare started.'

Matt scanned Jamie's face and saw that he was in earnest. He knew it was the sensible thing to do, but it went against the grain to back down and let Lord Kenning win. He moved to the window and looked out, common sense wrestling with inclination.

'Come on, Matt. You know I'm right . . .'

Matt sighed.

'OK. Thanks. Just for a while, maybe. Until things settle down a bit. But I've got a horrible feeling I may just have made things worse.' He told Jamie about his visit to the police station. 'It's entirely possible that Bartholomew is bringing up the subject of Kenning's relationship with Sophie as we speak,' he said ruefully. 'And there are no prizes for guessing who Kenning will blame for that.'

Jamie made a face.

'Oh dear.'

'Precisely.'

The door swung open and Kendra reappeared with the phone in her hand and tears glistening in her eyes.

'I can't believe it! He just won't listen. He says it's down to you to prove yourself, but it's like he's already made up his mind. I just couldn't get through to him.'

Matt could see that her inability to win her

226

father over was upsetting her almost as much as Brewer's unfair treatment of him, and he went to her, wrapping her in an embrace.

'It's all right, love. We'll sort it out.'

'But it's so unfair! I don't know what's got into him.'

'Well, I may be wrong, but I think Kenning's got a lot to do with this. I'm pretty sure he was behind that second drug test, and it could well have been him that tipped off the paper. In fact—I remember now—he hinted that it could happen.'

'But what are you going to do?'

Still hugging her, Matt explained about Jamie's moving out and, after an initial protest, she agreed that it might be for the best. What he didn't share with either of them was his growing determination that Kenning shouldn't be allowed to get away with the ruinous campaign he was waging.

What they didn't know, they wouldn't worry about.

*   *   *

Racing, the next day, was at Henfield, a smallish course on the Sussex Downs. Matt was booked to ride Cantablay for Kendra's father and a novice for Doogie McKenzie, but it seemed that Brewer's prediction was correct, for one other owner had jocked him off at the declaration stage and the only additional ride Josh Harper had managed to secure for him was on one of Westerby's horses.

'Sorry Matt,' his agent had said the night before. 'I don't think many people actually believe there's a problem with your riding, but they don't want to take any chances. It becomes a self-fulfilling

227

prophecy. But this horse of Westerby's is no slouch. It won a couple of useful races earlier this year. Certainly isn't another Khaki Kollin.'

Doogie's novice was Matt's first ride of the day, but it had never been on a racecourse before and ran very green. Matt coaxed enough of a run from it to pass the post in sixth place, which satisfied its connections, but would do little to redeem his besieged reputation.

Brewer's horse, Cantablay, was favourite to win the big race of the afternoon, and the businessman was in the paddock with Leonard when Matt made his way out to ride.

'The only thing capable of coming close is Louisiana Lou, and you beat her at Worcester the other week,' he reminded Matt. 'I don't want any foul-ups this time.'

'Yes, sir.' Matt kept his tone respectful with an effort. 'Any special instructions?' Brewer always left the issuing of directions to Leonard, and they both knew it.

'Just do your bloody job!' was the low-voiced reply.

As the trainer stepped forward to boost Matt into the saddle, he muttered, 'For God's sake, don't wind him up!'

Once on board and out on the course, Matt began to relax, feeling the tensions of the past couple of days dissipate in the wind that whipped past his ears. Cantablay felt strong and sensible, and although Louisiana Lou, with Razor on his back, looked fit and keen, she had been well beaten on their last meeting and, barring accidents, Matt could see no reason why the places should be reversed.

An accident was exactly what happened.

As usual, the bay travelled well, jumping cleanly and with enthusiasm. Matt kept him just behind the leaders until they approached the third last, where he eased the horse out of the pack to give him space to run on, but the fates were against him.

As he landed over the birch, the horse slightly ahead and to his inside pecked and pitched sideways, bringing Matt's horse down in a tangle of legs.

Seeing the ground flashing towards him, Matt swore, ducked his left shoulder, and rolled, turning two complete somersaults before he came to a halt.

Looking back, Matt saw that Cantablay had also rolled and was now struggling to his feet, but one despairing glance instantly told him that the bay gelding's racing days were over, his near fore dangling uselessly from below the knee.

'Steady lad,' he soothed, going forward to catch the trailing rein.

Not understanding what had happened to him, the horse tried to walk and almost fell, his eyes white-rimmed with pain and sudden fear.

'Whoah, steady. It's all right,' Matt lied, as the horse ambulance drew up on the other side of the rails.

*   *   *

How low can Mojo go? Matt quoted to himself gloomily, as he trudged back up the path to the weighing room. For the time being, he'd managed to avoid Brewer, but he knew he'd have to face

229

him sometime. The fall had been no fault of his—just one of the sad statistics of National Hunt racing—but, although it wasn't the first time it had happened to him and was unlikely to be the last, it was always distressing.

'Bad luck, mate!' someone called, and he raised a hand in thanks. There had been many such commiserations as he'd made his way back, and he appreciated them. Although newcomers were often horrified that a horse with a broken leg almost always had to be put down, most people at the tracks knew how poor the prognosis was for recovery from such injuries. Horses do not make good invalids, their physiology making them unable to lie down for sustained periods, and putting a limb in traction was impractical. With a return to full fitness unlikely, the kindest decision in most cases is swift euthanasia.

In the weighing room, the other jockeys were sympathetic, many of them having been through the experience themselves. Even Razor, to whom Matt's fall had gifted the race, seemed disinclined to crow. To most of their riders, owners, and trainers, these thoroughbreds were much more than a means to an end, they were individual characters and, over the years—in jump racing especially—real partnerships developed between animal and man, and a deep and genuine loss was felt at their passing.

Matt changed into the colours Westerby's horse was to carry, slipped a jacket over them to keep them clean, had a sandwich, and settled down to watch the intervening races on the jockey's TV until it was time to ride again.

He'd looked up the form on his last ride of the

day and found that Josh Harper was indeed right. The horse, a grey gelding called Maple Tree, had won over today's distance on two occasions and looked to be in with a chance, so it was with a palpable lifting of spirits that he went out to the paddock.

Westerby was waiting alone, huddled into a padded jacket against the sharp wind that had sprung up as the day progressed.

'Matt,' he said, nodding.

'Owner not here?' Matt enquired, his eyes on the deep-chested grey being led round the paddock by a tall, good-looking lad with sandy hair and a morose expression. The wind was lifting the horse's mane and rippling the corners of the warm rug he wore over his saddle.

'No. Unfortunately she's not in very good health.'

'Anything I should know about this one?'

'Take him steady down to the start,' Westerby recommended. 'Keep him handy and send him on round the last bend. He'll give you a good ride.'

'Let's hope so—you owe me one,' Matt observed, thinking of his last ride for the trainer.

Westerby pulled his collar up round his ears and didn't answer.

Following the trainer's advice, Matt took Maple Tree down to the start at a steady pace, his fingers loosely entwined in the grey's unplaited mane and resting on his prominent withers. The horse felt powerful and bold, and Matt prepared to enjoy himself. He had the promised ride on Peacock Penny the next day, and found himself wishing he trusted Westerby more, because the man trained some good horses and, in these uncertain times, he

231

might quite possibly need all the rides he could garner.

As the tape flew back, he managed to slot Maple Tree into the middle of the twenty or so runners, and there they stayed for most of the first circuit. The horse was indeed bold, jumping with more eagerness than care, but he seemed to have the scope to get himself out of trouble, and Matt would have thoroughly enjoyed the ride had it not dawned on him—as they flew the open ditch in the back straight for the second time—that all was not well with Maple Tree's saddle.

It wasn't easy to stay focussed on keeping the horse running straight over the short distance to the next fence when he had the growing conviction that the small synthetic pad was shifting beneath him. Risking a quick glance downward, he could see the horse's huge grey shoulders powering forwards and, further down, the rhythmic flash of his front hooves, but it was the position of the saddle that held his attention. Previously hard up against the rise of Maple Tree's prominent withers, it had moved back considerably and, in consequence, was now sitting on a narrower part of the animal's body.

Matt cursed and Rollo, who was racing alongside, glanced across.

'You all right?'

'Bloody saddle's slipped!'

'Oh, bad luck! Gonna pull up?'

'Would if I could,' Matt told him, but he knew it was a forlorn hope. The big grey was full of running and had no intention of stopping anytime soon.

'Could've done with a breast-girth,' Rollo

232

shouted, as his horse took off over the next fence.

Matching Rollo's horse, stride for stride, Matt and Maple Tree safely negotiated the next two fences but, with each enthusiastic leap, Matt felt his position become increasingly unstable.

Rollo was right—the grey could have done with a breast-girth, a webbing band that attaches to the saddle on each side, running across the horse's chest at the base of its neck, and held in place by a leather strap over the shoulders. As a horse takes off, its neck and shoulders stretch forward, elongating its body, which is what makes a breast-girth an essential piece of kit for many jumpers. If the horse hadn't been rugged against the cold wind in the paddock, it might have occurred to Matt to question its absence on such a big-fronted horse—but, then again, it might not. He usually trusted a trainer to know what tack the horse needed. For the second time in his life, Matt made a mental note to have words with Mick Westerby.

Had they been on the home straight, it would still have been within the bounds of possibility that he and his mount could finish the race together, but the final bend was fast approaching with all its potential jostling for position. Unable to slow the big grey, Matt knew that, realistically, it was not a case of *if* he came off, but when and how hard.

In the event, it was not the bend but the fence before it that proved his undoing. It was a simple, inviting birch, probably one of the smallest on the course, but, in the last couple of strides before take-off, the horse on his inside—perhaps getting tired—veered across Maple Tree's line, causing him to change direction as he took off, twisting a little in the air.

In mid-leap, high over four feet six of birch, the saddle slipped to one side and Matt went with it.

11

The first thing Matt hit, when he parted company with Maple Tree, was the rump of the horse who, by swerving, had sealed his fate. Rebounding, he dropped down behind the two horses and, because of the nature of the fall, wasn't able to tuck and roll, but landed heavily on his side, knocking the wind from his lungs and jarring every bone in his body. Lying helpless and vulnerable, he could do no more than close his eyes as the other runners touched down all around him, their aluminium-tipped hooves punching four-inch holes into the turf.

It was a testament to the effort that horses make to avoid riders on the ground that none of those deadly hooves scored a direct hit on Matt's sprawling figure. Amidst the ground-shaking chaos of noise and movement, something grazed his shoulder; he heard someone utter a shocked 'Christ!' and then the field was over and gone, like an express train thundering away down a track, taking urgency with it and leaving tranquillity in its wake.

As often, the whole experience was too swift even to justify relief at its passing and, as peace returned, Matt lay still, doing a mental inventory of his extremities. If they all retained sensation and movement, then the greatest horror was averted and all else could be faced and overcome.

They all did.

Matt opened his eyes to a vista of lush green, and supposed that he would have to try breathing at some point, but, just at that moment, it felt as though tight steel bands had been placed around his ribs. Footsteps swished towards him through the grass and a stout brown shoe appeared in his field of vision.

'Are you all right, sir?'

Matt nodded, but his attempt to tell the newcomer that he was merely winded came out as a hoarse whisper, so he drew in a painful half-breath and tried again.

'Just winded. Give me a moment.'

'Nasty fall, that.'

'They're never much fun,' Matt told the shoe, and, after a couple more shallow breaths, felt equal to the challenge of sitting up, aided by unseen hands.

Undoing the chinstrap on his helmet, he thanked the stout middle-aged lady who was crouching by his side; confirmed, in answer to her question, that there were no bones broken; and, with her help, presently made it to his feet.

*　　　*　　　*

The jokers in the weighing room had a field day.

'Trying out for the circus, Mojo?' one asked. 'Neat trick that. Think I saw the Cossacks do it, but, of course, they landed standing up.'

'I thought he was going to sit up behind me,' Tam Connelly reported. 'I mean, I know I had a good horse, but really a jockey should stick with the one he started on, don't you think?'

'He likes the course here so much he wants to keep getting up close and personal with it,' another voice suggested.

'No, I reckon he's got something going with one of the sheilas in the medical room,' Bully said.

'Yeah, yeah. Keep trying—you're almost funny,' Matt told them.

'So what did Westerby say?' Rollo asked, coming over. 'What excuse did he give for not having put a breast-girth on that animal? If ever a horse needed one . . .'

'I haven't seen him yet,' Matt said grimly. 'Surprisingly, he had made himself scarce when I got back, bloody man!'

'You're really not having much luck lately, are you? I saw that stuff in the paper yesterday. That was bang out of line. You should make them print a retraction.'

'Trouble is, it was basically true,' Matt said gloomily.

'You're kidding! Even the stuff about Brewer?' Rollo was astounded. 'I can't believe that! Ask anyone and they'd have said you had the most solid job in racing; especially since you took up with the governor's daughter. What's the matter with the man?'

'I have an idea it has something to do with our friend Kenning. I'm not exactly flavour of the month with him and you know what a toad-eater Brewer is when there's a title involved.'

Rollo shook his head.

'It still doesn't make sense. Brewer might be desperate for recognition, but he's not stupid. He knows damn well he was lucky to get you. Surely he wouldn't jock you off, even for Kenning?'

236

Matt shrugged. He was feeling sore and the loss of Cantablay still weighed on his mind.

'Brewer doesn't like it that I'm trying to help Jamie out. I think perhaps he's worried people will think I'm guilty by association. He says I haven't got my mind on the job, and, of course, it's sod's law that I'm having crappy luck at the moment.'

From the doorway, an official called the jockeys for the next race and Rollo had to go. Within moments, the weighing room had almost emptied, the heart of it going out with the chattering crowd of men bound for the paddock. Matt sat on the bench, half changed into his civvies, feeling drained of energy and purpose.

'I'm not surprised your saddle slipped.' It was Mikey who spoke from the other side of the room. 'I rode him a couple of times for Westerby last year and I'm sure he had a breast-girth on. You'd want one, wouldn't you, with a big front on him like that?'

Matt looked up.

'Are you sure? For Westerby?'

Mikey nodded.

'Yeah, I'm sure.'

'Right.' Matt stood up and reached for his shirt. 'I think I'm going to have a few words with Mick Westerby.'

As it happened, Matt's confrontation with the trainer had to wait, for, after asking a number of people, he was told that Westerby, with perhaps some precognition of trouble, had prudently already left the racecourse. Frustrated, Matt drew some comfort from the fact that Henfield was a two-day meeting and he knew that Westerby had a couple of runners the next day, one of them being the much vaunted Peacock Penny, whom Matt was booked to ride. Taking his leave of Leonard, who was still plainly very cut up over Cantablay's death, Matt eased himself stiffly behind the wheel of the MR2 and headed for home, thinking, as he did so, that the events of the day would have Dave Rossiter of the *Daily Standard* rubbing his hands in glee. He really wasn't looking forward to reading the sports pages the next morning.

*   *   *

Weighing out for the first of two races he was booked for the next day, it seemed to Matt as though he hadn't been away. By the time he'd got home the previous night, Kendra had gone out with Frances for the evening, leaving a curry simmering on the Aga, and, after he'd eaten, Matt had fallen asleep on the sofa in front of the TV with Taffy curled up next to him.

After coming home in the early hours, Kendra had still been in bed when he'd left for Rockfield that morning, although she had lifted her face for a sleepy kiss when he'd taken her a cup of tea. Matt got the impression that the company of her sister had done her a lot of good, and he left the house in a more positive mood than he had for several days. He felt, as long as he and Kennie were OK, he could face most things, a conviction that even survived Rossiter's best efforts in the daily sports round-up.

Now, at Henfield, it was an overcast day with a biting cold wind, and when, in due course, the jockeys were called into the paddock, he found Roy Emmett huddled in a sheepskin coat, with matching hat and gloves, and a red scarf wound about his neck. In spite of this, his eyes were watering behind his bottle-bottom glasses and his nose, which rivalled the scarf for hue, sported a glistening dewdrop. There was no sign of his partner, a tall, austere-looking man who rarely came to the races, and neither was Leonard in attendance, but Matt knew that Rockfield had two horses in the race, so the trainer was presumably with the owner of the other.

Matt approached Emmett with a degree of reserve, unsure as to whether he was one of the owners from whom Brewer claimed to have received complaints, but he needn't have worried.

When Emmett saw him, he beamed, the dewdrop wobbling dangerously as they shook hands.

'Good to see you, Matt. How are you?'

'Do you want my opinion or the one everyone read in the paper this morning?'

'Never take much notice of the newspapers, to tell you the truth. They're never happy unless they're raking up trouble. Giving you a hard time, are they? What's that about, then?'

'Oh, nothing I can't handle,' Matt said, devoutly hoping it was the truth. 'How's Coneflower today? Not getting too hot, I hope.' If Coneflower had a fault, it was a tendency to work himself into a lather before he even got onto the track, thereby wasting precious energy, but, as he was a tenacious stayer, it wasn't too big a problem.

'No, he's fine,' Emmett said. 'Shouldn't be surprised if he was growing out of that business. Here he is now.'

As he spoke, the good-looking black gelding

came into view, stalking round on his long clean-boned legs beside his handler, looking every inch the quintessential steeplechaser and, as Emmett had said, showing no sign of sweating up.

'We've got a good chance today, don't you think?' he continued, with barely a pause. 'I spoke to John a minute ago and he says he's been working well on the gallops. In fact, I went over to watch him work last week and he certainly looked the part . . .'

Matt let Emmett talk, listening with half an ear whilst he scanned the circling runners. Westerby also had a horse in this race but, so far, the trainer hadn't made an appearance in the paddock. When Matt finally identified his runner by the number he carried, he saw that the blond lad who had led Maple Tree round the day before had been replaced by a pale girl with straggling dark hair and an eyebrow ring.

The bell went for the jockeys to mount and, switching his attention back to the matter in hand, Matt accepted Emmett's good luck wishes and went towards Coneflower to meet Leonard and receive a leg-up into the saddle.

After the disasters of the day before, Matt was desperate for a good showing, and the black horse didn't let him down. He was a front runner who not only stayed the distance, but could also be relied upon to produce an extra burst of speed if challenged in the final furlong. On this occasion it wasn't necessary. By the time they rounded the bend into the home straight for the second time, Coneflower's ground-eating stride had left the other twelve runners struggling in his wake, and Matt was able to let him ease down towards the finishing post, which he crossed at not much more than a canter, six lengths clear of his nearest rival.

He rode into the winner's circle feeling triumph and relief in equal measures—perhaps his luck was on the turn at last.

*   *   *

Mick Westerby was still absent when Matt went out to ride Peacock Penny, and he was met at the entrance to the paddock by a wiry, middle-aged woman in a tired tweed suit, who introduced herself as Sue Westerby, Mick's wife, and walked with him towards the centre of the oval enclosure.

'So where's Mick today?' he asked casually.

'Called away, I'm afraid. Other business. You'll have to make do with me.' She gave him a thin smile, and Matt got the impression that, although Mick was the licensed trainer, as his assistant, his wife might well be the one who wore the trousers in the partnership.

'Oh, I'd rather hoped for a word with him.'

'About yesterday,' she stated. 'I'm not surprised. Bloody shambles! Can't apologise enough. It's been dealt with.'

It was quite remarkable, Matt reflected, that someone could utter such conciliatory words whilst not conveying the impression that they were sorry in any way, shape, or form. She obviously didn't intend to enlighten him as to *how* it had been dealt with, and he decided the girl with the eyebrow ring might be a softer target.

They were now drawing close to a serious-looking, bespectacled young man who looked painfully self-conscious standing on his own in the centre of the grass with faces crowding the rails.

'Let me introduce Kevin Rouse. His father owns Peacock Penny,' Sue Westerby said smoothly, producing the professional smile once again, and Matt realised that she had come to meet him early because she was wary of what he might say in front of the owner.

'Hello, Kevin. Nice to meet you.' Matt put his hand forward with a friendly smile. 'Do you come racing often?'

'This is my first time,' he replied, and Matt could see that, despite the suit and greatcoat, he was maybe only sixteen or seventeen. Wealthy father, buying a couple of racehorses as a status symbol, he surmised. That would explain the widely divergent abilities of the two horses he owned. Whoever had sold him Khaki Kollin had seen him coming, Matt thought sadly, but the mare, who was coming round in front of them now, had been a lucky acquisition.

'She's a fine-looking mare,' he told the lad— which wasn't strictly true, as she was a little light-framed and leggy—but Kevin was clearly pleased that Matt liked her.

Once Matt was on board Peacock Penny, Sue was obliged to drop back and watch with her owner as the stable girl led the mare once more round the paddock and off down the path to the track.

'So, where's the lad who was here yesterday?' Matt asked, as soon as he was settled into the saddle. 'Tall. Sandy hair.'

The girl glanced up at him.

'Rick Smiff?' she asked.

'Could have been. I got the impression he was

242

maybe head lad.'

'Was.'

'Sorry?'

'*Was* head lad,' she said, with emphasis.

'Oh. So what happened?'

'Got the boot, didn't he?'

'Because of what happened yesterday with Maple Tree?' Matt could see Sue watching intently as they passed and drew no little satisfaction from the fact that she would probably have given anything to shut the girl up.

'Yeah, that's right. The Governor said it was Rick's fault but . . .' She stopped, maybe belatedly remembering who she was talking to.

'But you don't think it was?' Matt prompted.

'I ain't sayin' nuffin'.'

'But you already have,' Matt pointed out reasonably. 'What were you just about to say? Come on, I won't tell on you.'

'She's watchin' me!' the girl hissed. 'I'll bloody cop it if she thinks I said anyfing!'

'So why don't you think it was Rick's fault?'

They'd turned down the path away from the paddock now and, maybe encouraged by the added distance between her and the Governor's wife, the girl gave in.

'Well, Rick's real careful, you know? All I'm sayin' is, I can't see him forgetting somefing like that.'

'Do you know where I can find Rick?' Matt enquired, as they approached the track.

'Look, you're going to get me into trouble.'

'Please, it's important.'

'What d'you want him for, then? 'Cos he's had enough grief as it is.'

'I'm not going to give him a hard time, trust me.'

'I dunno,' she said doubtfully, and Matt was left wondering whether she didn't know where Rick was to be found or whether she was undecided about whether to tell Matt.

With practised fluidity she released the lead rein and stepped away as the mare bounded forward.

Matt took up the slack in the reins, shifted his weight over Peacock Penny's withers, and put the previous day's drama out of his mind as he switched into work mode.

Less than twenty minutes later he was back, patting the little mare's sweaty neck as she slowed to a trot, having beaten a field of sixteen older and larger horses in a tight finish after one and a half circuits of the hurdles track.

The pale girl came out onto the track to meet him with a huge grin on her face, and whether it was because Matt had brought home the laurels or just because she'd had time to think, he didn't know, but, as she clipped the lead rein in place once more, she looked up and said, 'Rick's here, on the course. You'll probably find him near the bookies on the rails, but I never said that, OK?'

Matt smiled.

'OK. And thanks.'

The business of photographs, weighing in, and the presentation of the prizes all seemed to take an eternity, and, for once, Matt was glad that he had no more rides that day and was able to go in search of the unfortunate 'Rick Smiff'. Even so, that delay was made bearable by the excitement on the face of Peacock Penny's young owner and, when Rouse was borne off by the trainer's wife to further celebrate the win, Matt found himself thinking it was a shame that such a nice lad had landed in the clutches of such as the Westerbys.

Matt's progress through the crowds around the rails was hampered by a number of people wanting to congratulate him on his win. Normally, he could get by without being recognised when in everyday clothes, but, in this case, someone he knew quite well had precipitated the flurry of attention by calling his name far louder than was necessary and soon he was signing autographs left, right, and centre. Maintaining positive public relations was a part of the job he usually accepted with good grace, knowing how important it was for the advancement of his career, but today he heartily wished all the smiling faces would go and find someone else to pester; the more so because, if Rick had been anywhere nearby, he would now almost certainly have disappeared.

When the next race got underway, the crowd's attention was quickly transferred to the track, leaving Matt free to search for Westerby's ex-head lad, but this wasn't helped by the fact that he wasn't 100 per cent certain that he would even recognise the man if he did see him.

To the accompaniment of a crescendo of excited shouting, the race ran its course and people turned away from the rails, either joining the satisfied queues in front of the bookies or screwing up their betting slips in disgust. Matt began to think Rick had seen him coming, and was on the point of conceding defeat when, in one of the bookies' queues, he saw his quarry.

He waited until Rick had collected his winnings and was folding the notes into a back pocket, then stepped forward and spoke his name.

245

Rick glanced round enquiringly but, when he realised who had spoken, the expression turned to one of dismay. He put his hands up as if to ward Matt off and said, 'Look, I don't want any trouble. I'm sorry, OK? It was a stupid mistake.'

'But whose mistake was it? Yours or Westerby's?'

Rick's grey eyes narrowed and he cast a wary look to either side, as if checking that Matt was alone.

'What do you mean?'

'I mean that it's a pretty sizeable mistake to make, and, call me suspicious, but it seems strange that neither of you noticed that Maple Tree wasn't wearing his breast-girth. Who tacked him up?'

'Er . . . me. I did.'

'On your own?'

'Well, the Governor was pretty busy . . .' Rick's voice faded away uncertainly.

'Yeah, it doesn't sound very likely, does it?' Matt remarked. 'What could be more important on a race day than the horses? Why don't you tell me what really happened?'

Rick looked round again with a touch of desperation and, for a split second, Matt thought he was going to run.

'Please, Rick—I don't want to make trouble for you, I promise you. I just want to know what actually happened. Westerby saddled the horse, didn't he?'

'No, it was me.'

'I don't believe you. I think Westerby did it, and now he's blaming you. But what I don't understand is why you're letting him.'

Rick sighed and looked skyward, his face contorted by indecision, but finally, it seemed, honesty won out.

'I *was* there.'

'But it was Westerby who saddled the horse, yes?'

'Yes.'

'So he left off the breast-girth, and I'm guessing it wasn't an accident,' Matt said, taking care not to show the surge of triumph he felt. 'You must have noticed. Didn't you say something?'

'Yeah, I did . . .'

'So, what reason did he give?'

'He said . . .' Rick hesitated. 'Do you want to know exactly?'

'Yes, please.'

'Um—he said, "We're gonna give that arrogant bastard the ride of his life!" I wasn't happy about it, but what could I do? He's the Guv'nor. Was,' he corrected.

You could have reported him to the stewards or—at the very least—warned me, Matt thought, but, realistically, he wouldn't have expected it; the backlash would have been huge. He remembered the head lad's unhappy face as he led Maple Tree round before the race.

'We? Are you're sure he said *we*?'

Rick nodded.

'Yeah, 'cos I remember thinking—Count me out, psycho! I don't want no part of this. I knew how dangerous it could be, see?'

'What I don't understand is why you were still prepared to tell lies to protect Westerby, when he sacked you and left you to carry the can?'

Rick looked at his shoes, his sandy fringe flopping over his eyes.

'I got a police record, see?' he mumbled. 'Nicked

247

a couple of cars when I was a nipper. The Guv'nor said, if I told anyone about the girth, he'd put it about that he caught me stealing. So then no one would believe me and I'd never get another job neither, would I?'

'OK, then, if he knew you wouldn't blow the whistle, why did he sack you?'

'Well, to keep you off his back,' Rick replied. 'When he saw you get straight up from that fall, he got in his car and went home. You couldn't see him for dust.'

'Smart move,' Matt said.

He looked at Rick thoughtfully and then decided to back another hunch.

'Does Westerby have any connections with Lord Kenning? I mean, has he ever been to the yard or have you seen them talking recently?'

Rick pursed his lips and shook his head.

Matt wasn't overly surprised. It had been a long shot but, even so, he had to admit to a faint twinge of disappointment; it would have explained a lot.

'OK, never mind . . .' he started to say, but Rick interrupted him.

'Now you say that—I never saw him, but the Guv'nor did say something, a couple of days ago . . . He was looking right pleased with himself, and he told me, if I ever saw Lord Kenning on the racecourse, I should mind my Ps and Qs, 'cos, if we played our cards right, Kenning might be sending us some horses—to train, I mean.'

'Did he now?' Matt breathed, hardly able to believe his good luck.

'That's what the Guv'nor said, but I thought he was barking! I mean, Kenning was never going to send us anyfing in a million years, was he? But the

Guv seemed to believe it anyway. 'E was like the cat that got the sodding cream.'

'Did you win much?'

Rick was momentarily caught off guard.

'Sorry?'

'The last race—did you get a good price?'

'Not bad, I s'pose.' He patted the pocket where he'd put the notes. 'I had some on Peacock Penny, too. She's a smashing filly.'

'She is that,' Matt agreed. 'Look, I'm not going to offer you any money here—there are too many eyes, and it could get us both into trouble, but, if you get stuck anytime, give me a shout, OK?'

Rick looked taken aback.

'OK,' he said slowly. 'But I'm not telling anyone else what I told you. Especially not the police.'

Rick's expression clearly showed his opinion of the police and Matt sympathised with him. Bartholomew hadn't come over as a people-person in his dealings with Matt; with someone who already had a record, he imagined he'd be ten times worse.

'No police,' he agreed.

'So, what are you going to do now?' Rick asked. 'Are you going after Westerby?'

'I'm not sure. Not right away, anyway.'

'But you won't tell him what I said . . .'

'I won't tell him,' Matt promised. 'But where can I find you again—if I need to?'

'My mate runs a pub, just down the road from here—The Blue Lion. He'll always get a message to me.'

Pleased as he was with the information Rick had given him, Matt was under no illusions about whether it would prove easy to make use of. If it came down to the word of an ex-employee with a criminal record, against that of his former employer and a much-respected peer of the realm, it didn't take a Mensa candidate to figure out where the authorities would choose to place their belief. Even so, Matt hugged the tale of Kenning's possible involvement in Westerby's sabotage to him like a hot-water bottle on a cold night. At some stage, he felt sure, he would be able to turn the knowledge against them.

*　　　*　　　*

Matt left Henfield fairly content with his day's work. True, he had only ridden twice, but he had won twice, which should have given the doubters something to chew over.

Although he would rather have been racing, one advantage of finishing early was that he arrived back at the cottage before it was completely dark, with the pleasant expectation of a long, lazy evening with Kendra, a log fire, and a bottle of wine. To this end, when he stopped for petrol, he equipped himself with a large bunch of mixed flowers, smiling inwardly as he pictured her delight.

The house was in darkness when he drove into the yard, except for a faint glow that suggested a light on in one of the back rooms upstairs. Surprised, and hoping Kendra hadn't made plans for another evening out, Matt turned his key in the front door, but it wouldn't open—apparently bolted on the inside. He rapped on it with the horseshoe-shaped knocker, which set the dogs barking furiously, but no one came to open the door.

Deeply puzzled, Matt went round the back of the cottage and let himself in, switching the light on and fending off the excited attentions of Sky and The Boys. Fitting bolts to the new back door was one of the next jobs on his never-ending list, but, thankfully, he hadn't got round to it as yet.

Kendra wasn't in the kitchen, and he laid the flowers on the table, feeling even more bewildered. Remembering the light he'd seen upstairs, Matt went up, wondering if perhaps she was unwell and had gone to lie down with Taffy for company.

'Kendra?'

He paused at the turn of the stairs to listen for an answer, but there was none, only a faint clicking of claws, which heralded Taffy's approach over the uncarpeted floor. As Matt reached the landing, the sheltie appeared in the doorway of the master bedroom, and, when she turned and went back, he was hot on her heels.

He stopped just over the threshold. The light was on, but Kendra wasn't there.

Taffy was now standing in front of the door to the en suite bathroom.

'Is she in there?' he asked the dog, who glanced back at Matt before returning her attention solemnly to the door, as if by sheer patience she would eventually be rewarded by its opening. She looked as though she was prepared to stand there all night.

Matt went across and knocked lightly on the stripped wooden panel. Painting was one of many jobs waiting to be done.

'Kendra? Are you in there?' He leaned close, but

couldn't hear anything, and his heart began to thud with apprehension.

'Kendra! Are you all right?' Thanking providence that the lock had been removed for redecorating, Matt let himself in, following a close second to Taffy, who wasn't about to concede precedence to anyone.

At first it seemed as though the bathroom, too, was empty, but Taffy knew where she was going and, looking across, Matt could see a dark shadow, low down behind the semi-obscure door of the new shower cubicle.

'Kendra?'

Within moments, Matt had followed, sliding the door back, panic ballooning. And there, huddled—fully clothed—against the tiled back wall, was Kendra, her arms hugging her knees and her head bowed so that her face was hidden behind a curtain of blonde hair.

While Matt paused, his mind racing through the possible reasons for her hiding there, Taffy—ever practical—hopped over the lip of the shower basin and approached her mistress, pushing her nose under Kendra's arm to force her way into her embrace.

'Kendra—sweetheart, what's the matter? What's going on?' Matt's first thought was that something had happened to the baby.

At the sound of his voice, Kendra raised her head as if hearing it for the first time, and the expression on her face jolted him like a physical shock. Her eyes were huge, haunted, terrified, and she had clearly been crying.

'Oh my God, Kennie—what's wrong? What's happened?' He stepped into the cubicle, reached

252

down to her, and drew her to her feet, where she stood, leaning weakly against him, clutching the sheltie under one arm. Matt could feel her trembling and his own heart thudding.

'Talk to me,' he urged gently. 'What's the matter?'

'He said he was coming to get me,' she sobbed into the fleece collar of his jacket. 'I've been so frightened.'

'Who did?'

'I don't know—a man, on the phone. He said he knew where I lived and he was coming to get me.'

Matt was horrified.

'When? When did this happen?'

'This afternoon, when I got back from helping Mum. I didn't know what to do . . .'

'Did you call the police?'

'Yes, of course! At least I tried to, but the phone was dead.' She looked up at Matt through tear-filled eyes. 'That's when I knew they must be close—if they'd cut the phone line—so I thought I'd try and get to Dad's, but . . .' Her voice caught and she stopped and sniffed. 'I grabbed Taffy and made a run for the car, but it wouldn't start. It was like a nightmare!'

Matt kissed her forehead.

'You poor love! It's all right—you're safe now.' He rubbed her back. 'So you came in and locked the doors?'

'I didn't know what else to do . . .'

'Why didn't you use your mobile?'

'I couldn't find it. I must have left it at Mum's. And I kept thinking, if only Jamie was still here. Why did it have to happen today, when he's just gone?' She paused. 'Oh God! You don't think they knew that? That they've been watching and waiting until I was alone?'

'I don't know,' Matt said. 'I shouldn't think so.' Although it was what he'd been thinking himself, he didn't think it would help to say so. 'Did this man say anything else? I mean, did he say *why* he was coming?'

Almost imperceptibly, he felt Kendra stiffen.

'Yes.' She pulled back slightly. 'He said because of you. He said you'd ignored the warning. He said he didn't want to hurt me, but you hadn't left him any choice.'

'Oh God, I'm sorry, love.' It seemed woefully inadequate, but he didn't know what else to say. His mind was racing. Had this been one of the men from Saturday night, then? From what they had said, those two had been hired muscle, so perhaps, instead, this had been the man who had done the hiring, shifting from physical intimidation to emotional?

'But you'll stop now, won't you? This thing with Jamie and Sophie—you'll leave it to the police. Won't you, Matt? Please?'

When he didn't immediately answer, she twisted her neck to look up at him.

'Matt? Please ... ? I can't go through another day like today. It's gone way too far.'

'You're right. Come on, let's get you out of here. Let's go downstairs and I'll make you a cup of tea. You're safe now, anyway.'

Taffy had begun to wriggle, so Kendra lowered her to the floor, then, with Matt's arm round her shoulders, they went down, to be met at the bottom of the stairs by the other dogs, milling around with furiously wagging tails.

'Sky wouldn't have let anyone in, would you, lass?' Matt said, ruffling the German shepherd's thick fur.

Kendra sat at the table, clutching a handkerchief and still noticeably trembling, her face pale and tear-stained in the bright lights of the kitchen. 'I know she'd have barked, but I kept thinking, what if they had a knife? Or poison for the dogs? If they know all about us, they'd know about the dogs.'

Matt filled the kettle at the sink.

'To be honest, I don't suppose they ever intended coming in. I should think they just wanted to frighten you—to get at me.'

'Oh, so I'm overreacting, am I?' Kendra flared up. 'Making a fuss about nothing.'

'No—of course not! I didn't mean that, at all. I know how frightening it must have been. I was trying to comfort you.' Matt had a horrible feeling he was on a hiding to nothing.

'What, by making me feel like a pathetic female who's blown the whole thing out of proportion? Or was it to try and ease your conscience because you know bloody well it's all your fault in the first place? Because it is, you know. If you'd dropped this stupid private-eye thing when I asked you, none of this would have happened, and your career wouldn't be on the rocks. But—oh no! You had to play the hero! Well, I've had enough. I don't want to do this anymore.'

Matt left the kettle and went to crouch beside her, taking one of her hands in his.

'Of course I don't think you're pathetic. And I'm more sorry than I can say. If I'd had any idea it would come to this, I'd never have started it, I promise you.'

255

'So you'll give it up?'

'I would, but I'm not sure that'll help . . .'

'You *would*?' she repeated incredulously, snatching her hand away. 'You mean you're not going to? Even after what happened today?'

'Please Kennie, just listen. The thing is, I haven't really been doing anything anyway—not since that business on Saturday—but that hasn't made any difference, has it? They didn't wait to see if their warning had worked, so what's to say they'll stop now?' Done nothing, he thought guiltily, except speak to Bartholomew about Lord Kenning—but surely *he* wasn't behind this . . .

'*You* haven't done anything, maybe, but what about that Casey girl? They know she's helping you—what if she's been poking around?'

It was possible, Matt supposed, but she hadn't been in touch. He hoped she was all right. What if she was next in line for a dose of intimidation? What if she lived alone?

'Perhaps I'd better give her a ring,' he mused aloud. 'Check she's OK . . .'

'Oh, that'd be right!' Kendra jumped to her feet, upsetting the dogs, who all stood up with her in anticipation of an outing. 'Look after Casey, don't worry about your fiancée! Maybe Grace was right; she said it sounded like you were seeing a lot of her. Asked me if she was pretty.'

'Oh, for God's sake! You know your sister's got a vicious tongue! Since when did you take any notice of what she thinks?'

'So tell me why Casey's suddenly had a makeover—hair, clothes, the lot?' Kendra watched Matt's face for a long moment and then gave a short, bitter laugh. 'Oh my God! Are you going to try and tell me you hadn't noticed? *Come on!*'

Matt shook his head, vaguely remembering that something had struck him as different about the girl.

'I had other things on my mind on Saturday. Look, how did we get onto the subject of Casey, anyway?'

'You were going to ring her,' he was reminded tartly. 'Will that be before or after you drive me over to Dad's?'

'Tonight?' Matt queried.

'*Yes* tonight. Now,' she added, tears running freely once more. 'I love this house, but I don't want to be here alone anymore. I don't ever want to be that scared again.'

'And you won't be,' he stated. 'But stay here with me tonight and I'll take you first thing in the morning . . .'

She shook her head.

'Now. Please?'

'What about the police? We could use my mobile . . .'

'And spend all evening at the police station? No, thank you!'

'They might come here.'

'I just want to go home.'

The words cut deeply.

'I thought this *was* your home,' Matt said quietly.

'Home is somewhere you feel safe,' she retorted, her face pink.

With an effort, Matt checked his own instinctive response; nothing would be gained by a war of words. He sighed.

'All right. What about your tea?' He gestured at the waiting mugs and teabags. Anything to keep her there a little longer, to give her time to calm down, to maybe change her mind.

'No, leave it. I'll have some at Dad's,' she said, heading towards the stairs. 'I'll just grab some things.'

*　　　*　　　*

By the time Matt let himself back into the cottage later that evening, the pleasure he'd felt at the day's successes seemed a lifetime away. Even the dogs were subdued, looking past him into the darkness, as if waiting for Kendra and Taffy to appear.

They had spoken little on the journey to Birchwood Hall, Matt's efforts at conversation meeting with monosyllabic responses. They had never had such a serious row before and he was at a loss as to know how best to bring her round.

Using Matt's mobile to phone ahead, Kendra was met on the doorstep by her mother, who took the overnight bag from Matt with a commiserating half-smile and gathered her tearful daughter in, rather like a hen taking a chick under its wing. Taffy trotted in at their heels without a backward glance.

Left staring at the half-open front door, Matt kicked his heels for a minute or so and then pulled the door shut and turned away. Kendra's last words had been to suggest that he'd want to get back to feed the dogs. The implication was clear— for now, at least, he wasn't wanted.

At Spinney Cottage he shut the front door against a chilly wind and wandered into the kitchen, dropping his keys on the work surface and flicking the switch on the kettle. The two waiting mugs seemed to mock him and he put one away. On the wall, a pulsing red light on the telephone answering machine indicated messages left, and, while he waited for the water to boil, he listened to them.

There were four: the first from Josh Harper, who said he'd catch Matt later. One, incredibly, was from the telephone company—who he'd called before setting out. Then, they had told him that an engineer would call within the next two days, but their message said that the connection had been restored and they were testing the line. Next, Casey's Irish accent announced that she'd found out that the white van was owned by one Steve Bryan, who lived in Yeovil, but the usefulness of this information was limited by the fact that it had been reported stolen the evening Matt was attacked. The last message, left only ten minutes before Matt had got in, was from John Leonard and, instantly, something in his voice made Matt pause, teaspoon in hand, and look at the phone.

'Matt . . . er, well done today. Look, I'm sorry to have to do this to you, but the Guv'nor wants Ray on his first string for the rest of the week. There's Mr Monkey for you tomorrow, and those two novices of Emmett's on Saturday, but not a lot else, I'm afraid. I tried to reason with him, but . . . Well, you know what he's like . . . Sorry, Matt.' There was a short silence, where a sound like the rustling of papers could be heard, and then the click of the receiver being replaced. The machine told him that he'd reached the end of his messages, and invited him to listen to them again, but he reached out a hand to switch it off.

259

How the hell could Brewer justify jocking him off on the grounds of poor performance, just a few hours after he'd won two decent races? Matt picked up the handset, intending to ring Kendra's father, but stopped the call before it was answered. Even in his bitterly angry state, he recognised that now was probably not a propitious time to have what would almost certainly develop into a flaming row with the man. The thought of ringing Leonard was dismissed almost as quickly. He really couldn't blame the trainer for knuckling under to Brewer, who was, to all intents and purposes, his boss. Ruining his own working relations wouldn't do anything to help Matt. Seething, Matt hooked the phone back in its cradle and slammed the heel of his palm into the wall beside it.

Taking a deep breath to calm himself, he considered his next move. Kendra had said the man had phoned to threaten her, so the first thing to do was check caller display, just in case he'd slipped up and not withheld his number.

It was a slim chance and Matt wasn't surprised to find, among the numbers he recognised, one instance of a number not being left.

Scooping the teabag out of his mug, he stirred in milk and sat at the table, reluctantly coming to the decision that, whether Kendra liked it or not, Bartholomew must be called. He recognised, too, that, in doing so, the details of his own recent attack would inevitably be dragged out into the open and his knuckles be severely rapped for not reporting it at the time.

Hoping that Bartholomew would be off duty, Matt reached for the phone.

12

Shutting the door, rather more forcefully than was polite, on the DI's departing form, Matt put up a hand to rub his eyes and forehead, feeling—all at once—desperately tired.

Guessing that Bartholomew was almost certainly hotfooting it to Birchwood Hall, he felt it only fair to warn Kendra but, as luck would have it, it was Grace who picked up the phone.

'I'm afraid she doesn't want to speak to you,' she said, when Matt asked for Kendra. 'She's in a bit of a state. You really ought to take better care of her, especially in her delicate condition.'

So she'd told them her news, had she? Matt thought, with a touch of disappointment. What had happened to the big announcement they were going to make in a couple of weeks' time?

'Just put her on please, Grace. It's important.'

'Sorry. No can do,' she replied airily, clearly enjoying the moment. 'She's been crying her eyes out and now she's gone to bed. Boy, has your halo slipped, buster!'

'Well, she might want to get up again,' Matt informed her, keeping a check on his temper. 'I'm pretty sure DI Bartholomew is on his way to speak to her.'

There came the hiss of dramatically indrawn breath and Grace said, 'Oh dear, that won't please her. She told Daddy she didn't want to talk to the police. She's going to be seriously unhappy with you!'

'Just let her know, OK?' He itched to give Grace

a blistering set-down, but the knowledge that she would gain much satisfaction from knowing she had got to him kept him quiet.

He put the receiver down and stood staring gloomily at the wall. He supposed he'd better warn Casey, too, because Bartholomew now knew she had been a witness to the attack at Maiden Newton. As Casey had drawn a virtual blank with the registration number, Matt had left that particular detail out of his tale—partly to avoid getting the young reporter into trouble and partly because he suspected the knowledge would only add fuel to Bartholomew's anger at being kept in the dark. His remarks had been scathing enough as it was.

'My job would be a whole lot easier if I didn't have people like you making their own judgements about whether incidents are worth reporting or not! Haven't you ever heard of forensic science, Mr Shepherd?'

'Of course I have.'

'Well, if you knew a little more about it, it might have occurred to you that, by reporting your little fracas, you'd have given us the chance to possibly lift fibres off yourself or your clothes, which we could have compared with those taken from Sophie Bradford's clothing. If there's any chance that the men who attacked you had anything to do with her death, that could well have clinched it.'

'I'm sorry, I didn't think of that ...' Matt was genuinely contrite.

'Which is why I'm doing my job and you should stick to doing yours,' had been the acid reply. 'That kind of evidence can be invaluable. I suppose it's too much to hope that you haven't washed the clothes you were wearing?'

'Um . . . They were pretty dirty.'

Bartholomew tutted and shook his head. 'As I told you before—stay out of it!'

'Well, if I had, those guys wouldn't have come after me anyway, so you still wouldn't have got your evidence,' Matt had pointed out, the undeniable logic of which hadn't visibly improved the detective's mood.

Kendra's car had been trailered away, the forensic officer reporting that the reason for its not starting was that the battery had been disconnected. This information had brought with it the chilling realisation that the unknown caller had indeed been close and Kendra's fears completely justified. Matt remembered his own comments with a surge of guilt.

Now, a glance at the kitchen clock told him that, if he was going to get up to ride work the next morning, it was high time he went to bed, so he gave the dogs their supper, locked up, and headed for the shower.

In the bathroom, however, the sight of the white tiled cubicle brought the events of the evening sharply into focus, and, as he stood letting the hot water course over his body, he was tormented by the mental image of Kendra as he had found her— cowering, terrified in the corner.

The picture conjured up a mix of emotions in Matt: white-hot fury at the bastard who had caused her distress; frustration with his own inability to protect her; and—running through it all—a kind of dazed bewilderment at the speed with which his life seemed to be disintegrating around him.

263

Three weeks ago his most pressing concern had been how to keep up with the escalating demand for his services as a jockey in the coming season; now, that flood of demand had ebbed to a trickle, he'd been beaten up, threatened, had got on the wrong side of the police and the racing authorities, and his personal life was in crisis.

Oh God—Kendra . . .

The rest he could deal with, but the thought that he'd let Kendra down—that she'd felt the need to run to her family for comfort and reassurance— was something that seared through his mind like a physical pain. If only he could have seen it coming, he would have . . .

Here his self-chastisement ground to a halt. Just what would he have done? Abandoned Jamie to his fate? It wasn't in his nature to turn his back on a friend who so plainly needed him, but, on the other hand, had he really helped Jamie at all? He hadn't been able to stop the Irishman's career from going down the pan, and, as far as he knew, Jamie was still the prime suspect for the murder of Sophie Bradford.

Whichever way he looked at it, his actions—well meant though they undoubtedly had been—had achieved nothing of value, and the repercussions looked set to leave his life in tatters.

Out of the shower and wrapped in his bathrobe, the idea of an empty bed held no allure whatsoever, and Matt trudged back downstairs, to the delight of the three dogs who had settled down for the night. He found himself looking round for the fourth and swore under his breath; he was even missing Taffy, so much a part of his life had she become.

Out of habit, he filled the kettle and switched it on, then, moments later, switched it off again. His current mindset wasn't going to be remedied by a mug of tea or coffee. Somewhere, he knew, there was a bottle of whisky, given to him by a grateful owner at the Cheltenham Festival. Neither he nor Kendra drank spirits, as a rule, but he remembered having it in his coffee the evening he was attacked, and just now the enticing warmth and haziness it promised sent him hunting through the kitchen cupboards, banging doors and swearing when he couldn't immediately find it.

The bottle of Famous Grouse was finally run to ground in a cupboard in the sitting room and, retrieving a tumbler from the draining rack in the kitchen, Matt poured himself a generous measure, took a gulp and then, shadowed by the dogs and still carrying the bottle, went back and threw himself down on the sofa.

As the first mouthful of liquid burned a comforting trail down his throat and into the very core of his body, he took another, closed his eyes, and leaned back against the cushions, rolling the unfamiliar taste round his tongue.

A moment later, hearing a whine, he opened his eyes. Sky, the German shepherd, was sitting close, her head tilted to one side, watching him.

'What are you—my conscience?' he demanded. 'Go and lie down. I know what I'm doing.'

Sky flattened her ears uncertainly, but didn't move.

'What? I'm all right. Go and lie down!'

The dog obeyed the second part of the command, but not the first, curling up at the side of the sofa with her chin resting on the edge of the cushion.

Matt took a third mouthful and closed his eyes again, but he could still feel Sky's gaze upon him, making him feel unreasonably guilty. Why the hell shouldn't he get drunk? Didn't he have every excuse? Jamie had gone out on a bender, hadn't he?

Yeah, and what good had it done him? his logical self argued. Landed him in more grief, in fact. And who had it been who'd pointed out the error of his ways? Did that make Matt the sort of person he'd always despised? One of those who could dish out advice but not live by it themselves?

Stubbornly, he took another gulp, wishing he liked the spirit better. He craved oblivion. What was the point of thinking, when his thoughts just went round in circles and fetched up at the realisation that he'd made a total balls-up of everything and Kendra had left him?

Left him?

The idea caused a stab of panic. *Had* she left him? He didn't know. With his career on the skids, what could he offer her? Charlie had never really thought Matt good enough for his daughter. In her father's house, would she come under pressure to make the split permanent? Surely not, with a baby on the way . . .

Ignoring Sky's worried brown eyes, Matt drained the glass and refilled it.

*　　　*　　　*

Matt awoke stiff and cold, with a thumping headache. Opening his eyes, he couldn't, at first, make sense of the pattern of black and white stripes that crossed his field of vision, but they presently resolved themselves into the black beams on the sitting-room ceiling. He was still on the couch, still cradling the bottle of Famous Grouse, and an exploratory hand found the soft fur of the German shepherd, who had apparently not left his side.

With a groan, he sat up. On the sofa beside him the tumbler lay empty, a stain on the upholstery showing where it had overturned, and the discovery that the bottle remained four-fifths full meant he couldn't blame an excess of alcohol for his sore head. The mundane truth was that the intention to drown his grievances had been defeated by plain old-fashioned fatigue.

'Oh, God—look at me! Can't even get drunk properly,' Matt told the dog, in disgust. Sky stood up and wagged her tail happily.

The room was in that kind of half-light that results from drawn curtains in the daytime, the two shaded wall lights adding their golden pools to the total, and a glance at his watch showed that it was nearly half past eight. He'd missed riding work, then, even if he'd been expected, which—after Leonard's message—he doubted.

Standing the bottle on the coffee table, Matt got to his feet, stretching the kinks out of his muscles. Trying to keep his mind in neutral, he switched the lights off and drew the curtains back, then went into the kitchen to put the kettle on and feed the dogs, before heading upstairs for another shower.

While he was trying to summon up the enthusiasm to get something to eat, Leonard rang, wanting to know if he was all right to ride Mr Monkey that afternoon.

267

'I tried to ring earlier, but the line was busy . . .'

'It was off the hook,' Matt said, without apology.

'Er . . . I gather you and Kendra had a bit of bother yesterday,' Leonard ventured cautiously. 'The Guv said something about it. Everything OK?'

'I'll be there,' Matt said.

'Good, good . . .' Leonard hesitated. 'Look, Matt, I'm really sorry . . .'

'Yeah, well.' He well understood the trainer's predicament, but still couldn't find it within him to utter the words of forgiveness Leonard wanted to hear. Give it a day or two, maybe. 'See you later,' he said, and put the phone down.

Almost immediately, it began to ring again.

'Matt?' It was Casey.

With a rush of guilt, he realised that he'd never got round to ringing her the night before.

'Hi. Has Bartholomew been onto you?'

'No.' She sounded surprised. 'Why?'

Briefly, Matt explained.

'I meant to warn you not to mention the numberplate,' he finished. 'In case you got your contact in trouble.'

'Well, actually, it's the numberplate I'm ringing about. I've done a little digging on our Mr Bryan, and guess what?'

'Hang on, you've lost me already. Am I supposed to know who Mr Bryan is?'

'Steve Bryan,' Casey enunciated, with exaggerated care—as to one deficient in understanding. 'The man who owns the van, remember?'

'Oh, yeah. But you said it was reported stolen.'

'It was, but I've been thinking about that; I

268

mean, what's to stop him using it to set up the ambush on you and then dumping it somewhere and reporting it stolen. I told you it wasn't reported until later that evening, didn't I? But, anyway, the really interesting thing about Steve Bryan is that, until a year or two ago, he was in the army—and so was his brother! And guess who has army connections . . .'

'Who?' Matt's brain was lagging behind somewhat.

'Kenning, of course! Don't you remember? Father was a brigadier.'

'Yeah, but just because the morons that jumped me were wearing combat gear doesn't mean they were necessarily ex-army,' Matt contested. 'You can buy that stuff anywhere.'

'I *know* that. But it seems a bit of a coincidence, don't you think? And they had all the moves. I mean, if you were out to hire muscle, army types would be the obvious choice, wouldn't they?'

Matt supposed she was right.

'OK,' he allowed. 'So, what do you propose we do about it? We'll have to tell Bartholomew now.'

'Well, I've got Bryan's address. We could always go see if we can get a look at him. See if you recognise him.'

'Oh, no!' Matt said, without a moment's hesitation. 'I'm not going anywhere near Mr Bryan or his brother—and neither are you! Look, Bartholomew is certain to catch up with you today sometime—I think you should give him the registration number and let him draw his own conclusions. Let him think you haven't got anywhere with it. In fact, I should just give him the partial plate you got on Saturday and tell him I knew nothing about it. That way, *you* won't get into so much trouble for not reporting it straight away and *I* won't get into trouble for not telling him last night.'

'That seems a bit tame,' Casey complained. 'I thought you'd want to see it through yourself.'

'Well, I don't. All I ever wanted was to get the heat off Jamie—it was you who built it all up with that rubbish about the jockey turned sleuth, and look where it's got me. And don't go thinking you'll do this on your own, because, if it was this Bryan character who threatened Kendra yesterday, he probably wouldn't think twice about tracking you down too, and being a girl isn't going to save you.'

'He doesn't know who I am.'

'It wouldn't take an Einstein to work it out,' Matt told her, dryly. 'No, turn it over to Bartholomew and let him deal with it. Perhaps then I can start to concentrate on putting my life back together.'

*   *   *

In spite of adjuring Casey to leave the matter to the professionals, Matt found he couldn't stop himself turning the new information over in his mind as he drove to the racecourse later in the day.

The murder of Sophie Bradford had seemed, on the face of it, to be an unpremeditated attack—a spur of the moment thing. Somehow it didn't tally with the kind of organised retaliation of which he'd been on the receiving end. Was there more to it than met the eye? Or had the murder been committed in a flash of drunken temper by

270

someone who, now he'd sobered up, was mounting a careful cover-up operation?

If that was the case, he'd jumped the gun, because, as far as Matt was aware, he'd been nowhere near discovering the murderer's identity, and, in hiring muscle to scare Matt off, the man had potentially increased his own risk of being found.

Ex-army. Even though he'd debated its relevance with Casey, he couldn't stop his thoughts from returning to the fact, over and over again. It was quite possible that Kenning would still have contacts in the forces—in fact, hadn't Casey said something about his involvement in a charity for ex-servicemen? Could he really be behind all this? Matt's mind began to race. He returned to the idea he'd fleetingly considered, that Sophie had been blackmailing the peer in some way. From what he knew of her, it certainly wasn't beyond the bounds of possibility. Kenning hadn't been at the party, but then, if he *had* wanted her out of the way, it was difficult to imagine him dirtying his own hands . . .

But would he really employ someone else to kill for him? Matt found it hard to believe. Surely that would just lay him open to yet more serious blackmail.

Well, then, maybe murder hadn't been intended. What if the attack on Sophie had been intended as a frightener—along the lines of what Matt had been subjected to—but had got out of hand?

'For God's sake, Shepherd!'

Absorbed in the possibilities, Matt had almost collided with the object of his thoughts in the doorway of The Scales. He glanced up and, with a muttered apology, stepped aside.

'Mind still not on the job?' the peer queried, tutting his disapproval.

To retain at least some hope of salvaging his career, Matt stifled the urge to plant a fist in Kenning's aristocratic face and went on into the weighing room, where he found that the tale of his demotion had preceded him. It was not hard to see why—some five pegs down from his, Ray Landon stood, tucking the shirt-tails of Brewer's distinctive colours into the waistband of his breeches. He glanced in Matt's direction and then looked away, clearly feeling the awkwardness of his situation.

Returning the greetings of a couple of his closest colleagues, Matt dumped his kitbag on the bench and, taking a physical and mental deep breath, went over to Landon and laid a hand on his shoulder.

'All right, mate? You want to watch Trestle Table in the second. If you let him get too close to the wings, he'll sometimes duck out on you. Did it to me the first time I rode him.'

Landon turned a wary face in Matt's direction and the noise level in the changing room dropped a decibel or two as those nearest strained to hear what was said.

'Thanks,' Landon said, after a moment. 'Look—I know you must feel like—'

'Forget it,' Matt cut in, shortly. 'If it wasn't you, it'd be someone else. Just don't get too comfortable in my shoes, OK?'

With a final slap on the other jockey's shoulder, he turned back to his own peg to get changed for Mr Monkey.

'That was nice,' a voice said softly in his ear, and

Matt found Rollo beside him.

He shrugged.

'No sense in getting mad at him. Someone has to ride the horses.'

'Even so . . .' Rollo hesitated. 'Look, there's a rumour going round that you and Kendra are having a spot of bother—is everything all right?'

'Bloody hell!' Matt exclaimed, explosively. 'Who told you that?'

'I overheard some of the lads talking about it. Don't know where they heard. She hasn't really left you, has she? You two always seemed so tight.'

'No, she hasn't.' Matt gave Rollo the gist of what had happened. 'We thought it was safer if she stayed at her father's until this thing's sorted out, that's all,' he finished, praying that it was true. 'And I'd be obliged if you'd put the guys straight if there's anymore talk. Just as if it was any of their bloody business in the first place.'

'Hey, look—most of them are on your side, Matt. They think what Brewer's doing sucks. I wouldn't be surprised if you had a case against him—I mean, you've done nothing wrong. Why don't you get onto the JAGB?'

Matt pulled a face. The Jockey's Association was the closest thing they had to a union, and a great place to turn to in trouble, but, just at the moment, he was keen to keep his dispute with Kendra's father as low-key as possible.

'Excuse me—Matt?' Jim Steady, the valet, interrupted his thoughts. 'Mr McKenzie would like a word, when you have a moment.'

'Right-oh, thanks.'

Matt found Doogie McKenzie waiting just outside the building, his cloud of white hair

273

billowing in the stiff breeze. It seemed he too had heard of the growing rift between Matt and Charlie Brewer, and, although he expressed what Matt felt sure was genuine sympathy for his former protégé, it appeared it had come at a providential time for Doogie. Apparently his own regular jockey had broken his wrist in an accident on the gallops the day before, leaving Doogie in the lurch.

'Tried to ring you yesterday, but I couldn't get through,' he told Matt. 'But your agent said you'd be here, and would most likely be grateful for the rides, so I took a chance and left it. Can you help me out?'

'My pleasure,' Matt told him truthfully. And what better way to show Brewer that, in cutting his stable jockey loose, he was hurting no one but himself?

'They're not world-beaters, but neither are they without a chance,' Doogie said. 'Sage Counsel tends to give up when he's passed, but he's wearing blinkers today, so we'll see if that helps, and Delta Tango is a real honest stayer.'

'Delta Tango? Owner got army connections?' Matt queried, and then a thought struck him. 'Not another of Kenning's, is it?'

'Now, would I do that to you?' Doogie demanded reproachfully, bushy brows drawing down over his sharp blue eyes.

'Sorry. I've just had my fill of nasty surprises lately.'

'Actually the horse *is* owned by a retired army captain and his wife. You'll no doubt meet them later. Ex-SAS, I believe—but nothing to do with your friend Kenning.'

'SAS?' Matt frowned, wondering why that had

set a bell tinkling somewhere in the recesses of his mind.

'That's right,' Doogie confirmed. 'I tried out for the SAS once—did I ever tell you?'

'Many times,' Matt said dryly. It was one of the Scot's favourite drinking tales, and the ordeal he claimed to have endured grew more impossibly arduous with every telling.

'OK, well, I'll let you get on, lad. And thanks for stepping in. I never thought Charlie Brewer would be such a complete pillock, but he's done me a favour, so I'm not about to complain!'

With a wave of his hand, Matt went back to weigh out for his ride on Mr Monkey, feeling that at least something was working in his favour that day, even if at the cost of some other poor soul.

In the paddock he found Harry deputising for his father, who was on the other side of the central lawn, supervising Landon's debut as Rockfield's first jockey.

Matt wasn't sorry. He couldn't really justify the resentment he felt towards John Leonard, but, on the other hand, he wasn't ready to face him with a smile. For now, it was easier not to deal with him at all.

'The owner not here?'

'No, not today.' Harry greeted him with a rueful look. 'S'pect you're feeling like shit, aren't you?' he observed, in his disarmingly open way. 'If it's any consolation, the old man's not happy, either, but his hands are pretty much tied, you know. Brewer's got him over a barrel.'

Matt sighed.

'Yeah, I know. I'll have a word, later.' He glanced at the Rockfield second string as it approached on the cinder track. 'So, what can we expect from this lump of walking dog meat today?'

Harry grinned. Mr Monkey's cruel epithet had been earned by a series of uninspired performances during which Jamie had failed to coax anything better than a fifth place out of him. And even that was a joke, coming—as it did—in a race with only five finishers. The horse's middle-aged owner had been advised on numerous occasions to sell the horse and spend her training fees on something more promising, but she had formed an attachment to the animal and refused, point-blank, to do so.

'Mr Monkey is feeling quite on his toes today,' Harry reported. 'You never know—maybe this is the day he shows us what he's really made of . . .'

'Hmm. I'll believe it when I ride into the winner's circle.' Matt regarded the slightly built chestnut with a jaundiced eye. The race was a handicap hurdle and the handicapper had awarded Mr Monkey the number nineteen—lowest but one in the weights, which pretty much reflected his likely placing. The frustrating thing was that Matt had schooled the horse a time or two at Rockfield and he showed quite promising ability on the gallops.

Ten minutes later, mounted and out on the track, Mr Monkey exhibited every sign of eagerness heading down to the start, but, as soon as the race was underway, he dropped to the rear of the field and appeared to lose interest. It was almost, Matt pondered, as they swung round the second bend, as though he lost heart in the presence of the others.

With this thought in mind, as they moved into

276

the back straight, Matt eased the horse wide of the field until he was running a good fifteen feet away from the others, in the centre of the track. Almost immediately, Mr Monkey's longish ears pricked forward, and, with a little encouragement, he picked up speed until he was level with the leaders. As they approached the next bend, Matt moved the horse nearer to the others. It would be asking too much to run the whole race so far away from the rail and still expect to be in contention, but the success of the manoeuvre had given him food for thought.

Sitting behind the field for another half circuit, Matt again swung the horse wide on the back straight, with the same result, but this time he applied more pressure and kept the animal wide as they took the home turn. For a moment, it looked as though he'd given Mr Monkey too much to do, but, as the finishing post came into view, some three furlongs distant, the little chestnut was only a couple of lengths behind the leaders, one of whom was Landon's mount. With a clear view ahead of him, Mr Monkey responded to Matt's encouragement with a steady acceleration that took them past the post neck and neck with the favourite.

'Where the fuck did you come from?' Rollo demanded, as they slowed and turned back towards the stands. He looked sideways at Matt's mount. 'What did you do to that animal? Shove a rocket up its arse?'

Matt laughed, buoyed up by the unexpected success of his strategy.

'Don't know if I got you or not.'

'Not quite, I don't think,' Rollo said. 'But that

277

was pretty impressive. Didn't know the bugger had it in him!'

'Neither did I!'

Harry greeted Matt's triumphant return with an equal degree of pleasure.

'That's one in the eye for Charlie. He's going to look pretty stupid, and he won't like that.'

Matt wasn't sure that making your employer look stupid was the best way to campaign for reinstatement, but, just at that moment, he didn't care.

Harry reached up to slap Mr Monkey's steaming shoulder.

'So, you can do it when you feel like it. You just needed the right jockey.'

Undoing the girth, Matt shook his head.

'I can't claim any special powers. It just occurred to me that he was intimidated by the other runners, that's all. We'll have to pick courses with long run-ins to give him a chance.'

'But that's just it—you tune in to the horses; that's what makes you so good,' Harry persisted.

More used to trading insults with his friend, Matt felt mildly uncomfortable and replied with a tongue-in-cheek 'Aww shucks!'

*   *   *

Sitting in the weighing room watching the second race on the TV, Matt was glad to see that Landon had apparently taken on board his advice regarding Trestle Table and kept the wily old horse well in to the centre of each fence. Even so, Trestle Table had the last laugh, perhaps recognising his new jockey's relative inexperience.

Matt could see the warning signs as the pair approached the penultimate fence, and muttered, 'Pull your whip through! Keep him straight!' to the miniature figure on the screen, and then groaned as Trestle Table ducked left at the last moment, depositing his unfortunate jockey on top of the birch.

The camera followed the rest of the race to its conclusion, the commentator praising Rollo Gallagher's riding as he recorded his second win of the day, and saying that the smart money was on the Champion Jockey to retain his title at the end of the current season.

Matt turned away from the screen, his sympathy for Landon not entirely unmixed with satisfaction that things weren't running smoothly for Brewer and his new jockey.

'That looks good for you, right?' Mikey Copperfield had been watching beside him, standing—half-dressed—in breeches and a thin nylon jumper, his thick blond hair spiky and dishevelled. 'Leonard will be begging you to come back soon.'

'It's not really John's fault,' Matt told the youngster. 'It's down to Brewer. But you're right; it can't do any harm.'

He turned away to change into Delta Tango's colours. Delta Tango, whose owner was the former SAS captain. The acronym had been fluttering on the edges of his consciousness ever since Doogie had told him, and suddenly he knew why. At Hereford, when he'd quizzed Kendra's brother about his minder, Deacon had boasted that Delafield had been in the Special Forces. Whether or not that was true, Matt didn't know, but thinking of the powerful self-assurance of the man, he wouldn't be surprised to find that it was.

So—another person with an army connection, but had he been at the party? Matt couldn't remember seeing him there, although, knowing how he shadowed Deacon, it was hard to believe he could have been far away.

By the time Matt had changed and weighed out, his first flurry of excitement over the recollection had ebbed and died. As far as he knew, no link had existed between Deacon's minder and Sophie Bradford, and, if Delafield had been at Doogie's birthday bash, his movements that night would no doubt have been thoroughly checked out by DI Bartholomew and his wonderful computer, so, presumably, he was in the clear. All in all, Delafield looked a less likely suspect than Kenning, if that were possible.

Trying to relegate the matter to the back of his mind, Matt went out to meet Doogie, the retired SAS captain, and Delta Tango.

*   *   *

By the end of the afternoon, Ray Landon's fortunes had begun to revive. He had looked a little discomfited upon coming face to face with Matt after Trestle Table had dumped him, but Matt had merely said, 'Cunning bastard, isn't he?' To which the younger man had responded with a rueful nod.

Brewer's remaining two runners performed well enough, one netting a second place, but, as Delta Tango won that particular race for Matt and Doogie, it was unlikely to have aroused much joy

280

in the businessman's heart. Indeed, on the one occasion when their paths crossed, Brewer walked past Matt with his gaze fixed on some point away to one side.

'You're welcome to Anthony's rides until his wrist heals, if Brewer doesn't come to his senses before then,' the Scot told Matt as they walked back to the car park together.

'I appreciate that. I'll get Josh Harper to ring you.'

'If you would. I've got two runners at Wincanton on Saturday, if you're free, and don't forget you've got Woodcutter in the October Cup, Saturday fortnight. Did I tell you he'd been sold?'

Matt shook his head.

'Well, it won't make any difference. I haven't got all the details yet, but the new owner is keen that you should continue to ride him.'

'Oh, that's good.' Matt permitted himself a secret smile—he'd been counting on it.

'Good to see your mate out and about,' Doogie commented.

'My mate? Who?'

'Jamie Mullin. Didn't you know he was here? Saw him with Casey not ten minutes ago. You know—Casey McKeegan, daughter of the *Daily Standard*'s senior editor.'

'She's what?'

'Ah, she didn't tell you. Now I'll cop it.'

'I didn't realise you knew her . . .'

'My godchild,' Doogie announced, with a sideways look. 'Ah, you didn't know that either, did you? Who d'you think put it into her head to campaign on your behalf?'

'Well, I did wonder, at first,' Matt admitted.

281

'Thanks. Kendra would have it that she was sweet on me.'

'Och, she's that, too.' Doogie's eyes twinkled under his snowy brows. 'But she's young—she'll see sense.'

'So her father is editor of the *Standard*, is he? I wondered how she managed to get that job at her age.'

'You mustn't be thinking it just fell into her lap, lad. She's had to work for it, and she's got a rare talent, so I've heard.'

Doogie stopped as they came up to the old blue estate car that had borne him to and from the races for as long as Matt had known him.

'Anyway, you can tell Jamie that there's a couple of rides going begging next week, if he's interested—and if he hasn't put on too much weight from lazing about. If he puts up a good show, there could be some more, you never know.'

'I'll tell him,' Matt said, shaking the trainer's hand warmly. 'And thanks again.'

After Matt had waved goodbye to Doogie, he used his mobile phone to call Casey and, within five minutes, had tracked her down to a bar overlooking the course. The last race had just been run and she and Jamie were drinking coffee, amidst a sprinkling of people who were probably warming up after an afternoon spent yo-yoing between paddock, betting kiosks, and stands.

Having been alerted to the fact by Kendra, Matt could appreciate the ongoing transformation in Casey's appearance. Gone was the unruly mop of curls, to be replaced by a decidedly chic crop; her freckles were subdued under a dusting of make-up; and a fitted brown leather jacket had replaced the amorphous Puffa.

'You look very smart,' he said approvingly, and was rewarded with a demure, 'Thank you, sir.'

Matt turned to Jamie. 'So, what're you doing here?'

'Casey persuaded me. She wanted to talk and she suggested we meet here.'

'Well, it might just be the best move you've made for a long time,' Matt told him, settling on the other side of their table with a huge, indulgent cappuccino in front of him. He passed on Doogie's message.

Jamie was astounded.

'You're kidding!'

'Nope. Anthony Redman's broken wrist might well prove a godsend for both of us. Not that that'll be any comfort at all to *him*. I feel almost as if we should send him a thank you letter.'

'Christ! I'll have to do some sweating—I must have put on half a stone.'

'So, what did you want to see me for?' Casey wanted to know. 'Changed your mind about following up the lead on Steve Bryan?'

'No!' Matt said sharply. 'And I want you to promise you won't try it on your own, either.'

'But it's such a wasted opportunity,' she complained.

'Look, I've got something else for you to do, if you can,' Matt said, hoping to divert her mind. 'Can your contact find out whether a Niall Delafield was at the party the night Sophie was killed? I didn't see him there, but Deacon was, and, as he seems to act as his minder, it seems likely that Delafield was around, somewhere.'

'And we want to know this because . . . ?'

283

'Because he's the only person I can think of—other than Kenning—who has army connections.'

'Was he having it off with Sophie Bradford, too? Sorry, Jamie,' she added hastily.

'Not that I know of, but I couldn't say for sure,' Matt replied, glad to see that Jamie seemed to have taken Casey's unthinking remark in his stride. 'Will you be able to do it? I'd ask Bartholomew, but I don't think he'd tell me, and I don't especially want my head bitten off again.'

'Sure,' she said, airily. 'What's his name again? Delafield? How do you spell that?'

'As it sounds; one L,' Matt told her. 'So, who's your contact in the police force? No—don't tell me . . . Your uncle is the Chief Superintendent . . .'

'What?' Casey looked at him narrowly. 'Oh, I get it—you've found out about my dad. Who told you?'

'Your godfather.'

'Hang on a minute,' Jamie put in. 'I'm missing something here. Who is Casey's father?'

'Only the editor of the *Daily Standard*,' Matt said. 'Why do you keep it a secret?'

'That's rich! You of all people should know the answer to that one.'

This time it was Matt's turn to narrow his eyes thoughtfully.

'I won't tell if you don't,' he said after a moment.

'What about Jamie?'

Jamie responded with a shrug.

'Whatever. I don't know what you're on about anyway.'

'OK, it's a deal,' Casey said, getting to her feet and hoisting a hefty-looking shoulder bag into place. 'Right, I'll go see what I can find out about this Delafield blokey. See you later, Jamie.'

She leaned forward and gave her fellow countryman a kiss, waved to Matt, and headed for the door.

'And *are* you seeing her later?'

'We're going out for a Chinese,' Jamie said, watching Casey weave her way between the tables. 'So, what was that all about? You lost me completely at the end there.'

'Oh, it was just about wanting to be taken on her own merit,' Matt said, and she had every right to be, he reflected. As she had just demonstrated with her research on his own background, she was thorough to a fault.

*   *   *

Because he had two of Roy Emmett's horses to ride on the Saturday, in addition to Doogie's, Matt rode work for John Leonard the following morning, arriving in the same instant as Ray Landon, and it was a toss-up as to which of the three of them felt the most uncomfortable about the situation. Nothing much was said beyond what was essential to the business of the day, and Matt left feeling thankful that Kendra's father hadn't been there to further compound the awkwardness.

Matt was pleased to see that his old friend, Temperance Bob, was in normal work again, the problem with his back presumably sorted out, although, when he raised the subject with the trainer, Leonard put his recovery down to a combination of heat treatment and swimming. It appeared that Toby Potter hadn't come to see the horse after all.

Neither Matt nor Landon stayed for breakfast. Matt, unwilling to prolong the ordeal for any of them, made the excuse of wanting to get back to feed the dogs, a job which, normally, Kendra would have done.

A phone call to Birchwood Hall the previous night had again been fielded by Grace, but Kendra had rung back less than ten minutes later, and he was greatly reassured to find that she was clearly missing him. He didn't press her to return, but arranged to visit her at her father's the following evening after racing.

With no race meeting that day, Matt buried himself in working on the new kitchen, determined to have it ready for when Kendra returned. He didn't allow himself to dwell upon just when that might be.

At six o'clock that evening, he was cleaning paint off his brushes and hands when Casey rang and he hastily wrapped a cotton rag around his fingers to pick up the handset.

'Got your info,' she announced, with a justifiable touch of smugness. 'But I'm not sure it helps.'

'Oh.' Matt couldn't help feeling disappointed. 'Tell me anyway.'

'OK. Niall Anton Delafield: age thirty-seven; one-time medic in the Parachute Regiment; never married and only surviving family—his mother—lives in Devon. Disappeared abroad for a while and, as far as I can tell, he's been working for Brewer for about six months as a security consultant.'

'OK, I'm impressed. And was he at the party?'

'Yes, but only for a short while, apparently. He drove Deacon Brewer there and then went and had a kip in his car in the car park until Deacon came out, just before the trouble flared up between Jamie and Sophie. They were both seen coming and going on the security cameras in the club entranceway. Delafield told the police that they then went on to visit a friend in Warminster before going back to Birchwood Hall—presumably that's Brewer's place.'

'Yeah, that's right.'

'Well, it seems his story checks out. They stopped to get petrol at a station some six or seven miles away at about the time Sophie Bradford was killed. The car—with the two of them in it—was caught on the forecourt CCTV and Delafield himself filmed entering the shop and paying with his credit card. It all seems right and tight.'

'Damn,' Matt said. 'Back to square one. But thanks, anyway—brilliant work.'

'So what now?'

Matt sighed.

'I wish I knew.'

'Well, I still think we should check Steve Bryan out. It's the only real lead we've got.'

'But we don't even know for sure that he's one of the guys who jumped me.'

'Oh, *come on*, he must be,' Casey said. 'It was his van and he's ex-army—what more do you need?'

'Well, Bartholomew will have checked him out by now, if you gave him the numberplate. You did give him the numberplate?' Matt added, suddenly suspicious.

'Of course I did. But it wouldn't hurt to see if he ever served in the same regiment as Delafield, would it?'

'I guess not. And while you're at it, see if you can

287

find out if either of them have any connection, army or otherwise, with my friend Kenning.'

'Right. Will do,' Casey agreed, sounding much happier as she rang off.

*   *   *

If Matt had worried that his meeting with Kendra might be attended by a little embarrassment after the way they had parted, his fears were soon laid to rest. She met him at the front door and threw her arms around his neck before he had a chance to say a word.

'I'm sorry, sweetheart,' he muttered into her hair, and her reply was merely to hug him tighter.

When eventually she loosened her hold and stood back, her eyes were swimming with tears.

'We are all right, aren't we?'

'Of course we are,' he said, smiling, and she produced an answering smile.

Across the hall a door opened and a voice said, 'Oh my, how touching! The lovers reunited.'

'Ignore her,' Kendra advised, without turning her head. 'It's what annoys her the most. Will you stay to dinner?'

'Oh, I don't know.' The idea held little appeal for Matt. 'Your father and I, well . . .'

'But he's not here. He's away on business and won't be back till tomorrow. Please, Matt—you're expected. And Harry's here . . .'

Matt took a deep breath.

'OK. As long as you promise to defend me from Grace.'

'Idiot! You know you're more than a match for her. Come on, Mum's in the sitting room.'

288

Saved from the prospect of a painful confrontation with Charlie, and made to feel especially welcome by Joy, Matt enjoyed the evening, in spite of the occasional barbed comment from Grace. Harry seemed in good spirits and Matt wondered at the timing of his presence; apart from the barbeque, when all the Leonards had been invited, Harry had never been invited to a meal, as far as he knew. When the cat was away, he mused . . .

Kendra herself seemed relaxed and happy, and it was brought home to Matt with a sense of guilt just how quiet and depressed she had become over the last few days at Spinney Cottage. Had she hidden it well, or had he been too taken up with his own worries to notice at the time?

Deacon was present for the meal; it was the first time Matt had seen him since Hereford, although he was in one of his dreamy moods and contributed little to the conversation. However, when they moved to the drawing room with their coffees and Frances suggested they play board games, Deke became more animated and volunteered to unearth Pictionary and Trivial Pursuit from a cupboard in the hall. Even though the idea was greeted with groans from most of the company, the protest was half-hearted and, before long, they were all engrossed, entering into the spirit of the games with childish enthusiasm.

'Deke has the luck of the devil, doesn't he?' Matt observed later, as he and Kendra sat together on the green brocade settee, alone in the drawing room. When they had eventually tired of the games, the others had gradually drifted away, with the exception of Grace, who showed every sign of staying put, until her mother reappeared and removed her, on the pretext of needing her help.

'Mm—he's always been lucky,' Kendra replied. 'Did you think he seemed OK?'

'OK? What d'you mean? He was a bit quiet at first, but then he often is, isn't he? He seemed fine later. Why do you ask?'

'Well, Fran's a bit worried about him. I think it's this course she's on, it's turning her into a mental-health hypochondriac. Personally, I think Deke's always been a bit dippy, but he's a sweetie, so who cares?'

Matt shrugged.

'I don't really know Deke that well, but I shall be nervous now, if I catch Frances looking at me a bit hard.'

'Oh, she gave up on you as a hopeless case ages ago,' Kendra told him, bringing her feet up onto the settee and snuggling closer. Spotting a gap at the other end of the seat, Taffy jumped up and settled into it.

'Just like old times,' Matt observed.

'Mm. Do you *have* to go back tonight?'

'Yeah, sorry. I promised Doogie I'd do some schooling for him tomorrow, and, anyway, the dogs will be sitting cross-legged as it is.' He hesitated. 'Come with me?'

Immediately he felt a minute withdrawal.

'I can't. Please don't ask.'

He could have kicked himself for spoiling the moment. Giving her shoulders a squeeze, he apologised.

'I'm sorry too.' She sighed. 'When will all this be over?'

'I wish I knew. It can't be soon enough for me.

What has your father said about all this? I mean, you and me, and the situation with me and Ray Landon?'

Kendra shook her head.

'Nothing. I tried to talk to him about that, but he won't discuss it. He said it's a business decision, not personal.'

'And about us?'

She hesitated.

'What?' Matt asked, when she didn't answer. 'What has he said?'

Kendra shrugged.

'Nothing much.'

'That doesn't sound like him . . .'

'It doesn't matter.'

'Tell me.'

There was a long pause.

'He asked me if I wanted someone to go over to pick up the rest of my things.'

Matt sat up straight.

'You're joking!'

Again the shake of the head. She wouldn't meet his eyes.

'And what did you say?'

'I said no, of course. Do you really have to ask? I told him that, as soon as things have settled down a bit, I'll be moving back to Spinney Cottage. He just kind of grunted and walked off,' she added, correctly anticipating Matt's next query. 'I really don't know what's got into him. He seems constantly bad-tempered these days.'

*   *   *

Around eleven o'clock, when Kendra's eyelids

were drooping with tiredness, Matt shook her gently and told her he should be on his way.

'And you should be getting to bed, my girl—you're half asleep as it is.'

'Mm. I haven't been sleeping too well, but I'll be all right tonight,' she said, turning her head to kiss him.

'Good. Well, I'll just say goodbye to your mum before I go . . .'

'She'll probably be in the library. I think she was going to show Harry some old photos—I can't remember why . . . Something to do with a horse they were talking about earlier.'

'OK, I'll find her. You get to bed. I'll ring you tomorrow. By the way, did you ever find your mobile?'

'Yes, it was here all the time. Mum found it.'

'Good old Mum.' Matt pulled Kendra to her feet, where she drooped against him once more, tilting her face up to his.

'Love you,' she murmured, when they eventually separated.

'Love you too. Now, off with you, or you'll have junior yawning in there,' he added, rubbing her stomach gently.

He followed her to the hall and watched as she mounted the stairs with Taffy trotting solemnly at her heels. Moments later she had passed from view and he turned away with a smile on his lips.

He was still thinking about her when he knocked softly on the panelled door and walked into the library.

It would have been difficult to say who was more surprised—Harry and Frances, or Matt.

Harry had his back to the door when Matt

opened it, so it was Frances who saw him first, and, as the laughter died out of her face, it took a moment for the significance to hit Harry. When it did, he turned slowly, hanging onto the back of one of the library chairs, his other hand still poised to throw the small tasselled cushion it held.

What surprised Matt was not that they should be fooling around in such a way, but that Harry was on his feet, and the wheelchair was some six or seven paces away by the bookshelves that lined the side wall.

13

'Matt . . . hi.'

Harry seemed at a loss. He turned sideways and sat rather heavily on the arm of the wing chair, replacing the cushion where it belonged.

'Hi. I was, er . . . looking for Joy.' For some reason he wasn't sure he understood himself, Matt held back from commenting on the scene he had inadvertently walked in on. The atmosphere fairly crackled with unspoken thoughts.

Finally, Frances said brightly, 'I think she's in the dining room.'

She got up from her position on the sofa and advanced on Harry.

'Now, are you going to say a pretty please?' she enquired, then looked past him to Matt. 'He was being cheeky, so I removed his chair. But I suppose I'd better take pity on him . . .'

Matt smiled.

'Oh, I don't know. I should make him suffer a bit longer, if I were you,' he said. 'Do him good.

Anyway, I'm heading home, so I'll leave you to it. Goodnight.'

' 'Night, Matt,' Harry responded, and Frances waved a cheery hand.

Closing the door on them, Matt frowned. The explanation was plausible enough and he'd been careful to show no scepticism, but the truth was that he didn't believe a word of it. Although Harry had long been able to stand for a sufficient length of time to move himself in and out of his wheelchair, the manoeuvre had always caused him white-faced discomfort. The man who had turned to face Matt a moment ago had been smiling and relaxed.

Matt's pleasure at seeing Harry on his feet was mixed with confusion. It was clear that movement was no longer the agonising ordeal it had been since the accident that had ended his career, but for how long had he been improving, and why hadn't he shared the joy of his progress—even with his parents? Frances's pretence indicated that, whatever the reason, Harry wanted no one to know, and Matt felt a little hurt that he hadn't been considered friend enough to be taken into his confidence.

Shrugging the mood away, he made his way to the dining room, where he did find Joy, as Frances had suggested. She was standing by one of the long windows, looking out, and he had to say her name twice before she heard him.

'Oh, hello Matt. Are you off?'

'Yes. The dogs will be waiting to go out. Is everything OK?' He thought she looked a little distracted.

'Well, I'm not sure,' she said, pulling the curtain

aside once more and peering into the darkness. 'I can just see the yard from here and it looks as though there's a light on. I was trying to decide if it was the Hattery. I could have sworn I'd turned it off when I finished this afternoon, but it's just possible that I forgot.'

'Do you want me to check?'

'Oh, would you? You are an angel. I can't get Niall on his mobile and I was just thinking I'd better go myself, but it's raining.'

'No problem. If it is unlocked, I'll pop the key on the hall table before I go.'

'Brilliant—thank you.'

With an eye to the rain, Matt went out through the kitchen and utility room, which was a lot closer to the old stableyard than the front door. Turning up the collar of his jacket, he ducked his head and ran along the stone path towards the converted coach house which was the Hattery, but, as he drew closer, he could see that the light Joy had seen wasn't actually coming from the showroom or workshop, but further on. Matt wasn't sure what the next building was used for, but, having come that far, he supposed he might as well investigate.

An ill-fitting blind hung in the lighted window and, pausing as he came level, Matt was able to see round the edge of it. The room beyond appeared to be some sort of office, and was indeed occupied. Standing by the filing cabinet was a slim twenty-something man whom Matt had never seen before, and who was clearly deep in an impassioned conversation with someone out of Matt's line of sight.

At this point, with the rain circumventing his jacket's wholly inadequate defences, Matt's intention was to turn and make good speed in the direction of his car, but two things kept him by the window. One was the striking appearance of the man, who had alabaster skin, large, dark-lashed brown eyes, and long dark hair tied at the nape of his neck with what looked like a length of black velvet ribbon. He wore a three-quarter-length jacket of a silvery-grey material over a black shirt and slim-legged jeans, and the whole effect was more than a little effeminate. The other thing that kept Matt watching was curiosity about the identity of the person this vision was talking to.

Fortunately, he didn't have too long to wait. After gesticulating with all the drama of a silent movie star, the ponytailed one turned and moved towards the door, but, before he could reach it, another figure came into view, vaulting the desk, catching the young man by the shoulders, and turning him round.

Matt instinctively shrank back a little, but continued to gaze intently at the lighted cameo being played out before him, the rain forgotten. The second man seemed also to be gripped by a strong emotion and though, at first, Matt wasn't sure whether his intentions were violent, it soon became clear that nothing could be further from the truth. After addressing a number of rapid, fervent phrases to the man in the silvery jacket, he placed a finger under his chin, tilted his head up until the dark-lashed eyes looked back at him, and then kissed him full on the lips.

Matt felt a frisson of shock; not so much at the homosexual act as at the instigator of it, for it was none other than Charlie Brewer's security man, Deacon's bodyguard—Niall Delafield.

The kiss was unmistakably passionate, the young man slipping his arms around Delafield's neck to pull him closer, but, in the end, it was Delafield who broke the union, pulling away from the man and shaking his head.

This apparently incensed his lover. With brows drawn down and dark eyes flashing dangerously, he rattled off a furious tirade, punctuated by a number of ineffectual thumps on Delafield's arms and chest with his clenched fists. They were the hands of an artist or musician, not of a fighter, and the blows obviously didn't trouble Delafield at all. Half laughing, he caught the slim fists and held them still, which made the young man even angrier. When the diatribe came to an end, Delafield shrugged, shook his head, and lightly kissed him again before releasing him.

This time his reward was a stinging slap across the face, hard enough to make him take an involuntary step back, and the man in the silver jacket turned without another word and stalked across to the door.

Suddenly Matt realised the assignation was coming to an end and that, if he stayed where he was, he was in imminent danger of discovery. Although his encounters with the man had been few, he needed no one to tell him that being caught spying on Delafield in such a situation was probably not a good idea. Backing away from the window, he glanced hurriedly around and then slipped into the shadowed doorway of Joy's showroom.

He was only just in time.

The storeroom door was thrown open with such force that it hit the brick wall beside it and rebounded, almost hitting the slim figure that erupted from the doorway.

At this point, Matt deemed it prudent to turn his head to the Hattery door, aware that the pale skin of his face would very likely give him away.

'Joe—for God's sake, calm down! It's not going to be for ever, I promise.' That was Delafield.

'That's what *you* say—but you won't say how long.' The Scouse accent contrasted oddly with its owner's exotic appearance. 'So what am I supposed to do? Sit around waiting for you to call? You owe me more than that.'

'I know, and I'm sorry. But this isn't my fault, you know that.'

'Do I? I only know what you're telling me, but what if there's more to it? Is this really about you and me?'

'You know it's not. I just can't get away at the moment—I told you why.'

'Can't—or don't want to?' Joe demanded hotly. 'Perhaps you prefer to be with your precious Deacon.'

'Sshh! Keep your voice down!'

'Why? Brewer's not going to hear me in bloody Reading!'

'He's not the only one that lives here.'

'But who's going to be out here, in this? Besides, why should I care who hears us? If you're dumping me—what does it matter?' the younger man declared dramatically.

'Please don't start that again—I'm not dumping you. Things are a bit difficult at the moment, that's all. Look, I'll call you tomorrow, OK?'

'I might be in, I might not,' came the pettish reply.

'For God's sake, Joe—don't be childish!'

'Anyway—what if I tell him about that night?'

'You don't know anything . . .' There was a note of uncertainty in the response.

'Oh, I think I do. I'm not stupid, you know. I was with you when he phoned, don't forget. It wasn't really your night off, was it?'

There was a pause, when all Matt could hear was the rain hissing on the stone paving. He imagined the silver jacket darkening in the downpour.

'You wouldn't do that,' Delafield said, quite softly.

'Why not? I'd have you to myself then.'

'You mustn't do it. Believe me—you have no idea . . .'

'Call me, then. Come and see me.' The young man sounded at breaking point.

'I will, I said I would,' Delafield soothed.

'Call me.' The voice came from further away; there came the sound of running footsteps and then just the rain.

Heart thumping, Matt stayed where he was, hardly daring to breathe, and presently heard Delafield utter an emphatic, 'Shit!'

The door shut, a key turned, and then the security man headed back to the house, passing within a few feet of where Matt strove to meld his body into the doorpost.

When he was sure the coast was clear, Matt came cautiously out of hiding, glanced right and left, and then turned and hurried through the rain to his car, keeping in the shadow of the buildings until he had rounded the corner of the house.

Once in the MR2, he stripped off his wet jacket, pulled on a spare fleece that he kept behind his seat, and sat staring sightlessly in the rear-view mirror as the courtesy light faded and went out, his mind busy with the implications of what he'd just witnessed.

Exactly what was it that Joe was threatening to tell? It was certainly enough to seriously rattle Delafield. Who had phoned him? When? And what had been said?

Did Brewer know that the man he relied on to keep an eye on his son was gay? It was hard to believe he did, for Kendra's father was one of the most homophobic people Matt had ever met, but, from what had been said, it sounded as though he'd found out, somehow.

Matt's mind went back to the evening when he'd overheard a heated confrontation between the two men in Brewer's office. The words, which had meant nothing at the time, took on some significance in the light of the night's events. What was it Brewer had said? Something about having a right to be politically incorrect in his own home, wasn't it? And he'd told Delafield to get rid of someone—the exquisite Joe, perhaps?—or risk losing his job.

But Matt also remembered that Delafield had been confident that the businessman wouldn't fire him . . . Why? he wondered. What leverage did the security man have on Kendra's father that could possibly force him to overcome such a deep-seated aversion?

Whatever it was, it seemed that the two had reached an uneasy truce and Matt certainly wasn't about to ask Delafield about it. Maybe the security man had kept his job on the understanding that his lover stayed well away from Birchwood Hall?

It was the only explanation that made any sense at all, but it still didn't quite add up. For one thing, the word *compromise* was not one that Matt would usually use in the same sentence with Brewer. It was way out of character.

Shaking his head, Matt started the car and set off for home. All in all, it had been quite an evening.

*   *   *

The weather at Wincanton the next afternoon was blustery and cold, but the going was good to soft, a fact to which Matt could testify, as he trudged back down the home straight after falling at the last. The first of Roy Emmett's two promising novices had met the fence completely wrong, suffering a crisis of confidence and putting down for an extra stride when he should have been taking off. But the news wasn't all bad—the fall had been easy, the ground relatively soft, and both horse and jockey had come to their feet unharmed. Just another day at the office. All the same, Matt felt as though he'd had more than his fair share of falls lately.

With several runners from Rockfield, both Harry and John Leonard were at the Somerset course but, although Matt found it impossible to look at him without recalling the scene in the library, Harry seemed untroubled by any awkwardness, greeting him in his usual friendly fashion.

In the paddock for the next race, Matt scanned the field of six runners and was interested to see an old friend among them. It was Maple Tree, the horse of the missing breast-girth incident, although this time Matt noted that he was wearing a full

301

complement of tack. He looked round for Mick Westerby and saw him talking to a tall, middle-aged man in a grey woollen overcoat. Mikey Copperfield stood alongside, characteristically reserved.

'Who's the man with Westerby?' Matt asked Doogie, who, after a lifetime in National Hunt racing, was a font of knowledge when it came to owners, trainers, and horses.

'I'm not sure, but it isn't the horse's owner, I can tell you that much, because Glenda Naismith died last week. Shame—she was a nice old girl, ninety if she was a day and tough as boot leather. Maybe it's her son? I can find out for you. Is it important?'

'It might be,' Matt said. 'I could ask Mikey, but he tends to focus on the horses and everything else washes over the top.'

'He's a rare talent, though,' Doogie stated. 'I'd give him a job any day. OK, I'll see what I can do. Nice horse that grey. Shame Westerby's got it, I wouldn't mind training it myself. It'll be the one to beat in this race, I think.'

Doogie was right. Maple Tree was the one to beat, and, on this occasion, Matt's horse wasn't up to the task. They came a close second, though, passing the post less than a length behind the grey, and Matt slapped the younger jockey on the back as they slowed up.

'Nice work, Mikey! Hey, who's the guy in the long coat who was talking to Mick?'

Mikey shrugged.

'Not sure. The owner, I think. Somebody Naismith. Why?'

'Just wondered,' Matt said, hoping Doogie could find out more. He wouldn't mind a little chat with

Somebody Naismith, if he got the chance. He had an idea he might be interested to hear the sad tale of Maple Tree's last run.

When Matt joined Doogie in the paddock for the second of his two runners, the elderly trainer had a twinkle in his eye.

'Got the information you were after,' he announced. 'The chap with Westerby *was* Glenda's son. His name's Stephen Naismith and he's a lawyer. As the only child, he's expected to inherit his mother's horses, but it's not known whether he intends to keep them on. That's all anyone seems to know, at the moment. Oh, and he's currently entertaining our friend Mick in the bar upstairs.'

'Brilliant. Thank you.'

It was good news that Naismith had not, as yet, left the course, but slightly less promising, for Matt's purposes, that he seemed to be on such friendly terms with his late mother's unscrupulous trainer.

'Got some more news for you, too. Chris Fairbrother's retiring.' His bright blue eyes watched Matt closely. 'Thought you might like to know, considering he's given you a bit of a hard time of it lately.'

'But he's only young.'

'Well, it might just be temporary. His little girl is sick and he's taking her abroad for treatment. America, I think.'

'Poor bloke,' Matt said, genuinely sorry. Maybe that explained the steward's odd judgements of late. 'Christ, that'll cost him a pretty penny . . .'

'Ah, that's what I thought,' Doogie said. 'But it seems your good friend Lord Kenning is helping out. What do you think of that?'

303

What indeed? Remembering Fairbrother's strange behaviour the last time they had met, certain things began to slot into place.

'Well, well,' Matt said, thoughtfully.

Having partnered Doogie's second horse to a respectable third place, and with no rides in the next two races, Matt pulled his Q&S jacket on over his silks and went in search of Maple Tree's new owner.

Although Matt had no ride in the next race, he knew Westerby had a runner, and so could be fairly certain that the trainer would be in the paddock and not still in the bar with Stephen Naismith.

So it proved.

It appeared that Naismith had come to Wincanton on his own, and when Matt paused in the doorway of the bar, scanning the room, he saw him sitting at a table by the window, his grey overcoat thrown over the back of the seat beside him. Naismith was deep in contemplation of his racecard when Matt approached, and didn't look up when he stopped beside the table.

'Mr Naismith?'

'Yes?' Naismith glanced up blankly. He clearly didn't recognise Matt, even with the giveaway breeches and boots.

'Hi. My name's Matt Shepherd. I ride for Mick Westerby sometimes . . .' *Not anymore, he didn't.* 'Could I have a word?'

'Er . . . Yes—sure. Have a seat.' His voice was educated, pleasant, unaccented.

'I don't know whether you're aware, but I rode Maple Tree for your mother, when he last ran.'

'I'm afraid my mother's passed away.'

304

'Yes, I heard. I'm sorry. I never met her, but Doogie McKenzie told me she was quite a character.'

'She was,' Naismith agreed. 'So what can I do for you, Mr Shepherd?'

'Well, Maple Tree is—as you saw today—a very good horse,' Matt told him. 'But when *I* rode him, he wasn't allowed to run on merit; in fact, I believe he was sabotaged in an attempt to get at me . . .'

Quite suddenly Naismith's easy attitude was replaced by the needle-sharp gaze of a man for whom conflict and dissent were a part of everyday life.

'Perhaps you'd better start at the beginning,' he suggested. 'Would you like a coffee?'

*   *   *

Naismith listened with apparent interest to what Matt had to say, and ended by thanking Matt for telling him, without giving any intimation of what he intended doing about it—if anything. From his reaction to the story, Matt was led to suspect that the lawyer hadn't been wholly won over by Westerby himself, and he exhibited no sign of disbelief, even when Lord Kenning's name was introduced into the tale. He wanted to know where he could find Rick Smith and, reluctantly, Matt told him, whilst warning him that Westerby's ex-head lad might well refuse to see him. The encounter took far longer than Matt had envisaged, and, after answering a few very pertinent questions, he had to hurry back to weigh out for his next race, leaving Maple Tree's owner to digest what he had heard.

Kenning was at Wincanton, but kept his distance, and when, at the end of the day, Roy Emmett's second runner further redeemed Matt's fortunes by winning a novice chase in fine style, he made his way home feeling that, on balance, things were looking up.

*   *   *

Returning to Spinney Cottage after a satisfying schooling session at Doogie's yard the following morning, Matt collected the local paper from his letterbox, weathered a mobbing by his three exuberant dogs, switched the kettle on, and went upstairs for a shower. It was the old Sunday morning routine that he had followed quite happily until Kendra had moved in, but now it felt flat and dull. He really hadn't appreciated how much colour she had brought to his existence, until she had taken it away again. He missed her welcoming kiss; missed being able to discuss how the horses had worked—what Leonard had said; he even missed Taffy. Without him noticing, the streetwise little sheltie had become an integral part of his life, too.

Washed, changed, and the dogs fed, Matt settled down to drink a cup of coffee and read the papers, before going out to see to the horses. The dogs knew the schedule and sat, quietly watchful, on their beds, waiting for a sign that their master was on the move.

The *Daily Standard*'s racing pages had, among others, a picture of Mikey winning on Maple Tree the day before, and couldn't resist pointing out that, in doing so, the teenager had beaten Matt

306

Shepherd, who had had a very different result when *he* had last ridden the horse.

'Yeah, yeah,' Matt muttered, causing the dogs to prick up their ears hopefully. He took the jibe with resignation. It was the kind of observation that newspapers love to make, and he certainly didn't begrudge the young jockey his praise. Nobody could deny that Mikey had ridden the horse beautifully.

Moving on, in due course, to the local paper, Matt leafed through the pages, skimming over reports of land disputes, petty crime, and adverts for jumble sales and bingo in various village halls. There was little to catch his interest at first sight, but he would look through it again, if he had time, before it was used to light the wood-burning stove.

He had finished his coffee and was about to put the paper aside when his attention was caught by one of the photos. Frowning slightly, he turned back to look again.

The photo was of a willowy, pouting woman in a skintight skirt and a strapless top that appeared to be composed of a huge bow and not much else. Beside her was an equally slender young man in a three-quarter-length fitted jacket, with a large jewelled buckle on his jeans and tied-back dark hair. The striking, fine-boned face was, without a doubt, the one Matt had seen through the window of the storeroom at Birchwood Hall—the face he'd seen Niall Delafield take in his hands and kiss so ardently.

Swiftly, Matt scanned the text beneath the picture. Joseph Wintermann, the newest sensation in haute couture, was to show off his new season's designs in a charity fashion show that was to take

307

place in a marquee in the grounds of Kelsey Grange on Monday evening. Wintermann was becoming known, the article continued, for his imaginative and daring mixes of velvet, silks, and metallic fabrics. The rights to reproduce Wintermann designs for the general market were being fought over by several of the big names on the high street, he read, and Joseph, an enigmatic young man with dark, romantic looks, was certain to win numerous fans with his winter collection.

Matt was halfway through reading the piece a second time, when his mobile trilled. The display was showing Casey's name. He picked it up.

'Hi. I was going to ring you later.'

'How nice,' she said blithely.

'So what's new?'

'Well, not a lot, actually. Apart from the stuff I told you the other day, there's not much to find about your man Delafield. He seems to have gone off the radar a few years ago, then he turns up abroad, where Brewer found him. But I couldn't find anything at all to link him to Steve Bryan, the van man. They weren't in the same regiment, but I suppose—if you say Delafield was SAS—they might have run into each other there. I should imagine it'd be almost impossible to find out.'

'Yeah, I guess so.' With the shock of last night's discovery, the somewhat loosely linked chain of thought that had led to him asking for the information had completely fallen apart. He searched his memory. 'What about Kenning? Any link there?'

'Sorry. None I could find.'

'Oh well, it was worth a try. So, how did the date with Jamie go?'

'Which one?' she asked coyly.

'Ah! Say no more.'

When Casey rang off, Matt returned to the paper and stared long and hard at the photograph. In spite of the lack of any detectable link between the owner of the white van and Niall Delafield, it was obvious, from what Matt had overheard, that—quite apart from the matter of his sexuality—there was something very irregular about Charlie Brewer's security man.

Matt read the article again.

Kelsey Grange, if he remembered correctly, was a stately home somewhere between Bath and Yeovil. No doubt there would be a good deal of coming and going in the run-up to the fashion show; it was just possible, in the confusion, that there might be a chance to get close enough to have a word with the beautiful and talented Mr Wintermann. Quite what he was going to say, if he did manage such an interview, he wasn't entirely sure, but he felt he should at least make the attempt, if only to assure himself that the argument between Joe Wintermann and Delafield was a private affair and concerned nothing of significance to him.

If the young man was still in emotional turmoil, he might be ripe for pouring his troubles into a sympathetic ear. Matt had to repress a shudder at the thought. This was one task he would gladly have passed over to Bartholomew, but what reason could he give? Being homosexual wasn't a crime, whatever any individual might think about it. He knew nothing about Delafield that would remotely interest Bartholomew, all he had was a collection of disjointed facts and half-heard comments, and a hunch that they might possibly add up to an important whole.

*　　*　　*

After seeing to the animals, Matt once again spent the remainder of the daylight hours working in the new kitchen, leaving himself just enough time to take the dogs for a decent walk before the darkness closed in.

His evening meal was a reheated tagliatelli, which he ate in the sitting room with the TV on. The three dogs followed him in, flopping down at his feet and keeping an eye on his plate with varying degrees of subtlety. Without Kendra there to frown him down, Matt dropped the last three chunks of ham into their willing mouths and pushed the bowl to one side. It was a long time since he'd spent a Sunday evening at the cottage, and although the custom of going to Birchwood Hall every week had been irksome at times, it seemed infinitely preferable to eating yesterday's leftovers with only the dogs for company, much as he loved them. He'd rung Kendra when he'd finished work but, although she was plainly very happy to hear from him, she reported that her father's mood left a lot to be desired and discouraged Matt's intention to brave it and attend the family meal.

Even though he'd had plenty to occupy his thoughts that day, the conundrum that was Harry Leonard had kept creeping in. Matt found himself replaying the scene over and over in his mind. Was it possible that he'd been mistaken? However he looked at it, the answer was no. Harry had been

310

standing up, one hand on the back of the chair, weight on both feet, and sharing a joke with Kendra's sister. Matt was as sure as he could be that he'd had no further operations so, somehow, Harry had found some way to unlock the pain which had kept him confined to a wheelchair for the last eighteen months. But when had it happened, and how?

Frances would know, and he'd been sorely tempted to ring her, but, having covered for Harry on Friday, it seemed unlikely that she would give up his secret now.

The thought that his friend was on the road to recovery was wonderful, but a niggling worm of unease twisted through that pleasure—how long had he been mobile? Had he, in fact, lied to the police on the night of the party, when they had asked him about the wheelchair, and, if so, why? Wanting to keep his recovery a secret to surprise his friends and family was understandable, but not reason enough to mislead those engaged in conducting a murder enquiry. Matt knew that, secret or not, he was going to have to talk to Harry about it.

Realising that he had absolutely no idea why the woman on the television had just stormed out on her family and slammed the door, or even who she was, Matt switched it off and decided to have an early night.

*   *   *

With no racing the following day, there was nothing to prevent Matt taking a trip out to Kelsey Grange to try and track down Delafield's

311

boyfriend. It was not a thought he relished, not least because, if Delafield ever got wind of it, Matt had an idea he might turn rather nasty, and, long before he arrived at his destination, he had decided that an alias might be a sensible precaution.

Kelsey Grange was a grand but not particularly beautiful Bath stone building in the Adam style, and home to—according to the guidebooks—a quantity of mosaic flooring of international importance.

As Matt drove up, he found the house partly obscured by a large white marquee and the numerous vehicles standing on the parkland immediately in front of it. The marquee was billowing in the brisk breeze and the scene was one of frenetic activity with people scurrying in all directions: some in overalls, some in casual workaday clothing, and one or two looking as though they had stepped out of the fashion pages of a cutting-edge magazine.

No one took any notice of him as he parked the car, slotting it carefully out of sight between a huge, spotless 4x4 and a pink van that bore the legend 'Marcell's Event Catering' and promised— rather ambiguously, he thought—'Party food you'll remember!'

Trying to look as though he had every reason to be there, Matt locked the car and made his way towards the marquee, where he encountered the first sign of security in the form of a beefy-looking individual in worn jeans and a black tee shirt, the short sleeves of which strained round a pair of powerful, tattooed biceps. He had frizzy gingerish hair dragged back into a ponytail and small, steely-

312

grey eyes that Matt felt uncomfortably sure had singled him out as an impostor the moment they had spotted him.

He sauntered up, producing what he hoped was a relaxed smile, but was met with no answering gleam. Although the gingery one wasn't actually physically blocking the tent opening, he was standing close enough to leave would-be unauthorised entrants in no doubt that they would be repelled.

Matt rethought his initial plan of keeping his head down and following someone else through and walked straight up to the big man.

'Is Joe inside?'

Ginger looked him up and down from his extra six inches or so.

'Who wants to know?'

'Friend of a friend,' Matt said mendaciously.

The piggy eyes narrowed still further.

'Mr Wintermann don't want to see no journalists till later. Come back at six o'clock.'

'I'm not a journalist,' Matt began, but, before he could say anything more, a new player erupted upon the scene in the person of a middle-aged man in skintight leather trousers and a white polo-neck jumper. He appeared in the marquee entrance wearing shades—even though the day wasn't bright—and with his unconvincingly black curls partially hidden under a red baseball cap.

'At last!' he cried, beckoning to Matt with a clipboard. 'You certainly took your time. I was just going to ring the agency again. Come along in.'

Unwilling to pass up this fortuitous chance, Matt smiled again at Ginger and followed the clipboard man into the subdued light of the tent.

313

Walking slightly sideways, the man looked back at Matt and kept up a continuous chatter as he led the way towards the catwalk, which was laid out in an elongated T shape from a stage at one end of the tent.

'Shouldn't you be taller? I specifically asked for over six foot. Joseph's designs cry out for height. Honestly, these people are imbeciles! It's hardly rocket science, is it? Six foot or over, I said, and they send me—what are you? Five nine, five ten?'

Matt nodded, a little bemused. 'Five nine,' he confirmed.

The man stopped in his tracks and, close up, Matt could see that, despite the youthful style of dressing, he was well into his fifties if he was a day.

'There, what did I say? Why don't they just say if they can't fulfil the fucking brief? What are we supposed to do? Take all the clothes up? I mean, it would spoil the lines completely—even if we had time, which we don't. Not that you haven't got the look ...' He put out a hand and caught Matt's chin, turning his face to profile. 'Mm. You might do for our summer range, I suppose. Shame you didn't grow a bit more,' he said, his tone leaving Matt in no doubt that his lack of inches was entirely his own fault.

The man shook his head, tutted, and led the way forward again.

'It's no good. I shall have to get onto the agency again. You'll stick out like a sore thumb. Fucking hell! If it wasn't enough having Joseph in floods of tears every five minutes ... He's had a row with his boyfriend, you see,' he confided, over his shoulder. 'I expect it'll all come out all right in the end, but it's lousy timing.'

314

In the corner they were approaching, a table and chairs were set up out of the way of the bustling crew. On the table were a laptop computer, several more clipboards, and a couple of mugs half full of tea or coffee with skin forming on the top.

A young man sat on one of the chairs, but, to Matt's disappointment, it wasn't Wintermann. This man had chin-length platinum blond hair, angular features, a pencil-slim body, and a sulky *whatever* expression that made it a fair guess that he was a model.

'This is Juno,' Matt's companion said, waving a hand. 'And you are—what did you say your name was?'

'Er—Luke,' he said, giving his brother's name.

'Luke ... ?' The clipboard man waited, expectantly.

'Yes, that's right,' Matt said unhelpfully. 'Actually, I'm not from the agency, I was looking for Joe.'

'Not a model?'

Matt shook his head.

'You're not a journalist?' he said, lowering his voice suspiciously.

'No, I'm a friend of Niall's.'

'But Joseph's not here. I thought he was meeting Niall—he said he was.'

'Oh, damn. I must have just missed him then,' Matt said. 'Look, if I give you my number, could you get him to ring me? It's rather important. But tell him it would be better if he didn't mention me to Niall. I don't want to cause any more problems—especially with all this going on. Er ... have you got a piece of paper ... ?'

The clipboard man favoured him with a narrow-

315

eyed look and then gestured to an A4 pad on the table.

'You can write it down there. They're all things he's got to sort out when he gets here—if he's got time, that is. I can't believe he's not here now, after all the work we've put in to get this thing up and running. Here, use my pen,' he added, passing Matt a cheap blue biro which bore signs of having been extensively chewed.

Drawing a line under the previous memo, Matt wrote down his alias followed by his mobile number, and then, in brackets, 'Niall's friend'. Whether the gamble would pay off, he wasn't sure, but, hopefully, the idea that the mysterious Luke had links with Joe's lover would be tantalising enough to do the trick.

* * *

His failure to speak to Delafield's boyfriend left Matt feeling some disappointment, but a far larger measure of relief. His plan, such as it was, had been to bluff Wintermann that he knew more than he did, hoping to frighten the highly strung designer into betraying something. With that opportunity taken away from him, he didn't really know which way to turn, and he doubted that Wintermann would phone him, even if the message didn't get lost in the flurry of preparations for the show.

By the time he'd reached home, Matt had decided that, if he didn't hear anything by the following day, he would contact Bartholomew, lay before him all the facts he had gathered, and wash his hands of the whole business, trusting that, in

316

the end, justice would be done. Whether it would prove to be in time to save his relationship or his job at Rockfield, only time would tell.

He wandered into the new kitchen and stood looking unexcitedly at the paint pots and piles of sandpaper for several minutes, before turning his back on it all and shutting the door. Plugging in his laptop for the first time in days, he logged on to check his e-mail and found, to his surprise, one from Sophie's flatmate, Tara Goodwin. He vaguely remembered having given her his address, in case she thought of anything new, but he hadn't really expected her to make use of it.

The text read simply: *Some photos arrived for Sophie today. She must have taken them on holiday with one of those throwaway cameras. I've passed them on to the police, but I've scanned a couple I thought you might want to see. Don't know if this is Mosie . . . Love to Kendra. X*

Matt scrolled down to find three very amateurish photographs, two shot at the poolside of a towering white hotel that could have been located in one of several hundred resorts, and one in a hotel room. The two outside ones featured Sophie herself, wearing a barely-there bikini and lounging on a sunbed next to an older man. The inside one was blurred, as if the camera hadn't been held steady, but showed the same man decked out in a woman's black and red negligée set, complete with suspenders and love hearts on the knickers and bra. He had put his hand forward in an attempt to block the lens, but, even so, there was no mistaking the lean features of Matt's nemesis, Lord Kenning.

317

14

After sending Tara a heartfelt electronic thank you for the photos, printing off copies, and shutting the computer down, Matt found the prospect of DIY even less attractive. His head was buzzing with the implications of this new information, so he pulled on boots and a coat and took the dogs for a good long walk.

What occupied Matt's mind was not so much what the photos revealed, because the suspicion had been there for some time, but more what to do with the information, now he had proof. Or could he actually do anything? After all, Tara had said that she was turning the originals over to the police, so, presumably, Bartholomew would be having further words with Kenning about his relationship with the dead girl.

Another session on the golf course? Matt wondered. It was hard to imagine how the conversation would go. With irreverent amusement, he pictured Kenning and the DI strolling down the fairway, and Bartholomew asking, 'So where *did* you get that lingerie? Would they have it in my size, do you think?'

For his own part, he couldn't see how to make use of the knowledge, but it occurred to him that there was one person who might, and so, when he returned to the cottage, he scribbled a note and put it, with the prints, into an envelope to post.

After Matt had done the evening rounds of feeding horses and dogs, he found himself standing in front of the fridge with the door open, completely devoid of any inspiration as to what to have for his own meal. Part of the trouble, he knew, was that he wasn't looking forward to spending another evening alone. If Kendra had been away on holiday or out with friends, he would have settled down, quite happily self-sufficient, with the dogs for company, but the knowledge that they were separated by emotional issues made it much harder to accept.

'Sod it!' he muttered aloud, slamming the fridge door. They were both missing each other—why should they be apart? If Charlie Brewer didn't want Matt at Birchwood, he would take Kendra out for dinner—somewhere romantic, with candlelight and music.

He lifted the telephone receiver and selected the phonebook entry for Birchwood Hall.

'Hello, Matt.'

It was Grace. Damn!

'Hi, Grace. Can I speak to Kendra?'

'Oh, I'm sorry. I don't think she wants to speak to you at the moment.'

Her tone was apologetic, but it didn't occur to Matt for an instant that it was sincere. He gritted his teeth.

'Well, could you at least ask her?'

'She's in the bath at the moment. I'll ask her when she gets out, but it won't do any good.'

'Just ask her, OK?'

'Of course.'

Matt put the phone down feeling even more unsettled than he had before. There was no way he was going to sit down to a solitary supper now. He wasn't too worried about what Grace had said, because he knew her for a troublemaker, but it

319

rankled that she should get away with interfering in their relationship. Had her father encouraged her to do so? he wondered. Charlie's readiness to try and break Kendra's bond with Matt had, quite frankly, surprised him. Although Matt had always known the businessman didn't think he was good enough for his daughter, as Matt's career had taken off, Brewer had seemed to become reconciled to their relationship.

He looked at his watch.

Half past six. Dinner at Birchwood Hall was normally at eight, so Kendra wouldn't have eaten yet. If he changed and set off straight away, he could ask her out in person. Immediately feeling more positive, Matt headed upstairs.

* * *

Having taken a little time to smarten up, it was nearly half past seven when Matt parked the MR2 in front of the Hall, and he was in a thoughtful mood. Thinking about Brewer's animosity of late, it had occurred to him that, having frightened Kendra away from Spinney Cottage, the mystery caller had not repeated his threats. Had the separation been his goal? Surely it couldn't have been Charlie Brewer's doing, could it? Matt well knew the businessman's colossal determination when he set his mind on something, but why the sudden resolve to ruin Matt's life? Arrogant he could certainly be, but Matt had never suspected him of being cruel or vindictive.

Greening answered the front door promptly, and Matt thought he looked a little surprised at the identity of the visitor—as well he might, Matt

320

thought, on reflection. As a long-term employee, he would be just as aware of the goings-on in the household as anyone else. However, the butler recovered his calm composure, returning Matt's greeting, but adding the unwelcome information that all three girls had gone out.

'Oh.' Matt felt a stab of disappointment. 'When?'

'About half an hour ago, sir.'

'For the evening, would you think?'

'They *were* all dressed up.' Greening hesitated, then ventured the information that he had heard mention of a fashion show.

'Ah.' Kelsey Grange, perhaps. Ironic. 'Did Mrs Brewer go too?'

'I think Mrs Brewer is in her workshop, sir.'

'OK, I'll go and find her, then. Thanks, Greening.'

Turning away, Matt descended the steps and set off along the front of the building. In the yard, he found the doors to the Brewers' huge garage standing open, and a glance into its lighted interior showed him that several of the cars were missing. It seemed that the girls weren't the only ones out tonight. Suppressing the urge to switch the light off, he turned his back on it and headed for the Hattery. The house had had lights glowing behind almost every window, too—typical of a family who had presumably never had to worry about the electricity bill. It had taken him several weeks to train Kendra out of the habit at the cottage.

Knocking softly on the showroom door, Matt let himself in. He could see Joy bending over her bench in the workshop beyond, apparently not having heard him.

'Hi,' he called.

321

Joy started and looked up quickly, a length of stiff blue ribbon in her hands and a couple of pins between her lips. She was wearing a red guernsey jumper and a Puffa waistcoat, her blonde hair caught up in a loose knot at the back of her head. Seeing her visitor, she removed the pins.

'Hello, Matt.'

After her initial surprise, she seemed almost disappointed, he thought.

'Were you expecting someone else?'

'No—that is—I wasn't expecting anyone. You startled me a bit, that's all. I'm afraid Kendra's not here. They've all gone to a fashion show at Kelsey Grange.'

'Yes, Greening said he thought they had. I'm surprised to find you here. I would have thought Joseph Wintermann would be right up your street.'

'You've heard of him, then?'

'Saw it in the paper.'

'Well, I probably would have gone, but I've got an order to finish for a wedding at the weekend.'

Matt leaned one hip on the bench and watched her quick fingers at work.

'Do you enjoy doing that?'

'Sorry?'

'Hat-making—millinery.'

'Oh, sorry. Yes I do—when I'm not under pressure.'

Picking one of the ornamental hatpins out of the ceramic vase, Matt examined it absent-mindedly.

'I rang earlier. Grace said Kendra didn't want to talk to me ...'

Joy didn't answer, and, after a moment, Matt glanced at her. She appeared lost in her work.

'Has she said anything to you?' he asked.

322

'Who?'

'Kendra. Grace said she didn't want to speak to me.'

'Oh, you know what Grace's like. I shouldn't say it of my own child, but she's a troublemaker. I don't know why she's got like that, unless it's jealousy.'

'Jealousy?' Matt stabbed the pin into an offcut of polystyrene foam.

'Yes. Of you and Kendra. Grace has never been very good at relationships—mainly because she goes into them for the wrong reasons.'

'For status?'

'Yes. She takes after Charlie in that. In fact, that's part of the problem. She's always trying to win her father's approval; I think she thinks Kendra's his favourite. But, anyway, I wouldn't worry too much about what she says.' She finished arranging the ribbon and selected a silk flower from a pile on the bench.

'I wouldn't, normally,' Matt said. 'It's just that things are so weird at the moment, I don't know what to think.' He jabbed at the foam extra vigorously, enjoying the texture of it.

'It'll be all right, Matt. I'm sure of it. You have to remember that her hormones are all over the place with the baby, and, of course, there's been a lot happening lately. It's not surprising that she found it all too much and ran for the family home. She's still young and she's had a fairly sheltered life until now. Just be patient and I'm sure things will turn out fine.' Joy gave him an encouraging smile and, for the first time, he noticed that she was looking tired. For once she actually looked her age. He wondered whether she had problems of her own.

Maybe Charlie's uncharacteristic behaviour of late had its roots in some deeper crisis.

'Joy, is everything OK?'

She looked up sharply.

'Why shouldn't it be?'

Matt shook his head.

'No reason, I just wondered.' He picked the polystyrene up on the end of the pin and looked at it. 'Actually, I thought you seemed a little stressed . . .'

'Just working too hard, I expect,' Joy said lightly. After several attempts, with fingers that shook slightly, she threaded a needle with blue thread and began to sew the flower onto the hat, next to the blue ribbon bow.

There was silence for a short while as she worked, and Matt slid the foam off the pin and began to perforate the other side, his mind drifting. He supposed he'd better call it a day and return to the cottage—maybe pick up a takeaway en route. He'd worry about working off the excess calories in the morning.

'Oh, for God's sake, stop doing that!' Joy snapped suddenly, then rubbed a hand over her face. 'Sorry, I'm tired.'

'No, *I'm* sorry.' Contrite and a little taken aback, Matt removed the hatpin from the foam and put it back in the vase with the others. 'I didn't realise—I mean, I thought it was just an offcut.'

'It is; it's just—you kept stabbing it with that bloody pin and it reminded me . . .'

Watching her closely, Matt saw her eyes begin to fill with tears. He straightened up and put out a hand to touch her arm, deeply concerned.

'Something *is* wrong, isn't it? What did it remind

324

you of?'

Joy shook her head, shrugging his hand off and bending over her work again.

'Nothing—just leave it, please Matt.'

'No. You can't tell me it's nothing. You're all on edge. What's the matter?'

After a moment's silence, Joy gave in.

'It's Deacon's cat. Did Kennie tell you about that?'

Matt nodded. 'She said it was run over.'

'Well, it wasn't. It was killed with one of those—a hatpin. Someone stuck one right through it. But you can't say anything,' she said, rushing on. '*Please* Matt—you won't, will you? No one's supposed to know.'

'Why? What's going on, Joy? Who did it?' Matt's mind was racing through the possibilities. 'Oh no . . . not Deacon?'

Joy's expression confirmed his fears.

'Oh, Joy . . .'

'How did you guess? Did he say something?'

'No, I had no idea. But I did know Frances was worried about him—Kendra told me the other night. I didn't think any more of it, to tell the truth.'

Joy nodded.

'I wondered how long it would be before Frannie guessed the truth, but, to be honest, the way Deacon's been lately, someone was bound to start asking questions. I told Charlie we needed more help, but he wouldn't hear of it.'

'So what's actually wrong with him?'

Joy looked down at the worktop.

'I shouldn't be telling you . . .'

'But you've already admitted something's wrong.

You can't stop there.'

Joy took a steadying breath, then looked Matt full in the eyes.

'Deacon has schizophrenia.'

He'd been expecting something of the sort, but the confirmation was still shocking.

'When? I mean, how long has he had it? When did you find out?'

'About nine months. It started while he was at university. We were getting reports that he was having problems concentrating and seemed increasingly withdrawn and depressed. The doctor on campus was worried about him, and eventually his roommates admitted that they'd been experimenting with drugs a time or two. I don't suppose it was anything more than a bit of grass, but it may just have been enough to trigger it. Apparently it can happen that way, sometimes.'

'I didn't know.'

'Nor did I. I don't suppose many people do. Deke was just unlucky. We brought him home and consulted a specialist. When he made the diagnosis, Charlie was devastated. At first he didn't believe it—didn't want to believe it, really. He's our only son, Matt, and Charlie had such plans for him. He took Deacon abroad to a special clinic so no one would know. We invented the story that there'd been kidnap threats and that he'd gone to stay with friends. It took a while to get his medication right. Deacon was gone for three months or more and, when he came back, Niall Delafield was with him.'

'Delafield's a *doctor*?'

'Not exactly. But he was an army medic, once upon a time. I'm not entirely sure where Charlie

326

found him—someone's recommendation, I think—but he's been a godsend. On the surface a security man and minder, but also a nurse. You see, the problem is that, when Deacon's on his medication, he feels fine, and, before long, he becomes convinced he no longer needs it—schizophrenics *can* recover, you know. And, anyway, they aren't normally violent. A lot of sufferers don't have psychotic episodes at all.'

'But not Deke.'

'No.' Joy shook her head sadly. 'The trouble is, it's such a fine balance. The medication has a sedative effect and, when he's on it, he tends to be dreamy and lethargic; he seems to have no real motivation and, some days, he gets the shakes. He hates taking it but, when he doesn't, the symptoms come back.'

'What happens then?'

'Well, mostly he's very withdrawn and depressed. He'll sit for hours, apparently doing nothing except muttering to himself or rocking to and fro. But then he can become jumpy and unpredictable, and, just occasionally, he has flashes of temper. It's scary, Matt—like dealing with a stranger. He's my own child and I feel I don't know him at all. Worse still, I can see that he's in torment and I can't help him—just can't help him at all.' Her eyes filled with tears and she stood staring sightlessly at the hat in her hands.

'I'm so sorry,' Matt said, putting a hand out to cover one of hers. Words just didn't seem adequate, but his touch seemed to recall her from the private hell she was gazing into.

'It was Charlie's idea to tell people he's on pills for a migraine problem and that he mustn't have

327

alcohol for the same reason. Alcohol makes it much harder to get the dose right.'

'And Delafield keeps an eye on him and makes sure he takes his medicine?'

'He tries to, but Deacon is getting more and more cunning in finding ways to outwit him.'

'And is that what happened when he attacked the cat?'

'We think so. It's the only explanation. I came in here early that morning and found the poor thing on the floor. Oh, Matt—it was horrific. It made me physically sick. The pin was pushed right through from one side to the other—the poor little thing ...' Her face contorted as she recalled the gruesome find. 'And it's so sad, because he loves cats, and, once he was back on his medication, he had no memory of what he'd done. But every time I look at him now, I remember ... Niall was marvellous, he offered to take the blame; told Deacon he'd accidentally run the cat over. There was a huge row.'

Stabbed with a hatpin, Matt thought with revulsion, remembering the jokey conversation Deacon had walked in on, the night of the barbeque. Had that, in fact, planted the idea in his subconscious? He tried to recall who had started it, and had a horrible feeling it might have been himself.

'I find it hard to believe that you've kept all this from the girls—his illness, I mean. Is that fair? Is it safe, even?'

Joy looked uncomfortable.

'Charlie insisted that we did. He dreaded the secret getting out—said, if the girls knew, then, sooner or later, one of them would let it slip and

328

then everyone would know. He said Deacon would be all right as long as he took his meds. Oh, I argued with him, I can tell you. I thought it was wrong—but he was adamant; you know what he's like.'

'It *was* wrong,' Matt stated with conviction. 'What if it hadn't been the cat he turned on? What if it had been one of his sisters?'

'I know,' Joy said miserably. 'I've thought of nothing else ever since, but you have to understand, this was the first time he'd been violent. He'd never done anything like that before. But now even Charlie has admitted that something has to be done. Niall's adjusted his medication, but that worries me too. I mean, Niall's been very good, but he's not a proper doctor, or even a trained psychiatric nurse, and sometimes I think Charlie forgets that. Anyway, Deke's been fine on the higher dose, until . . .'

'Until what . . . ? What's happened?' Matt was watching Joy closely and saw her eyes flicker towards the window, almost involuntarily. Suddenly all the individual anomalies of the evening began to connect in his mind. Greening's surprise, the missing cars, and Joy's obvious anxiety; seen together they became ominous. With a chill premonition, he asked, 'Joy—*where's Deacon now?*'

'That's just it,' she admitted, miserably. 'We don't know. He was in his room resting and then he was gone. Niall says he was upset and asking about the cat again this afternoon. He wonders if he was beginning to remember—can you imagine how terrifying that would be? Oh, Matt, I'm so scared! He's such a gentle person—knowing he'd

329

done something like that would tear him apart. I'm afraid . . .' She didn't finish the sentence, her face crumpling as a desperate sob broke past her guard.

Matt was pretty certain he knew what she couldn't bring herself to say. She was worried that, for someone with Deacon's sensitivity, the knowledge that he was capable of doing such a thing might prove impossible to live with. Much as he would have liked to reassure her, Matt couldn't. He was very much afraid she could be right. He turned, instead, to the practicalities.

'How long has he been gone?'

Joy took a deep shuddering breath and pulled a tissue from a box on the worktop.

'Um . . . we think he must have gone about the same time as the girls did. With all the commotion of them setting off, he must have slipped out without anyone seeing him. Niall and Charlie are out looking for him now.'

Matt consulted his watch.

'So, about forty minutes or so. Is he—I mean, has he taken his medication?'

'Yes, I think so. Niall says so, anyway.' She sniffed and wiped her nose. 'I just thank God Niall's here.'

Matt wished he shared her faith in the ex-army medic and wondered whether her husband had told her about Delafield's sexual tastes. He shrugged the thought away. After all, it had no bearing on the present problem.

'Has Deke taken a car?'

Joy shook her head.

'No.'

Matt thought of the garage, wide open and inviting. If Deacon had doubled back, he could have helped himself to whichever of the vehicles he fancied—always supposing he could lay his hands on the keys. But then that would be the action of someone who was thinking logically and who had somewhere in mind to go, and Matt wasn't sure either factor applied in Deacon's case.

'Have you told the police?'

'No. He's been gone less than an hour. They won't be interested.'

'But—with his condition . . .'

'No! Charlie doesn't want anyone to know.'

'But surely Deacon's safety is what matters?' Matt felt exasperation rising.

'Of course it is! I know that, but they're sure they'll find him. I mean—he can't have got far on foot, can he?'

'The longer it takes, the further he will get,' Matt pointed out. 'Look, can I help? Which way have they gone, do you know?'

Joy shook her head helplessly.

'I think Niall was going towards the town, but I'm not sure where Charlie went.'

'OK, well there's nothing I can do here, so I'll go back by way of Rockfield and up over the hill by the gallops. I'll leave my phone on, so let me know if there's any news.'

Joy thanked him and promised she would, and he left her drying her eyes and went out into the bitter wind to collect his car, scanning the vehicles in the garage on his way past. As far as he could see, they were all there except for Brewer's car, the Land Rover, and the Porsche that Grace liked to be seen in—presumably the girls had taken that. Just to be on the safe side, he paused long enough to turn the light off and operate the electronic closing mechanism on the wide rollback door.

In the MR2, he turned the heating up and, as he pulled away, a few pellets of icy rain bounced off the windscreen.

'So much for global warming,' he muttered, hoping that Deacon had found somewhere out of the cold wind.

There was little traffic on the back road to Rockfield, where Matt hesitated before turning into the drive that led to the farmhouse and yard. He thought it unlikely that Deacon would have gone there, but, for the sake of five minutes, it seemed worth checking, just to be sure.

John Leonard answered his knock, blinking slightly, as if he'd just woken up. He looked surprised to find Matt on his doorstep.

'Matt. Er . . . come in.'

'I won't, thanks. Actually, I'm looking for Deacon. I don't suppose he's been here, has he?'

'*Deacon?* No. Why?' Leonard looked understandably mystified; Deacon wasn't a frequent visitor to the yard.

Unable to think of a convincing lie, Matt opted for the partial truth.

'He seems to have gone AWOL and, as I was passing, I promised to pop in and ask if you'd seen him.'

'Good for him, I say,' the trainer growled. 'Time he showed a bit of spirit.'

'Yeah.' Matt didn't know what else to say. A couple of hours ago he would have agreed wholeheartedly. 'Well, I'll see you in the morning.'

Back in the car, Matt left the farm and took the narrow lane that led up the steep hill parallel to the gallops. Just over a car's width wide with passing spaces, it was flanked by fields fenced with barbed wire and hawthorn hedges of varying density and, to Matt's knowledge, led nowhere except to a group of isolated farm buildings standing on the very top of the rise. A couple of miles further on, the lane curved round the head of a deep valley before descending to the village of Langford Combe.

As the car climbed out of the dip, the wind drove another scattering of ice particles against the windscreen and Matt's mobile phone gave a loud *ding ding* to indicate a message left. Operating the keypad clumsily with his left hand, Matt's attempts to retrieve the message whilst on the move were interrupted by another call.

'Hello?' he said.

'Luke?'

Matt just managed to check the instinctive denial, remembering that it was the name he'd used on his visit to Kelsey Grange.

'Er, yes—speaking.'

'Is he there?' the voice demanded, and something about it sounded familiar. In the background Matt could hear the thumping rhythm of a pop track.

'Who?'

'Niall. Is he with you?'

'No. Why would he be?' Matt had placed the accent now; it was indeed Delafield's boyfriend.

'Well, he's not *here*,' Wintermann said, with an audible tremor. 'So, if he's there, you can tell him—from me—that I'm through being fucked around, and I never want to see him again! You're welcome to him, OK? He's let me down one time too many. Well, this is the last fucking time!'

Taking advantage of a pause in the emotional deluge, Matt said quickly, 'Hang on a minute, Joe. I told you, he's not here. And anyway, Niall and I are just friends.'

'Niall doesn't have friends,' came the bitter reply, 'he just uses people.'

'Well, I'm no threat to you, I promise. I'm straight—I have a girlfriend.'

'So how do you know him, then? Were you in the army together?'

'No, we just work for the same bloke.' Matt steered the car into the side of the road, took it out of gear, and applied the handbrake, searching all the while for a way to gain the designer's confidence. To prolong the conversation, he asked, 'So what's happened?'

'Well, he didn't come, did he? He promised to be here and he didn't fucking come!'

'Your fashion show . . .'

'Yeah, of course—my show. I saved him the best seat—should've known better, I suppose. Now everybody knows I've been stood up. I feel so bloody stupid!'

'He's a shit,' Matt agreed. 'Did you try and ring him?'

'Of course I tried, but he wouldn't speak to me. Said he was sorry, but he was too busy to talk, and then he cut me off. Now he won't answer at all. Well, sorry just doesn't cut it anymore. Where does he think he gets off, treating me like that?'

'Did he tell you he was with Deacon?' Matt asked provocatively.

'No.' Warily. 'Is he?'

'Well, I know he was looking for him. You do *know* about Deacon?'

'Oh God, do I ever? It's all I hear—Deacon this, Deacon fuckin' that. When his precious Deacon calls he has to drop everything and run. It happened the other day. First time we'd had a night out for ages and then the phone rings and he's off. Left me outside the nightclub and told me to get a taxi home. We'd only just got there. Bastard!'

'He *didn't*! And you think it was Deacon who called?'

'I know it was. Niall used his name. He was trying to calm him down.'

'And why was that? Did he tell you?'

'No, but I guessed. You see, I don't think he had the night off at all,' Wintermann confided. 'I think he'd left Deacon somewhere and the kid had got himself in trouble. I reckon Niall was shitting himself in case the big chief found out he was shirking. He's onto a cushy number there, and there's no way he wants to lose it. But I'm getting sick of it, you know? It's like his bloody job means more to him than I do.'

'When *was* that—can you remember?'

'Um, I don't know ... about three weeks ago, maybe? What's it to you?'

'Was it a Saturday?' Matt held his breath. Three weeks ago, on a Saturday night, was when Sophie was killed. Surely that couldn't be a coincidence?

'Yeah ... Why?' The reply came slowly, cautiously.

'And that's all you heard?'

'It was a nightclub; it wasn't exactly quiet in there,' Wintermann pointed out.

'Have you ever met Deacon?'

There was a pause.

'No. Why . . . ? Look, what's all this about?'

'Did he ever tell you what happened that night?'

'Not really. I asked, but he said it was all taken care of.'

'So, what nightclub were you in?' Matt could tell he was pushing it, but he had to try. If the nightclub had CCTV, the police would have the evidence they needed that Delafield had lied to them.

It was a question too far.

'No, look—you're fucking me about! Who are you? You're not Niall's friend. Leave me alone.'

'Joe, please—it could be important . . .' Matt began, but his phone bleeped to signal a lost connection and the display showed call ended.

Lost in thought, he stared out at the section of hedge illuminated by the beam of his headlights. Twigs and brambles danced in the gusty wind and now and then the car was hit by sleety rain. The engine was still running, the heater pushing out a comfortable level of warmth, and he hoped that, wherever he was, Deacon had found some sort of shelter.

Deacon.

Why had he phoned Delafield in a panic on the night of Doogie's party? Matt would dearly have liked to know what time that had been. According to Casey's contact, the minder's story had been that he and Deacon had left the party together, and the police had apparently been satisfied that the footage from the CCTV at the garage backed that up, but what if the figure in the car hadn't been Deacon but Wintermann? The two young men were of a similar build and colouring. On grainy videotape, it would probably be impossible

336

to tell who was who. If Joe was telling the truth—and there seemed to be no reason for him to lie—then Kendra's brother had been left at the party to amuse himself while Delafield pursued his own pleasures. Deacon had certainly been there when he and Jamie arrived, Matt remembered, but for how much longer? What kind of trouble had he got himself into that Delafield should have dropped everything—including the unfortunate Joe—to hurry to his rescue?

The answer that immediately sprang to mind was horrifying but refused to be dismissed. It was clear that—like Jamie—at the time Sophie had been attacked, Deacon's whereabouts were unaccounted for and the police weren't aware of the fact. At best, the troubled young man may have been a witness to her killing; at worst . . . It took no very great leap of imagination to see that someone who, in the grip of psychosis, could deal out a cruel death to a beloved pet, could also have been responsible for the death of Sophie Bradford.

Without medication, Deacon was prone to 'flashes of temper', his mother had told him earlier. Had he taken his medication on that Saturday night?

Reluctantly, Matt picked up his phone again. He didn't have Bartholomew's contact number with him—the card was under a fridge magnet in the kitchen at Spinney Cottage—but a directory enquiries company put him through to Charlborough Police Station. At this point he suffered a check. Asking for DI Bartholomew, he was told that he was at present unavailable. Declining to speak to anyone else, Matt gave his name and requested that Bartholomew call him back as soon as possible.

Frustrated, he cut the connection. Thinking of Joy had presented him with another dilemma. Should he tell Deacon's parents what he'd found out from Wintermann and warn them that he'd contacted Bartholomew? He shrank from the thought of Joy's distress, but it was inescapable. And what of Charlie, who was so desperate to present a normal front to the world that he had kept his son's illness a secret—even from his daughters? How would he react to the possibility that Deacon had been responsible for Sophie's death?

While Matt was debating his next move, a movement caught his eye. Away up the lane, at the dim limits of the car's headlights, a figure was climbing over a gate from one of the fields. Even though it was too distant to be distinct, the idea that it was anyone other than Deacon didn't occur to Matt for a second. Wearing only jeans and a pale tee shirt, in spite of the bitter wind, the person was slender but unmistakably male. As Matt watched, the man glanced back down the lane towards the car, shielding his eyes with his hand, and then set off, half walking, half running, in the other direction.

Losing sight of him round a bend in the lane, Matt put the car in gear and drove slowly in pursuit. Just as his headlights picked out the hurrying figure once more, his mobile phone began to trill. He picked it off the seat with his left hand.

'Is that Matt Shepherd?' It was Bartholomew.

'Yes. Thanks for getting back to me.'

'Well, strictly speaking, I'm off duty. I just

popped back to the office for something, but my sergeant said this sounded important.'

'Yes, it is—but . . .'

Ahead of Matt, Deacon picked up speed and, worried that he was panicking the youngster, Matt pulled in and stopped the car at the side of the lane, its two nearside wheels on the verge.

'Look, can you hold on for a moment?' he said into the phone and, without waiting for an answer, dropped it back onto the seat and opened the car door. Stepping out into the biting wind, he shouted, 'Deacon wait! It's Matt. Wait for me.'

To his relief, Deacon slowed and turned, squinting against the lights as he continued to walk backwards with short, jerky steps.

Realising that the lights were intimidating, Matt reached in and switched them to dipped beam, turning the hazard warning lights on at the same time.

'Deacon, stop! I just want to talk.'

This time Deacon hesitated.

'Who is it?'

'Matt—you know, Kendra's boyfriend.'

Leaving the car door open, he stepped round it and walked forward a few paces.

Deacon looked blankly back.

'Where's Kendra?'

'She isn't here, Deke. She's gone out with Grace.'

'I can't see you—I can't see your face. Who are you? Stay away from me!' Panicking, Deacon started to back away again, his own face sheet-white in the glare.

'It's all right. I'll stay here. I won't hurt you.'

Through the open front of his leather jacket the

339

wind was cutting through the fabric of Matt's sweatshirt as if it didn't exist and, even at a distance of several feet, he could see that Deacon was shuddering with cold, hunching his back and hugging his bare arms, his dark hair whipping around his head. Matt remembered that he had his new fleece in the back of the car.

'Deke, stay there. I'll get you a coat. Just hang on.'

Keeping an eye on the figure outlined by the lights, he retraced his steps and reached in. On the passenger seat his phone was emitting a tinny voice and he picked it up.

'I'll be with you in a moment,' he told it, without preamble. 'Please hang on. It's really important.'

Moments later he was advancing cautiously towards Kendra's brother, the navy fleece, with its red and white logo, held before him, invitingly.

'This'll be warm, Deke. Come on, take it. Put it on.'

Although Deacon looked longingly at the garment, he made no move to reach for it, but neither did he move away as, approaching as if to a nervous horse, Matt drew closer. Finally, stepping slightly to the side, he held the fleece up and Deacon obediently slipped first one arm and then the other into the sleeves.

'Good. That's better,' Matt said.

'Matt?' The word was spoken on a note of discovery.

'That's right. What are you doing out here, Deke?'

Deacon looked away across the darkened landscape and, for a moment, Matt thought he wasn't going to answer, but then he said, through

340

chattering teeth, 'I had to try and find her.'

'Who? Kendra?'

Deacon shook his head.

'The girl. She was pretty—really pretty. She was dancing.'

Matt was touched by dread.

'Do you mean Sophie, Deke?'

'Sophie . . . ?'

'The dancing girl. Was her name Sophie?'

Deacon looked away again.

'Where's Frannie?'

'She's with Kendra,' Matt said, beginning to shiver himself. He wasn't sure whether Deacon's slightly irrational state of mind was the result of too much medication, or not enough. 'They've gone out for the evening. They'll be home later.'

'Frannie's kind. She's my favourite.'

'Why don't you come and sit in the car and I'll see if I can get Frannie on my mobile,' Matt suggested. 'It'll be warmer in there.'

The temptation was to try and lead Deacon back onto the subject of the dancing woman, but he wasn't at all sure it was either wise or in the lad's best interests. As it turned out, his thoughts drifted back that way without prompting.

'She wouldn't wake up,' he said suddenly.

'Who wouldn't?' Matt's heart began to thump heavily.

'The dancing girl. She had pretty hair—long and blonde. She sat down and went to sleep. I didn't know what to do.' He turned towards Matt and there were tears running in sparkling trails down his thin face. 'She wouldn't wake up.'

'So what did you do, Deke?'

'I just wanted to talk to her. She looked so

341

pretty, dancing.' Then, with a sudden shift, 'I was smoking—you won't tell them, will you?'

Matt assured him that he wouldn't.

'I knew you wouldn't. I like you, Matt. *You* wouldn't hurt me, would you?'

'Of course not. Why? Who's hurt you, Deke?'

Deacon's face screwed up like that of an upset child and he started to walk again, turning away from the car and its promised shelter.

'Niall said I mustn't talk about it.'

'Has Niall hurt you? What has he done?'

'He took care of her.'

'Took care of the girl?'

Deacon nodded.

'He says I mustn't talk about it or I'll be locked away. He says he'll tell everyone I'm mad and they'll take me away. Can he do that?'

Matt shook his head.

'No, of course he can't,' he said, with more conviction than he felt. Delafield could certainly set things in motion—cause questions to be asked—but, unless Matt was very much mistaken, the minder would be just as reluctant to have his charge committed to an institution as Deacon would be to go. If Matt's suspicions were correct, then just under the troubled surface of the youngster's mind were memories that could have Delafield consigned to a cell for a good few years to come. Took care of the girl, did he? Hefted her body over the side of the bridge and down into the undergrowth, more likely.

'When did he threaten you?' he asked. 'Was it today? Is that why you ran away?'

'Yes. No. It was the dream . . . Oh God! I can't get it out of my head.'

342

Deacon's hands flew to his temples and he stopped so abruptly that Matt passed him and had to turn back.

He saw the lad's fingers curl tightly into his dark hair and heard the tormented groan that he uttered.

'It was horrible,' Deacon said brokenly. 'And I keep thinking—what if it wasn't a dream? What then? What if I really killed Benjy without even knowing it? What kind of person does that make me? Oh, God, I wish I could just remember, instead of seeing things—pictures—that don't make sense. It's like it's all there on the edges of my mind but, when I try to look at it, it slides away. What's the matter with me?'

Matt was way out of his depth, but he felt that, whatever Deacon had or hadn't done, this wasn't the best time or place to try and exorcise his demons. He put a hand on the lad's arm, but the contact made Deacon jump as if an electric shock had passed through his body.

'Come on,' Matt urged gently. 'Come back to the car, Deke. There's nothing that can't be sorted out.'

Deacon shook his arm free, moving sideways a pace.

'You don't understand. I loved Benjy. How could I do that? *How*? And the girl—she's in my head, too, kissing me, smiling at me. I thought she liked me.'

In spite of himself, Matt said, 'And then what happened?'

Deacon tilted his face to the night sky, where windblown scraps of cloud scudded across the darker vault. One or two stars showed, and a three-quarter moon.

'She smelled wonderful. I tried to hold her, but she pushed me away . . .' He put a hand up to his face again, running his fingers down his left cheek.

Matt remembered the stinging blow Sophie had dealt Jamie.

'Did she slap you? Is that what happened?'

'I pushed her and she sat down. I only wanted a kiss. She wanted it, too—didn't she? She was so pretty, and now . . . now she's dead.' Deacon's gaze dropped to Matt's face, his eyes gleaming in the light from the distant car. 'Was it me, Matt? Did *I* do it? I can't remember.' His voice began to rise in an apparent agony of frustration. 'I can't bloody remember! Did I kill her? Oh God, I wish all this stuff would get out of my head and leave me alone!'

Deacon started to walk again, weaving from side to side as though drunk, but nevertheless swiftly putting distance between himself and Matt, who stood helplessly watching him go.

He was rapidly moving beyond the reach of the car's headlights and, fearful of losing him completely, Matt decided to go back to the vehicle and bring it closer.

Breaking into a run, he retraced his steps and slid behind the wheel of the idling MR2. Shutting the door, he shifted the gear lever into first and was about to pull forward off the verge when a glow in the rear-view mirror signalled the approach of another vehicle.

Hoping that it was either Brewer or Delafield, Matt lowered the side window and signalled for it to slow down, trusting that the driver would see his hazard warning lights and pull up alongside.

344

It didn't.

Barely slowing to pass Matt's car in the narrow lane, a four-wheel-drive vehicle whooshed by, its full-beam headlights instantly picking out the moving figure on the brow of the hill, the red and white target on his borrowed jacket bobbing with each stride.

Matt's first thought was to thank God that he'd loaned Deacon the highly visible fleece, his second, bewilderment that the other driver didn't appear to be slowing at all.

'Slow down . . . For God's sake, slow down!' he muttered. 'What the hell are you doing?'

Frantic, he leaned on the car's horn, watching with growing horror as the vehicle rapidly closed on the walking man. Whether Deacon heard the warning or not, Matt would never know. The bulk of the 4x4 hid him from view in the last few moments before—with no attempt to brake—it hit the youngster with a sickening thud that was clearly audible where Matt sat, frozen in his seat, some sixty or seventy yards away.

15

'No!'

Matt's cry was worthless, coming eons too late and going unheard by anyone but himself. Seconds later, he was once more out of his car and running to the scene of the collision, still struggling to believe that the driver of the 4x4 hadn't seen Deacon before he had run into him. Had he been on the phone perhaps, or fiddling with his radio? Whatever the case, reality was in the motionless form at the side of the road, its outline just visible to Matt in the glow of the vehicle's reversing lights as it backed up.

The 4x4 stopped, slightly slewed across the lane, a few yards from Deacon's body, and, as Matt drew nearer, the driver's door opened and someone stepped out, but instead of immediately hurrying to see what—if anything—could be done for the casualty, he stood stock-still, with one hand on the door, watching Matt's approach.

Shock, Matt supposed, slowing as he reached the scene.

'What the hell were you doing?' he demanded. 'Didn't you see him?'

Deacon lay partly on his side, face down in the frosty grass of the verge, with one arm outflung and both legs hideously misshapen, the thigh bones curving impossibly.

'Ring for an ambulance!' Matt instructed, and then knelt down, wishing he had a torch. The moon was free of cloud now, but Deacon was in the shelter of the hedge and his face and upper body lay in shadow. There was no way Matt was going to move him; Kendra's brother was in a pretty good approximation of the classic recovery position, and experience with racing falls had taught him that you don't touch if you don't have to.

Putting a hand lightly on Deacon's chest, he felt the shallowest of rise and falls, and, giving up on the silent bystander who still hadn't moved, he unzipped his jacket and reached into the inside pocket to find his own phone, only to remember that it was lying on the passenger seat of the MR2.

A beam of light fell on Deacon's face, and, with

renewed hope, Matt looked up. The 4x4 driver had found a torch and was coming closer.

'Is he dead?'

'Not yet, but he will be if we don't get an ambulance here!' Matt told him, urgency rendering his voice sharp. 'I haven't got my phone.'

The torchlight transferred to Matt's face, catching him full in the eyes.

'Get that bloody thing out of my face!' he snapped, blinking.

'He's wearing your jacket,' the voice beyond the light said in a faintly accusing tone.

'Yeah, well he was cold,' Matt replied unthinkingly. 'Look, have you got a mobile or not?' He was beginning to think he was dealing with a second case of mental imbalance. Surely everyone had a mobile phone these days; certainly you'd expect the driver of what appeared to be a fairly modern Land Rover to have one, so why on earth didn't he use it to call for help?

The driver ignored his question, and the light stayed, infuriatingly, on Matt's face.

He stood up.

'Phone . . . ? All right, I'll get mine. Look, don't just stand there! Have you got anything to put over him? He needs to be kept warm but, whatever you do, don't move him.'

'You've fucked everything up now!'

The driver's voice was vehement, but so low that, for a moment, Matt wasn't sure he'd heard the words aright over the noise of the wind. He paused in the act of turning to run back to his car.

'You what?' he demanded, squinting against the torchlight which was still shining in his face.

'Giving him your fucking jacket! What did you go and do that for?'

'I told you—he was cold. He only had a tee shirt ...' As he began to speak, recognition came to Matt. The slightly gruff tone, the Land Rover, the fact that the man had recognised what was, after all, a fairly new coat—the man with the torch was Niall Delafield.

Suddenly, the full, chilling significance of his remarks was borne home to Matt. Delafield had *meant* to hit the running figure; and not because he'd thought it was Deacon but because, in that distinctive jacket and having just passed the MR2, he had mistaken him for Matt.

Almost involuntarily, he took a step back, glancing down at the motionless body at his feet. What to do now? The very fact that Delafield had drawn Matt's attention to his mistake augured badly for the future. By not attempting to pass the deed off as an accident, he had, in effect, signalled his intention of finishing the job.

'Look—he's still breathing. If we can get him an ambulance, he might still be all right.'

'Do I look like I care? He's a fucking fruitcake— he'd be better off dead. Tidier all round.'

Matt took another step back. He was loath to leave Deacon to the mercy of Delafield, but he had no choice. The lad needed an ambulance and his erstwhile minder was clearly not going to call for one. Added to which, if he was reading it right, his own situation was looking increasingly precarious. For both of their sakes, he needed to get to his phone, but all at once the car seemed a frighteningly long way away.

'You can't just leave him,' he said, mentally

poised to run and trying to disguise the fact. 'After all, *you* ran him down.'

'Ah, yes. A shame, that,' came the answer, and Matt sensed rather than saw the accompanying shrug. 'Just stepped out in front of me with no warning. Off his head, poor bloke; suffering a psychotic episode, no doubt. Who's to argue? There'll be no witnesses . . .'

Matt swallowed, his mouth dry.

'They'll know you're lying. The forensic people can tell exactly what happened.'

'Why don't you let me worry about that?' Delafield suggested calmly. 'Time they get their act together, I'll be long gone.'

There didn't seem to be anything more to say, so Matt ran.

He'd expected Delafield to give chase, and hoped that his own fitness would give him the edge he needed over the bulkier man; what he didn't expect was for Delafield to give chase in the Land Rover. Matt had barely covered twenty yards when he heard the powerful engine roar, and twenty more when the headlights caught him, sending his running shadow leaping fifteen feet ahead of him down the road.

How the hell had he got the damned thing turned round so quickly in the narrow lane?

Matt ran harder than he'd ever run before, desperate to reach the relative safety of the car and the phone that represented a lifeline for Deacon and himself.

Slipping slightly as he decelerated on the gritty surface of the lane, Matt grabbed the car's door handle and pulled it open, glancing back at the oncoming Land Rover as he did so. In that instant he realised that, as before, Delafield had no intention of slowing. He was aiming the 4x4, like a lethal weapon, squarely at the front of the MR2, and Matt had no illusions about which vehicle would come off best in the encounter.

Casting one regretful look at the mobile phone on the passenger seat, he abandoned the idea of retrieving it and concentrated, instead, on his own personal survival. His instincts were shrieking at him to get away from the car, given the speed at which the Land Rover was travelling, to go behind it was clearly suicidal, and to move to the side a moment too soon would make him an easy target should Delafield swerve to follow him.

He had only fractions of a second to play with and, in the end, he left it one crucial moment too late—his dive to the right being thrown off course by the reflex action of the open door as the Land Rover ploughed into the nose of the silver sports car.

Tarmac, hedge, and sky barrelled crazily round Matt and he fetched up on his back at the side of the lane with his head and shoulders resting on the grass verge. From there he had a grandstand view of the Land Rover as it mounted the bonnet of his car like some giant copulating metal monster. The sound was horrific as the sleek bodywork collapsed under the strain and the windscreen imploded, showering the interior with glass.

The impact had driven both vehicles several yards down the road, the Land Rover finishing up with its front wheels dropping into the seating compartment of the MR2, a chilling affirmation of the wisdom of Matt's decision. For a moment, there was relative silence, broken only by the small sounds of settling machinery. The Land Rover engine had stalled, but any hopes Matt might have entertained that the danger was past were swiftly routed as Delafield attempted to restart it. Obediently, the 4x4 hiccupped back to life and, with a creaking groan of distressed metal, Delafield began to rock it to and fro in an attempt to break free.

Pushing himself up into a sitting position, Matt saw to his dismay that the manoeuvre showed every sign of success; with each pull backwards the Land Rover rose higher, and it looked to be only a matter of time before it would have all four wheels on the tarmac again. While it couldn't be said that Matt's brain was functioning at full power after being thrown across the lane, his self-preservation instincts were unimpaired and they were unequivocal in urging him to put as much distance as he could between himself and the Land Rover as quickly as was humanly possible.

Scrambling to his feet, Matt was relieved to find his limbs were all in working order—if a little bruised. He glanced up and down the lane in momentary indecision and came to the rapid conclusion that his best hope was to head back down the lane towards Rockfield, though he knew he had little chance of reaching it on foot before the Land Rover caught up with him. Even a practically unachievable goal was better than no goal at all, which was what he would face if he went the other way, past Deacon Brewer's inert form and on into the no-man's-land beyond.

Seconds later he was sprinting past the revving 4x4—still riding high on the mangled remains of the MR2—and away round the bend in the lane.

With the wind in his ears, Matt couldn't hear anything except his breathing and the slapping of his soft-soled shoes on the road, and the sensation that the Land Rover had broken free and was bearing down on him began to prey on his mind to the extent that he had to keep checking over his shoulder. He had covered the best part of two hundred yards and glanced back half a dozen times when he finally saw the sight he'd been dreading— the oncoming lights of a vehicle.

There was never any doubt in his mind that it was the Land Rover; quite apart from the fact that traffic was rare on this road, this vehicle was dragging a section of metalwork beneath it, scraping over the tarmac with a horrendous screech, and sparking like the fifth of November.

Whatever was caught under it didn't seem to be slowing the Land Rover much, and, desperately, Matt searched the dark line of the right-hand hedge for a thin patch as he ran. He was instinctively looking to the right because that way, albeit a good mile or more distant in the valley bottom, lay the farmhouse and stable yard of Rockfield. However, as the roar of the pursuing vehicle grew ever louder, he would have taken any route that offered.

Finally, just when Matt had begun to think his luck had run out, a gap appeared in the blackthorn and, stepping up onto the verge, he launched himself through in a flying leap designed to clear any wire that might span the opening.

There was indeed wire, its barbs making themselves felt in a burning pain down the length of his right leg as he caught his toe in the top strand and sprawled untidily onto the spiky stubble

352

headland of the field beyond. The lights that had chased him down the lane followed him still, shining above his head as the Land Rover bumped up onto the verge and ploughed into the fence in its turn. At this point, the wire—which Matt had been roundly cursing just moments before—now earned his gratitude, as the three strands combined to bring the heavy vehicle to a halt, its engine stalling and its headlights illuminating nothing but empty acres of ploughed earth and a couple of startled pheasants.

'Fuck!' Delafield said plainly into the sudden silence that followed, and, keeping low, Matt raised himself onto all fours and scuttled closer to the hedge, where he paused to catch his breath, taking in the lie of the land while he waited to see what Delafield's next move would be.

On this side of the hedge the wind was bitingly cold and Matt could feel the chill of evaporating sweat on his body. Above, the moon was sailing in a sky that was now clear of all but the wispiest ribbons of cloud, and it was plain to Matt that any attempt to cross the huge open field would leave him horribly exposed. Looking to his right, he could see a dark cluster of farm buildings on the skyline, but he'd driven past them many times and knew there was no farmhouse amongst them. The barns and stables might offer a place to hide, in the short term—always supposing he could reach them unseen—but they offered little in the long term.

While Matt racked his brains for a plan of action, the Land Rover engine turned over twice and came back to life. Twanging free of the wire, the 4x4 reversed and moved off up the lane, but slowly—as if searching for something. That something turned out to be a gateway and there was clearly no gate to hinder its progress, for, as Matt watched with a sinking heart, its headlights blazed out across the field once more, some twenty yards further on, and began to swing round in an arc that would inevitably bring them towards his position by the hedge.

It was time to be moving again.

Standing up, Matt bent the top strand of wire down as far as it would go and stepped carefully over. Back on the tarmac, the need to make a decision about which way to go became imperative. His idea of heading for Rockfield had lost some of its feasibility but, then again, he didn't have a better one, so he set off at a run along the lane once more, hoping that the next field might perhaps be less accessible to the Land Rover and gain him a little leeway.

Slowing down as he reached the first gateway, he peered round the gatepost and saw the Land Rover in the far corner but heading back. It looked as though Delafield was doing a sweep of the whole field, driving round the perimeter to avoid the uneven plough.

Matt hesitated. The long metal gate to the field was opened right back against the hedge and he toyed with the idea of shutting it, to buy him some precious time. On the other hand, it would be a clear signal of his whereabouts, so, resisting the temptation, he stepped back and ran on.

Pounding over the tarmac, Matt was grateful for the endurance fitness that his profession required, but aware that a prolonged game of catch-me-if-you-can with a motor vehicle could have only one ending. He had to get off the road and out of sight; after all, surely Delafield couldn't afford to remain in the area for too long, with the evidence of what he'd done laid out for any chance passer-by to see. On the other hand, where could he go? As the only witness, did Delafield think that removing Matt would solve his problems? Matt couldn't believe he'd be that short-sighted. He must know that he'd burnt his bridges, so his determination to silence Matt could only be to buy himself time in which to make a clean getaway.

Spotting a gap low down in the hedge to his right, Matt stopped, threw himself to his stomach, and began to wriggle under the bottom strand of wire. A knobbly root made the manoeuvre extremely uncomfortable, but that was forgotten when, halfway under, Matt felt his jacket snag securely on one of the barbs. His attempt to tear his way free was unsuccessful—the thick leather withstood all the force he could bring to bear from his restricted position and all he succeeded in doing was to gouge a painful furrow in the skin of his back. Neither did it seem possible to shrug the garment off, his arms necessarily being in front, in order to help pull him through the narrow gap.

Directing a stream of invective at whomever it was who had invented barbed wire, Matt fought back panic and tried to think rationally, an attempt that was routed when he heard the roar of the Land Rover, plainly back on the road and bearing down on the spot where he lay.

Shit! Would Delafield see him? What portion of his legs still protruded from the untidy line of blackthorn? Should he throw everything at the struggle to get under the wire or should he lie still

355

and hope that he wouldn't be seen in the shadow of the hedge? In spite of the risk, Matt chose the latter, aware that nothing draws the eye like movement. Even so, it was as much as he could do to lie perfectly motionless as Delafield drove closer, and he found himself imagining the agony of having the 4x4 run up on the verge and over his outstretched legs. He'd had brutal evidence that the deed was well within the ex-army man's capability and it would be a sure-fire way of ensuring that Matt ran no further.

By the time the Land Rover thundered past, Matt was shaking like a washing machine on spin cycle. He let out the lungful of breath he'd been holding, but there was no time to celebrate his narrow escape for, seeing the empty road ahead, Delafield would soon realise that he had overshot the mark and almost certainly return, no doubt driving more slowly and searching the banks and hedges for any sign of Matt.

Reaching awkwardly behind with one hand, he managed to locate the part of his jacket that had caught on the wire and, by dint of wriggling backwards an inch or two, unhook it. Even as he started to crawl forward once more, he heard a screech of tyres as the Land Rover's brakes were savagely applied further down the lane.

Moments later, Matt was out the other side of the hedge and getting to his feet. With relief, he found he was in a different field. This one was laid to pasture, if the short-cropped turf could be called that, and, in the pale light of the moon, he could see a number of irregularly shaped dark objects a little way off. At first he thought they might be cows, but, as he stood up, the movement attracted their attention and he could see by their size and the length of their necks that they were, in fact, horses—carthorses, to be exact—feeding from a big circular hay rack.

As the Land Rover began its return journey, Matt walked calmly towards the group of horses, talking in soothing tones as he went. The equine giants watched him with interest but no apparent alarm, jaws still winding in long streamers of hay, and one of them even fluttering its nostrils and uttering a low whickering sound.

'Hello, lads,' he said, reaching a hand up to caress the nearest lowered nose. He thought they were probably shires. A good two hands, or eight inches, taller than the thoroughbreds he was used to, these draught horses were bigger in every way—long roman-nosed heads set on massively crested necks, barrel-shaped bodies, stout legs feathered with a mass of long hair, and hooves ten or twelve inches across.

Matt counted five horses in total as they gathered round him in anticipation of possible titbits. Glancing in the direction of the lane, he could see the lights of the Land Rover approaching the field gate. He dropped to a crouch as the beams swung towards him, illuminating the galvanised metal feeder behind which he hid, and haloing the horses, who blinked uncomfortably. Confident that he couldn't be seen, Matt stayed still and, after a minute or so, heard the vehicle back away and continue up the lane.

Letting out his breath in a shaky sigh, Matt considered his position. Fairly safe for the moment, he could conceivably stay where he was all night, if necessary, or at least until Delafield

357

gave up the search. However, it wasn't only himself he had to think of—although in a bad way, Deacon had been alive when Matt had last seen him, and he couldn't square it with his conscience not to do everything possible to get him some help.

Thinking about the option of returning to the lane once more, and not liking it at all, Matt stroked the neck of the nearest horse and noticed—for the first time—that three of them were wearing headcollars. He continued to stroke the animal, thoughtfully. If one was contemplating riding, a headcollar wasn't much use without a rope, but was he *really* contemplating it?

He rather felt he was. On the back of a horse, he could move a good deal faster and would feel a lot less vulnerable than on foot.

Looking around him, he saw that the hay the horses were pulling at was in the form of three or four bales, which the farmer had dumped into the feeder wholesale, binder twine and all, probably earlier that day. At any other time, Matt would have deplored such carelessness, worried for the safety of the feeding animals, just now, though, he sent a blessing winging in the man's direction. A length of orange twine, whilst not ideal, could be fashioned into a makeshift rein that might just provide the means for his getaway.

It proved necessary to climb into the feeder to retrieve the string, but, even so, in less than two minutes he had attached a piece to either side of the headcollar of his chosen horse and was preparing to climb onto its broad back. This he did with the help of the feeder, talking quietly all the while, and trying not to allow his tension to communicate itself to the animal who, for all he

358

knew, might never have been ridden before.

In the event, it wasn't an adverse reaction he had to worry about as much as no reaction at all. Beyond turning an ear in his direction, the horse took no notice whatsoever of Matt's presence and continued to eat hay unperturbed.

It took a fair amount of unattractive kicking and hauling to coax the animal away from his feed, but, eventually, Matt managed it, and even succeeded in bullying the animal into a reluctant trot. His plan—if plan it could be called—was to ride the horse down the field in the hope of finding a way out at the bottom. Failing that, then at least he would be close enough to make his way to Rockfield on foot.

For twenty or thirty yards or so, the animal trotted, head up and showing a strong inclination to turn back to his companions if Matt would let him, but then fate, in the shape of the other four horses, took a deciding hand.

Matt didn't realise they were following until one of them kicked up its heels and cantered past, causing his mount to veer sideways. Slipping a little, Matt grabbed a handful of rough mane to steady himself. The shire's back felt acres wide compared with the lean thoroughbreds he rode everyday, and his legs didn't reach far enough round its girth to grip effectively. Being herd animals, the sight of one of their number running got them all going, and soon the other horses joined in the fun, running alongside Matt's horse, bucking and snaking their heads.

Matt cursed. Steering a horse with string attached to its headcollar was never going to be a very precise art and relied a good deal on the willing co-operation of the animal; with five horses on the run in a ten-acre field on a windy night, he might just as well have tried to convey his wishes by Morse code for all the notice the shire took of them. Caught up with the exhilaration of this wild charge, the five heavy horses got faster and faster, thundering down the field towards the boundary fence in the valley like massive warhorses going into battle.

Matt hauled on the orange twine until it felt as though it would cut through his fingers, but to no avail. Carried along with the others, the horse he had chosen swung right to follow the line of the fence before turning inexorably back up the hill again. Even the option of baling out was taken from him, as the five animals stayed closely bunched together, and to have landed amongst their pounding hooves would have been tantamount to suicide. Helpless to do anything but hold on grimly, Matt found himself carried back up to the top of the hill, but any hope that the horses would slow and stop by the feeder were dashed as they raced by, apparently still full of running, heading for the other side of the field.

For one awful moment, Matt thought he was going to have to endure a second circuit and quailed at the thought. The shire's back might have been broad and well covered, but his withers were prominent and bony, and Matt feared they were doing untold damage to an extremely delicate area of his anatomy. Instead of swinging right-handed along the top hedge, however, the lead horse made for the very corner of the field, chivvied all the way by one of the others, mouth open and teeth bared.

As the five animals converged, funnelled into a rapidly decreasing space, Matt renewed his grip on the shire's mane and prepared for a rough ride. There were slip rails in the corner, but Matt didn't discover them until the first horse launched itself into the air and the second horse didn't, smashing through the top pole and almost coming to its knees. Matt's own mount made an ungainly leap over the remaining pole, throwing him forward onto its neck, and the next moment they were all streaming along the unploughed headland of the adjacent field, galloping hard. It occurred to Matt that there was now a certain purpose about their progress; they seemed to know where they were going. Regaining his seat, he saw, looming close, the dark bulk of the barns he'd seen earlier, and the next moment the five horses charged through the open yard gate and came to a slithering, bone-shaking halt in front of the stables.

Matt slid thankfully to the ground. Presumably, the horses were on occasion stabled in this yard, and had come here now, instinctively, in expectation of being fed. That being so, he had little hope of being able to persuade the somewhat stubborn shire to carry him any further, even if he had wanted to, but he had no intention of subjecting the horse to the danger of confronting Delafield and the Land Rover.

A shadow raced across the yard and, looking up, Matt saw a bank of cloud moving across the moon. In theory, he knew the darkness should benefit the hunted rather than the hunter but, even so, some age-old subconscious dread made him shiver and look around warily.

He wasn't given long to suffer, and the danger—

361

when it came—came, not creeping stealthily, but with lights blazing, as the Land Rover appeared junketing down the short track from the lane, its headlights strafing vertically as it traversed the deep potholes.

Matt took one look and then ran for the nearest barn. It was a huge structure, boarded partway up each side and then open to the elements under the arched roof. Running in through the full-height opening that served as access, he found it three-quarters full of hay bales and began to climb, hoping against hope that Delafield had pulled in as part of his general search, and not because he'd witnessed Matt arriving with the horses.

The hay smelled warm and earthy, a familiar smell to Matt, and he climbed swiftly, feeling his way in the deeper darkness of the barn and expecting, any moment, to be picked out by Delafield's torch. The Land Rover engine was silent now, and the only sounds from the yard were the horses' hooves tramping restlessly in the gritty mud.

The first few layers of bales were stepped but, as Matt climbed higher, he came upon a sheer wall of hay that apparently spanned the width of the barn. Jamming his fingers and the toes of his shoes in between the bales, he was able to continue upward until, right at the top, he hit a very real problem. Just a few inches short of the metal cross-beams, the last layer of bales had no weight on top to hold them in place and, as Matt reached to haul himself up and over the edge, the bale under his hand tilted precariously and threatened to fall.

Hanging on with his other hand, Matt tried to push the loose bale back into its place, but it had tipped beyond the point of no return and, with a jolt of fear, he watched its inexorable slide towards him—fifty-odd pounds of dead weight destined to test his powers of adhesion to the limit. Pulling his body as close to the side of the stack as he could, Matt turned his head sideways and pressed his cheek to the bristly wall. Although it wasn't a sheer drop to the barn floor, the thought of landing upon the stepped lower levels, after a fall of twenty-five feet or so, didn't appeal overmuch.

Finally toppling, the heavy bale caught him a glancing blow on the shoulder as it fell, loosening the grip of one hand and swinging him away from the stack, before it dropped into the gloom, bouncing off the stepped bales below to land with a dull thud on the barn floor.

Matt grabbed wildly at another handhold to save himself and then clung tightly for a few seconds, before making use of the gap left by the dislodged bale to complete his climb. In the darkness under the corrugated roof, he laid spreadeagled, face down, while he waited for his rocketing pulse to steady and his breathing to slow. Somewhere in the darkness of the roof space, he heard the anxious fluttering of a number of birds, but his stillness apparently reassured them and they settled once more. Matt drew in a deep, calming breath and let it out slowly, but he would have been far happier if he could have been sure that the falling bale hadn't alerted Delafield.

He waited in silence for what seemed an age, the barbed-wire gash on his leg smarting and his ears straining to hear any small sound that might denote the other man's presence down below. Such was his level of tension that, when he did hear the hollow thunk of a footfall on a loose plank, it was almost a relief. Then, without warning, a strong beam of light played along and over the edge of the stack, partially illuminating the arched roof above Matt and, caught unawares, he shrank backwards, unsure if he'd been seen.

Whether or not he had, he was never to know, for his quick movement was the last straw for the roosting pigeons, and they erupted into noisy flight, their wings sounding like a salvo of pistol shots in the silence.

When the pandemonium had died down, Matt held his breath, praying that Delafield would ascribe their panic to reaction to his torchlight, but it seemed not.

'Ah, so you *are* up there, Shepherd.'

Matt didn't answer. He could be bluffing.

After a moment or two, there was a low chuckle and a slow handclap.

'Absolutely right. Don't give away your position. Well, I guess I'll just have to come and get you.'

Matt's heart rate leapt up a few notches. Was the man mad? Surely no one with half a brain would start to climb, knowing that the person who waited above could start throwing bales down at any time. Or perhaps Delafield didn't believe that Matt had the stomach for such potentially lethal tactics. If that was the case, Matt thought grimly, he was going to find that he had been sadly mistaken. In his eyes, the ex-army man had forfeited any right to mercy when he'd run Deacon down and, although Matt was in no way a violent man, he had a healthy desire to look after his own interests.

As tense seconds multiplied and no further

sound came from the floor of the barn, Matt realised that the drawback of his position was that, while Delafield had no clear idea of where he was hidden, the same was true in reverse, and it wasn't a comfortable feeling. Was he still in the barn, or had he perhaps started to scale one of the outer walls of the stack?

Matt edged forward and hitched an eye warily over the rim.

Niall Delafield was over halfway up the hay wall, less than fifteen feet below Matt and climbing fast, his torch in his waistband.

Not giving himself time to waver, Matt got to his knees, took hold of the outermost bale by its string, and rolled it off the edge.

Delafield was lucky. The bale wasn't directly above him and only brushed him in passing. It was enough to make him hesitate, however, and whilst he clung there, looking up, Matt tipped another over.

This time it did the job. Landing squarely on the climber's head and upper arms, the weight of it loosened his precarious hold and both he and the bale plummeted to the bottom of the stack, bouncing and rolling over the stepped section on the way.

Matt stifled a decidedly unphilanthropic urge to cheer. As far as he could see in the poor light, Delafield was lying face down and still. Matt watched intently for half a minute or so, but could detect no movement at all, and the only sound was the wind whistling through the open-sided building and the odd restive hoofbeat from the horses outside.

Still he waited. He didn't trust Delafield. It had

been a nasty-looking fall, but the floor of the barn was carpeted with the fallen chaff of many seasons, and the bales that had broken the man's fall were essentially soft. How incapacitated he was would depend on whether he'd fallen awkwardly, and Matt just wasn't sure. What he did know was that he'd have to take his eyes off Delafield as soon as he started the descent, and that would make him horribly vulnerable.

He thought hard, trying to second-guess Delafield. If he *were* faking injury, would he really have waited that long for Matt to come down? Considering what he'd done, Matt was astonished that the man had stayed in the vicinity this long. How long had it been since he had run Deacon down? Fifteen minutes? Twenty? His determination to silence Matt seemed out of proportion to the extra getaway time it would gain him. If Delafield had made no attempt at all to catch him, it would still have taken Matt a good ten minutes to reach the main road and flag down a car. This way he risked discovery at any moment. Surely he didn't think he could fool the police with some elaborate cover story?

Coming to a decision, Matt moved back from the edge of the stack, turned round, and wriggled under the cross-beam into the next bay. With his back to the yard, he moved cautiously across the bales to where the corrugated roof curved down to within inches of the hay. Turning round, Matt sat back and pushed hard with his feet until he dislodged the outermost bale, sending it tumbling away into the darkness. Moments later he heard the soft thump of its landing and eased himself under the edge of the roof, sincerely hoping that

366

fate didn't have something similar in store for him.

Because the stack had been constructed properly, with interlocking layers, the top bales were the only unstable ones, and Matt was able to begin his climb from the gap he had made with no fear that the first bale would topple under his weight. The hay on this exposed edge was damp and musty smelling, and some of the seed had germinated, sprouting soft grass. Months of rain and wind had started to decay the bales and finding secure hand- and footholds was nowhere near as easy as it had been inside. The bitter wind buffeted Matt, cutting through his clothing as if it were lace, and he was truly thankful when his feet found the top of the boarding, a third of the way down. From there, clinging on for dear life, he let himself down to the full extent of his trembling arms and, praying that he didn't land on some item of farm machinery hidden in the long grass at the base of the boards, he let go.

Dropping some six feet or so, Matt landed on his feet and fell sideways. His first discovery was that the long grass wasn't, in fact, grass at all, but nettles, and his second was that his recently injured ankle wasn't really up to such stunts.

Picking himself up, rubbing at his smarting hands, he set off in a limping run towards the end of the barn, his mind on the Land Rover parked on the other side. Climbing over a rusting metal gate that spanned the gap between two barns, Matt moved cautiously to the corner nearest the yard and peered round.

An unseen hand grasped the front of his jacket and jerked him forward so that his face connected painfully with the metal upright. In the next instant his feet were swept from under him and he went sprawling in the mud.

16

Many years of experience in the art of falling ensured that Matt didn't stay down and helpless for very long. No sooner had he hit the ground than he was rolling, legs and arms drawn in, and coming to his feet once more.

In this instance the manoeuvre quite possibly saved his life, for, as he stood upright and backed away, the moonlight gleamed on a wicked-looking five- or six-inch blade in Delafield's hand.

Matt's chest constricted in fear. The muscular ex-army man would be a daunting opponent at any time but—armed with a knife? He stood slightly crouched, holding it almost casually, blade pointing to the sky, and, with his other hand, he beckoned. As Matt took another step backwards, he saw Delafield's lips draw back in a thoroughly unpleasant smile.

'I've hunted down guerrilla fighters in Bosnia and South America, you didn't really think you were going to get away, did you?' he asked, and, in that query, Matt found the answer to the question that had been nagging him. Pride had kept Niall Delafield from cutting and running. A veteran of the Special Forces, he couldn't bear the thought of being bested by a mere civilian.

Matt cleared his throat.

'Bartholomew's on his way,' he said, wishing with all his heart that it were true. 'The police know what happened with Sophie Bradford.'

Delafield shook his head.

'I have an alibi, remember?'

'Not any more. I was talking to Joe earlier.'

That had shaken him, Matt observed with satisfaction, as he saw the other man straighten up and pause.

'Joe doesn't know anything about it.'

'You underestimate him. He's not stupid, and he's very, very angry. Seems you broke one date too many.'

'He wouldn't talk to the police,' Delafield asserted.

'He already has,' Matt lied.

Distracted by the conversation, Delafield's next move caught Matt off guard and he had to jump back so hastily to try and avoid the slashing blade that he caught his heel and almost fell again, stumbling into the nearest of the horses, which, in turn, jostled the others. They shifted warily, their ironshod feet churning the dirt.

'Not quite quick enough, eh? Mister hotshot jockey.'

Matt had felt nothing more than a tug at the front of his sweatshirt, but even as the meaning of Delafield's words registered, so did a fiery streak of pain across his ribs. Without taking his eyes off the other man, he put an exploratory hand through the unzipped front of his jacket and encountered a gaping slash in the fabric. It felt wet to the touch and his fingers came away bloody. Clearly, the blade of Delafield's knife was razor sharp, and Matt was in big trouble.

Suddenly, behind him, there was a commotion amongst the horses and one of them burst away from the group in a flurry of stomping hooves. Matt took little notice; he had more important things on his mind and it was doubtless just a little rank-pulling, but his interest sharpened as he saw the reaction of the man facing him.

Niall Delafield, ex-minder, ex-Special Forces, was unmistakably terrified of the horses. Seeing his wide-eyed apprehension, Matt recalled Deacon's comment at the races one day: 'If I wanted to lose him, I'd just go down to the stables. Niall won't go near the horses—he's allergic.'

Was he was allergic to horses or just plain scared? A bogus allergy would be one way to save face, Matt thought, and, empowered by the discovery that his super-tough adversary had an Achilles heel, he searched for a way to use this weakness to save himself. Getting back on board the shire—even if it could be accomplished—might save his skin, but would only return the situation to stalemate. What Matt needed was the Land Rover and, to get to it, he had to get past Delafield.

The horses had settled again, but Matt knew it would take very little to set them off, and he intended to provide a lot. He glanced over Delafield's shoulder to check the position of the Land Rover, and saw that it was—to all intents and purposes—blocking the exit from the yard. It was also pointing the wrong way for the ideal getaway vehicle, but that couldn't be helped.

Delafield noticed his glance and smirked, happier now the horses had stopped moving.

'Fancy your chances, do you?' he asked, jerking his head in the direction of the gate. He moved a step closer and Matt's heart rate accelerated off the scale. He'd survived the first lunge, but he was pretty sure that it hadn't been meant as a killing blow. Something told him that, when Delafield attacked again, it would be with the intent of finishing the business. Just how he would deliver the fatal cut Matt didn't know, and wasn't especially keen to find out; he did know that he hadn't a hope in hell of stopping him.

'It wasn't me that killed that tart,' Delafield said. 'The boy did it.'

Aware that he'd used conversation as a distraction the last time he'd struck, Matt didn't answer.

'Fuckin' idiot had been drinking. He knows he's not allowed. If that woman had crooked her finger, he'd have gone with her like a shot. Had to live like a bloody monk, the way the old man kept tabs on him. Not surprising he flipped, if she led him on. Did she fall or did he push her? He doesn't remember, but, whatever happened, she smacked her head on the stone wall. He was sitting beside her trying to wake her up when I got there,' Delafield added with contempt.

'So you dumped her body over the edge, took her credit cards, and planted them in Jamie's car,' Matt said, drawn in, in spite of himself. 'And I suppose it was you who beat Jamie up and stole his car that night in Bournemouth.'

'Well, I had to make sure the cops found the evidence, didn't I?'

'And the two thugs you sent after me?' Matt asked, and, playing Delafield at his own game, leapt back and sideways, mid-sentence, to plunge into the midst of the horses.

'Go-arn!' he shouted, waving his arms in the

371

faces of the nearest ones and slapping the rump of another.

The horses threw up their heads and split into two groups, stampeding away from Matt in momentary panic. Out of the corner of his eye, Matt saw Delafield shrink back, gazing wildly around as the startled animals shot past him on either side. Finding the exit blocked, the horses bunched together and milled round before setting off with one accord to circumnavigate the yard once more. Once Matt could see which way they were going to run, he ran to meet them, spreading his arms and shouting to throw them into even more confusion, and, under cover of this, he made it to the driver's side of the Land Rover, opened the door, and slid behind the wheel.

The downfall of this plan would have been if Delafield had removed the keys, but the gods were with Matt on this occasion, and, with a low-voiced 'Yes!', he started the engine, flicked the lights on, and put the vehicle in reverse, familiar with the controls from his own, albeit older, Land Rover at home.

Flooring the accelerator, he backed, at speed, a little way up the track down which he had recently ridden, braked, and then drove forward, steering hard right to make the turn into the gravel track leading to the lane. Catching its nearside wheels in a pothole, the 4x4 tilted so violently that, for one heart-stopping moment, Matt thought it would roll, but somehow it recovered, settling comfortingly back onto four wheels, if somewhat skewed across the track. Matt stamped on the brakes, wrenching the wheel back the other way, and, as the Land Rover straightened out, he heard a thump from the passenger side. The inner light came on and, glancing across, he was in time to see the door swing open and Delafield start to pull himself inside, the knife held between his teeth.

Once again he steered hard right and had the satisfaction of seeing the other man jerked back, wildly off balance and forced to clutch at the doorframe, but, within the narrow confines of the track, Matt soon had to swerve back the other way. The rapid change of direction and the deeply pitted surface of the track combined to shake Delafield's grip loose and throw him bodily against the inside of the windscreen and then down onto the seat.

'Motherfucker!' he growled, and Matt's desperation at not having got rid of the man was tempered by the realisation that, to have articulated the words, Delafield must have dropped the knife.

A second attempt to throw him out by swerving was thwarted by the door having slammed shut. The Land Rover bumped and jolted down the track, becoming airborne more than once, and, after smacking his head on the front shelf a time or two, Delafield gave up trying to search for the weapon in the footwell and launched an attack with his fists, catching Matt with a stinging blow to the side of his head, which, in turn, resulted in him hitting the other side of his head on the window beside him. Seeing stars, Matt stamped savagely on the brakes and had the satisfaction of seeing Delafield impact heavily with the windscreen for a second time.

It didn't improve his temper or his language.

Jamming the gear lever into first, Matt

transferred his foot to the accelerator and the Land Rover leapt into the harness once more. Ahead, the lights picked out an apparently solid obstruction spanning the width of the track, and it took him a moment or two to realise that it was the hedge on the other side of the road. Within seconds they would be on the tarmac and he would have to make the choice of whether to go left or right—and what then? On the smooth, narrow lane, how long would it be before Delafield recovered the knife?

In the event, he found out even sooner than he'd feared, for, as the Land Rover bucketed over the last few yards of gravel, Delafield came upright again and this time he had the blade in his hand.

Matt made a snap decision. Applying the handbrake, he dragged the wheel round to the left, forcing the locked back wheels to describe a 180-degree arc around the front end. The vehicle crossed the lane travelling backwards with a deafening screech of tyres and hit the bank on the other side with a whip-cracking jolt. The stunt had effectively pinned Delafield against the passenger door and Matt's intention, in the absence of any better ideas, had been to open the driver's door and take off on foot once more, but, before he could implement this part of the plan, the cab was filled with dazzling light and something hit the Land Rover, broadside on and very hard indeed.

When the chaos of noise and movement stopped, Matt found himself on Delafield's side of the vehicle, half-lying against the man, his eyes assaulted by a flashing blue light, and the hissing sound of escaping steam in his ears. Broken glass littered the seat and cascaded from his clothing as he cautiously sat up, whereupon he could see that Delafield's head was lolling out of the side window.

The driver's door was wrenched open and a uniformed policeman shone a torch in.

'You all right, sir?'

Matt nodded, hardly believing it. He felt a little light-headed and there were a few decidedly sore spots, but he'd had a lot worse.

'Yeah, I think so,' he said, beginning to edge towards the open door.

The policeman put a helping hand under Matt's elbow as he stepped down onto the road, wincing a little as his injured ankle took his weight, and a green-jacketed paramedic passed him en route to go to Delafield's aid. They made their way round to the other side of the Land Rover, where another paramedic was asking the unresponsive Delafield if he could hear him. Here, Matt discovered that the vehicle that had crashed into them was, in fact, a police car. Behind it, parked on the verge of the narrow lane, were a police Range Rover, a paramedic's car, and a dark-coloured saloon. Edging past them, blue lights still flashing, came an ambulance. It seemed that the cavalry had arrived, en masse.

'Well, Mr Shepherd, you've certainly been busy,' a familiar voice observed, and DI Bartholomew hove into view.

Matt would never have believed he could be pleased to see the detective, but the circumstances were indeed extreme.

'How did you know where to find us? Did someone call you?'

'You did,' Bartholomew stated dryly. 'You left

your phone on and there seemed to be something major going on, so we took a fix on it, and here we are.'

'And just in time,' Matt remarked, wishing he could sit down.

'We aim to please. Wait a minute . . .' The DI put out a hand to move Matt's jacket front a little. 'Can we have a medic over here?' he asked, raising his voice.

'It probably looks worse than it is,' Matt told him. The knife wound had paled into insignificance in the frantic struggle for survival that had followed.

'Nevertheless . . . So, would you like to tell me what's been going on here?'

'Oh my God! Deacon!' Matt said, suddenly remembering.

Bartholomew nodded soberly.

'Yes, we found him.'

Matt didn't miss the significance of the tone.

'Is he . . . ?'

'I'm afraid he didn't make it.'

'I tried to call an ambulance . . .'

Bartholomew shook his head.

'From what the medic said, they wouldn't have been able to save him had they been here when it happened.'

'Poor bastard!' Matt said bitterly, and all at once the events of the evening seemed overwhelming and pointless. He looked up at Bartholomew, wanting to explain about Deacon's illness, about how Delafield had run him down by mistake, but somehow he couldn't focus on the big man's face. He frowned, blinking to try to clear his vision, and felt the road tilt under his feet.

Someone caught him as he fell and the last thing he heard before he passed out was Bartholomew shouting, 'Where's that bloody medic?'

*   *   *

It was a mellow late October day, and Matt was circling at the two-mile start on Henfield Racecourse, along with fifteen other jockeys. It was normal for the adrenalin to start pumping through his veins at this point, but today, deep inside, fizzed an extra excitement, for it was the day of the prestigious Henfield October Cup and he was riding Woodcutter. They had been circling for a minute or two already, because the seventeenth runner, Rollo's mount, had spread a plate, or lost a shoe, in layman's terms, and the farrier had been sent for.

Woodcutter was taking the delay well, as were the two runners from Rockfield: Inkster, ridden by Ray Landon; and Jamie's mount, Secundo.

Jamie caught Matt's eye as he passed.

'You really think that little half-pint animal is going to beat the mighty Secundo?' he enquired derisively.

'We'll see,' Matt replied. Jamie had received a formal offer to ride for Rockfield just a week ago and it was good to have the Irishman back on side. For Matt's part, his relationship with Kendra's father had undergone something of a change since Deacon's death and the revelations that came hot on its heels.

Walking the little bay horse round with the autumn sunshine warm through his thin silks, his mind drifted back to the days following that terrifying night.

He had awoken in the ambulance on his way to hospital, but, after the examination and stitches in the knife wound and wire tear, he'd succumbed to fatigue and slept through the night and half of the next day.

Waking in a hospital room, the first person he'd seen had been Kendra, who was sitting in the easy chair at his bedside, staring out of the window with reddened eyes. He'd softly spoken her name, and the hug she gave him—if a little physically uncomfortable in the circumstances—reassured him that, whatever else might fall apart, their relationship wasn't about to.

Deacon's death had hit the family hard, coupled—as it was—with the shock of discovering his involvement in Sophie Bradford's killing, but after three weeks, Matt was relieved to see that what could have split the family asunder had actually united them more strongly. Even Grace, not usually a team player, had seemed to rise to the occasion, although, as Frances remarked wickedly to Matt, in her case there was plenty of scope for upward motion.

Delafield was still in hospital with head injuries and the knowledge that DI Bartholomew was eagerly awaiting his discharge. Matt wasn't looking forward to the inevitable court appearance, but knowing how slowly the wheels of the justice system rumbled along, he was able to relegate it quite comfortably to the back of his mind for the time being.

When the police had finished questioning Matt, there had been a very difficult interview with Charlie Brewer to endure. Matt could recall it with uncomfortable clarity. The businessman had asked him to come to his study, offered him a seat; a drink, which he had refused; and then stood looking out of the window whilst apparently searching for the words to begin. In the end, Matt had taken pity on him.

'I know why you did what you did,' he said. 'I don't condone it and I find it hard to forgive just at the moment, but I do understand why you tried to cut me out of the picture.'

Brewer swung round.

'It wasn't my idea. Niall told me to get rid of you. He said, if you stayed, you were bound to work out the truth about Deacon and then we'd all be up on charges.'

'It was that evening I heard the two of you in here, wasn't it? That's when it all started to go belly-up.'

'So you did overhear,' the businessman said. 'I wondered if you had . . .'

'Not much, frankly, and what I did hear didn't make much sense, but I could tell that Delafield had something on you.'

'I'd just found out that he was gay,' Brewer said, his face twisting into an involuntary expression of distaste. 'I wasn't going to have that kind of influence around my son, so I told Niall he'd have to go. That's when he told me what Deke had done. He threatened to go to the police with it; said he'd tell them that I'd known all along. What could I do? I couldn't just hand my own son over to the police.'

'He needed proper help,' Matt pointed out. 'Didn't it occur to you that it might have been better for him, in the long run? Bartholomew says

379

he'd probably have got off on diminished responsibility; it would have been manslaughter rather than murder. And, anyway, didn't you ever think of the girls?'

Brewer had cast him a look of deep anguish.

'Of course I thought of the girls—they were constantly on my mind—and God knows I'd never have put them in any danger, but ... Well, Niall said it was probably an accident—the Bradford girl, I mean. He told me that Deacon gave him the slip and went off with the girl. The boy was naïve, a dreamer. If she led him on and then got scared ... Maybe they struggled and she fell ... ? I don't know. But Niall said, if the police found out about Deacon's illness, they'd lock him up and throw away the key. And well—he's my son, for God's sake!'

'Delafield has no idea what happened,' Matt stated. 'He wasn't even there—I bet he didn't tell you that. He left Deacon and went out with his boyfriend. The whole thing was his fault, and he would have said anything to keep his job.'

Brewer nodded miserably.

'I know that now.'

'And the cat? Was that an accident, too?'

Brewer flinched as if Matt had hit him.

'That was later. Until then, I didn't know he was capable of something like that and, by that time, I was in too deep.' He hesitated, then said dully, 'You don't think the girl was an accident?'

Matt shook his head.

'I don't know. I don't suppose we'll ever know now. Deacon couldn't remember. He just seemed totally bewildered by what had happened.' He paused, looking at Brewer contemplatively. 'I still

380

find it hard to believe that you'd go along with a vicious bastard like Delafield. Ruining my career was bad enough, but trying to turn Kendra against me—frightening her like that!'

'I didn't know he was going to do that,' the businessman protested. 'You know I would never have agreed to anything like that.'

'But you weren't above making use of it to try and separate us.'

Brewer met Matt's eyes for a moment and then looked away.

'I know it was wrong. I'm sorry.'

'I was never good enough for her, in your eyes, was I?' Matt stated without heat. 'A commoner. A steeplechase jockey. You wanted a title, or, at the very least, money.'

Brewer turned back.

'All right, I admit it, I did want more for her. I wanted the best, what father wouldn't?'

'No, you're wrong there. Most fathers want their children to be happy. And the bottom line is that if you hadn't been so worried about what the world would think, none of this mess would have happened.' Matt had stood up, intending to leave before he said something that would irrevocably damage their future relationship; after all, the man was going to be his father-in-law one day, however little either of them relished the fact.

'Do you think I don't know that?' Brewer demanded. 'Do you think I don't blame myself every waking moment? It's *my* fault that the girl is dead and it's my fault Deacon is dead, and, whatever you may think of me—I did love him. I love all my family, and all I've done is fuck things up for everybody!'

Matt sighed, moved to compassion in spite of himself, but he couldn't truthfully think of anything comforting to say. He turned his back and went to the door.

'I don't blame you for hating me,' Brewer said. 'But, for Kendra's sake, can't we try and start again? I'd like to offer you your job back, on whatever terms you like. Will you consider it? The horses run better for you than for anyone else.'

Matt paused on the threshold, reluctantly impressed. He was only too aware how much the admission would have cost Brewer, after all he'd said in the past.

'I'm sorry. The answer's no,' he said, after a moment. 'I'll ride for you, when you've got something good to offer, but I don't want my job back—not yet awhile, anyway. I've a fancy to stay freelance. Why don't you give it to Jamie?'

*   *   *

Now, Matt sighed. The whole business had been so destructive; he had no idea how long it would take for the repercussions to die away. As well as Delafield, Charlie would be facing charges in due course, but it was expected that the courts would show a degree of leniency in the circumstances.

A quickening in Woodcutter's pace alerted Matt to the fact that Rollo's horse had been reshod and things were on the move, so he shrugged off the memories, shortened his reins, and pulled down his goggles. He was confident that the little bay was good, but there was no excuse for handicapping him by missing the jump-off at the start.

'Jockeys!' The familiar call set his nerves atingling and Woodcutter began to canter in a rocking-horse motion on the spot. Within moments, the tape flew back and they were away.

Woodcutter hadn't run on a track since Matt's win with him at Maiden Newton, and, although he'd exercised him a number of times at Doogie's, he hadn't shown any great enthusiasm on the gallops. This was clearly a horse that saved his best for the racecourse.

Keen and yet biddable, he had the ability to take the race on from the front, yet allowed Matt to play a waiting game, slotting in a third of the way down the field, on the outer edge to keep clear of trouble, and jumping as if there were prizes for style. Matt's only worry was that some unforeseeable problem would crop up, such as a loose horse taking him out at one of the fences, but it didn't happen, and Woodcutter gave him the ride of a lifetime.

Turning into the final straight with two to jump, his heart was singing. The little bay was placed fourth, tracking Secundo, Inkster, and Rollo's chestnut, and, as Matt let him have a little more rein, Inkster quickly dropped out of the equation. Woodcutter took the last level with the chestnut, but he was quick in the air and landed half a length clear.

'You've got him, Matt!' Rollo called as he fell behind and, hearing him, Jamie glanced over his shoulder before stepping up the pressure on the favourite.

Secundo responded willingly, but Matt knew he was on the better horse. With half a furlong to run, he finally gave Woodcutter his head and had to stifle a cry of pure exhilaration as the little bay lengthened his stride and passed Jamie's horse as if it was standing still.

Crossing the line, some four lengths the winner, Matt stood in his stirrups and punched the air. The October Cup was theirs, but that was quite plainly only the start of what this horse was capable of achieving. This was a one in a million kind of horse and, if Matt had his way, no one was ever going to ride it but himself; he was entitled to celebrate.

Back in the winner's unsaddling area, Jamie was magnanimous in defeat, seeming almost as excited as Matt was about the horse's performance, and later, after the presentation, he accompanied Matt, Doogie, and Woodcutter's new owner to the bar for a celebratory tonic water.

When the race had been relived half a dozen times and ambitious plans mooted for the little horse's future, the talk turned to the other hot topic of the day. It was rumoured that Lord Kenning had, citing ill health, stepped down from his position at the Jockey Club. No one was sure of the facts, but the peer was noticeably absent from what was one of his local meetings.

Matt had his own ideas about Kenning's sudden decision and when, as they left the bar, he spotted Stephen Naismith in a queue at the Tote kiosks, he excused himself from the company of the others and went across.

'Matt, hi!' Maple Tree's owner smiled. 'Caught in the act!'

'Collecting on Woodcutter's win, I hope,' Matt said.

'And placing a little sum on Maple in the last,' he

replied, nodding. 'It's all rather worryingly addictive. I see what my mother saw in it now.' In a lower voice he added, 'What do you know about a mare called Peacock Penny? I'm told she'd be a good investment.'

'Is she for sale?' Matt asked, surprised. He remembered the serious young man who had been in the paddock the day he'd ridden the mare.

'Apparently. Her owner is rather put out by Westerby's imminent retirement from training, and has decided to sell both his horses and buy dogs instead.'

At this point he reached the kiosk and stepped forward to conduct his business, leaving Matt to digest the information he had imparted. Joining Matt again, minutes later, he folded a wad of cash into his back pocket with an evident air of satisfaction.

'I hadn't heard about Westerby,' Matt said thoughtfully. 'When did you hear?'

'Last night, when I visited to finalise the arrangements for removing Maple to Mr McKenzie's yard. The greedy sod tried to garner commission for putting me onto Peacock Penny!'

'This wouldn't have anything to do with Lord Kenning's sudden retirement, would it? I'm assuming we have you to thank for that . . .'

'Ill health, so I heard.' Naismith assumed an expression of innocence.

'And the rest!'

'Well, all right, I might have pointed out to him the benefits of a dignified withdrawal from the public eye, but, actually, when the facts were presented to him, he didn't really have much option. And I had a couple of aces to play.'

385

'The photos?'

'Those, and the little matter of a witness to his involvement with Westerby.'

'*Not Rick Smith?*'

'Yes, indeed. Nice lad. He was very helpful and good enough to sign a statement indicating his willingness to testify in court, if the need arose.'

'How on earth did you manage that?' Remembering the head lad's reticence with him, Matt could hardly believe it.

'Merely by offering the services of a top-class lawyer, if it should transpire that he needed one—not that I thought he would for a minute. Any half-competent judge would easily recognise how he'd been manipulated.'

'And how would a lad like Rick be able to afford this top-flight lawyer, may I ask?'

Naismith looked a little sheepish.

'Oh, well, there's this one guy I know who has been known to take on the odd case for a pittance, now and then, in the interests of justice.'

'*A guy you know,*' Matt repeated, eyebrows raised.

'Yes. Actually, it's not as noble as it sounds. Often the mere threat of his involvement is enough to see the case settled amicably, as now,' he observed.

'And Kenning's vendetta against me—all to hide his smutty little secrets?'

'Ah, but, you see, he'd had word there could be honours in the offing,' Naismith said. 'Needless to say, he won't be accepting—if the question does arise!'

Matt shook his head, smiling, but his attention was caught by Jamie, who had apparently hooked

386

up with Casey McKeegan, and who was now standing by the door to the premier stands, trying to convey, by way of hand signals, that they were going up to the Brewers' box.

'You're wanted,' Naismith said, following his gaze.

'In a minute. Why don't you come up for a drink?'

The lawyer shook his head.

'Thanks, but I'm here with a party—my wife and some colleagues. I'm trying to drum up some interest in forming a syndicate,' he confided, with a smile.

'OK. Well, I'll let you get back to them,' Matt said. 'And thank you for what you've done. Racing can do without people like Kenning and Westerby.'

'The *world* can do without them, if you ask me!' Naismith suggested, his eyes twinkling. 'But I suppose we must be content with less drastic measures.'

Matt laughed.

'I guess so.'

'Oh, and Matt—I don't have to ask you to keep this under your hat . . . ?'

'Of course not, and I'll look forward to seeing you at Doogie's.'

He waved a hand and, as he turned to follow Jamie and Casey, Woodcutter's owner left Doogie McKenzie and fell in beside him.

'Come up to the box,' Matt invited. 'There's someone I want you to meet.'

'Is this the best time? I mean—owner of the horse that beat theirs . . .' The man was a couple of years older than Matt, and an inch or two taller. He was dressed smartly in a suit, his tie bearing the red and white logo of Q&S Holdings.

'You're my guest,' Matt said, slapping him on the back. 'Anyway, quite apart from anything else, you represent my sponsors. You've every right to be there. Come on, faint heart.'

The box Charlie Brewer had hired was, predictably, the most expensive on the course, being both spacious and directly opposite the finishing post. In spite of its size, however, it was well peopled, hosting—at that moment—the whole Brewer clan, Rupert Beaufort, Jamie and Casey, John, Reney and Harry Leonard, and—somewhat surprisingly—Toby Potter and a red-headed woman, unknown to Matt, who was presumably his partner.

Kendra spotted Matt first, weaving her way through the crowd to his side. He slipped his arm round her and gave her a kiss. Since his return to racing, ten days ago, she hadn't missed a single meeting, knowledge of his deadly duel with Niall Delafield altering her attitude in a way even *she* was at a loss to understand.

'Do you know—I actually enjoyed watching that last race,' she told him, adding to his companion, 'That's the first time I've been able to watch the whole thing without hiding behind my hands. I'm getting better!'

Matt laughed, kissing her again.

'Luke, this—you will have gathered—is my fiancée, Kendra. Kendra, this is the head of Q&S Holdings UK Ltd, my brother Luke.'

They leaned forward to exchange kisses, Kendra saying archly, 'Ah, you must be the good-looking one of the family . . .' for which she earned an indignant slap on the behind from Matt.

Just then, someone rapped on one of the tables with the handle of a knife, and they all turned to see Frances standing, a little pink-faced, beside Harry's wheelchair. Harry himself appeared to be more interested in his hands, which he held clasped in his lap.

'Er, Harry and I have something to tell you,' she began, turning pinker under the interested scrutiny of family and friends.

'Not another wedding to pay for!' Charlie said, in horrified accents, and Joy frowned at him.

'Is it, Frannie?' she asked, looking more animated than Matt had seen her at any time since Deacon's death.

'Well, that's part of it,' Frances admitted, and, for a moment, any further revelations were drowned out by the mass of congratulations.

Then Harry raised his voice.

'Can we have some quiet, please? I *have* asked Fran to be my wife, and—for some reason known only to herself—she has accepted.' He paused while several disrespectful comments were passed. 'But I was determined that I wouldn't do so until I could do one thing . . .'

Matt held his breath, almost certain he knew what was coming.

Harry put his hands on the arms of his wheelchair and pushed himself upright, as he normally did when transferring to a chair or his car, but there was no other support within reach.

Matt looked across at Harry's parents and saw the bewilderment in their faces; he had obviously been successful in keeping his progress from them. Reney even took a step forward, as if to help her son, but John put a hand on her arm, watching

Harry intently.

'I told Fran that I would only marry her when I was able to walk down the aisle and stand by my best man for the ceremony,' he said, breathing a little faster than normal. 'Well, I'm not quite there yet, but we've booked the church for six months' time,' he added, and, fixing his gaze on the table, some eight feet away, walked six wavering steps through an anxious silence to reach it.

Once there, he leaned thankfully on a chair back, breathing hard, and smiled radiantly. As if that was the signal, the assembled company broke into delighted applause, with the exception of Reney, who burst into tears.

'But ... but how? When did this happen?' his father asked above the tumult. 'Why didn't you tell us?'

'I wanted it to be a surprise,' Harry said. 'At first, when I thought there was an improvement, I didn't want to say anything until I was sure it would continue, and then—when it did—I decided I'd wait until I'd got something really impressive to show you.'

Fran had moved to stand beside him now, clearly enjoying his moment of triumph just as much as he was, and Joy went over and hugged them both, her eyes shining with unshed tears.

'But, hang on,' Harry spoke up again. 'There's a very important person I have to thank for all this— besides Frannie, of course—Toby Potter, my craniosacral therapist. That's spelt Q U A C K to you, Charlie,' he added, laughing. 'But, seriously, without his healing hands, I'd still be stuck inside my self-limiting circle of pain and fear—to quote his wise words. Toby—come forward and take a bow.'

The vet went across, shaking his head and smiling.

'I should be thanking this fella for taking a chance on a horse doctor, and letting me practise my new-found techniques on him,' he remarked. 'But his recovery was 10 per cent therapy and 90 per cent determination. He just needed the belief.'

'Hey—you didn't tell me you were just practising, I thought you were a pro!' Harry exclaimed, and suddenly everyone was crowding round, talking and laughing, and wanting to hear about Toby Potter's miracle-working.

Having added his own congratulations and given Frances a hug, Matt squeezed out of the throng and made his way back to his brother's side, arriving in the same moment as Charlie Brewer.

'Ah, Charlie—this is Woodcutter's new owner, my brother Luke.'

Charlie raised an eyebrow and inclined his head.

'Well, congratulations on an impressive win—even though you beat my horse.'

'Thanks. Yes, sorry about that. I'm new to racing, but Matt told me Woodcutter was a good investment, and today I realised he was right. Even *I* could see that the horse is something special.'

'Matt, you didn't tell me your brother had bought the animal. I assumed it was your sponsors,' Charlie said then.

'Luke *is* Q&S Holdings,' Matt told him. 'At least, he's the UK branch. It's a family company.'

Brewer's face became very still as he took in this information.

'Your family owns Q&S Holdings International?'

'That's right,' Matt said lightly, enjoying the

moment. 'Queenbury and Shepherd—Q&S. My father is the managing director. Dick Queenbury died last year and we bought his widow out.'

'We . . . ?' Charlie asked faintly.

'Yeah. Like I said, it's a family company. Equal shares—though I don't take a regular wage, being something of a sleeping partner, so to speak.'

Charlie was looking at Matt as if seeing him properly for the first time, and it was Kendra who spoke up, linking her arm through Matt's and laying her head on his shoulder.

'So you see, your little girl didn't do too badly for herself after all, did she?'

'Why did you never tell me?' her father asked.

'I didn't know,' she replied simply. 'And, anyway, it's never been about money for me. The guy I'm marrying is going to be the next Champion Jockey, and that's far more exciting!'

β

41 61 81
    62 82